Meet Me at Pebble Beach

BELLA OSBORNE

avon.

Published by AVON
A division of HarperCollins*Publishers* Ltd
1 London Bridge Street
London SE1 9GF

www.harpercollins.co.uk

A Paperback Original 2020

3

First published in Great Britain by HarperCollins*Publishers* 2020

A catalogue copy of this book is available from the British Library.

ISBN: 978-0-00-833127-6

Typeset in Minion Pro by Palimpsest Book Production Limited,
Falkirk, Stirlingshire

Printed and bound in UK by CPI Group (UK) Ltd, Croydon CR0 4YY

MIX
Paper from responsible sources
FSC™ C007454

This book is produced from independently certified FSC™ paper to ensure responsible forest management.

For more information visit: www.harpercollins.co.uk/green

For Julie – Everything a sister should be and more.

Chapter One

Regan knew it was going to be a bad day when she awoke to find she was using a half-eaten kebab as a pillow.

'You're going to be late *again*,' said Jarvis, giving her shoulder a poke.

Regan opened a bleary eye and tried to focus it on the alarm clock. 'I've got loads of time.' She harrumphed and pulled the duvet over her head. The work do the previous night had been dull so she'd drunk more than she intended to.

'But I thought you were taking Cleo to the airport?'

'Shiiiiiiit!' Regan got out of bed so fast she forgot to put her feet down, and instead tumbled to the floor face first. Jarvis guffawed. 'Ow! That bloody hurt.' She jumped up and thrust her face up to the mirror. 'Shit. I've got a carpet burn on my nose.' She gave it a rub and removed a piece of lettuce from her cheek.

'Remember you're picking Cleo up from her studio and not the apartment.'

'I know.' Regan hadn't remembered this, but being reminded by Jarvis was a daily irritant. She began picking things up and flinging them in all directions. 'Shittity shittington . . .'

'Regan, please don't leave the apartment in a state,' said Jarvis, adjusting his tie. She was doing a passable impression of the Tasmanian Devil as she tried to decide what she needed to do first. 'I hate coming home to a mess.' He sighed deeply. 'Perhaps we need to have another discussion about this later. Hmm?' A bra sailed past his ear.

'Pants,' said Regan, decisively. Pants were always a good starting point. She began pulling underwear from her top drawer. 'No, actually I need a wee first.' And she dashed off to the bathroom, taking a clean pair of pants and yesterday's clothes with her in the hope she could get dressed whilst sitting on the loo to save some time.

'You really should allow more time,' said Jarvis, with a tut. Regan gave him a sarcastic smile and shut the bathroom door. Jarvis was lovely, but he could be a pompous arse sometimes. It didn't help that he was frequently correct.

Right now she needed to accomplish as many things simultaneously as possible. She could brush her teeth sitting down too. The Lean Methodology expert at work would be proud, she thought, as she snatched up her toothbrush.

'Bye then. We'll talk later, all right?' Jarvis called through the bathroom door, his voice overflowing with exasperation.

'Oh kweee,' mumbled Regan. It was the best she could do with a mouthful of toothbrush and one leg in her pants.

She heard the front door bang shut and relaxed a little. It was like living with her dad rather than her boyfriend. She surveyed the bathroom floor, strewn with an assortment of her clothes, a couple of towels and the oozing toothpaste tube. She'd just have to make sure she was home before Jarvis. She couldn't stand another lecture on her slovenly ways, but she didn't have time to sort it out now.

A few minutes later she was hurtling across Brighton in her battered Fiesta shouting obscenities at anyone in her way, which was essentially everyone. A quick check in the rear-view mirror reminded her that she hadn't brushed her hair – she resembled a one-colour version of Cruella De Vil.

There was nowhere to park at Cleo's studio, as usual, so she abandoned the car in the middle of the road and sprinted up to the door. She banged hard until Cleo appeared. 'Come in. I've been calling you,' said Cleo, kissing her lightly on the cheek.

Regan frisked herself as she stepped inside. 'Shit. I forgot my mobile. Sorry, Cleo.'

Cleo gave her a forgiving look. 'It's fine. I told you an hour earlier than I needed anyway because I knew you'd be late.'

Regan was going to protest, but a quick glance at where her watch should be, followed by a squint at the clock on the studio wall, told her Cleo was absolutely right to have done this. 'Sneaky – but good call.'

Regan was notorious for being late. She tried not to be, but she had long ago resigned herself to the fact that timekeeping simply wasn't one of her talents.

'What have you done to your nose?' asked Cleo, peering at Regan.

Regan's hand automatically shot to her face. 'Carpet burn. Still need to hurry you up because the car is blocking the road.'

Cleo raised an eyebrow. 'Interesting. Let me just do one

last check and we can go.' Cleo swept away. She was dressed elegantly in clothes that adored being shown off on her willowy frame. Even the way she walked was sophisticated. She was the fashion opposite to Regan, who often looked like her wardrobe had vomited on her.

Regan stopped slouching. 'Why did you want picking up from here and not your place?' Cleo was an artist with a swish flat in Hove but this was her studio in Brighton, where she worked.

'I stayed at The Downs Hotel last night. There was an exhibition at the racecourse, but I didn't expect you to remember all that so the studio seemed easiest.' Regan pursed her lips, but she wasn't offended. Cleo was right; she wouldn't even have remembered to come to the studio if Jarvis hadn't said. 'And anyway I've let out my flat. Daddy suggested it as I'm away for two months. It made financial sense.'

'Of course,' said Regan. Nothing made financial sense to her. Finance meant numbers, and she wasn't good with numbers. Which explained the credit card juggling act she had to do at the end of each month. Although, thanks to Jarvis and his austerity measures, this was now more under control.

Regan scanned the small studio. It was filled with canvases: some blank, some finished and a couple somewhere in between. There was a high-arched window, which filled the space with light. It seemed to fall like a spotlight on Cleo's latest work. Regan peered at the large brown mass in the picture, tilting her head at an uncomfortable angle. 'I don't know what you find so fascinating about—'

'We've no time for any of that,' said Cleo, pulling her Louis Vuitton case as if she too were on wheels and she shooed Regan backwards out of the studio. Cleo's art baffled Regan; she wasn't an arty sort. The two of them had met when Cleo had taken a part-time job as a waitress to impress her rich father with her work ethic. Regan had been working there with no other ambition than not to get fired before payday. They were an unlikely pairing, but curiosity on both sides had brought them together – that and a mutual love of coffee and tequila shots.

After she'd set an alarm and checked the door, Cleo poured herself gracefully into Regan's car. 'Got everything?' asked Regan.

'Because *I'm* the one who forgets things,' said Cleo, playfully arching a perfect eyebrow. 'Here,' she said, handing Regan her keys. 'Alarm code fourteen fifty-two. The year Leonardo da Vinci was born.'

'Why do I need to know that?' Regan was instantly uncomfortable with the responsibility.

'Because there's an issue with the boiler and the landlord is sending a workman over . . .' Cleo was speaking slowly as if Regan was remedial.

'And you need me to be here tomorrow to let him in. I hadn't forgotten,' she lied. She tried to repeat the number silently in her head so she'd remember it. She wished she hadn't forgotten her phone – putting a reminder on there would have been useful.

'I'll send you a text,' said Cleo, pulling out her mobile. She gave her friend an indulgent smile.

Regan noticed Cleo twang the hair bobble on her wrist. She kept it there to help with stressful situations. 'You okay?'

'Not looking forward to the flight . . . or being away for so long.'

Regan set off; she was now far more relaxed knowing

she had a little time to spare and she also stood half a chance of not being late into work. 'Remind me again where you're off to this time?'

'Dubai, Hong Kong, Japan and Taiwan,' said Cleo, without a hint of any enthusiasm.

'Wowsers.' Regan had always wanted to travel. The furthest she'd strayed in recent years was the Isle of Wight – Jarvis's favourite holiday destination. She couldn't complain, because he usually paid the lion's share due to her cash flow issues. 'You'll have the best time. Post loads on social media so I can live vicariously.' She didn't really need to ask because Cleo lived her life on whatever social media platforms were the hottest. Her timeline was filled with photographs of beautiful people in amazing places, and she had a gazillion followers on Instagram. Whereas, Regan had eighty-four, and an alarming number of those claimed to be single males very high up in the American armed services, which everyone knew was code for fraudster.

Cleo raised a perfect eyebrow. 'It is work. It's not a holiday.'

'Still,' said Regan, braking hard for a bus that pulled out at the same time as it indicated. 'It'll be five-star hotels, cocktails, *à la carte* dining and comfy beds all the way.' She gave a small sigh. She wouldn't have to think very hard before trading places with Cleo.

'How's your job?'

'Still duller than a black-and-white party political broadcast. But like Jarvis says, it's secure and it pays the bills.' There must be more to life than that, thought Regan.

'You should try staring at a blank canvas for hours. That's dull too.'

'I guess.' Regan knew Cleo was just trying to make her

feel better. As an artist, Cleo's life was two extremes: she spent a large part of her time alone in the studio painting, but then she also travelled the world to attend exclusive exhibitions of her work, as well as being invited to all the trendy star-studded parties because she was very much part of the art scene glitterati. Regan loved hearing all about Cleo's glamorous life, even if it made hers look crappier by comparison.

They pulled into the airport shuttle drop off zone and Regan hopped out to get Cleo's case from the boot. 'Have an amazing time . . .' said Regan, and she could see Cleo was about to interrupt her, '. . . at work. But remember to have fun too. Love you.'

'And you,' said Cleo, kissing her cheek and giving her a tight hug that went on a fraction longer than usual.

Regan held her at arm's length. 'You okay?' She could sense there was something not quite right.

Cleo's face was deadpan for a moment and then a smile appeared. 'Of course. It's just that two months is quite a long time. I'm really going to miss you.'

'No, you won't,' said Regan, passing her the case handle. 'You'll be far too busy with *work* cocktails and *work* parties and other wonderful worky type things.' Cleo looked skywards. 'FaceTime me tomorrow.'

'Of course. And please remember the boiler man. Saturday. Ten o'clock,' called Cleo over her slender shoulder and she sashayed into departures.

Regan watched her go. She wished she were going too. She needed a break, and some sunshine would be lovely. There was nothing she'd miss for two months – with the possible exception of her dad – but he was all loved-up these days, so she rarely saw him anyway.

Beep, beep, BEEP!

The blast of a horn brought her back from her daydream. She gave a sickly-sweet smile to the large shuttle bus trying to get in behind her, whilst in her mind she was sticking her tongue out at him.

She had time to stop for petrol on her way into work, which was unheard of, so she treated herself to a Mars bar. The person in front of her in the queue asked for a lottery ticket. Regan couldn't remember the last time she'd bought a lottery ticket. Jarvis had decreed that she needed to cut out all extraneous spending in order to repay her credit cards; her lottery and online bingo habits were the first to go. Jarvis called the Lotto a 'fool's tax' because only stupid people played something with odds of forty-five million to one.

'Which pump?' asked the man behind the counter.

Regan had to check. 'Two, please, and this,' she said, passing him the Mars bar. Jarvis wouldn't be impressed with her having chocolate for breakfast either. He was cutting down their sugar intake. 'And a Lotto lucky dip for Saturday night, please,' she said, feeling a tiny bit rebellious.

'Good luck, love,' said the man on the till.

'Thanks,' said Regan, putting the ticket in her purse.

It was a short drive into town. Regan waved as she entered her usual coffee shop, the Hug In A Mug, and Penny behind the counter did a double take. Regan braced herself for the sarcastic comments about her being earlier than usual. 'You been evicted?' asked Penny, chuckling whilst she made Regan's usual order. 'Wet the bed then?'

'Had to take a friend to the airport,' Regan said, with a giant yawn. 'Actually can I have an extra shot in mine today, please?'

'Sure thing,' said Penny. She put it through the till and Regan paid with the joint account card. She liked contactless payments on the joint account because it wasn't like real money. The only price she had to pay was Jarvis tutting over the statements.

There was a bang on the window of the coffee shop, followed by the cringe-making sound of nails on glass moving slowly down the pane. Penny and Regan winced and turned quickly to look. A large dog was standing on its back legs with its giant front paws on the window. It was the height of an average human.

'Christ, what is that?' asked Penny. They both watched, mesmerised by its large fangs and open slathering jaw.

'Ah, that is Kevin's new friend. I met him yesterday. Some bloke tied him up and left him, according to Kevin.'

'Poor thing,' said Penny, and they watched it lick the glass with its huge pink tongue. 'What sort of dog is it?'

'I think it's a werewolf,' said Regan. It certainly looked the right size. She grabbed some sugar sachets, slung them on the cardboard tray and headed for the door, calling 'Bye!' as she left.

Outside, the giant mutt was waiting for Regan, but thankfully, so was Kevin. Kevin was homeless. Regan had walked past him every day since she'd started her job at BHB Healthcare and he always told her *carpe diem*, which was Latin for 'seize the day' – she'd looked it up. He never asked for money, which had been what had triggered her to start getting him a coffee each morning, and the smile she got from Kevin when she handed it over kept her going for hours.

'Hey Kevin. You might want to keep your dog off the glass. Don't want him getting into any trouble.' She gave Kevin his coffee and he beamed at her. The dog sniffed her groin and retreated. She couldn't blame him – she hoped her lack of a shower didn't have the same effect on her work colleagues. She made a mental note to spray herself liberally with perfume when she got there.

'Thank you. *Carpe diem*,' said Kevin, cupping his coffee reverently. Regan tried not to stare at the scars lacing their way across Kevin's hands.

'I will.' She turned to walk away and then spun around. 'Oh, has your dog got a name yet?'

'I've called him Elvis,' said Kevin proudly.

'Because he's in the ghetto?' asked Regan.

Kevin looked baffled. 'No,' he replied, 'because he's a hound dog.'

'Genius!' said Regan, and it kept her laughing most of the way to work.

Chapter Two

Regan waltzed into the office with a whole twenty minutes to spare. She worked in a small team, which dealt with late invoices. The only break from the unrelenting tedium of doing the same thing every day was her mate Alex. He had a sense of humour, which made him infinitely more likeable than anyone else in the office.

'Blimey, did they put the clocks back?' asked Alex, pulling his coffee from the cardboard tray Regan offered him, then picking up the sugar sachets and a stirrer.

'Your stand-up routine needs work,' said Regan, taking her seat and switching on her computer. 'I need to leave early tonight.'

'What, because of the extra eighteen minutes you've put in this morning?'

'No, because I left in a hurry and basically trashed the place.' She needed to make it back to the flat, or 'apartment', as Jarvis liked to call it, to have a quick tidy-up before Jarvis got in.

'Jarvis won't like that.' Alex tutted in an uncannily Jarvis-like manner.

'Precisely why I need to get home before him.'

'Why so early if you were in a rush?' Alex was screwing up his face.

'I dropped my friend Cleo at the airport.'

'Artist. Posh sort?'

'Yep, that's the one. She's jetting off for two months to Dubai, Japan and some other awesome places.' Regan flopped back in her seat. 'I wish I was going with her. She has the best life.' She turned her head towards Alex. 'Would you like to travel?'

'I do travel.' He looked affronted. 'I go to Skegness every year.'

'Hmm. Not quite the same.'

Alex gave a twitch. 'Japan may have the edge on Skeggy.' They both sighed together.

'Ooh,' said Regan, pulling her purse from her bag. 'Look what I got.' She held up the lottery ticket and gave it a wave. 'It's a rollover on Saturday. Ten million quid. Think what you could do with that.'

They both paused for a moment, lost in thought, until their boss, Nigel, tapped on his glass office door and they both quickly got back to work.

Regan liked Alex. There was no romantic pull on her part, but she knew he was quite fond of her thanks to some slurred words after too much tequila at the Christmas party. In any case, he made the day go quicker: they kept the tedium at bay by winding each other up on a regular basis. Nothing major; just the usual office pranks like hiding each other's mouse, changing chair adjustments and unplugging equipment. It was quite childish, but it made work marginally more entertaining.

Most of the day was uneventful. In the afternoon, Regan found herself dozing off in a very dull meeting about discounting and promotions. Alex gave her a nudge and she turned what she feared was a snore into a cough. A few heads spun in her direction.

'Terrible hay fever,' she muttered, pulling a tissue from her pocket. Alex shook his head at her.

She could see he was furiously scribbling things down on his pad; she eyed him with suspicion. Alex was like her in a lot of ways; neither of them usually put in any particular effort at work, although Alex still fancied himself for a promotion. Regan couldn't really see the point. She'd get paid very little extra at the end of the month, but have a load more responsibility. No, she was all right just doing what she needed to and no more. She understood why sales people worked harder for a bonus, or people who ran their own company, but it totally foxed her why an ordinary employee would do any more than the minimum required.

She leaned over and tapped a finger on Alex's pad. He tilted it for her to see. The title at the top jumped out at her: 'Lottery Rollover – What I'd do if I won.'

'You don't even have a ticket,' she whispered.

He shrugged. 'I've got loads of time to get one.'

She pulled the notepad from his grasp and had a read. It was fairly standard stuff. She handed it back and began jotting down her own. Regan chewed the end of her pen and made some crossings out as her imagination soared.

- *Live in a ~~big~~ ~~huge~~ awesome home*
- *Help Dad out*
- *Get a pedigree puppy*
- *Save ~~the tiger whale~~ some important animal*
- *Run my own successful company*

- *Bask on a deserted island and drink cocktails served to me by bare-chested waiters*
- *Go out and enjoy myself*

She had another scan of Alex's list. He'd put down 'Hook up with celebrity females'. Regan snorted and Alex turned his pad away. She studied her own list. Where did Jarvis feature? After how he'd annoyed her that morning, did he feature in her lottery fantasy life? She added an extra item to the list. It was only a laugh after all.

- *Get new hot boyfriend who doesn't nag or wear button-up pyjamas*

'Regan?' asked Nigel, their manager, who was standing at the front, his expression one of knotted puzzlement. Alex gave Regan a nudge and knocked her pen from her hand, making her jolt upright.

'Er, yes. Sorry. I was concentrating on my notes,' she said, reaching down and scrabbling on the floor for her wayward pen. Alex kicked it and it disappeared. She glared at him.

'How many queries do we get relating to errors in discounting?' Nigel repeated.

'Um,' she scratched her head, 'Alex?' She looked pleadingly at him.

He grinned. 'Regan is the data guru on this.'

Thanks for nothing, she thought. She'd definitely get him back later. 'A couple a week. Maybe.' She didn't really record them like she was supposed to, so it was a complete guess.

'When I last checked the figures, they were much higher than that,' said Nigel.

Regan wondered if that was the column on the end

that she added lots of ticks to at the end of the week. 'It's quite variable,' she said. 'Peaks and troughs.' Nigel nodded and she relaxed. She needed to pay more attention, but it was hard when meetings were this boring.

Back at their desks, Alex was still tittering about Regan's questioning in the meeting. Regan started plotting her revenge. It needed to be something hilarious. She zoned out trying to come up with a suitable penance for Alex while she did some data input. When he went off to a meeting she put a sticky note over the sensor of his mouse so it wouldn't work and flipped his login screen upside down. They were only temporary measures, but they would at least put him off the scent that she was planning something bigger.

Regan paperclipped her lottery ticket to the wish list she'd drawn up.

'Predictable,' said Alex, returning to his desk and flipping his screen back. 'What are you doing?' he asked, nodding at the lottery ticket.

'I'm not giving Jarvis any additional excuses to moan about me spending money. And if I win it's probably safer here.' She stopped short of adding that replacing Jarvis was an item on her wish list.

Alex made a grab for it. 'Do the numbers mean something?'

'Nope. It's a lucky dip. Statistics show you're likely to win more money with a lucky dip.'

Alex looked momentarily impressed. He pulled out his phone and took a snap of the ticket. 'Hey,' she said snatching it back. 'What are you doing that for?'

'So I'll know if you're lying when you ring me on Monday and tell me you're on a beach in Barbados.'

‘As long as you don’t buy a ticket with the same numbers. I don’t want to share with you.’ She put the ticket and wish list safely in her desk drawer and locked it.

Alex stuck his tongue out at her. ‘Remember we’ve got a director’s visit tomorrow. Don’t be late.’

Regan pulled an unimpressed face. She didn’t like anyone telling her what to do and just because Alex was slightly older and squarer than her still did not give him that right.

‘Ah yes, it’s your big opportunity to impress,’ said Regan. Alex had been chosen to meet the visiting director and she hadn’t. Not that she was bothered – she wasn’t. But Alex was clearly making plans to improve his career prospects.

‘He’s meeting everyone,’ said Alex, breaking eye contact and chucking his stuff into his desk drawer.

‘Yeah, but you’re special.’ He glared at her. She did her best solemn Confucius impression. ‘Just remember the higher the monkey goes up the tree, the more it shows its bum.’ He took a swipe at her and she ran for the door.

Regan was still plotting her revenge on Alex as she walked through the market place en route to her car, which she had parked in the cheapest car park possible. The market traders were packing up for the day and she was astonished by the amount of waste she saw as the grocery stallholder piled up the veg he couldn’t sell next to the bins. He caught her staring at the racks of tomatoes a little past their best.

‘Help yourself, love,’ he called to her. She thanked him but declined. Jarvis would not be impressed if she took home a crate of dodgy tomatoes, but it did seem like a terrible waste.

* * *

As soon as she opened the front door she could hear Jarvis tutting. He'd beaten her home. She went to check her watch and for the umpteenth time that day cursed that she'd left home without it. She didn't know exactly what time it was, but she guessed he must have left work earlier than usual, probably just so he could beat her home and have something to moan about. She took a deep breath and prepared herself for some grovelling.

'Hiya, you're home early. I need to get straight on with the tidying,' called Regan, scooting through the flat. She met Jarvis in the kitchen already shaking his head.

'Regan, you promised you'd not leave my apartment in a state. And what did I come home to?' It irritated her that he always managed to highlight that it was his place.

'I was going to tidy up before you got back, but you're early.' She was trying to keep her cool, but the condescending look on his face was seriously annoying. 'I'll do it now.'

'But it's too late. I couldn't bear it a moment longer, so *I've* tidied up *your* mess.'

This was the bit where he expected her to thank him. She wasn't going to. 'You didn't have to. You could have come home at your usual time and there wouldn't have been a mess.'

'We both know that was never going to happen.'

'Er, yes it was. Because I'm home now and that would have given me . . .' she looked at her bare wrist again, '. . . shitting hell . . .' she checked the kitchen clock, '. . . twenty-three minutes. I could easily have tidied up in twenty-three minutes, but as you *chose* to do it, I don't need to. So we're all good.' She responded to his confused expression with a cheesy grin and went to have a shower. She wasn't sure how much longer she could stand living with Jarvis and his endless irritating lectures. In the initial flush of a new relationship she'd ignored his quirks, but now they just seemed to grate on her.

Next morning, the sound of a car horn made Regan stir. She opened one eye. Jarvis wasn't in bed. She stretched out and was dropping off again when a stab of conscience made her turn over and check the time. She blinked at the clock. 'Shittity shittington!' That couldn't be right. She was seriously late for work and shitting Jarvis must have known and left her to her fate. Regan scrambled out of bed, keen not to repeat the carpet burn of yesterday. It would be another day without a morning shower, she thought, grabbing up her clothes from their floordrobe and dashing for the bathroom, tripping over Jarvis's precious rug in the process. Bloody thing.

Despite her lateness, Regan never missed getting a coffee. It was the only breakfast she had, and she justified her coffee purchase because it was also a commitment she had made to Kevin. And, more importantly, she couldn't face a day of terminal tedium at work without a decent shot of caffeine. She flew into the little coffee shop and found Penny was already on the case. Within minutes Regan had swiped her card, grabbed her tray of coffees and was heading for the sugar sachets.

'New process,' said Penny. 'No more sugar in little packets because some buggers keep nicking them. There's a sugar dispenser on the side.'

Regan was thrown by the new process. Trust Alex to have sodding sugar in his. She wrenched off the lid of his cup, tipped some in and quickly replaced the lid.

Kevin was outside, his hair and beard wet as they often

were in the morning. She puzzled over why that was; she had no idea where he would go for a shower. The irony that he had had a shower and she hadn't wasn't lost on her.

'Morning, Kevin,' trilled Regan, her pace virtually a jog. 'Morning, Elvis.'

Elvis barked his reply. The sound was loud enough to loosen her fillings and she very nearly threw the tray of coffees in the air. Kevin grabbed his quickly. 'Thank you. *Carpe diem*.'

'And you, Kevin,' she called over her shoulder and she speed-walked in the direction of the office.

When she arrived, Alex was hovering by their desks wearing a smart white shirt, dark tie and khaki chinos. Regan smirked at his outfit. He was definitely trying to impress the management. She could see he was looking flustered as she approached. 'I'm sorry. Jarvis is playing games. The shit let me sleep in.'

'You could set an alarm clock,' said Alex, pulling his coffee from the tray.

'I don't like—' but Regan didn't get to finish her sentence. Alex pulled the coffee from the tray and it got a few centimetres from the desk before the lid parted company with the cup. The cup bounced on the desk and, in spectacular fashion, doused the front of Alex's trousers with hot coffee. Alex gulped in air, making a noise like a train braking. Regan tried hard to stifle her laughter, but it was too funny.

Chapter Three

Alex stared at the stain spreading across his trousers.

'They're very absorbent,' said Regan, grabbing a box of tissues from the desk opposite. 'At least it missed your keyboard.'

'You utter cow.' Alex's voice was a low grumble.

Regan's grin slid from her face. 'What did I do?'

He pointed at his coffee-stained groin. 'You did this on purpose.'

'No, you did that all by yourself, pal.' She shook her head. She understood he was cross, but she wasn't taking the flack for something that wasn't her fault.

'You loosened the bloody lid!'

'No, I di . . .' Regan thought back to the new sugar process. 'Ah, no. You see the sugar isn't in the little packets any more—'

But Alex wasn't listening. 'Just because I kicked your pen in that meeting. You do this?'

She wished he'd stop pointing at his groin. Regan did feel a sense of responsibility, but she didn't like his assumption that she was this vindictive.

'It was an accident, Alex. You need to calm down.'

He opened his mouth to speak, but an office door

opened at the other side of the room. Managers and the visiting director spilled out. 'You'll need to take my place. But then I'm sure that's exactly what you planned.'

'Shit. No. I'm not taking your place. Man up and say you spilled your coffee. I don't want to go to some dull meeting,' said Regan, throwing the soggy tissues in the bin.

Alex quickly sat down and wheeled himself under the desk to hide the large coffee stain. It was a smart move. He then leaned on his mouse mat and froze. Regan glanced in his direction. 'What?'

Alex slowly lifted his arm to show that his once-pristine crisp white shirtsleeve now had a soggy brown coffee patch. 'Whoops,' said Regan, cringing. 'Think I missed a bit.'

'You are unbelievable,' said Alex.

The herd of management made their way over. Thankfully, someone more ambitious than Regan led the discussion. Alex was quiet; he kept his lower half under his desk and intermittently scowled at Regan. She shrugged. It was unfortunate, but she couldn't feel too guilty about it. It was only a meeting – it wasn't like he'd missed the last lifeboat.

'And Alex will be joining us to give an overview of the challenges he and his colleagues are facing with invoicing,' said Nigel, with a confident nod in Alex's direction. He seemed puzzled as to why Alex was facing the wrong way.

Alex twisted in his seat. 'I, um . . .' He frowned hard. 'I think Regan should attend instead of me. She knows the department and its challenges as well as I do.'

'Oh, well. Regan. Um. That's . . .' Nigel appeared to have

developed a facial tic. Regan's mouth lifted at the side. He was clearly dreading the thought of her being let loose in a meeting with the grown-ups.

The director tipped his head. 'Regan is an unusual name. From Shakespeare, isn't it?'

'Yes,' said Regan, surprised that he recognised it. Most people assumed it was her surname. 'It's from *King Lear*.' Her mother had had ideas well above her station so had saddled her with a name she felt was interesting and unusual. For Regan it was pretentious and annoying, but something she was lumbered with because she was too lazy to change it.

'Excellent,' he said. Nigel gave an uncertain smile of agreement. 'We'll see you later then, Regan.'

'Can't wait,' she said, holding her smile in place as they filtered away. Once they were safely in the lift, she turned to Alex. 'Ugh, thanks for that. I don't . . .' she began, but Alex got up and stormed off.

She decided she'd buy him a doughnut at lunchtime. That usually cheered him up. She'd get Kevin one too.

Her phone – which she'd remembered today – buzzed into life. It was Cleo on FaceTime. Without thinking, Regan answered it. 'Hi.'

Despite hours on a flight, Cleo still looked perfectly coiffured. After a few minutes on the Isle of Wight ferry, Regan usually looked like she'd been mauled by hyenas.

'This is the hotel,' said Cleo, scanning the phone around a room about the same size as Jarvis's entire flat.

'What country?'

'Dubai.'

'Is that a bath in the bedroom?' asked Regan, catching a glimpse as the camera moved past.

'Jacuzzi bath. So I can lie here and admire the view.'

Cleo turned the camera and Regan took in the vibrant blue sea. 'I'm on what they call the Palm.'

'It's amazing,' said Regan, trying to stop her mouth from falling open. 'What was business class like? Did you get—' But her questioning was interrupted by a cough behind her. Regan turned to see Nigel scowling at her and running his fingers down his tie. It was the same tie he wore every day; that, or he had a whole rack of the same one at home, but Regan doubted from the iffy stains on it that that was the case. Nigel poked a finger at her phone. That was the trouble with FaceTime; it was on loudspeaker, so it had obviously alerted everyone around her and now they all looked like meerkats on parade. If only she'd remembered her ear buds.

'Sorry, got to go.' Regan hurriedly ended the call.

'Regan, we've spoken before about personal calls. Haven't we?'

Regan wondered if Nigel went to the same school of condescending arses that Jarvis had studied at. 'Sorry. Won't happen again,' she said, but they both knew it would.

'If you're not busy, perhaps you'd replenish the printer paper stocks and get me a coffee?' He gave her a reptilian smile and she begrudgingly went to do as he'd asked. He wasn't the worst manager she'd ever had, but he was quite picky, self-important and always seemed to be on Regan's case, which – some of the time – wasn't justified.

The meeting with the great and the terminally dull was a lot less taxing than she'd feared. Alex had handed over his notes and figures, so she simply reeled them off when asked, while everyone nodded and her boss gave a deep sigh of relief. Really, these people had no faith.

She nipped out at lunchtime and bought three exorbitantly priced doughnuts, but it was on the magic contactless joint account card so it was fine. She wanted to drop one off with Kevin, though he was trickier to find at lunchtime because he often got shooed away from the market during the day by the manager. Eventually, she managed to track him and Elvis down to the supermarket car park, where occasionally a benevolent shopper would give him something from their trolley.

There was a fancy concrete bench affair outside and they sat there to eat their doughnuts together. Regan liked Kevin. He was probably a similar age to her dad, but it was hard to tell with the beard. Unlike her dad, he had a calm way about him. Like he'd seen it all and done it all. She never liked to ask him too many questions, although it didn't stop her being curious about his situation.

'I haven't had a doughnut for years. That was tasty, thanks,' said Kevin, letting Elvis lick the sugar from his fingers. 'It's funny the things you miss.'

'Like what?' asked Regan, trying hard to avoid jam dripping down her top.

'Eye contact,' he said with a wan smile. He and Regan exchanged knowing looks. The homeless were somehow invisible to most people. Kevin tilted his head back. 'I miss my mates, sofas . . . and those little chipped potato things . . .'

'What, chips?'

'No,' said Kevin, with a chuckle. 'Sort of cube shaped. I used to like those.'

'What about your family?'

Kevin took a deep breath. 'Goes without saying that I miss my folks, but . . .'

Regan felt compelled to fill the silence. 'Families are complicated, right?'

Kevin turned his gaze towards her. 'I couldn't bear to disappoint mine again.'

Regan opened her mouth to speak and was surprised by the loud bark that erupted until she realised it was from Elvis, who had spotted someone with a tray of coffees walking past.

'I best be off. Thanks again,' said Kevin. '*Carpe diem*.' And he made his way across the car park, Elvis lolloping after him.

She felt there was so much more to Kevin than just some homeless guy. Regan sighed to herself then looked at her watch. 'Shitterama!' Did someone fast-forward her life when she wasn't looking?

Back in the office she waved the doughnut bag in front of Alex's face. 'By way of apology for the earlier *accident*.'

Alex's shoulders slumped. 'Okay. But that was over the line for a gag, Regan,' he said, swiping the bag.

'Not a bloody gag. Why won't you believe me?' She was getting irritated now.

Alex looked in the bag. 'Ooh, chocolate dreamcake. You're forgiven.'

'Thanks,' said Regan, a little reluctantly. She still didn't like being falsely accused.

The rest of Friday was uneventful, with the exception of another lecture from Jarvis, but it was easier to take because she had a beer in her hand and a plateful of her favourite Chinese takeaway. Jarvis had also apologised for not waking her when he'd left, which had smoothed the waters somewhat. Despite his lectures, he wasn't a bad person, and she knew he had her best interests at heart. Even with his slightly obsessive need to keep the flat immaculate at all times, she was very fond of him; and nobody was perfect. It was yin and yang – she was spontaneous, he was a planner; she wanted to have fun and be a Bond girl, he wanted quiet nights in and government bonds . . . whatever the hell they were. She vowed that when she got to work on Monday she'd cross the 'get a new boyfriend' task off her list, because that was unfair.

As expected, on her arrival in Dubai, Cleo was liberally splashed across all social media platforms. Various pictures of her looking unspeakably glamorous accompanied by other beautiful people in stunning locations kept popping up on Regan's phone, all accompanied with masses of hash tags (something Regan didn't really understand). #LivingMyBestLife was one that kept popping up. Regan had to agree that Cleo really was living her best life. Work, my arse.

Jarvis left early for a golf match on Saturday, but not before he'd woken Regan with a strong coffee, enabling her to be at Cleo's studio with five minutes to spare before the boiler man was due. Regan had wondered if Cleo had told her the wrong time again, so she'd taken a magazine with her in case she had an hour to kill. She stuck the key in the lock and opened the door. Instantly the alarm sounded; a shrieking noise that made her eardrums rattle. 'Shi . . .' She flipped the cover on the alarm – but what was the code? She'd not written it down. She quickly scrolled to Cleo's last text message: **Boiler man at Studio 10am Saturday – DON'T FORGET**

No mention of the alarm code. Regan closed her eyes whilst the alarm echoed through her brain. Why couldn't Cleo use her birthday like everyone else? Cleo had said something about the code being related to a famous person.

'Good morning,' said a cheery man in navy overalls, making Regan flinch – she hadn't heard him approach thanks to the relentless racket of the alarm. 'You got a problem?'

'No, it's my alarm clock. Of course I've got a problem!' He pulled a face. 'I'm sorry,' she shouted over the alarm. 'I can't remember the code.'

'Try 1234. It's usually 1234.'

'No, it's something to do with a famous person. Leonardo . . .'

'DiCaprio?'

'No, the artist bloke.' Her head was throbbing in time to the incessant alarm. A few people passing by were glaring. 'Leonardo da Vinci!' shouted Regan as recollection struck her.

'Born fourteen fifty something and died fifteen something-or-other.'

Regan was stunned. She eyed the boiler man again – who'd have thought he'd know something like that? It was a reminder that she should never judge people on first impressions; although of course she absolutely did. She began inputting numbers and on the third attempt she struck gold – 1452 worked, and silence reigned. *Hallelujah*, she thought. And then: *Oh poo, now I'm going to have to change the code AND think of a reason to tell Cleo why I've had to change it.*

Her head continued to buzz, but she went inside and the boiler man followed. After a few minutes hunting for the boiler, she left him to it, while she raided the solitary cupboard for coffee. There was a tiny fridge but, sensibly, there was nothing in it apart from a half-used jar of pesto, so she made two black coffees and settled down in the only chair to read her magazine.

'Is this what goes for art these days?' asked the boiler man whilst unscrewing something.

Regan eyed the large canvas nearby. 'Yep. She makes a mint.'

He paused. 'Really? What are they?' He tipped his head at the large pinkish brown circle on the canvas. 'Abstract, is it?'

'Nipples,' said Regan and she disappeared behind her magazine.

The rest of Saturday was quite dull. Jarvis had insisted on having a bit of a spring clean, changing the bed linen and the towels, and it felt like that had taken up most of the day. When she'd finally flopped in a chair, Jarvis had hold of the TV remote and was flicking through the channels. The winning lottery numbers flashed up and she yelped.

'What?' he asked.

Regan realised she had no idea what her numbers were, and the ticket was safely locked in her drawer at work. Oh well; she'd have to wait until Monday to check them. 'I thought the thing before looked interesting.' She wasn't going to let on that she'd bought a lottery ticket.

'*Wheeler Dealers*? Okay,' he said, changing the channel back. She sank into the chair in defeat.

Regan spent most of Sunday in the kitchen: half the time cooking, and the rest trying to keep on top of the mess she was creating. It was such a shame that society didn't see her ability to make a mess as a talent, because she really was very good at it. Jarvis tapped on the door. 'Dare I come in?' he asked.

Regan scanned the room. 'Mmm, okay but don't freak out.'

'Now I'm already freaking out,' he said, pushing the door open a crack and peering cautiously inside. Apart from a few sticky patches on the worktop and some onion skins on the floor the kitchen was tidy.

'Ta dah!' she said, flailing out her arms and whacking a spoon resting in a saucepan of toffee, which sent a dramatic splatter up the wall. 'Shit!'

'And it was going so well,' said Jarvis, cracking a smile as he grabbed a cloth from the sink.

'It really was.' Regan's mouth turned downwards. It had taken a lot of effort to keep the mess at bay; she seemed to be able to make it multiply without any particular effort.

'When's dinner ready?'

'Ah,' said Regan, retrieving the gooey spoon from the floor and trying not to stand in the puddle of toffee it had left. 'I'm not making dinner.'

'But you've been in here ages.' Jarvis rinsed the cloth and had another go at the toffee that now appeared to be firmly attached to the paintwork.

'I'm making "special" toffee apples for Alex at work.' She indicated a tray of four toffee-coated balls covered in chocolate sprinkles with lolly sticks sticking out of them.

'Why special?' he asked, frowning at the toffee patch, which wasn't going anywhere.

'They're not apples. They're onions.' She did her ta-dah

hands again and narrowly missed the toffee spoon, so she shoved her hands in her pockets for safety.

His eyebrows knitted together. 'Why?'

'Because he dropped me in it at a meeting and kicked my pen across the floor. *Then* blamed me for him spilling *his* coffee *and* made me go to a director's meeting. It's payback.'

'It's juvenile.' He returned to trying to shift the toffee.

'It's funny,' said Regan, feeling deflated. It had taken a few coats of toffee to disguise the white of the onion but they looked just like innocent toffee apples now. She smiled to herself. She was pleased with her subterfuge, and it would be hilarious in the office tomorrow when Alex bit into one. What did Jarvis know? Having fun was definitely not one of his talents.

Regan had set two alarms for Monday morning so that she didn't have to rush with the toffee onions. She had carefully stowed them in a cake box because the thought of dropping them was too upsetting and most definitely something she was likely to do. In fact, dropping things was another of her many talents. Someone had once suggested she might be dyspraxic but she'd never bothered to investigate it further. She rested the box on the coffee shop counter while Penny fetched her usual order.

Her phone rang – it was Jarvis. 'Regan, did you remember to put the washing on?' he asked.

'Good morning,' said Regan, trying to think of an excuse.

'You forgot, didn't you?'

She'd been far too focused on the safe delivery of her toffee onions. 'Yeah, sorry. I'll put it on later.'

'But you won't,' said Jarvis. 'You say you will but you

won't. I'm fed up with everything being left to me. I do everything around the apartment. I cook, I clean and I do all the tidying up.' Regan rolled her eyes. 'I'm fed up with it. It's like being a student again.'

Regan had loved being a student. 'I'm sorry. All right?' She was in a good mood bubble and he was the prick that was going to spoil it.

'No, Regan, it's not all right. Things need to change.' And he put the phone down.

A bang on the glass made her jump and knock the cake box. 'Shit, Elvis,' she said, seeing the large hound with its feet up on the glass. 'Actually Penny, can you do me a small warm milk for Elvis?'

'Sure, on the house. But don't tell the boss.' She slotted the cups into the tray and passed them to Regan. 'Is it your birthday?' She pointed at the cake box.

Regan grinned. 'No, it's a surprise for a friend.' She tried to hide her smugness as she placed the coffees on top of the box and went outside.

'Morning, Kevin,' said Regan, passing him his coffee.

'Thank you. *Carpe diem*.'

'Elvis, sit,' said Regan, and the mutt's butt hit the floor like a soldier under fire. 'Good dog,' she said, impressed with his response. She looked at the small cup of milk and then at the large, gaping jaws of Elvis. She hadn't thought this through. 'I got him some milk,' she said lamely to Kevin.

'Thank you,' he said, pulling the small cup from the tray. He put down his own drink, took the top off Elvis's milk and carefully tipped a little into the dog's mouth. His tongue began working overtime even though it was fairly redundant because no lapping was required. The drink disappeared in seconds.

'Kevin, that was brilliant,' said Regan. Such a tender act of kindness. Elvis gazed adoringly at Kevin. They were a match made in heaven. 'Take care,' she said.

'You too,' called Kevin and Regan left with a spring in her step and a happy heart.

She took a moment before she walked into their office space because if she was grinning like a mad clown Alex would know there was something up. Once composed, she walked in with her shoulders back and her head high.

'Good morning,' she said to the back of his head. He jumped.

'Regan, you're early.'

'Only a couple of minutes. Here.' She passed him his coffee and then opened the cake box. 'And I made you these because I still felt bad about the coffee *accident*.' She emphasised the last word because she wasn't apologising for it. She stepped back and tried to control her excitement.

'Er, right. Thanks. But there's something far more important.' Regan puckered her eyebrows; her plan was getting derailed. 'Did you check your lottery numbers?'

'No. The ticket's in my desk drawer.'

'Open it, open it!' said Alex, beginning to bounce about like a toddler on too many Haribos.

'Why?'

'Because I took a picture of your ticket and I've checked your numbers and . . . I think you've won.' His words came out in an excited screech making Regan recoil.

'What?'

'I think you've won. But you need to check it. Check it now!'

'What? A couple of quid?' But she could tell from Alex's

body language that he was way too hyper for it to only be a few pounds.

Bubbles of excitement fizzed in her gut. She'd always secretly thought that one day she would win. Most people hoped they would, but she'd had a feeling that she couldn't quite explain. A luxury lifestyle of parties and cocktails felt like her destiny far more than working in a dull office drinking coffee out of paper cups.

'Open the bloody drawer!' said Alex, pulling her from her thoughts. She fumbled in her bag and pulled out her desk key. Inside the drawer was her ticket paper-clipped to her wish list. She pulled the ticket free. 'Here,' said Alex, thrusting his mobile at her. 'Here's Saturday's winning numbers.'

She tried to look at the ticket and back at the phone but the numbers kept dancing about. Her pulse was racing and she was starting to shake. She took a deep breath and checked the people around her. It was early and most hadn't settled at their desks yet. Nobody was watching them. She splayed out her hands in a calming motion and took Alex's phone. He continued to bob up and down beside her. Regan put her finger under the first number and checked it to Alex's phone. It matched. The second one, the same – it matched. And the third, fourth and fifth. She could no longer control the shaking. With a trembling finger she checked the last number. It was a match. 'I've won.' It was like fireworks going off in her head. 'I've bloody well won!'

'I know!' said Alex.

She threw her arm's around him and he stiffened. She held him at arm's length. 'How awesome is this?'

'Totally awesome,' he said, through a broad grin.

'Alex,' called the finance manager. 'Can I have a word?'

'Sure,' called back Alex. He turned to Regan. 'Don't do anything. I'll be back in five minutes. Okay?' he said, still grinning.

'I'm not telling anyone.' She certainly wasn't going to share any of her winnings with the other office dwellers – most of whom looked down on her anyway. They wouldn't be looking down on her any more. This was it. This was the turning point in her life. Everything was going to change.

Chapter Four

Regan was on autopilot. She switched on her computer and stared into space as it loaded. She didn't know how much she'd won. She pulled up the lottery website and checked the draw information for Saturday. She had another quick check of her numbers. They all matched. Something flipped in her stomach. This really was happening. She clicked on 'Prize Breakdown'. There was one winner for Saturday's draw and they'd won ten million, three hundred and thirty-seven thousand, four hundred and ninety-two pounds. And that winner was her. She stared at all the numbers that followed the pound sign.

Her phone rang and it was Jarvis. A spike of something unpleasant coursed through her. 'Regan, I'm sorry if I was harsh earlier but you really wind me up—'

'You really wind me up too, Jarvis. So shall we call it quits? I think we both know this isn't forever. No hard feelings. You get on with your neat and tidy life and I'll get on with mine. Okay?' She was shaking; she wasn't sure if it was the effect of the lottery win, or adrenaline at finally having the courage to exit a relationship that wasn't going anywhere.

'What? You're dumping me because of an argument over the washing?' he said, with a chuckle.

'Nope. I'm ending the relationship because it's pointless. We've been muddling along for a while now and . . .' she realised her manager was hovering at her shoulder '. . . hang on, Jarvis.' She tilted her head up.

'Is that a personal call?' Nigel asked, his grubby tie flapping dangerously close.

'Yes. Yes it is,' she said, with a broad smile. Oh, this was going to be so much fun. 'So if you could give me a minute that'd be great.' She shooed him away with a flick of her wrist.

'Jarvis. Our relationship has run its course. I'm sorry but I think it's for the best. I won't be coming back tonight.' She'd already decided that she'd book herself into the Grand Hotel for a few days while she worked out her next steps.

'But . . .'

'Oh and don't worry about my stuff. You can give the lot to a charity of your choosing. I'm making a whole new start so I won't be needing it. Find someone who appreciates your planning and tidying skills. And be happy because you deserve to be. Take care, Jarvis. Bye.' She ended the call. There was a touch of sorrow in her heart. They'd been together for almost two years and she was fond of him, but she knew she was doing the right thing. They'd only annoy the crap out of each other for a few more years, end up loathing each other and then split up anyway. She was just speeding up the process. This was the best decision for both of them.

She spun her chair around to face Nigel, who appeared to be simmering gently by the colour of his face. 'Right, now. How can I help you?' she said, in her most pleasant telephone voice.

'Shall we go into my office?'

'Yes, let's,' she said, propelling herself from her wheelie chair. Nigel stalked off. 'Hang on,' she said, snatching up her winning ticket. The last thing she needed was to lose that. She put it carefully in her back pocket.

She entered the office and shut the door behind her.

'Have a seat,' said Nigel, his jaw tight. Regan sat.

'Regan, you really are skating on thin ice. You do the bare minimum and your attitude—'

'Actually, Nige.' He looked like he'd been whacked in the face with a dirty dishcloth. 'Can I call you Nige?' He didn't respond. She leaned forward. 'Nige, I've been meaning to tell you a few things for quite some time. Firstly, you really are an irritating little man.' He started to bluster and she held up her palm to stop him. 'This is a pointless little carbuncle of a company and you are the tiniest, most meaningless barnacle on that carbuncle.' She was probably mixing her metaphors but she didn't care, she was on a roll. 'I have spent the last three years slaving my guts out,' okay, slight exaggeration, 'for no thanks, very little pay and a cheap mince pie at Christmas. Well, today that all stops. I don't give a crap about my job, this company or you. So you can stick your boring, shitty, low-paid job right up your bottom hole because I don't need it any more.' She stood up and relished the look of total shock on Nigel's face. 'In case you didn't get that: I quit. And lastly, you really should change that tie occasionally. It's very unhygienic. Bye.' She left the room and did a Bridget Jones style sashay across the office. It felt good. Better even than all the times she'd imagined it in her head – and that was quite a few; mostly when she was meant to be working.

She patted the ticket, which was still safely in her back

pocket. She was going to go to her dad's. She wanted him to be the first to know about her Lotto win, and she wanted to see his face when she told him. Partly because her dad didn't react to anything, so this would be a big test. Plus, she was planning on getting totally wasted on the most expensive cocktails available and she'd need someone she trusted to get her back to her luxury hotel.

I hope they have those big suites you see in films, she thought whilst she filled an empty printer paper box with the contents of her desk. She swiped the stapler, because they could hardly sack her for nicking it, and she wanted some sort of memento from this chapter of her life. She picked up her lottery wish list and nestled it reverently on the top of her things – she was going to need it. There wasn't a lot to show for three years and, for a moment, it felt a little sad. She straightened her shoulders; that was all going to change. From here on out she had money to sprinkle like fairy dust on her life. It felt amazing.

She scanned the office. Almost all heads were down; everyone was busy working. They were oblivious to the massive life-changing event going on in their presence. There was no sign of Alex. She left a Post-it note on the cake box, which read EAT ME, and grinned to herself. She'd call him later. Maybe he could join her after work for cocktails.

'Bye, losers!' she hollered, then she strode out of the office, out of the building and into her new life.

Well, she would have done if she hadn't had an altercation with the bloody revolving doors. Trying to get through with her box was more than tricky. She got the box wedged and the door jammed. She reversed back out, ignored the sniggering receptionist, and tried again. Halfway round she heard someone call her name.

'Regan!' It was Alex and he was waving frantically at her. She staggered out into the street clutching her box and waited for him to join her.

Alex flew out of the revolving door looking puffed. He took a second to get his breath.

'What the hell are you doing?' he asked.

Regan jolted backwards in puzzlement. 'I'm ditching this shithole and starting my new life. I told Nigel to stick the job up his arse and change his filthy tie. You should have seen his face.' She snorted at the memory. That was a picture she would savour for a very long time. 'Oh and I've told Jarvis we're over. It was going to happen sooner or—' The colour was draining from Alex's face and it made her pause her story. 'Are you all right?'

'Regan . . .' He shook his head. Well, it was more of a wobble.

'What?' He was acting very strangely and he was delaying her starting her celebrations. She thought she'd try a cosmopolitan cocktail first – she'd never had one and had always wondered what they were like. Then she would order lots of expensive champagne.

Alex held a lottery ticket aloft. Regan peered at it. 'Oh, did you win something too?' He couldn't have shared the jackpot, because she'd already seen on the website that there was just one winner. And it was her – eek!

Alex was shaking his head. He really didn't look very well. He took a deep breath. 'You've not won the lottery.' He swallowed hard.

Regan grinned at him. 'Yes, I have.' She pulled the winning ticket from her back pocket. 'We've both checked the numbers.'

He shook his head; his expression was solemn. 'That is not your lottery ticket.'

'Yes, it is. It was locked in my desk drawer.' She frowned at him. He wasn't making any sense.

'This is your ticket. I switched them,' he said, his face ashen. 'I have your spare desk key. The ticket you have does have the right numbers but it's for *next* Saturday's draw. I bought it this morning.' Regan's grin vanished and a wave of nausea swept over her. She opened her mouth to speak but she had no words. 'I was getting you back for the coffee. It was just a joke. A prank. I didn't think—'

Regan was shaking her head like a bobble head strapped to a racehorse. 'You're lying.' Her stomach felt like a washing machine on spin cycle. The sounds around her were muffled, like she'd been immersed in water.

'Check it,' he said, calmly, and pointed to the ticket she was clutching. She studied the lottery ticket that she thought had changed her life. She blinked at the date. He was right – it was dated for next Saturday. The realisation of what she had done hit her. An icy sensation went over her like she'd just done the ice bucket challenge. She had walked away from her job, her boyfriend and all her possessions. All because of a stupid prank. She slowly looked up. Her whole body started to shake uncontrollably. 'You bastard!' she yelled, dropping the box of office stuff and launching herself at Alex.

The force of her sent him flying backwards into the revolving doors and she followed, screaming like a banshee with its hair on fire. She pummelled him with her fists whilst he held his arms over his head to try to protect himself. 'I'm sorry!' he shouted. Regan grabbed his head and began banging it on the glass, the momentum of which started to turn the revolving door.

'Ow! Ow! Ow!' hollered Alex, each time his head hit the glass.

'You fart-brained shitbungle!' yelled Regan.

Someone grabbed Regan from behind and hauled her off Alex. With her arms still flailing she turned around to have a go at whoever had interrupted her. 'Woah!' said a broad-shouldered guy. 'You need to calm down.'

'You need to keep out of this,' snapped back Regan.

'I'm a police officer.'

'Then arrest him. He's ruined my life!' She spun back to have another go at Alex but he had managed to push the revolving door round so he was trapped in the middle section, where he was safe from her assault. 'Argh!' she beat her fists on the glass in frustration making Alex wince like a trapped animal.

Inside the security guard was heading towards the doors. 'Come on,' said the police officer, who wasn't wearing a uniform. 'You don't want to get arrested.'

'You need to arrest *him*.' She shot the police officer a glare, but stopped short when she noted his stony response. She was in enough of a mess. He was right – she didn't want to get arrested, although at least she'd have somewhere to sleep tonight if they locked her up. The thought was a sobering one.

Chapter Five

Regan watched the police officer picking up her scattered items and returning them to the box. It was like watching someone else's life scattered across the pavement – fragments of her minor achievements that had now been rendered completely useless by Alex's practical joke.

'Come on, let me buy you a coffee,' said the officer, standing up.

Her whole body was trembling with shock. She watched Alex scramble out of the revolving door into the safety of the lobby and speak to the security guard. He still looked scared but he was telling the guard he was all right. She wanted to kill him. She'd never felt like that in her life before. She hadn't known she was capable, but right now she wanted to do Alex serious harm.

The police officer took hold of her arm. 'Come on,' he said, giving her a tug to make her walk. She reluctantly dragged her glare away from Alex and walked in step.

Regan was in a daze. Her life was ruined. Everything wiped out. And for what? Payback? A laugh? She turned on her heel and began heading back to the office.

'I am going to kill Alex.' It was the only solution.

'Hang on,' said the copper, with a firm grip on her arm,

making her swivel round. He was surprisingly strong. 'You're looking at an actual bodily harm charge. He's not worth it.'

'He's worth doing time for murder,' said Regan, wrenching back her arm in frustration.

'I tell you what: seems like you need something stronger than a coffee, so I'll buy you a drink. You tell me exactly what's happened. And if you still feel the same, I'll hold him still for you. Deal?' He gave her a cheeky grin. If her world hadn't just imploded she'd have found it cute, but right now it was simply annoying. 'I'm Charlie, by the way.'

'Regan,' she said.

'From *King Lear*?'

She frowned. Had there been a recent adaptation on the telly or something? 'Yeah. That's right.' It wrong-footed her enough that she stopped resisting and found herself being towed along by Charlie, who was still gripping her hand.

In a nearby bar she regaled him with the whole sorry story, accompanied by animated arm-waving for full effect. When she reached the end she felt like she'd hit the bottom of a well.

'What can you charge him with?' she asked, hopefully.

Charlie pursed his lips and shook his head. 'I'm pretty sure there's nothing he could be charged with. He's done nothing against the law.'

'But . . .' her voice faded. She knew he was right. 'It'll be all round the office by now.' She cringed at the thought of the water cooler gossip.

'He may keep it to himself.'

'That's not how offices work. It'll be the biggest thing since Chris got a beard trimmer in the secret Santa draw.'

'Didn't he like it?'

'No, *she* didn't.' Regan stared at the small glass of brandy and large coffee Charlie had bought her.

'Life has a funny way of making you look at things differently.' He leaned forward a little.

'Oh yeah. It's shitting well hilarious.' She shook her head. This guy was no help. Regan downed the brandy and when it hit the back of her throat she grimaced. She noted the slight tremor was still there in her hand as she returned the glass to the table.

'You might not see it now, but this might end up being the best thing that's ever happened to you.' Yep, this guy was nuts.

'Charlie, I'm sure you are a well-meaning person, and I guess looking out for members of the public is your job, but I fail to see how losing *literally* everything in approximately ten minutes could be the best thing that's ever happened to me.'

She picked up her coffee, appraising Charlie over the rim. If she hadn't felt so miserable she would have been far more appreciative of his easy good looks and stubble-swathed jawline. He was having a rummage in the old printer paper box, which now contained everything Regan had left in the world. He pulled out her lottery wish list and managed to give it a quick scan before she hastily snatched it off him.

'I saw this when I picked up your things. There's some life-changing stuff on this list. What's stopping you doing those things anyway?' he asked.

'Erm. Oh, let me see,' she said, her voice dripping with sarcasm. 'The lack of ten million quid for a start.' Just saying the amount out loud made her feel sick. She'd lost ten million pounds. She couldn't imagine anyone else on the planet had lost so much money in such a short space of time. A little voice in her head unhelpfully pointed out that she'd never actually had any winnings, but that wasn't the point; she had genuinely thought she'd won the money – and now every single penny was gone.

'You don't need money to enjoy yourself,' said Charlie, taking a long sip of his coffee.

Regan was too tired to argue. Her whole body was fatigued. She wanted to curl up in a ball, but she wasn't going to do that in front of a complete stranger – she still had her pride, if nothing else. 'I need to get back to my car. And then . . .' Then what? She stared at Charlie.

'Is there a friend or a family member who could be with you?'

Cleo sprang into Regan's head, but she was thousands of miles away living her hashtag-best-life. A life Regan had thought she was about to share. Next, she thought of her dad. She didn't want to bother him; but what choice did she have?

'I'll drive over to my dad's.'

'I can give you a lift.'

'No, don't worry. Turning up in a cop car is the last thing I need.' She forced a brief smile.

Charlie's forehead puckered for a second, and then it was gone. 'I'm off duty. No cop car. You promise you won't go after that Alex guy?'

'I promise,' she said, begrudgingly. She finished her coffee. 'I should get going.' She had absolutely no need to get going – other than that she needed a bloody good mope away from this kind stranger.

'Sure thing. Look . . .' He opened his wallet and pulled out a card. He took a pen from her box and wrote his name and mobile number on the back. 'This is a group that might interest you. Help you focus on the here and now and what's good about it.'

Regan read the card. 'Mantra – mindfulness for beginners? It's a full mind I'm suffering from – it's full of how quickly my life has turned to shit.' She could see he was trying to help. 'But thanks. I'll think about it.'

'No, you won't,' said Charlie, which was unexpected.

Regan narrowed her eyes at him. 'I might.' She was feeling dogmatic.

'We'll see. Anyway . . .' he got to his feet. 'Nice to meet you, Regan. Take care of yourself.' He held out a hand to shake.

The odd formality of it made her smile. 'You too, Charlie. Thanks for not arresting me back there.'

'What? Oh, my pleasure.'

She watched him leave. The feeling of being totally alone swamped her and she quickly picked up her box and left.

Regan hurried through town clutching her belongings like her life depended on it. When she reached the market, it was in full swing: stallholders shouting out the day's best bargains; elbows out enabling others to get to the front; busy people swerving in and out on their way to somewhere important. The burger van hissed as a fresh batch went on the griddle and a chill wind blew through the stalls, making all the coverings slap about wildly. Everyone and everything had a purpose. Apart from her. She was surrounded by bedlam and yet she'd never felt more alone in her life.

Regan wasn't sure if it was the brandy, but her head started to swim. The noise, the bustle and the smell were all too much. She was going to pass out. She reached for a stall, but she wasn't close enough. Her legs buckled and she dropped her box, but someone grabbed her securely around her waist and kept her upright. She shook her head to clear it.

'You're not well. You need coffee,' said a kind voice.

'Kevin?'

She was about to protest but the feel of something wiry under her fingers pulled her concentration. Elvis was standing the other side of her, his head under her hand. He looked up, his sad eyes appearing concerned.

Kevin and Elvis guided her out of the main thoroughfare and to the Hug In A Mug coffee shop. Kevin took her inside.

'Customer,' he called. 'You'll be all right now,' he said, and he scuttled out of the door before Penny appeared.

'Hey, what's happened to you?' asked Penny, coming from behind the counter. Regan didn't know where to start: from nowhere, the tears started to pour. She had always been irritated by crying – in her mind it served no good purpose. She didn't believe those people who said you'd feel better after a good cry. It made your face blotchy and your nose run and quite often it gave you a thumping great headache to make you even more miserable.

'Sorry, no tissues.' Penny offered Regan a bundle of serviettes instead, which she took gratefully. 'I'll get you a coffee and you can tell me all about it.'

Regan took a moment to pull herself together while Penny made her a coffee and left the other waitress to field the couple of customers who had come in. 'Here,' said Penny, handing Regan a cup and pulling up a chair.

A loud bang on the glass right behind Regan's head made her almost jump off her seat. She spun around and came face to hairy face with Elvis. Kevin popped his head round the coffee shop door, pushed Regan's box inside and gave her a tentative thumbs-up. 'You okay?' he asked.

Despite everything, she couldn't stop the smile appearing. She responded with a thumbs-up and Kevin beamed back at her. Kevin really did have nothing and no-one, and yet he was still able to smile. It touched her that he'd come to her rescue and gone back to pick up her box, which she'd all but forgotten about. Penny opened her mouth but Kevin took the hint before she said anything and retreated outside to join his dog.

Penny was lovely, but Regan didn't want to spill out the whole story again. What good would it do? The more she went over it the more stupid it made her feel. What an idiot to have been taken in by such a moronic prank. She waited until she felt a little better, thanked Penny and headed off.

Hugging her old paper box to her chest, Regan tapped on the glass of her dad's front door. She'd taken some time in the coffee shop to order her thoughts and calm herself down. More than anything it had been an almighty shock – one that it would probably take her a while to recover from – and in the meantime she needed a roof over her head. She knew she could go back to Jarvis's flat, but as he hadn't called or messaged her since their earlier conversation, he obviously wasn't desperate to have her back; plus she didn't like the idea of using him just because things had gone spectacularly wrong, and if she went back now that would be all she was doing. She also had a large dose of stubborn pride that was stopping her: that, and the thought of having to put her tail between her legs and admit she'd messed up again – no, she couldn't go back to Jarvis's. The sentiment that had underpinned her decision to end their relationship was the right one, although the timing could have been so much better. They had been treading water for a while and, whilst this approach was most definitely more akin to ripping off the plaster rather than soaking it off gently, it was still the right thing to do.

The chill of the April breeze made her shiver. She took a deep breath and tapped on the door again. She could see movement through the opaque glass.

'Who is it?' Her father sounded annoyed.

'It's me, Dad.' He opened the door and hastily beckoned her inside. He was wearing his dressing gown but had socks on his feet. It was an odd combination for the middle of a Monday afternoon – or at any time, come to that. 'Are you all right?'

'Er, yeah. I'm fine. What can I do for you?' He tightened his dressing gown cord and hovered near the door. Her father lived in the same one-bedroom maisonette that he had bought after her mother had left him and taken everything (except Regan) with her.

Regan balanced her box on the back of his sofa. 'I'd kind of like to stay if I can?'

Her father's eyes widened. 'What? Here?'

It wasn't the welcome she'd hoped for. 'If that's all right.' It was feeling very much like it wasn't all right at all. She knew she'd be on the sofa, but that'd be fine for a few nights while she licked her wounds and sorted a few things out.

'Have you had a row with Jarvis? Because I'm sure you can sort that out.' Graham adjusted his dressing gown again whilst his eyes darted about. There was definitely something wrong.

'Not exactly, but—'

A noise from the bedroom stopped her mid-sentence. She turned to listen, and then turned back to her father. He was biting his lip. 'Is there someone else here?'

He nodded sheepishly. 'Tara just popped round . . .' He broke eye contact and Regan surveyed her father's attire afresh.

Tarty Tara was there. Regan knew exactly what *she'd* popped round for. She suddenly had a horrible thought that under his dressing gown he was probably not wearing anything at all. She almost knocked her box to the floor in her haste to snatch it up. 'Oh, I've just remembered something.' She lurched for the door, desperate to escape before embarrassment ate them both alive.

'Right. Okay then,' Graham called after her, enthusiastically. 'If you're sure?'

'Yes. Certain. I'll be fine.'

'Maybe next time give me a call first?' he said, hiding behind the door as he opened it for her.

'Yes. Good idea. Thanks. Bye.' Something made her pause. She leaned round the door and kissed his cheek. 'Love you, Dad.'

'Um, yes. You too, Regan.' He gave her an awkward smile before closing the door. She heard hysterical laughter erupt behind the glass and rolled her eyes at them behaving like teenagers.

That was her only family member in a fifty-mile radius. Now what?

Chapter Six

She trudged back to her car and sat there thinking. Her phone pinged to indicate she had a message. It was from Alex.

V sorry. Hope UR OK.

Regan shook her head and deleted the message. Worst-case scenario; she could sleep in her car. It wasn't ideal, but at least she wouldn't be joining Kevin and Elvis on the streets tonight. Although it would still be a bit chilly in the car. A thought struck her. Perhaps she'd sit it out? Tarty Tara would likely be off home soon. Yes, that was a good plan. Wait for Tara to clear off, then she could try to explain again to her dad what had happened and kip on his sofa. She reclined her seat so it was a bit more comfortable, and she waited.

Two hours later her phone rang, pulling her from a delicious dream about swimming in an infinity pool with a pet hippo and Liam Hemsworth. Her neck was stiff and she wasn't sure where she was for a moment. Then she remembered, and a little dark cloud seemed to hover above her. She picked up her phone – it was Jarvis.

'Hi, Jarvis.' She prepared her resolve.

'Regan, I just wanted to check you're not having some sort of breakdown.'

Regan closed her eyes and tried to keep her irritation levels at a manageable level. 'No, I'm fine thanks, Jarvis. But I am sorry if it was all a bit sudden.'

'No, not at all. I mean I was a little surprised that it was *you* instigating it rather than me, because I've been considering it for quite some time . . . I just didn't know how to broach it.'

Great, thought Regan, *another blow to my dwindling self-esteem*. 'Well, I'm glad you finally approve of one of my decisions.'

'Anyway, I don't think I should be responsible for giving your belongings to charity. I don't want to get caught out legally. So I've packaged them up for you to collect whenever suits.'

'Thanks.' It was a small thing, but at least she had her stuff back even if she didn't have anywhere to put it.

'When would you like to collect it?'

So much for whenever suits you. 'I can come straight over now.' She glanced up at her father's front door. There didn't seem to be any sign of Tarty Tara leaving; her tarty Toyota was still parked outside. Maybe she'd be gone by the time she got back.

'Great. I'm off to Waitrose, so please lock up properly and push your key through the door.'

'Will do. Bye.' It was some consolation that she hadn't broken his heart with her phone call this morning – although had he been a little more upset, it might have helped her feel a bit more valued than she currently did.

Regan was dashing about Jarvis's kitchen when Cleo FaceTimed. Her phone was on the counter so she hit the answer button.

'Regan? You there?'

Regan picked the phone up from the counter. 'Hiya, I'm just . . . I'm . . .' She realised she couldn't drop all her woes on Cleo – she'd only fret. And what could she do when she was thousands of miles away? 'How are you?' asked Regan, trying to sound bright and carefree.

'I'm okay.'

'You at another party?' It looked like a hotel lobby in the background.

'Yeah. I've stepped out for a bit of a break.' Cleo looked like she was stifling a deep sigh, or a yawn.

'What time is it there?' Regan opened and closed kitchen drawers.

'Nearly three in the morning.' She looked tired. 'I could go but I loathe being in a hotel room alone. I think I might be a bit homesick.'

'Blimey. Ow!' Regan was only half listening. 'Bloody skewers.' Regan sucked her finger.

'Are you cooking?'

'Don't look so surprised!' said Regan. 'No, I'm not cooking, but I could be. I'm looking for a corkscrew.'

'What else are you doing? Remind me what normal people do.'

'It's riveting. I'm having a mug of soup.' Regan held up the mug as evidence whilst she moved around the flat picking things up and stashing them in a black bag.

'Soup?' Cleo chuckled.

'Yeah. It's hot and nutritious.' *And I don't know when I'll get to eat again*, she added in her head. Regan squinted at the screen. 'Is that Elon Musk behind you?'

'Oh, I expect so. I'm so bored with celebrities. Oscar wheels me around like a kid in a supermarket trolley introducing me to anyone who might get us more social media coverage. They're like playing cards. On one side is a pretty picture: bright, colourful and engaging; but on the other there's very little at all and what's there is bland and functional.'

'Wow, that's deep,' said Regan, pausing with a gin-scented candle in her hand. It was hers, but did she really need it?

'Unlike most celebrities,' quipped Cleo.

Regan watched a parade of beautiful people mill about behind Cleo. *That could have been my life*, she thought dreamily. 'Oh, Cleo, you're so lucky.' Cleo opened her mouth to protest. 'No, please don't get me wrong; I know you've worked so hard for this, but to get the chance at a life like yours is millions to one and I'm so happy for you. Tell me how fabulous it is?' She knew she was staring at her like a child anticipating a bedtime story.

Cleo took a moment to answer. Her smile seemed forced. 'Yes, of course it's fabulous. Let me show you the view.'

Regan made a series of awestruck noises as Cleo panned around the sights of Hong Kong harbour. It was quieter outside and Cleo found somewhere to perch.

'Okay, well you'd better get back to the party,' said Regan. 'Have a brilliant time.' Still holding her soup, Regan moved out of the kitchen and into the hallway – she didn't have long before Jarvis returned and she wanted to avoid a face-to-face confrontation if she could.

'Hang on!' Cleo's voice sounded a bit desperate and it drew Regan's attention. Cleo was silent for a moment as if trying to think of something to say. 'How did it go with the plumber?'

Regan shrugged. 'Fine.'

'Er . . . Any difficulties?' Regan shook her head. 'All fixed then?'

'Yep.'

'And you locked it all up properly?'

'Yep. No problems. The studio is all locked up safe and warm.' Regan frowned as a thought struck her. 'It'll be there empty just waiting for you to get home.'

Cleo appeared sad for a moment. 'I guess so. I miss my little studio. It's my safe place, where I feel most at home.'

'Actually you could live there if you wanted to. Couldn't you? It's got virtually everything a person could need.' Regan could feel her eyes widening as she spoke.

'Not really. It's against the terms of the lease so I'd get kicked out. And there is a loo but there's no shower. No cooker, no washing machine, no—'

Regan was waving at her to stop. 'Right, well, I need to . . . um . . . dash,' she said.

'Are you sure you're all right?' Cleo peered at her through the screen.

'Me? Yes, brilliant. Top banana! Don't you worry about a thing. I'll check on the studio for you if you like?' Regan leaned in closer to the camera.

'No need.'

'It's no bother at all. You leave it with me. Anyway, cheers!' said Regan, holding up her mug and liberally splashing soup over herself and the screen.

'You're bonkers! Cheers,' replied Cleo, holding up her champagne glass. The call ended.

'Shitterama . . .' Regan stared down at her feet and at Jarvis's beloved rug. The pale cream wool was now liberally doused in tomato soup. A few more trickles dripped from her hand, landing like paint on a new canvas. She rushed back to the kitchen in a panic, knowing that Jarvis would think she'd done this on purpose.

How on earth am I meant to clear this up? she thought,

scanning the cupboards for something to clean it with and grabbing a cleaning spray and a cloth. The quicker she acted, the better chance she had of saving the rug. She sprayed the cleaner liberally over the stain but on the third squirt she halted mid-squeeze. 'Green!' The cleaning fluid now overlapping the orange soup stain was bright green. 'What the . . .' She checked the label. 'Oven cleaner.' Discarding the bottle, she began rubbing the orange and green together in the valiant hope the green would somehow magically eliminate the orange. It didn't. After a few minutes she leaned back on her haunches and surveyed the rug. It looked worse than when it was just the soup stain. Now, thanks to her vigorous rubbing, the stained patch had a certain fluffier quality than the rest of the rug. She shook her head. This was hopeless. As usual, she was only making things worse.

In desperation, she laid the best part of a roll of paper towel on top of the rug in an attempt to draw out all the moisture whatever its colour. That seemed to help a little bit. She put some fresh kitchen roll on top. There was nothing else she could do – she could almost hear Jarvis's voice telling her sarcastically that she'd done more than enough.

She fired off a quick text to him: **Sorry. Had a bit of an accident in hallway. Take care and be happy. Regan.** This way it wouldn't be a total surprise and hopefully he would realise it wasn't her being vindictive. She quickly grabbed the bin bags Jarvis had left, as well as a few more essentials she needed like shampoo, coffee, biscuits, the Easter Egg she'd not scoffed yet and his spare razor – whatever happened, she liked to keep her underarm hair under control. She also took the pen he kept by the phone – not because she needed one, but because she knew when he went to use it and it wasn't there it would drive him disproportionately crackers.

She hurried from the building trying not to think about the good times she'd had there. It would only upset her and she needed to stay positive and look to the future. She grinned to herself as she headed off – not towards her dad's place as she'd originally planned, but instead towards her Plan B, which she was mightily proud of.

Chapter Seven

This time Regan was thinking ahead. The alarm code for Cleo's studio was now Regan's birthday, so she could at least remember it. Once she had managed to sneak all her stuff in to the studio without attracting any attention she shut the door and waited for her racing pulse to settle, feeling like an MI5 agent on a top-secret mission. She looked around Cleo's studio. This was to be her home for the next two months, unless of course she got discovered and kicked out. *That absolutely must not happen*, she thought. Cleo would be terribly upset if she lost the studio – Regan knew how much she loved it, having been with her the day she'd found it. Back then it had been a dirty, dusty sanctuary for spiders and rodents, having been used previously as a store for a nearby garage. Now it was clean and critter free – thanks to a lot of TLC from Cleo.

She sat herself down in her friend's comfy chair: an oversized, slouchy, modern affair. Perfect. She could definitely sleep here, she thought, pulling out the teddy bear throw she'd taken from the flat and drawing it over herself. Cosy . . . What more could she need?

She smiled to herself. The place was a bit paint-splattered but otherwise clean and dry. Her eyes landed on Cleo's latest canvas of a large nipple and the smile became a pout. That was a little off-putting. It felt as though it was studying her . . . Judging her. She closed her eyes but it was no use – she knew it was there. She opened one eye. The nipple was still staring at her. Regan pulled off the throw and huffed. She'd have to move it. Carefully, she lifted the nipple picture and leaned it, nipple side down, against the opposite wall. *Much better*, she thought, and snuggled back under her cosy cover to try to get some sleep.

She woke up super early. Typical: on the one morning she could actually have a lie-in; although lie-in was stretching it, given her position was more hunched up than lying down, but that wasn't the point. It was the first time in years she wasn't meant to be up and out for work, and she'd woken up mega early. What sort of sick reality was that?

Her positive mood from the night before was apparently only temporary. She felt weighed down with a sense of impending doom that was no longer impending but fully *in situ*. She hadn't got much sleep because her mind had been far too busy panicking about the situation she was in. One that – for once – was not entirely of her own doing. *Bloody cockwombling Alex*, she thought. A fresh wave of anger and injustice engulfed her and she paced the studio saying out loud all the things she wished she'd thought of yesterday. Why did the perfect insult always wait twenty-four hours before appearing in your head?

She threw insults around like pebbles but they didn't make her feel any better. This was all so unfair. And on top of everything, there was no milk, so she'd had to have black coffee again.

She stomped about the studio for quite some time until she got tired and the adrenaline powering her subsided, at which point she flopped into the chair. The fury that had kept her going had turned to despondency as the reality of the mess she was in truly hit home. She no longer had somewhere to live. The studio was a very temporary setup until Cleo came home; even more temporary if anyone caught her living there.

She no longer had a boyfriend – although if the latest stream of texts from Jarvis were an indicator, she would be hearing from him again very soon via his lawyer regarding what he termed the criminal abuse of his rug.

She didn't have a job, and that meant she had zero income. She also didn't have any savings as such – just a few quid in her bank account that she had been holding onto so she could buy Jarvis a birthday present. At least that was something.

She was also surprised to discover that, on top of everything else, she'd lost her purpose – and this was most shocking of all. She hadn't liked her job, but then who did? Moaning about bosses, colleagues and too much work was par for the course, but when it suddenly wasn't there it left a great big nine-to-five-shaped hole.

Regan spent a while mulling over whether to call Nigel and ask for her job back. Eventually, she swallowed her pride and rang Nigel's number, but as soon as she'd been put through to him he went into corporate mode, listing all her faults and making it very clear that returning was most definitely not an option. She thanked him kindly and hung up.

Regan sat there staring at one particular brick in the bare Victorian wall. This brick wasn't like the other red bricks; it wasn't a perfect little clone like the rest. The surface of this one was rougher; pock-marked, almost. It didn't have defined angular corners and sharp edges. They were worn and rounded, partly due to it being slightly out of alignment. It didn't quite fit, so someone had chipped bits off it in an attempt to wedge it in, but had simply managed to scar it instead.

That brick was her. She was damaged and scarred. She didn't fit.

She closed her eyes. She was losing the plot. She needed to get out before she went totally Jack from *The Shining*.

She'd been pleased that her dad was at home when she'd telephoned, and frankly delighted to hear that he was alone and she was welcome to pop round.

After the usual niceties, she followed him into the kitchen and he put the kettle on.

'What's up, Regan? You never come round in the daytime.'

It was like the time she got found out for smashing next door's greenhouse; he was giving her the same look of disappointment.

'It wasn't my fault,' she said, remembering too late that her defence of the greenhouse situation had started with the exact same words. 'I thought I'd won the lottery and it turns out I hadn't, but because I thought I had . . .' He was watching her intently. She swallowed hard. 'I dumped Jarvis, quit my job and moved out of the flat.' She bit her lip and waited for his response.

'Coffee?'

Not the response she was expecting. 'Er, yes please. So . . .'

He shrugged his shoulders in a slow movement. 'That wasn't very smart. Was it?'

And the award for stating the bleeding obvious goes to Graham Corsetti. 'I know that, Dad, but like I said I thought I'd won the lottery.'

'Money's not everything, Regan.'

'I know.' It was like being in a parallel universe. Why were parents so obtuse sometimes? And especially when you needed them to help you get to a solution 'So what do I do?'

'Get another job?' His face was stoic.

'Yes.' That was the most logical thing. 'What else?'

He scratched his greying temple. 'I don't know.' He brightened up and squeezed her arm. 'You'll think of something.'

She blinked rapidly. Clearly he was not comprehending the huge shitstorm her life had become. In fact, shitstorm didn't really cover it – this was more global shit tsunami with extra-large fans.

'I feel like a pea in a river – too small to swim against the tide.' She felt quite poetic and proud of her analogy.

Her dad screwed up his face. 'You'd like to pee in a river?'

'No. A pea . . . Oh never mind.' *Why was it so hard to explain?* 'It's like someone's slammed the brakes on my life.'

'Hmm.' He was pulling a doubtful face, but she continued unperturbed.

'I mean, I was hurtling along and suddenly I've come flying off the rails.'

'I see,' said Graham, in a tone that said he wanted the conversation to end. He was a rather logical, straightforward person, lacking the encumberment of extremes of emotion – an unkind soul may have called him 'odd'. He was still pulling a face as he passed her a mug of coffee and opened a fresh packet of cheap chocolate digestives.

'What?' asked Regan, catching sight of his twisted lips.

'Well, I'm not being funny, Regan, but it's not like your life was motoring along at a pace, now was it?'

'Oh, thanks a bunch.' She snatched a biscuit from the proffered packet.

'No, what I mean is, in life's race, you're less Aston Martin, more Nissan Micra – slow and steady.' He was smiling, like he thought this was a compliment.

'Bloody hell, Dad. You're not helping my self-esteem here.' She'd been called lots of things in the past, but never a Nissan chuffing Micra. She knew he had a point though, however harshly worded. She'd liked to think she was pootling along taking the scenic route in life, but she could hardly claim that when on her life's journey so far there really hadn't been anything worth seeing – dead ends of jobs, a scrap heap of relationships and a junk yard full of mistakes. She dunked her biscuit and half of it disintegrated into her coffee. She frowned and tried to scoop it out with the other half of the biscuit, making the situation infinitely worse.

Graham was frowning. 'Where are you staying?'

'Cleo's place.' She didn't like lying, especially not to her dad, but technically she *was* staying at Cleo's – just in her studio and not in the flat where he had obviously assumed she meant, judging by the relief on his face. She knew he was secretly pleased that she wasn't going to put him in the awkward position of making excuses as to why she couldn't stay at his.

'That's good then. But you know if you're desperate you're welcome to stay here.' His shoulders tensed.

'It's fine, Dad. It's only temporary. Just until I get myself back on my feet.' He looked relieved.

'You okay for money? Because I've a little put aside.'

She doubted he had very much put by. He worked part-time in a newsagent's and it was sweet of him to offer but she needed to sort this mess out on her own. 'I'm fine.' If she said it often enough with conviction there was a possibility that she might start to believe it herself. 'Really. Fine.'

Three days later, she was all out of self-belief. And ice cream. All too quickly, her world had been turned upside down, and she had no idea how to right it. She knew the answer wasn't to drink her troubles away, and she couldn't afford alcohol anyway, so she had eaten a skip load of ice cream instead. Regan had been spending a lot of time with her new best friends Ben and Jerry, but sadly she didn't find any answers at the bottom of the cartons – only brain freeze and a little self-loathing.

She decided that this was what rock bottom felt like. She'd heard from no-one with the exception of one FaceTime call from Cleo that she'd had to reject for fear of her spotting the familiar background of her own art studio. They'd had a text chat instead, which was nowhere near the same. No-one else had called. Nobody had noticed she had slipped off the planet. Not one other person cared.

She hadn't showered in days and felt wretched, tired and lethargic – though some of it may have been down to too much ice cream. She had no telly, no WiFi and no future. Everything felt too difficult. There was so much that needed sorting out, but every time she thought about it, she thought her head might pop with the overload. So it was easier not to do anything at all.

Regan found herself at a new low when she tried to eat

a pot noodle using two coffee stirrers for chopsticks. It was a tough challenge, but at least it was warm and kind of like a meal, although she wasn't sure how much nutrition there was in the reconstituted dust and noodles. She counted three dried peas, which definitely didn't get her close to her daily government-suggested fruit and veg targets.

She wondered at how quickly she'd lost everything, and if this was what had happened to Kevin. How had he found himself living on the streets? If it weren't for Cleo's studio being empty, that could have been her. The thought frightened her. She pulled over the box she'd filled in the office on That Day – which now seemed like ages ago – and sifted through the contents, sniffing her derision at the useless things inside. A stolen stapler; what good was that to her now? Unless she used it for stapling Alex's testicles to his desk – but he wasn't worth the staples. She found the Mantra card from Charlie, the gallant stranger who had pulled her off Alex. She turned it over. Saturdays at ten at the community centre. Charlie had said mindfulness might help her focus on what was good about the here and now. She gave another derisory snort – there was nothing good about her life.

Regan bit the inside of her mouth and pondered. She had nothing planned for Saturday – or the rest of her life – so there really was nothing to lose.

She sniffed her armpit, whipping her head back from the nasal attack. She couldn't go anywhere smelling like that. What had she become? She straightened her spine. This had to stop, and it had to stop now, before she drifted into a pot-noodle-induced coma and was found in a giant spider's web being nibbled on by rodents.

'Right,' she said out loud, giving herself a start because

her voice was all croaky from not having spoken for days. She felt herself galvanising for action. What to do first? She caught another whiff of her armpit. Getting showered was definitely priority number one.

Regan had her most favourite trip to the gym ever and was pleased that her membership card still worked. With any luck, it would take Jarvis a while to realise he was still paying for the joint membership; and since he was still paying, it would be a shame not to get some use out of it.

In the past she'd only ever had a quick shower after a gym session and dashed out, but today she could set a more leisurely pace. She made the most of the free shampoo, conditioner and body wash and took her time drying and styling her hair – taking care not to make it too fluffy for fear of it looking like she was wearing a motorcycle helmet. She felt a lot better for it and a bit of a spring returned to her step.

Back at the studio, she washed her clothes in the sink using Cleo's Molton Brown hand wash and hung them over Cleo's three easels to dry. She'd bought a local paper, so she made herself a black coffee and sat and circled a number of potential jobs. This was progress. She had a tall mountain to climb, but she had a foothold and the only way was up.

However, a few hours later she started to feel like she was slipping back down the mountain. A phone call to a recruitment agency had her stumped at the first hurdle when they asked her for her home address. After a long pause she gave her dad's details and explained it was temporary. The second hurdle was a bit more difficult – they wanted her to upload her CV to their website.

She had no computer and she was dangerously close to her monthly download limit on her mobile. She felt a mudslide sweep her back down the mountain and went again in search of ice cream.

Chapter Eight

After another uncomfortable night sleeping in the chair and a now-permanent ache in her neck, Regan woke to face another day staring at four brick walls, a couple of nipple paintings and a gloomy looking future. She gave herself the best wash she could manage in the tiny sink and made a strong coffee. She didn't have the solution, but she at least knew diving back into the ice cream wasn't the answer.

She brushed her hair, checked her armpits and headed off for the mindfulness session with an open mind – and, if she was honest, a spark of interest in seeing Charlie again. She told herself she needed to thank the kindly policeman, but it wouldn't do any harm to check whether he was seeing anyone. If anything he might make a pleasant distraction.

The community centre where the session was held wasn't far, and she decided to walk to save the meagre amount of petrol she had in her car in case she needed it to get to a job interview – she was trying to remain hopeful. The community centre was a simple affair, so it was easy to find the large room with a circle of chairs and a hotchpotch of locals milling about. She watched the interesting mix of people through the glass in the door and began to reconsider. Was this really for her?

'Hello, I'm Cressy,' said a tall woman with neat grey hair and a long, flowing cardigan. 'First time?' Regan nodded. There was no sign of Charlie and she was starting to wonder if this had been a bad idea. 'Tea or coffee?' asked Cressy, beckoning her inside.

'Um . . .' Regan checked her pockets for the fiver she'd brought in case there was a charge.

'It's free, and there's biscuits. Custard creams this week.' Cressy had a warm smile.

'Coffee, please. Lots of milk.'

'You take a seat. Pop your details on here,' she said, handing Regan a clipboard, 'and I'll get your drink.'

Regan scanned the form. It was all basic stuff. She began filling it in but the pen was running out. She scratched it on the edge of the paper and it worked, but as soon as she tried to write in the boxes it stopped. She sighed. Why did pens do that?

'I had that problem,' said a nasal voice to her left. 'I'm Chris. That's me.' He leaned over and ran his finger along the line above Regan's. She gave a tight smile and gave up on the form. She scanned the people taking seats. These weren't her kind of people. What was she even doing here? There was no point staying just in case Charlie showed up. He wasn't that cute, it wasn't worth it.

She stood up to leave, but Cressy took the clipboard from her and swapped it for her coffee.

'Biscuits are on their way round,' she said, taking a seat nearby. If she left now she'd miss out on a free biscuit. She'd stay for a bit.

'Welcome to Mantra, everyone,' said Cressy. The chatter

ceased and everyone looked in her direction. 'While we're finishing drinks . . .'

The door at the back of the hall creaked open and Charlie rushed in. He took a seat, nodding greetings to some of the others until his eyes alighted on Regan. He gave her a slow, almost regal nod. She liked that he was surprised to see her. She twitched an eyebrow in a 'See, told you so' response.

'Sorry I'm late,' said Charlie.

'That's fine. I was just welcoming our new members,' Cressy peered closely at the form, 'Chris and Reg?' Regan sprang to life, almost spilling her coffee. She held on tightly to the mug and tried to ignore Charlie, who was tittering nearby.

'Hello, I'm Chris,' said Chris.

Regan felt all eyes land on her. 'Hi. I'm Regan.'

'Oh,' said Cressy, studying the form. 'It says Reg.'

'The pen was running out,' Regan tried to explain, but nobody seemed to hear.

'Like the president?' asked an older woman in a brightly coloured kaftan.

'If you mean Ronald Reagan,' started Regan, and the woman nodded, 'then no, that was pronounced Ray-gun. Mine's Ree—'

'I had an Uncle Reg.' A man with Harry Potter-style glasses cut her off. 'Jolly nice chap. Nice to meet you.' This set off a series of welcomes from around the circle and ended with Charlie.

'Lovely to see you again, Reg,' said Charlie, failing to control a smirk.

Great, thought Regan. She'd have her free coffee and biscuit, if the packet ever made its way around to her, and then she'd escape.

'Would someone like to share what mindfulness means to them?' Cressy looked hopefully around the group.

'I will,' said the lady in the kaftan. 'I'm Wendy and I had a stroke six months ago. So for me, mindfulness is about teaching my brain to keep focused. It's about staying calm, not getting frustrated about all the things I can't do, and focusing on the many things I can do.'

'Thanks, Wendy. Anyone else?'

The man in Harry Potter specs put his hand up. 'This is only my fourth session. I'm getting over a breakdown. I'll probably always suffer from depression and low mood, but mindfulness helps me to spot the simple pleasures in life rather than giving all the attention to the bad stuff.'

'Thanks, Joel.'

A bearded face leaned forward. 'I'm Mandeep and coming to Mantra makes me sleep better.'

A young woman gave a little wave and Cressy nodded at her. 'I'm Ellie and I'm in remission from cancer and I live in fear of it coming back. Mindfulness helps me take time to order my thoughts and feel calmer.'

Regan knew she was staring. She didn't know what she had been expecting, but these revelations from these poor people about everything they were going through was definitely not it. On first superficial look they had all seemed perfectly healthy.

She felt like a complete fraud. What did she have to worry about? A few things swamped her mind. Okay, there was stuff to worry about, there always was, but her problems weren't life-threatening. What these people were dealing with was serious stuff.

'Thanks, everyone. Right, let's start with a full body scan,' said Cressy. 'Please can you move your chairs to the side and get out the yoga mats.'

Regan was unsettled; she hadn't been expecting to do yoga, and apart from a couple of people in trackies, nobody else looked like they'd dressed for it. 'Here you go, Reg,' said Charlie, putting down a yoga mat for her next to his own.

'Actually, I'm not sure I . . .' she began, but Cressy was talking so she copied Charlie and sat down on the mat with her legs crossed.

'Now, Chris and Reg,' said Cressy, and Charlie stifled a laugh. Regan glared at him and he turned his laugh into a cough. 'Don't be alarmed, this is really easy. All you need to do is lie down and listen to my voice. Okay?'

Regan and Chris both nodded. Lying down she was good at and, after a few nights scrunched up like a hamster in Cleo's chair, the opportunity to lie out flat was a welcome one. She stretched out and was pleased with how comfortable the mat was. She wondered if they'd miss one if she borrowed it for a bit.

A few people produced pillows and took off their shoes. Cressy waited until everyone was settled. 'Close your eyes. Empty your mind. I want you to focus all of your attention on your feet . . . Specifically your left foot . . . and your big toe . . .'

Regan grinned. This was all a bit bonkers. 'Keep your focus on your big toe . . . Think about how it feels.' Cressy had a melodic voice, which thankfully was pleasant to listen to, and whilst Regan found herself tuning in and out she did try, as Cressy suggested, to keep pulling her attention back.

Cressy moved their focus from the big toe to other parts of the foot, and eventually over the whole body, until they were focused on their breathing. When someone on the other side of the room snored, Regan couldn't stop a snort of a giggle. Cressy continued unperturbed. Despite the giggles, Regan did feel calmer; she probably wasn't far from nodding off herself. She was interested by how difficult it was to keep her mind focused on Cressy's voice, and how easily it was distracted by the minutiae of life that littered her brain like plastic in the ocean.

They finished the body scan and Cressy went on to tell them about practical ways of using the techniques. She suggested losing your temper was a good opportunity to deploy mindfulness. Regan had a sly look in Charlie's direction and he was staring straight at her. Rude. She didn't make a habit of pummelling people's heads on revolving doors, but, in his defence, he didn't know that. She smiled and he smiled back. Cressy went on to teach them some other practices, but then all too soon the session was over and people were packing away their mats.

'So, Reg,' Charlie appeared at her shoulder, 'what did you think?'

'Hmm.' She wanted a moment to consider her thoughts.

'Actually, let's get a drink and you can update me. Okay?' He was already walking for the door.

She had nothing else planned. 'Why not?' she said, with a lazy shrug. She didn't want to look too keen.

She suggested her usual coffee shop and they walked through the bustle of the Saturday market. The market always had a vibrancy that buoyed Regan. Whether it was the sights, smells or banter of the stallholders she wasn't sure, but there was something about it that brought her to life. When they neared the coffee shop, she spotted Kevin hunched in a doorway. He was hugging his knees and rocking. Elvis was leaning against him as if trying to comfort him.

'I'll get the coffees,' said Regan, when they went inside and joined the short queue.

'Sorry. The rule is that whoever suggests it pays. So I have to pay.' Charlie nodded sagely.

'Thanks, but I want to get a couple of extra drinks for my friends.' She nodded towards the doorway.

'That's cool, I'll get theirs too. It's near payday so I'm flush. Order away.'

Regan thought about standing her ground, but with only a few quid in her pocket she wasn't in a position to be stubborn. 'Cheers, that's kind of you.' And generous, she thought.

Penny wasn't about so another woman took her order. When the drinks arrived on the end of the counter, Charlie took his and Regan's. 'Shall I get us some seats? I'm assuming you're not going to run out on me.' He gave a pout, which made him look rather sexy.

'I'll come back, I promise,' said Regan, giving him an equally flirty look. This was fun.

She almost bounced over to Kevin and crouched down next to him. Elvis towered over her and was very excited that she was within licking distance. She scratched his head to try to keep him occupied, although his focus was on the paper cups. Kevin's eyes were tight shut and he was muttering something inaudible. 'Kevin, you okay?'

His eyes popped wide open in an alarming fashion, making Regan almost topple backwards. 'Birds,' he said, in a whisper.

'Birds?' She looked about her. There was a pair of wood pigeons pecking about nearby.

'They get in my head.'

His hunted expression was bothering her. 'Here, have a coffee. I got milk for Elvis.'

Kevin blinked a few times and seemed to almost come to. 'Thanks . . . I bet you think I'm mad, don't you?'

'No, but you had me a bit worried there.'

He smiled at her. And then he froze. 'Listen.' There was a buzz of background noise from the hubbub of the nearby market.

'Yeah, always noisy on a Saturday.'

'No. Listen to the birds.' His eyes were wide and he was worrying her again.

Regan closed her eyes and concentrated. Could she hear birds? 'I can hear a pigeon.' Its rhythmic coo of 'da-dah-da-da-dah-dahhh' was easy to pick out.

'Yes, yes, that's it.' They listened together. 'Can you hear what they're saying?' Regan gave a slow and slightly bewildered shake of her head. Kevin spoke along to the pigeon's tune. 'You *can't* do it, Kevin. You *can't* do it, Kevin!'

Regan would have laughed if Kevin's face hadn't been etched with horror. 'Come on,' said Regan, helping him up. She needed to find him somewhere away from the wood pigeons; all the scraps from the market must have drawn them in from The Level, so they'd be there for a while.

They walked until she found him a wall to sit on. 'There are no birds here.' She gave him the drinks. 'Here.' The dog was now slathering wildly and had not left her side.

Kevin's eyes darted anxiously about and then he seemed to relax a little. She sat next to him while he sipped his drink.

'Not seen you this week. You been on holiday?' asked Kevin, now seemingly almost back to normal.

'No, I quit my job.'

'For a better one?' Kevin tilted the milk cup for Elvis and he wolfed down the contents.

'Er . . . no. I'm in between jobs. But it's okay.' She nodded and Kevin nodded too.

'I wouldn't want to be cooped up in an office.' He was staring straight ahead. 'I enjoyed working in the fresh air too much. The smell of the sea.'

Regan was curious. 'What line of work were you in?'

'Engineer.' His voice had taken on a clipped tone.

'Did you enjoy the work?'

Kevin looked at his scarred hands. 'Yeah, most of the time.' He snapped his head back. 'Anyway, thanks for this.' He held up Elvis's empty cup.

'You're both very welcome. And thanks for taking care of me the other day. It was kind of you.'

Kevin shrugged a shoulder. 'Ditto.' They smiled at each other. 'Well, *carpe diem*.'

She figured that was her cue to leave. 'You too.' Seeing Kevin kept reminding her that she was only one more bad decision away from being on the streets herself, and it scared the life out of her.

Charlie was watching the door when she returned and looked relieved to see her. She sat down and picked up her drink. 'That'll be cold by now, let me get you a fresh one,' he said, getting up from the table. She noted his empty cup. 'I need another coffee anyway.' She didn't argue.

He returned with the drinks and a couple of muffins. She went to protest but he waved it away. 'I was hungry. Okay?'

'Okay.' She picked up the cake and began eating. It tasted divine but it crumbled everywhere. She could see Charlie was amused by it. So unlike Jarvis, who would have been on level two tutting by now.

'So,' he said, when he'd finished eating his, 'are you coming back to Mantra?'

She tilted her head to one side. He was one big incentive to go back, and not just because of the free muffin. He was very easy on the eye and, from what she could tell, he appeared to be totally lovely to the core. It was hard not to compare him with Jarvis. He was so much more easy-going. And he was patient. There was no way Jarvis would have waited in a café on his own like Charlie had done. Charlie was generous too, she thought, whilst she savoured her muffin. He was so much more fun than Jarvis. She liked the easy rapport they'd quickly developed.

So was she going back to Mantra? 'Yeah, I think so. It was a bit weird but I liked it.'

'The trick is to practise. It's like any new skill; you need to keep doing it and you'll get better.'

'How long have you been doing it?' She noticed his eyebrows twitch. It had been ages since she'd flirted, and it was like flexing a little-used muscle. She popped the last of the muffin in her mouth and mourned its end.

'Five months. I miss a few because of shift patterns but I'm usually there most weeks.' Now she knew where she'd be most Saturday mornings too. 'What's new with you?' He looked bright with anticipation and she hated to bring down the mood.

'Not a lot. I've been looking for a job but it's tricky with no WiFi, no computer and no fixed abode.'

His expression changed to concerned. 'You said you had somewhere to stay.'

'Yeah, I do, but it's a friend's business premises. Living there is against the rules and she doesn't know I'm doing it. It's all a bit precarious.' When she thought about it she got a bit panicked so she sipped her drink to try to distract herself.

'Did you know the computers at the library are free to use?'

'Thanks, that's good to know.'

'Look, Regan. I know we've only recently met, but if you'll let me I'd like to help you get back on your feet. What happened to you was really . . .' He looked like he was searching for the right word.

'Shitty,' she offered.

He laughed. 'Exactly. What do you say? Will you let me help? No strings.'

Right now she could do with people she could trust on her side. He'd been right about the mindfulness and it couldn't harm to have a police officer on her side. Especially one with such a long list of positive attributes. 'Sure, why not?'

'Okay. Let's have a look at local jobs.' He scooted his seat round to her and cosied up, and she noted he smelled of aftershave and coffee. He pulled up a website on his phone. 'HGV driver? Maybe not.' He eyed her cheekily.

'You don't know. I might be qualified,' she said, making him tilt his head in question. 'I'm not, as it happens, but I do like a Yorkie. Next.' She leaned over his screen and got another whiff of aftershave. This was a good way to spend a Saturday.

'Sous chef or carpentry lecturer?'

'A bit niche.'

'Recruitment consultant. How ironic,' he said. 'Assistant drainage engineer?'

She wrinkled her nose. 'What's a production operative?' she asked, touching the screen. They both read the details together. Picking, packing and labelling boxes. It wasn't glamorous but it was probably the only one she didn't need qualifications or experience for. He took a screenshot of the details, they swapped full names and phone numbers and he sent it to her. She typed his name in next to his number – Charlie McGee.

Chatting with Charlie was making her feel buoyed and ready for action. She'd had a great time with him but now it was time to leave. As they were exiting the coffee shop, a man the same size and shape as the doorway loomed over him. Regan feared there was about to be trouble.

'Hey Debbie, what you up to?' he asked.

Regan was confused. Had he mistaken her for someone else? But, before she could question him, Charlie spoke. 'Hiya, Beanstalk,' he said. 'Beanstalk, this is my friend Reg.'

Regan didn't argue; everything was already too strange. 'Nice to meet you, Beanstalk.'

'You too, Reg.' He gave an unsubtle head tilt in her direction and winked at Charlie.

'Bye, Beanstalk,' said Charlie, slapping the large fellow on the back when they passed in the coffee shop doorway.

Beanstalk turned back for a second. 'Hey, Debbie, I heard you got a bollocking from the station commander about Thursday's shout. Tough call,' he said with a wince, before disappearing inside.

'You wanna tell me what went on there . . . Debbie?' asked Regan, failing to hide her amusement.

Charlie screwed his face up. 'It's a work thing. Pretty much all of us have nicknames.'

Regan grinned. 'And yours is *Debbie*?' By comparison, Reg didn't seem bad at all. 'Oh, Debbie McGee.' The penny dropped. 'That's genius.' She laughed.

'Isn't it?' said Charlie, not looking that impressed; but he'd likely witnessed this reaction before.

'And what did you get a bollocking about?' It was

reassuring to hear about others making a hash of things at work, although it was unlikely to be on the same scale as hers.

Charlie rubbed his stubbly chin. For a moment he appeared vulnerable, making her warm to him even more. 'I didn't exit a burning building when I was instructed to.'

Regan was surprised. 'A burning building? Like one on fire?' *How brave was this copper?*

Charlie looked like he was chewing the inside of his mouth. 'I may not have been entirely truthful with you when we first met.' He looked suitably chastened. 'I said I was a police officer so that you'd listen to me and stop pummelling that bloke's head in. But I'm actually a fire-fighter.'

'Right,' said Regan. She wasn't entirely sure how she felt about this news, but her instant reaction was one of distrust. Clearly he wasn't totally trustworthy or he would have owned up to this a lot sooner. 'So you lied.'

'I figured you wouldn't take any notice unless you thought you were about to be arrested,' said Charlie. 'I'd forgotten about it, which was why I didn't put you straight. I'm sorry.'

Regan didn't need people she couldn't trust. He no longer looked quite so appealing. 'Yeah. Me too,' she said, with a disappointed smile and she walked away.

Chapter Nine

Sunday in the studio was lonely. Its location was off the beaten track but in the week there was the sound of traffic to make her feel like she had some connection to the rest of the universe. On Sundays, not so much.

Yesterday, thanks to Charlie, she had gone to the library after she'd left him and got herself registered so she could use the computers. She'd managed to produce a reasonable-looking CV and fire it off for a couple of vacancies, as well as uploading it to some job websites. She'd also been able to check out some books, which at least meant she had something to do in the evenings other than stare at bare walls or nipples.

This morning she'd been to the gym, taking care to avoid Jarvis's usual timeslot, and had really enjoyed her time on the bike and the treadmill because she'd been able to watch some telly, which now seemed like such a treat. She'd used the yoga area to have a go at practising her mindfulness technique and ended up having a little nap. She'd also had a shower so she was clean too – she had a lot to be thankful for.

The spring weather was notoriously changeable and it had turned a bit chilly. The drop in temperature was noticeable in the studio: its high ceilings whisked away any warmth and, whilst the boiler was doing its best, the two radiators didn't provide much heat. She moved the chair so that she could lean against a radiator, got out one of the library books and started reading.

Three lines in, her phone rang. It was Charlie. She considered cancelling the call but she knew she'd probably acted a little hastily yesterday. 'Yep,' she said, her tone curt.

'Delivery for Reg Corsetti. Where should I deliver to?'

'Delivery of what?' She was more than suspicious after his revelation.

'Chinese takeaway and chocolate cake. It's my way of apologising.'

Regan knew it was going to be hard to stay mad with this guy for long, especially when he brought food as an apology. Could this be a match made in heaven? She gave him directions to the studio on the proviso he wouldn't alert anyone to the fact she was living there.

Regan tidied her stuff into the corner and covered it with the throw, because old habits died hard. She waited excitedly for her knight in shining armour to appear, complete with chicken chow mein.

There was a gentle tap on the door and she whipped it open making him flinch slightly. 'Shhh,' she said, beckoning him inside and shutting the door quickly. It was raining and a chill wind was picking up. Charlie put down the bags on the drainer and looked about.

'Welcome to my temporary abode.'

He was giving reassuring head bobs but she could see he was taking it all in. He pulled two bottles of wine from one of the bags. 'I didn't know if you preferred red or white, so I bought one of each.'

'That is exactly what I prefer,' she said, getting two mugs off the mug tree.

Charlie gallantly let Regan have the chair, whilst he perched on an odd little wooden stool with a round seat that you had to spin to get it to go up or down. Regan had forgotten to point out that she didn't have any plates or cutlery, but Charlie had brought free chopsticks and passing the containers to each other and eating directly from them was actually quite fun.

'See, no washing up,' she said, when she could eat no more. 'Although I will wash up the chopsticks – they'll come in handy.' They were a step up from the coffee stirrers.

Charlie sipped his wine and surveyed the studio. 'I know you said it was basic but . . . I kind of expected you'd have a bed.'

'Nope. This is it. But it's more than a lot of people have.' A picture of Kevin out in the wind and rain instantly sprang to mind.

Regan tidied up the cartons and used an odd-looking arty tool of Cleo's she'd found to cut the cake into slices. 'So, firefighter, huh?' She took a bite of the cake to stop herself from making any lame jokes about firemen's poles or long hoses.

'All my life, apart from brief stints as a waiter and a dustman.'

'That is pretty awesome, being a firefighter . . . not a dustman.'

Charlie gave a modest shrug. 'I'm not academic but I've always known I needed to have a job with a purpose. Something that added some value to other people's lives.'

Regan felt instantly inadequate. She'd never felt like that at all. She was starting to think her dad was right about the whole Nissan Micra analogy. 'I don't know what the hell I've been doing with my life.' She finished her cake and licked her fingers.

Charlie chuckled. 'I'm sure you've done plenty.'

'Nope. I've been bumming around, basically, doing as little as I can get away with.' She marvelled at her own honesty. She took a swig of her wine, wincing at both the clash of wine with chocolate cake and how little she had achieved. Friends from school were married and had kids in tow but that had never been an ambition of hers. If she thought about it she'd never really had any ambition. Even the school careers advisor had suggested a job as a fishmonger might suit her, and whilst that was a perfectly good job, it wasn't exactly setting her sights high. She feared invoices clerk at BHB Healthcare had been the peak of her career. She chuckled to herself and Charlie scrutinised her.

'So, what now?' he asked.

Regan drank more wine and sighed slowly. 'I fired off some job applications from the library. Thank you for that tip,' she said. 'I've uploaded my CV to a few job sites, too, so hopefully in a couple of days they'll be beating my door down.' She tried to sound optimistic but she didn't believe it herself.

'There are other options.'

'Like?'

Charlie looked like he was going to lean back on the stool and then thought better of it. He put down his wine and went over to the corner to the box Regan had brought from the office – not as well tidied as she'd thought. He returned with Regan's lottery wish list.

'I keep thinking about this,' he said, waving it near her but just out of reach.

'Don't remind me.' She drained and refilled her Cookie Monster mug.

'I think this is an excellent thing to have done.' If Regan had worn glasses she would have been looking at him from over the top of them right now. 'Bear with me. You wrote this because, like all of us, when we think about winning the lottery we think it is the key that unlocks all our dreams. So this list,' he tapped the paper, 'is a true list of the things you really want to do with your life.'

'*If* I won the lottery,' she added.

He shook his head. 'Regardless of winning. You still want to do them; you just need to find a way of achieving them without the money.'

Regan laughed and then saw his expression was serious. She needed more wine. Charlie topped up both their drinks and picked up his Hong Kong Phooey mug, eyeing her speculatively.

Regan snatched up the list. He was being ridiculous. She scanned them. 'Which of these is even vaguely possible without tons of cash?'

'Well, the bottom one is, but we'll come back to that.' She scanned it quickly; the last item was 'Get new hot boyfriend who doesn't nag or wear button-up pyjamas'. She looked back up again slowly; this was a promising development. Charlie was looking thoughtful now. He tapped a bullet point towards the top of the list. 'How could you help your dad out?'

'Suggest he dumps Tarty Tara.'

Charlie was grinning broadly. 'Tell me more about Tarty Tara. I think I love her already.'

Regan shook her head. 'Where to start . . . She's ten years younger than my dad. She works part time so she's round his all the time. I'm sure she's bleeding him dry moneywise.'

'Any redeeming features?' Charlie was looking amused.

Regan screwed her face up in thought. 'Hmm, she puts the hoover round. That's about it, though.'

'So what does he need help with?'

'He's only got a one-bedroom flat. I was thinking I would buy him somewhere nicer. I definitely need lottery money for that.'

Charlie was nodding. 'Could you make his flat nicer in any other ways?'

Regan was feeling put on the spot. 'Dunno.' Charlie was watching her expectantly. 'It needs redecorating and his kitchen is really dated but I don't think there's much I could do there without ripping it all out.'

Charlie leaned forward. 'But the redecorating wouldn't cost much – only your time and a bit of paint.'

Regan waved her mug at him and the contents sloshed about, making her realise she was probably a bit more drunk than she'd thought. 'You forget that paint costs money and I have none.'

'I've got friends in the trade. They have half tins left over all the time. I'll speak to one of them if you like?'

Regan studied him. He was ruggedly handsome with very good teeth. He'd got her out of trouble when she could have quite happily brained Alex. He'd bought her a takeaway and wine, and here he was offering suggestions of how she could help her dad. She found herself ticking off a list of everything she wanted in a partner and Charlie was it. This guy was sent from heaven. 'You're brilliant,' she said, feeling it was a pretty good summary.

Charlie went coy. 'Just being a friend. I'm a big believer

in karma. You know, that the good you do will come back to you eventually.'

He used the 'f' word. Friend. That was unfortunate, because right at that moment she wanted to snog his face off. 'Do you really believe that?'

'I have to.'

Her booze-addled brain was trying to process what he'd said when he got unsteadily to his feet. 'I should go.' He picked up his jacket and pointed to the door.

'It's been a great evening. Thanks for dinner and everything.' She stood up and held on to the wall to steady herself. How much had she drunk?

She followed him to the door and when he spun around to say something they both froze as their faces were so close to each other. Regan didn't stop to think. She kissed him. She didn't have to wait for his reaction. He kissed her back, hard. They were soon up against the brick wall exploring each other in a frenzy of booze-fuelled lust.

'Ow,' said Regan, grazing her back on the rough brick-work.

'Sorry,' said Charlie through a gasped breath. 'Chair?' he suggested after scanning the bare room.

'Okay.' They made it to the chair, their lips still attached. Regan paused. How was this going to work? She sat in the chair and Charlie awkwardly kneeled next to her and they resumed their feverish kissing. The chair rocked precariously. Regan clutched the sides whilst still mid-kiss. Charlie's weight shifted and so did the chair, tipping them both unceremoniously to the floor.

'Ow,' said Charlie. 'Dodgy joint,' he explained, getting to his feet and rubbing his knee. 'Old injury.'

'Actually that was killing my back,' said Regan, and they paused to look at each other rubbing their separate sore patches. They both dissolved into hysterics. 'That killed the mood.'

'Maybe it's for the best. We've both drunk quite a bit,' said Charlie, planting a kiss on her forehead. 'I'll see you soon. Okay?' He gave her a look that made her go weak at the knickers.

It was more than okay with Regan; the sooner the better.

Regan was settling down to sleep when she saw she had new emails. Maybe it was a job interview. She yawned and flicked through them. Nothing about any jobs, but there was one from Cleo. She opened it expecting to see photos of fabulous places, but instead it was late-night ramblings.

Hey You!

Hope you're okay and not missing me too much lol. My brain's a bit foggy because we had a long flight and an even longer car journey . . . Followed by a meal where I was expected to engage with people. I tried my best but Oscar informed me that it was a woefully inept performance and I need to improve before we meet the next round of prospective buyers. But that's the least of my worries. A top art critic saw an early preview of my new collection in Japan and to say they slated it would be too much praise. There wasn't a thing they liked about it. They said: The colours held as much vibrancy as mud. The style felt like a poor copy of Cleo's earlier work. Even the size of the canvas in their opinion was wrong. Or as they put it, 'obese'. They concluded that I've had my day and my moment in the sun is over.

Oscar is furious. I'm a bit torn. Part of me is happy to retreat back into the shadows and paint. Leave behind the madness of the celebrity lifestyle and be normal. But now it's happened, it's a far bigger blow than I'd ever thought it would be. Financially, it's not great, and all the anxiety I've carried about being an imposter, a fraud, just a lucky chance that I once painted something that was okay . . . now that's come crashing down on me too.

Coupled with that, there's also Oscar's temper to deal with. He swore at me last night. Wanted to know if I'd said something out of line about the reviewer that may have got back to them. Oscar believes this particular person is vain enough to take out their revenge via a review. I know I haven't said anything out of place but I've still been awake all night going over every conversation I can remember that could have in any way been misconstrued. And I've drawn a blank.

Everything's a mess and I'm virtually on the other side of the planet from you. And I know, unlike Oscar, you actually care about me. I miss you. Tell me everything's going to be okay?

Love

C

x

Regan typed a hasty reply:

Everything is going to be okay.

Love

R

X

P.S. Oscar is a twat.

P.P.S. Will write properly later.

Chapter Ten

While Regan tried to drown her hangover in coffee, she studied her lottery wish list with fresh eyes. Charlie had a point about how genuine this list was. It was all the key things she really wanted to change in her life. Could some of them really be possible without winning the lottery? She'd certainly enjoyed herself last night without spending a penny. Although obviously Charlie had and she wasn't expecting him to pay for everything going forward. It made her think of Charlie and a warm glow lit her up inside – and this time it wasn't being caused by the wine. He was quite simply perfect. He was the whole deal physically, and also everything she didn't even know she wanted in a companion and a relationship. At least something good had come out of this disaster. Whether he was entirely worth it . . . only time would tell.

She'd had another uncomfortable night in the chair and her neck ached. If she wasn't careful she'd have a permanent disfigurement from sleeping curled up like a cat. What she needed was a bed. She was almost fantasising about having a bed again. And not just because of the fun she and Charlie could have in it . . . right now a decent night's sleep was even more appealing than sex, which was saying something.

A good night's sleep: that was her goal. It was an odd place to get motivation from, but motivation it was.

Regan pulled her attention back to the list. She decided the island with bare-chested waiters would have to wait, as would the pedigree puppy, but the idea of running her own company was sparking something inside her brain. She had always wanted to be her own boss. At school, her Olympic-level laziness had been much maligned by teachers but practically worshipped by her peers, and so it had been something she was extremely proud of. Now she could see it hadn't done her any favours over the years. It would be a hard habit to break, but if she was working for herself, all the time and effort she put in would directly benefit her – something that had an even greater appeal than doing nothing.

If she were to set up a company, what sort of thing would she do? She put down the list, hugged her coffee mug and thought. It would have to be something that made money; otherwise what was the point? Her mind was blank. She looked around the studio. Cleo had a gift for painting. Some of the things she'd painted over the years had been stunning, but it was the nipple work that had brought her fame and, most importantly, fortune. She could tell by the tone of Cleo's email that she was worried about the bad review, but nothing bad ever happened in Cleo's life so Regan doubted it would be anything more than a bump in the road. Regan's road was one giant bump, and she had to work out how to overcome it. If she was to work for herself she needed a breakthrough idea. She needed her own nipple, so to speak. But for now, it eluded her.

Regan's phone sprang into life. A FaceTime from Cleo. Regan panicked and scanned the room quickly. She couldn't cancel it knowing how worried Cleo had sounded in her email. The toilet door was pretty nondescript. She dashed over to it, pointed the phone at a suitable angle and answered the call.

'Hiya.' She beamed at the camera and then realised how manic she looked and tried to calm it down. 'I'm at my dad's,' she volunteered, trying hard to appear normal.

'Oh, right. Is he all right?' asked Cleo, her expression one of concern.

'Yeah, he's fine.'

Cleo was frowning. Her perfect skin puckered. 'Shouldn't you be at work? I thought it was about eleven in the morning at home.' She seemed quite confused.

Shit, thought Regan. 'Yes. Yes, it is eleven o'clock on Monday. So that makes it what time where you are?'

'It's seven in the evening. But is your da—'

'And where are you exactly?' asked Regan, brightly talking over Cleo in an attempt to distract her, because she had absolutely no idea why she would be at her dad's in the middle of the day barring medical emergency or catastrophic disaster.

'Japan,' said Cleo, bluntly. She was still frowning. 'Why are you at your dad's?'

She clearly wasn't going to let it go and the odd camera angle Regan was having to maintain to avoid the bare brick studio wall was making her already achy neck spasm. A thought struck her. 'Tara! Tarty Tara has . . .' *Come on, brain, what the hell has Tarty Tara done?* pleaded Regan. She scanned the studio for inspiration. '. . . got her tits out.' *Really? Is that the best you could do?* she admonished her brain.

'She's done what?' asked Cleo, looking suitably horrified.

'She . . . um . . . boob-flashed someone. Yes, that's right,' said Regan, so far out of her comfort zone it was like rolling naked on a cheese grater. 'Tara was out with a friend. She'd drunk too much. Mixed red and white wine,' she said, taking inspiration from last night's empty bottles. 'And she flashed her boobs at some guy in the street. Only it wasn't some guy, it was an off-duty police officer and she got herself arrested.' Regan gasped for breath. She'd told the whole made-up story on one lungful of air and was now quite exhausted.

Cleo was shaking her head but a smile was creeping across her features. 'That's hilarious.'

'It's not,' said Regan.

'So what happened exactly?'

Regan was getting grumpy. 'I've told you what happened.'

'Yes, but did she get a caution or a fine?' Cleo was grinning broadly. At least she looked happier than she had when Regan had answered the call.

'I don't know the details, but Dad was devastated so I came straight round.'

'Is he there now?'

'Er. No . . . he's popped out for . . . some milk.' She was talking like she was doing a hostage video under duress. 'Anyway, how are you?'

'Not great. I've been panned by a critic and Oscar is having a meltdown about it.'

'I know, I read your email. I'm sorry.' Regan could tell this was more serious than she'd realised. 'What can you do?'

Cleo pursed her delicate pink lips. 'Nothing. I can't magic a new collection. We've got to ride it out and hope the buyers aren't too heavily influenced by the piece.'

'I'm sorry, Cleo. That's rubbish. If there's anything I can do, you just have to say.'

'Thanks. I might need you to pop round to the studio.'

'Er, okay. Any time. Just let me know. Sorry, but I'd better go. Keep me posted on everything. And I'm here if you need me. And I can be at the studio any time.'

'Thanks, that makes me feel better.'

Regan ended the call and put down her aching arm. That was a close call.

Regan had a rubbish week. Charlie was working – or at least she really hoped he was, because he said he was on six-until-nine night shifts so she couldn't see him, but they'd had some great text exchanges, which had reassured her that she hadn't imagined the spark between them. Being on her own was making her more than a little paranoid. She'd had two job rejections without even an interview, and both were jobs she had loads of experience for. There'd been no approaches from the jobs websites she'd signed up to, apart from an office cleaning job which, despite not being the most exciting, she had decided she would apply for; until she'd found out it was at BHB Healthcare and her pride wouldn't let her.

She'd been round to her dad's twice. Both times, Tara had turned up almost as soon as Regan had sat down with a cuppa. The second time, she'd come in carrying a massive dress carrier and taken it through to the bedroom; Regan had spotted a shifty look on her face as she did so. Knowing her dad was instantly on edge when Regan and Tara were forced to share the same air, she'd downed her drink and left. All in all, her plans to get herself off rock bottom were not going well.

Saturday trundled around again and she found herself

looking forward to Mantra. It made her feel that she was a bit of a lost cause if that was the highlight of her week. She'd thought about the people on the course off and on all week, especially the ones who had suffered with illnesses. They had been helpful for her mental pep talks and to get some perspective. She was fit and healthy, apart from all the ready noodles and ice cream she'd consumed, and her health was a lot to be thankful for.

Charlie had assured her he'd be there on time and had suggested they go for a walk along the beach afterwards, which sounded like a couply thing to do and a stride in the right direction. She'd done an early session at the gym so she was clean and preened and, in her enthusiasm to see Charlie, she got to the community centre early and joined a couple of others in the kitchen. Embarrassingly, she couldn't remember their names, but they happily reminded her that they were Wendy and Joel. Regan's brain immediately filled in the details of their medical conditions – Wendy had had a stroke and Joel suffered with depression. Wendy was wearing another wonderfully bright kaftan and they struck up a conversation about it.

She hadn't realised she'd been keeping an eye on the doors but as soon as there was a figure on the other side, Regan recognised it was Charlie and felt herself light up. Charlie gave a broad smile when he saw her and she had to stop herself from doing a slow motion run into his arms. There was something very special about Charlie. Nobody, and certainly not any previous boyfriends, had made her feel like this. Maybe it was the situation she found herself in? Maybe that was magnifying anything that was vaguely pleasurable against the rest of the giant whiffy pile of poo that was currently her life. Or maybe they were perfect for each other.

She made her excuses to Wendy and greeted Charlie. They grinned at each other like idiots for a few moments before Charlie went to make himself a coffee.

'Sunday night was fun,' he said, dunking his Hobnob.

'Yeah, we should do it again.'

'Great,' said Charlie. He went to say something else but Cressy interrupted by chiming her bell and calling the session to order. Everyone picked a chair and Charlie and Regan sat next to each other. Charlie reached his fingers down and gave her hand a squeeze. When he let her fingers go she felt bereft. She was falling for Charlie. A spiral of panic uncoiled in her gut – she hoped he was feeling the same.

This was moving very fast. They'd only met a few times, but Regan had an innate feeling that the two of them were meant to be together. She wasn't the slushy sort and certainly hadn't felt like this with Jarvis. It was exciting and scary at the same time. Her mind drifted off and she fantasised about holding his hand as they walked along the beach. Regan took a steadying breath and tuned in to Cressy.

'Can everyone please hold out their hand, palm up.' Cressy had a bowl and a teaspoon and she went around and placed a sultana in everyone's palm. Regan was grinning wildly.

'Blimey, that's portion control for you,' said Regan, eyeing her sultana.

'It's mindful eating,' whispered Charlie.

Cressy took them through a step-by-step process where they studied the surface of their sultana, sniffed it, squeezed it gently and held it up to the light. At this point Regan struggled not to laugh. They all looked like they were presenting a miniature offering to the gods. Eventually

Cressy told them they could place it on their tongue, but they weren't to eat it. They had to think about the texture and what they could taste before biting into it. When they were allowed to eat it, very slowly, Regan was amazed by how good it tasted. Her senses were on high alert and the sultana tasted better for it.

'Wow, that is weird,' said Regan, marvelling at the intensity of flavour. It made her wonder if there was such a thing as mindful sex. If there was, she very much wanted to give it a go.

After lying down for the same body scan technique they'd done the previous week, it was the end of the session. Chris, the other new member from the previous week, came over to speak to Charlie and while they chatted Regan put their yoga mats away. She couldn't wait to go for their walk and spend some time with Charlie. He was an addiction she wanted to feed.

'Thanks,' said Chris, as Regan returned. 'Good luck with yours,' he added, before giving Charlie a knowing look and leaving.

'What's he wishing you luck for?' she asked. She had a sneaking suspicion it had something to do with her.

Charlie looked cagey and steered her out of the community hall. Outside, he took hold of both her hands.

'Regan, you are something else. I knew the day I met you that you were someone very special.' She could have floated away on his words. It made her so happy to know he'd spotted the connection they had too. 'Look . . . there's something I should have told you. But I really don't want it to change anything between us. Okay?'

'Okay,' said Regan. She racked her brain for anything he could tell her that would change things. A wife? A dozen unruly children? He was a spy? If it wasn't the wife, she was pretty sure she could cope with anything else.

Charlie looked down and bit his lip. She could not adore him more. He slowly looked up and fixed her with his gaze. 'I've got a brain tumour.'

Regan realised she'd been grinning. The grin fell from her face. She wanted to ask if he was joking but she could tell he wasn't. Her stomach lurched and her head swam to the point of dizziness. 'But . . .' She looked back at the others leaving the centre. That was his connection to the group; he had something very wrong with him too. 'But they can operate on tumours, right?'

Charlie gave an almost imperceptible shake of his head. 'The odds of me surviving an operation are not in my favour. So I'm not taking the risk. But we can still have fun for as long as I'm here. Can't we?'

Unexpected tears sprang to her eyes. Her one chink of light in the darkness had just had the blinds pulled down over it and the shutters nailed closed. They say the universe only gives you as much as you can handle. *The universe must think I'm hardcore*, thought Regan, *but I'm not*. She gasped in a breath. How wrong she had been before about reaching rock bottom.

Chapter Eleven

Regan and Charlie had abandoned their walk on the beach because Regan had too many questions spinning around her mind. They went to the Hug In A Mug café and drank coffee like they had done the previous week – but this time everything was different. Now she knew that Charlie had a brain tumour everything had changed. She was struggling to make any sense of what he was trying to explain to her. It was like her own brain was in shock.

'So what do you want to know?' asked Charlie. The odd thing was he was exactly the same. His demeanour, his attitude, his smile – all unchanged. How was he so jolly when he was walking around with a time bomb in his head?

'Only what you're comfortable to share with me.' She went to pick up her coffee mug but realised she was shaking, so she hastily put it down again.

'I'm comfortable sharing it all with you, Regan. I'll tell you anything.'

Somehow this didn't give her any comfort. 'How long have you known?'

'Seven months. I took a nasty blow to the head at work. I know, it explains a lot,' he said, with a cheeky grin. Regan couldn't pull a smile however hard she tried. 'And they sent me for a brain scan. That's when they spotted it. It's extremely close to my spinal cord so any operation could kill me or leave me paralysed. I decided against surgery because that's not how I want to spend my life. I'd rather just enjoy my last months.'

'Months?' It came out as a croak.

Charlie sipped his coffee. 'Nobody's really sure but it looks like it's growing at a pace.'

'Why are you still working?'

'I've got no symptoms. I've declared it to the Fire Service and my station commander is really supportive. My crew know so if something was to happen at work they would make sure there was no impact on the public. And I love my job and really need to stay busy.'

An icy shiver ran up Regan's spine and she shuddered. 'I don't know what to say.' She couldn't take her eyes off him. He was young, fit and appeared healthy – none of it made sense.

'Don't look at me like that. Like I'm at death's door. I feel fine and as long as I do then I want to carry on with a normal life. I want to squeeze as much fun as I can into every day.'

Regan joined some dots. 'That's why you're so kind. Why you believe in karma.'

'Hey, I'd be kind without the tumour,' he scolded, but he was smiling. Always bloody smiling. 'But you're right. I'm on a bit of a mission to spread some kindness.' He gave a self-conscious shrug. 'I figured someone upstairs might let me stay on earth a little bit longer if I did.'

Regan was choked. How could this lovely man be dying? He looked the picture of health. 'Are you sure there's not been some horrible mistake?'

'Nope. I've seen the scan pictures. Bloody great lump. But, you know, I'm still really lucky.'

Regan shook her head. 'How on earth do you figure that?'

'Because I know my time is running out. I have a chance to make my last few months count. Some people are taken just like that.' He clicked his fingers and Regan jumped. She wasn't seeing the bright side he seemed to have discovered. 'I want to spend some time with you, Regan. Nothing serious, just some fun. But if it's all too much, I'd understand.'

Regan was choked with emotion and didn't know how to answer. Yes, she wanted to spend time with him, but the thought of what would happen when his time was over was too much to take. 'I don't know if I can do this. I can't think straight. I'm sorry.'

He reached out and covered her hand with his. 'No apology needed.'

Regan popped to the loo, and switched her phone to camera to check her eyes weren't too puffy. Her face was a bit blotchy, but if she held the phone further away it wasn't so bad. She leaned back against the cool of the toilet door and pressed the button to FaceTime the one person she always told everything to.

A pleased-looking Cleo answered. 'Your timing is perfect. I'm at a very dull drinks reception. Let me duck outside.' Regan caught a glimpse of a stony-faced Oscar as Cleo made her apologies. 'Right,' she said, when the background had changed to sky. 'How are things with you?'

'I want to talk to you about this guy I've met. He's called Charlie.'

Cleo blinked rapidly. 'What about Jarvis?'

The name gave Regan a physical jolt and the phone slipped. 'Sorry, I almost dropped you then.' Regan tucked her hair behind her ear multiple times. 'Um, we've kind of split up.'

Cleo's mouth actually made a shocked 'O' shape. 'What? Why didn't you tell me?'

Regan could hardly say *Because I'm secretly sleeping in your studio and I feared if I told you about Jarvis the rest of it would come out*. She searched for something else plausible. 'I didn't want to bother you when you're away working.'

'I hate not being there when you need me. When did this happen?'

Regan felt sheepish. 'A week and a bit ago. I didn't want to worry you. It's not like you can do anything. And for the record *I* dumped *him*.'

'Right. Wow. I wasn't expecting that. You sometimes moan about Jarvis, but otherwise you seemed to rub along okay. Are you all right?'

Regan nodded nonchalantly. 'Yes. Totally. Completely fine.'

'So who's this new bloke?'

Regan took a deep breath and retold Charlie's sad story. Cleo listened intently until Regan stopped talking and her shoulders slumped. Cleo blew out a breath that whistled through her perfect white teeth. 'I wish I could teleport home.'

'I wish you could too.' Regan longed to have a proper chat to Cleo. FaceTime was okay but it wasn't the same as curling up on a sofa for a few hours.

Cleo appeared to be processing what Regan had told her. 'Are you sure it's not a line?' she asked.

'You're a sick individual,' said Regan.

'Hear me out. I'm just thinking that if it were a line . . .' Regan was rolling her eyes. 'I said *if* it were a line then it's pretty well guaranteed to get him a lot of pity sex over the next few months.'

Regan shook her head. 'Charlie's not like that.'

'You said he lied about being a policeman. I'm getting a bad feeling about this guy.'

'But he's a fireman. That's still an emergency service so it wasn't a massive lie,' said Regan.

'I'm not so sure. I don't want you getting sucked in by some sob story. I've been there and it's not fun.'

'It's not a sob story.'

'And you've met him how many times?' Cleo had a look of her mother about her.

'Four.' Regan's voice was barely audible. 'I've met him four times.'

Cleo shook her head. 'Where is he now?'

'He's gone. He's agreed to give me some time to think it over. Not rush into anything. I don't know what to do.'

'You need to get his story checked out.' Cleo tilted her head in a teacher-like way as she spoke. 'He could be a total con man out to fleece you.' Regan opened her mouth and then closed it again. 'Just be very careful. That's all I'm saying.'

Regan nodded her glum face. 'I really like him. It's so sad.'

'If it's true,' said Cleo, waving away Regan's protest before it came. 'Where are you?' Cleo leaned in closer to the screen.

'Coffee shop disabled toilet.'

'That's a relief – I thought you were going to say you'd moved already and it was your new place.'

Cleo was a bit too close to the mark with her guesswork and it made Regan jolt herself upright. 'Shitting hell!' yelped Regan, dropping the phone and scoring a direct hit in the toilet bowl.

Regan trudged out of the toilet with her phone wrapped in so much toilet roll it looked like she'd mummified it.

'You okay?' asked a harassed-looking Penny.

Regan shook her head. 'Not really.'

Penny glanced at the queue and then at the clock. 'I'm rushed off my feet. Kasia has strained her Achilles. But when I've cleared this lot we can have a natter if you want?'

Regan nodded miserably. 'I can give you a hand if you like?' She'd been coming there every day for the last three years so she knew her way around the coffee menu. She'd not worked a coffee machine since her days at the restaurant where she'd met Cleo all those years ago, but coffee was coffee and not much had changed.

Penny looked like she was going to kiss her. 'Actually, that'd be great. Thanks.'

Regan grabbed an apron, more so she looked the part than to protect her clothes, and got to work. Penny shouted the orders and Regan soon found her way around the small area. She frothed and sprinkled until Penny declared the shop was closed. 'What can I get you?' asked Regan, with a mug in her hand.

'Coconut flat white, please,' said Penny, flopping into the nearest chair.

Regan quickly made their drinks and ferried them over. 'Here you go.' She'd made herself a large latte. She figured she'd earned it and she wasn't sure what was for dinner tonight.

'You're a star,' said Penny, appraising Regan. 'Not seen you for a few days. Holiday?'

'Nope. I quit my job.' Regan hoped she didn't ask any further questions.

'I don't suppose you want one here?' She said it through a laugh as if expecting Regan to dismiss it.

Regan jolted upright. 'Yeah. I'd love to work here.'

'Really?' Penny was frowning hard.

'Unless you were joking . . . then this is kinda awkward.' She hoped she wasn't joking.

'No. The job's real all right. But weren't you something in pharmaceuticals?'

Regan puffed out a sigh. 'It's a long story . . .' When she'd got to the end, Penny was looking suitably stunned.

'My God. That's awful.'

Regan shrugged one shoulder and lifted her large coffee to her lips. She paused. 'Do I get the job?'

'Definitely. As long as you don't mind that it's only until Kasia is back on her feet. Doctor says at least four weeks for a strained Achilles.'

'Excellent,' said Regan, and then realised that for Kasia it wasn't. 'Sorry. I'm just pleased to get a job.'

Penny waved her faux pas away. 'It explains why you looked so glum earlier.'

'Ah . . . that's a whole other long story with a very much sadder ending.' Penny hugged her mug, enthralled.

It was actually nice to be able to talk to someone. Being alone in the studio had made her realise how much she needed other people. She understood now why old people went to the supermarket just to get human contact.

Regan relayed Charlie's situation and was pleased with how she kept it together at the end without triggering the waterworks. Repeating it to someone else made it seem even more real.

They sat in silence for a while. Penny appeared shell-shocked.

Eventually she spoke. 'There's a big guy comes in here. He's a firefighter. Talks nonstop and I rarely tune in. But a while ago he told me about a colleague who'd been diagnosed with a brain tumour. I remember it because I thought how unfair it was for them to get something like that when they risk so much for other people. Must have been Charlie he was talking about.'

Penny had described Beanstalk. *So it's true*, thought Regan, although she hadn't doubted Charlie for a second. A dark cloud was settling above her and she feared it would be a very long time before it moved on. Oddly, she would have been happier if Charlie had been peddling her a line – because even though it would have made him a lowlife at least he wouldn't be facing a death sentence.

Regan felt like she was being twisted inside. Part of her was thrilled to have a job, but the rest of her was tormented by Charlie's news. She had been beyond frugal since she'd left Jarvis, thanks mainly to the terror of realising the few quid she had in her bank account was all she had in the world. She wanted to celebrate her new job with a couple of beers, but she questioned if she should. Somehow it didn't feel right to be celebrating after hearing Charlie's revelation.

Regan had no plans for the rest of her day off. There was nothing and nobody waiting for her back at the studio, so she set off on a mammoth walking tour of Brighton. She strode past the pier and the distant joyful cries of children on the rides, along the seafront, dodging slow walkers and dog leads. The sea air whipped her hair into her eyes, so she left the sea front and walked through the splendour of Regency Square. She loved the white-fronted townhouses that flanked the once private gardens; she liked to imagine what it must have been like to live there when they were first built. Today, though, she couldn't think about anything except Charlie. She put her head down and marched on.

She trundled through The Lanes. The quirky little shops and narrow alleyways were like something out of a fairy tale. It was somewhere that usually cheered her up, but today Regan wanted to scream at the happy people walking past her. She'd never really noticed the smiles, the laughter and the carefree tones in voices before, but she noticed now. There were miserable faces too. People who had likely spent their whole lives being miserable. Why wasn't it one of them with a tumour and not Charlie? She felt awful for thinking it but she couldn't help it. What was happening to Charlie seemed so unfair. She really liked him. Who was she kidding? Her feelings were already further up the scale than 'like'. If she was honest, some of her sadness was at what she was potentially losing. She'd seen something special in Charlie from the start and their relationship had built so quickly. What if he was The One?

She plodded on, her mind elsewhere, until she reached the market. The smell and sounds of the place always took her mind off things, but today would be a big test. Stallholders were laughing and joking with each other as they packed up for the day. She walked past the bins and today's unwanted fruit and veg – onions, cabbages and nectarines were the unpopular choices this time. She kicked at a cabbage to release her frustration but missed and almost fell on her backside. She was angry at everything and everyone, but mainly at the unfairness of life and the indifference with which tragedy struck.

Regan stopped near the cash machine and kicked at the wall. The pain shot up her toe and she hopped away swearing under her breath. A loud woof caught her off guard. Elvis bounded over and hastily sat in front of her looking up expectantly. Despite everything, it made her smile.

'Sorry, Elvis. I've no milk on me today.' She petted his head. Kevin sauntered over. 'Good news, Kevin. There'll be coffee again next week. I've got a job at the coffee shop.'

Kevin beamed a smile. 'Thank you.' He made it sound like she'd got the job just to get him free coffee. 'You okay?' he tipped his head at the wall she'd been assaulting.

'Yeah, fine. Letting out my frustration.'

He bobbed his head in understanding. 'There's a band playing on the pier tonight. And it's low tide.' He was looking at Regan as if this should mean something. 'Me and Elvis sit under the pier and listen for free. The band's pretty good. You can join us if you like. It might cheer you up.'

'Oh, Kevin. You're the sweetest person.' He went all shy and gave Elvis a sturdy pat on his side. Elvis didn't seem to notice; he was still staring at Regan. Emotion spiked through her. Whilst she really wanted to hate the world and everyone in it right now, how could she? 'Thanks. I'd love to join you.'

Regan had been surprised to see that her bank balance was a lot higher than it had been. All she could think was that BHB Healthcare must have owed her some money because nobody else paid in to her account. She decided she'd treat herself and Kevin to a fish and chip tea later, and so Elvis didn't feel left out she bought some dry dog food when she bought a pack of beers.

Back in the studio, she tried her hardest to push the Charlie conundrum to the back of her mind – it was simply too hard to deal with right now. She washed and changed and put on a splash of make-up – she'd not been out in ages. She bundled up a large plastic sheet for them to sit on that she'd found amongst some spare easels, rolled up the throws and grabbed her carrier bag of beer and dog food. She opened the studio door cautiously, as she always did, to check the coast was clear. To her surprise, leaning in the doorway was Charlie.

They both stared wide-eyed at each other. 'You weren't answering your phone—'

'Dropped it down the toilet,' she said, and he raised an eyebrow. 'I really did. It's drying out in some rice now. Penny said it might work.'

Charlie looked relieved. 'Not ignoring me then?'

'No. Of course not.' Just looking at him made her sad. 'I wouldn't do that.'

There was a difficult silence that stretched between them. Regan feared this would be the first of many times she wouldn't know exactly what to say. Charlie frowned at the tarpaulin under her arm.

'You going camping?'

'No. Much better.' She stuck her neck out further: there was nobody about. 'Come on. We're going to have a fun evening, I promise.' She locked up the studio, linked arms with Charlie and they set off for the pier.

Chapter Twelve

Kevin's face when she presented him with his fish and chips was a sight she'd never forget. He rubbed the tears away from his eyes. 'Thank you,' he said, nodding heartily.

'You're welcome, Kevin. This is my friend Charlie,' she said, introducing the two men.

'Nice to meet you,' said Charlie. Elvis thrust his nose into Charlie's groin. 'Woah, and you too,' he said, going up on tiptoes.

'This is Elvis. He's my dog,' said Kevin, proudly.

Charlie took charge of setting out the plastic sheet and throws and they settled down for their meal. It was early in May so the evenings were still a little cool but, with the throws over her legs, Charlie one side and Elvis the other, Regan was quite warm.

'We're celebrating,' she said, getting out the beers. 'I've got a new job. Four weeks' work at the coffee shop.' She was really looking forward to it, and the thought of some money coming in was a huge relief.

'Congratulations,' said Charlie. He bent his head as if he was about to give her a quick kiss and then thought better of it. The gesture broke her heart just a fraction.

Their fledgling relationship had been so easy, and now she felt like she needed to remember every little moment in case he wasn't here tomorrow. She swallowed hard. She had to get a grip on her emotions. She still hadn't given him a final answer about their future, and it was hard to think straight when she knew Charlie's own future had an end date.

Charlie popped the top off three bottles and passed them round. She watched Kevin lift the beer to his lips, his eyes closed. He took one long swig and seemed to pause. Regan wondered if she'd done the right thing getting alcohol. 'Kevin, I've got Coke if you'd rather.' Although, from his expression, he was definitely enjoying the beer. She'd sometimes seen homeless people drinking alcohol on the streets, but she'd never seen Kevin with anything other than coffee or water.

He shook his head. 'Haven't had a beer for years. Wasn't allowed with my medication. But I don't take that any more.'

'That's good,' she replied.

'I still have my ups and downs, but nothing like before,' said Kevin.

Regan nodded her understanding. She didn't like to probe.

Someone speaking into a microphone on the pier above drew their attention. She couldn't make out exactly what was said because they weren't able to get directly underneath where the band were playing, due to the sea, but it was followed by applause. Then the band started.

After a couple of songs, the day's warmth was ebbing away and the sea breeze made her shiver.

'Come on,' said Charlie, lifting his arm for her to snuggle. She hesitated for a moment. What harm could it do? She cuddled up to Charlie. Elvis rested his head on her lap and looked at her adoringly. *Fickle creature*, she thought. He was only like that because she'd filled him full of dog food.

The music echoed above them and she was lost in it. It was an indie rock band playing a mix of covers and originals. As the sun packed up shop for the day and the moon started its shift, Regan watched the light dance across the surface of the water as if accompanying the music. Everything seemed so perfect – except for one thing. She cast an eye at Charlie and he gave her a similar look to Elvis. A spark of happiness glowed inside her for a moment, but it was snuffed out like the sun slipping into the sea. She closed her eyes tight. She had a choice to make, and it would be the hardest she had ever faced – embark on something with Charlie that had the potential to be very special but would likely shatter her heart, or go for the self-preservation option and walk away.

Kevin was really knowledgeable about music. He and Charlie chatted like old friends about one-hit wonders and their favourite lyrics. Regan listened to them, happy to be in the moment, sitting on the beach in the moonlight, sipping a beer and sharing an evening with friends. It was far easier to think about now than what the future might hold. Now was clear and easy and tangible.

When the music had finished they packed up their things.

'Where are you staying tonight?' Regan asked Kevin whilst Charlie rolled up the plastic sheet.

'It looks like rain, so I might head for North Street. There's some cover by the shops there.'

It didn't feel right when she had a roof over her head. 'Do you want the plastic?'

'We'll be fine.' Kevin patted Elvis as he spoke. She wasn't sure what else she could do.

They said their goodbyes to Kevin and Elvis and strolled back along the pebbles. The soft zhush of the tide calmed Regan's senses; the salt air cleared her mind. She loved living by the sea and couldn't imagine being anywhere else.

'Do you have some kind of bucket list?' she asked.

Charlie laughed. 'Nah. I don't want the pressure. I want to live each day as best and as normally as I can. It's an odd thing, but I've been much happier since I was diagnosed.'

'That is bloody odd,' said Regan.

'I know. I wasn't happy at first. I wanted to pick a fight with everyone. Then I kind of went to pieces. I got some help and was referred to Mantra. And that was what made me think differently.'

'Really?' Regan wasn't convinced. She'd enjoyed the sessions, but they weren't exactly life-changing.

'It made me focus on the here and now. And that's all I can be certain of, so I need to make the most of it.'

'You make me wonder what the hell I'm doing with my life.' Regan sucked air in through her teeth.

'You've got a new job. That's a good start.'

'For four weeks. I've got a job for just four weeks and a roof over my head for another five and a half. The clock is ticking.'

'Okay. What about running your own business?' Regan laughed at his joke but he stopped walking and turned to face her. 'I'm dead serious . . . no pun intended.' She smiled at his dark humour. 'It's on your wish list. What's stopping you?' She opened her mouth but he carried on. 'And don't say money.'

Regan gave a brief pout. 'I wouldn't know where to start. I've never run a business. I don't even know anyone who does.'

'Where do big companies start?' he asked, and they began walking again.

'Don't know. With big loans, I guess.'

'Do they? Or do they start small and build up?'

Regan's mind was whirring. 'I read something once about Marks and Spencer starting as a market stall.'

Charlie became animated and almost dropped the rolled-up plastic from under his arm. 'That's it! That's where you should start. Get a stall on the market. Brilliant idea!'

A bubble of excitement fizzed inside Regan. A market stall sounded doable. 'But what would I sell?' The fizz went flat.

Charlie was still bubbling. 'Anything you want to.' His eyes were darting about the night sky as if he were joining up the stars. 'What's the latest craze? You could buy stuff in from China and sell it on.'

'Doesn't the post from China take like forty days?'

'Oh yeah. I ordered an inflatable sheep off eBay once and that took about three months to arrive.' She gave him a look. 'Don't ask. What about flowers?' he suggested.

'There's already a well-established florist on the market. And a gardening stall with pot plants and stuff.'

'Veg? Clothes? Cosmetics?' His voice seemed to bounce higher with each suggestion.

'Already there.' She tried not to feel glum, but for a moment she'd really thought they'd hit on something.

'Hmm. Okay. But this is still a really good idea. The coffee shop job can fund the market stall while you get it set up. We just need a good idea for what you can sell.'

She loved his optimism and it was rubbing off on her. She knew that in theory she could walk away from him. But life was precarious anyway, she thought; nobody knows how long they've got left – we only presume. There was no pressure from him to start a relationship, but something was already compelling her to be with him even if it was all as temporary as love hearts drawn in the sand. There was something about the way she felt when she looked at him which was very different to anything she'd ever felt before, and it had nothing to do with his health situation. She took a deep breath.

'Charlie . . .'

'Yeah?' He beamed his usual smile at her and it seemed to force one onto her face too.

'You and me. I want to do this. I want to be in a relationship with you for as long as . . .' She didn't want to finish the sentence.

Charlie dropped everything he was carrying and lifted her into his arms. He swung her around, making her squeal, and finally enveloped her in a hug. 'Regan Corsetti, you've made my day; my week; my life.'

'I've not bloody well proposed,' she said, through a giggle.

'You might as well have done. You've made me so happy.' His lips met hers and she was sure his happiness was infectious because the feeling that swamped her almost reduced her to tears.

They kissed with abandon until a whoosh followed by

a wet sensation travelling up from her shoes made her stumble backwards. 'Tide's coming in!'

They grabbed up their things and in a bundle of laughter and happiness they ran up the beach as fast as the unstable pebbles would allow.

Chapter Thirteen

Regan was on time for work the next morning, despite hardly sleeping – thanks partly to Cleo's bloody chair, but mainly because her mind was awash with images of Charlie and ideas for what to sell on a market stall. It was a surprisingly heady combination.

'Blimey. You look happy – or did a face-lift go very wrong?' asked Penny, throwing an apron at her.

'Today everything changes,' said Regan.

'Okay,' said Penny, not looking convinced.

'I'm going to work here and then I'm going to run my own market stall.' Regan raised her eyebrows in anticipation of Penny's reaction.

'Good.' Penny continued to dash about. 'Opening in twenty minutes. Need to unpack the milk delivery and stock up.'

Regan couldn't help but be a bit disappointed by Penny's lack of reaction. But she had a job here and she needed to keep hold of it. 'Okay, boss. Ooh, actually, can I take Kevin a coffee?'

Penny straightened her shoulders. 'You only get free stuff for you.'

'Oh, right. Sorry.' Regan was a little surprised by Penny's

attitude. She kind of thought working for Penny would be a bit like working for a friend. They had got to know each other over the last few years and their chats had got longer and longer.

Penny's expression softened. 'Mr Hughes would sack the pair of us if he found out. But look, there's always errors on orders—'

'Hey, I did all right yesterday.' Regan was mildly offended at Penny's assumption.

'No. Not you, the customers. They order one thing then change their minds or think they've ordered something else. When that happens we chuck it away, but if it's not mad busy you could run one of those out to him.'

'Perfect,' said Regan.

'Just no deliberate mistakes. Okay?' Penny gave her a look she'd seen on many a teacher in her past.

'Cross my heart,' said Regan, crossing her chest and hoping it was a morning of customer errors because she'd already promised drinks to Kevin and Elvis.

The morning rush was exactly that. Lots of shouting and running about interspersed with blasts of steam, the gurgle of the coffee machine and all of it steeped in the smell of hot milk and coffee. Regan found it quite exhilarating. *I'm dying for a coffee*, she thought, and then a picture of Charlie popped into her head and she swallowed hard. Maybe she wasn't quite that bad.

'Large cappuccino to go,' called Regan, placing the cup on the collection counter.

'Decaf?' asked a slim man with a gruff voice.

'Nope, fully leaded,' said Regan, with a smile.

'I asked for decaffeinated,' he said, checking his watch.

Regan frowned but Penny was already there. 'No

problem, sir. Sorry about that. It'll just be a minute.' Penny guided Regan back to the coffee machine. 'See. Like I said. It's his mistake – he didn't ask for decaf. Do him another and then run this one out to Kevin.'

Regan grinned. This was brilliant. She had some milk that she'd already heated and now it was cooling down it had to be thrown away, but instead she tipped it into a cup for Elvis. Once the customer was happy with his large *decaf* cappuccino Regan spied her chance and nipped outside. She scanned the street in both directions and her eyes alighted on the market stalls all setting up for the day. She could barely quell her excitement. That could be her. If she could just get her shit together and come up with a good idea, that really could be her. She watched them, transfixed for a moment whilst her mind wandered off to picture herself running her own stall.

A loud bark heralded Elvis's arrival and pulled her out of her daydream. She was sure the dog could smell milk from a mile away. Today it was a very wet Elvis; he merrily showed Regan *how* wet by doing a full body shake in front of her and showering her in the process. 'Oi!' she said, through spluttered laughter. Kevin wasn't far behind and he was shaking his head in a similar fashion to Elvis. 'You guys been for a swim?' she quipped.

'Beach showers.'

'What, those ice-cold ones?' She knew the ones on the beach. She'd seen tourists dancing about underneath them in the summer months. She'd even stuck a toe under one once, but the chill had soon had her retreating. She admired his ingenuity and was once again thankful for Jarvis continuing to pay the joint gym membership so that she could have a regular hot shower. She handed Kevin his coffee.

His eyes widened at the large cup. 'Thank you. *Carpe diem*.'

'I will,' she said, and she was pretty sure of it.

'Regan!' came a shout behind her. A fire engine was pulling up to the kerb and Charlie was leaning past the driver. 'Wait up.'

He jumped down from the cab and ran over whilst his fellow firefighters hurled some banter after him. She'd not seen him in uniform before and it was all she could do to stop her brain from slowing down the images and putting a musical soundtrack over the top as he jogged towards her. He looked very tasty indeed. 'Ignore them,' he said, giving her a light kiss. 'Here.' He handed her some printed pages of A4. 'I did a bit of research on market stalls last night and I printed this off. It might be helpful. Oh, and I've got a lead on some paint for your dad's place.'

'Great.' She kissed him because she was grateful and he was her hot new boyfriend.

'Gotta go.' He gave her another kiss, which triggered more catcalls, before jogging back to the engine. Regan waved them off and then scurried back inside, her cheeks as warm as the glow in her heart.

When it was finally time for her break she took her free toasted panini and large latte out to the small room at the back and studied the printouts that Charlie had done for her. It was from the Brighton Open Market website and contained pretty much all the information she needed about setting up a market stall. She hurriedly read through it all, surprised by her own enthusiasm. There was a lot to take in, but most exciting was the list of stalls they would like to see on the market. She read it carefully whilst she munched on her panini. It read:

Brighton Open Market is open to a wide range of products and services. We are very happy to advise but in general pretty much anything you make or bake, that is unique or quirky, that appeals to collectors, or is glittery and shiny, that makes people look or feel fabulous, is vegan or vegetarian, is green or healthy, that tastes incredible, or feels lovely, anything artistic, designed, or creative! If people want it, we want to help you sell it!

Regan took out a pen and underlined a few key words – quirky, shiny, vegan – and then put rings around 'tastes incredible' and 'people want it'. She sipped her coffee and stared at what she'd highlighted. She felt the key to her market stall was there. She just needed an idea to miraculously pop into her head. She stared and stared at it, but no ideas came. This was far harder than she'd thought it would be.

Regan returned to the counter and took the highlighted piece of paper with her, having stowed the other printed sheets in her bag. Perhaps inspiration would strike whilst she was working. Penny looked over her shoulder. 'Who's a quirky, shiny, vegan who tastes incredible? I could do with one of those.'

'It's what the market is looking for from a market stall. I need to work out something that ticks those boxes and I'm off the starting blocks.' Right now, she was so far from the starting blocks it was more like she was still in the changing rooms trying to work out how to put on her pants.

'So you're going to bake stuff?' asked Penny in between the next couple of customers.

'Maybe,' said Regan. 'It all seems to point at something home-made.'

'Can you bake?'

'Er, no. But that's just a slight – major – flaw in the plan.' It wasn't something Regan had overlooked so much as stuck a hat on and pretended wasn't there. Penny's eyebrows were doing a dance without music, but she didn't say anything. She didn't need to.

After work, Regan headed to the library and baulked at the number of messages from Cleo. She opened the first email:

> *Hi Regan, Sorry it's another email from the sleep-deprived brain of yours truly. I've been thinking about you and your brain tumour guy. Please be careful. Some people are very good at putting on a show when they are completely different underneath – and I should know. I don't want you to get hurt.*
>
> *I've had a rubbish day. I knew something was up as soon as I got in the car with Oscar this morning. My bad situation with the art critic has got worse. Walkers have cancelled. They're a large, well-established gallery in London who had previously stocked my bigger pieces and sold them to investors. And worse still, Oscar dropped the bombshell that in his words 'Something interesting has come up . . .', which I'm guessing is a new client, and he's flying home tomorrow and leaving me to finish the tour without him. I thought I was going to pass out in the car when he said it.*
>
> *I don't think I can do it.*
>
> *C x*

Regan fired off a quick reply:

Hi Cleo, You're not a quitter. You can do this. You're stronger than you know. If nothing else, do it for me. See Japan, treat it as a holiday – it's free!

In the nicest possible way – please don't come home!

Love you

R

X

P.S. Charlie is the real deal <3

Regan opened the next email and clicked on the video link. This was something different. Cleo's face popped up and it felt odd that it wasn't FaceTime and she couldn't interact with her.

'Regan. Why aren't you picking up my messages or my calls?' She looked distraught. She tugged at her hair with her free hand.

'I dropped my phone down the loo,' Regan whispered at the screen. She looked up to see an elderly man on the opposite computer eyeing her suspiciously. She smiled and slunk down behind the monitor. She wished it was FaceTime and Cleo could hear her.

Onscreen, a harassed Cleo continued: 'I've spent almost two hours trapped in the car with a grumpy Oscar and my escalating anxiety. The driver kept looking at us through the rear-view mirror because I spent most of the journey begging Oscar to stay in Japan, but he refused to be swayed. I know Oscar has other clients and I understand he needs to fill the gap my art, and associated commissioned income, leaves, but dumping me in a foreign country was a kneejerk reaction which is not acceptable. I'm not you. I don't thrive when I'm chucked in the deep end. I sink. I doubt I'll be able to leave the hotel room let alone finish the tour.'

Regan could tell Cleo's anxiety was escalating by the speed of her speech and her strained expression. She wanted to reach into the screen and tell her it was going to be okay.

'Then we pulled up at this fancy place.' She turned the camera and gave a fleeting panorama of a building, with a New England, whitewashed look to it – not what she had been expecting from Japan at all. 'This delightful Japanese gentleman met us, Mr Yomoda, whose English and demeanour put me in mind of Yoda, but thankfully he was a healthier colour. Oscar went into full-on schmooze mode and took control of the conversation. And it turns out this is a university.' Cleo panned the camera round to a large window where a number of young faces were staring out. A couple of them waved. 'A university!' repeated Cleo, turning the camera back to herself. 'It's a total mess. Oscar is furious. He's ranting at poor Mr Yomoda right now.' Cleo pushed her hair off her face. 'What do I do, Regan?'

Regan shook her head and then checked the sound was as low as it would go. She didn't want to get chucked out of the library.

'Apparently the students have been following my work. Mr Yomoda said my art is an inspiration.' Cleo bit her lip and looked away from the camera, back at the faces at the window. 'I don't even know what a university visit entails, but I'd quite like to meet the art students. Being an art student is at least something I can relate to—'

'Right. We're leaving. It's a total shambles,' said Oscar, marching over. Cleo fumbled the phone but it kept filming. Oscar turned to a small Japanese gentleman who Regan took to be Mr Yomoda. This was better than a soap opera. 'So sorry to have wasted your time,' said Oscar. He began ushering Cleo back to the car, but she stood firm.

'No, Oscar. We can't just leave. These young people were expecting to meet me. We have nothing else planned for today. I can spare them a couple of hours.'

'Go Cleo!' said Regan, punching the air. She coughed and huddled back down in front of the screen so she didn't miss anything.

Oscar's face was stony. He checked his watch, then his phone and then his watch again. 'There might be some good photo ops. Possibly a different angle to explore.' Regan could almost see his mind whirring. 'Okay. Half an hour.' He put his smile back in place. 'Let's do this, Mr Yomoda.'

'Gotta go,' whispered Cleo. 'Wish me luck.' And the video ended.

'Good luck,' whispered Regan and she placed her hand on the screen. Poor Cleo. This was her worst nightmare.

Leaving the library, Regan was tired. She was amazed to find she was enjoying her job and that was mainly down to Penny. It had been full-on, but Penny was a lovely manager and fun to be around. She was very different to the people she'd worked with in her old job and most other jobs she'd had. Usually everyone moaned about their job; about having too much work, about the bosses, about colleagues and pretty much anything they could think of to grumble about. Working in the coffee shop was different. Penny was the manager; the owner, a Mr Hughes, rarely visited and seemed to leave the day-to-day running entirely to Penny – and wisely so, because Penny was hardworking, enthusiastic and great with the customers.

Regan felt she could learn a lot from her, hopefully some of which she could use on her market stall.

Regan couldn't remember a day she had been so engaged in a job. She was looking forward to scoffing the about-to-go-out-of-date chicken wrap and two cakes for her tea. She'd not get paid until the end of the week, and she still had to be frugal because she needed every penny to set up her business venture.

She walked through the empty market, her head buzzing with possibilities, and something caught her eye. She stood and stared at the pile of thrown away fruit and vegetables. Today it was cauliflower, radishes and rhubarb. She went over. There was loads of it and most of it looked okay. Not Waitrose okay, but not ready for the bin either. An idea pinged into her head. This was it. She was going to use the thrown-away fruit and veg to make something quirky, shiny and vegan. All she had to do now was work out what that was.

Chapter Fourteen

A couple of evenings later, Charlie had come up trumps with some magnolia paint. He was waiting for her when she pulled up at her dad's place.

'Hiya,' she said, joy swamping her at the sight of him. His grave expression and downcast body language quickly had her worried. 'What's wrong?' Her stomach flipped while she awaited his reply.

'It's work. Bad accident on the A23.'

'Oh.' She tried to hide her relief that it wasn't about his health. 'Was someone hurt?'

He gave the tiniest of nods. 'A baby.' She pulled him into a hug and held him. She wondered if he'd hoped to be a dad some day, then banished the thought because it was too upsetting to dwell on.

She couldn't imagine the horrors that he must have witnessed being a firefighter and she didn't want to. She knew it was something she would never be able to deal with. Anyone who worked in the emergency services was a hero in her mind.

He pulled back out of the hug and appraised her, his eyes full of warmth. 'You're something else, Regan Corsetti.'

'Nah, I'm average at best.'

'Not to me.'

'You okay to do this?' She tilted her head towards her dad's front door.

Charlie took a deep breath and pulled back his shoulders. 'Sure thing. It's just sometimes it's . . .' There was a long pause. 'Anyway, let's get painting.' He said it with forced enthusiasm.

Regan loved her dad but she knew he was sometimes a bit offbeat, and frequently peculiar. She felt she needed to warn Charlie. 'You know every family has an oddball?'

Charlie tilted his head. 'Mine doesn't.'

'Right, well . . . they usually do. And my dad is the one in our family.'

'Okay.' Charlie didn't look convinced.

'I bet your family has one. Have a think.'

He shook his head. 'Nope. We're all perfectly normal. No oddballs.'

'In that case the oddball is probably you.'

'Hey,' he said, but at least now his usual smile was back in place.

Regan knocked on the door and her dad appeared. A troubled expression was etched on his features, his shiny face not looking at all happy. 'Hiya, Dad. We've come to start the decorating.' She held up a paint pot and he viewed it as if it was a severed head.

'I'm not sure about this,' he said, his tone pure Eeyore.

'It'll be fine. This is Charlie,' she said, proudly, and she waited for her dad's reaction.

'Not very sure about this at all,' he said, retreating inside.

Charlie gave her a look. 'I did warn you,' whispered Regan.

Regan marched off to the bedroom, noting the row of stilettos lined up in the bottom of the wardrobe. Tarty Tara was making herself very at home here.

'Where are you going?' Graham sounded alarmed.

Regan looked over her shoulder. 'Cupboard to get the old curtains we use for decorating. You've still got them, haven't you?'

'Oh, yes.' He seemed relieved. 'But I'll get them,' he said, almost pushing Regan out of the way. He dashed into the bedroom and gave her a suspicious glance before shutting the door sharply.

Charlie was staring open-mouthed. Regan gave a shrug. This was embarrassing; her dad was acting even odder than usual. 'I can see what you mean,' whispered Charlie.

The kitchen was pretty small, and with only a clock to take off the walls it was quite simple. Charlie started on the ceiling and Regan set to work doing the tricky bits around the edges. Graham stood and watched from the doorway looking apprehensive.

'No T . . . Tara today?' She had to catch herself; she was so used to referring to her as Tarty Tara, she feared one day she'd say it out loud.

Graham's expression changed to one of suspicion. 'Why do you ask?'

'Because I'm being nice and showing an interest.' *Which is more than you've done, and I've been here twenty minutes and introduced you to my gorgeous new boyfriend*, she added in her head.

'Oh. I see,' said Graham, and she saw Charlie hide a smile.

'Sooo, where's Tara?' asked Regan.

'At hers. I told her about the decorating. She wasn't sure about it either.' The light caught his bald patch and Regan realised he was getting older.

'It'll be fine, Dad.' She patted his arm.

'You will be finished before bedtime, won't you?'

'Of course, Mr Corsetti,' said Charlie. 'We're proper little worker bees when we get going.'

'I don't like bees,' said Graham.

Eventually Graham left them to it.

'Sorry,' said Regan. 'He's all right when you get to know him . . . Actually, I don't know if that's true because obviously I've known him my whole life, so I guess I'm used to him. Maybe after a few months you'll get used to him too.' She smiled and then what she'd said made the smile slide away. Charlie might not have a few months to get to know Graham. Every time she made one of these faux pas it hurt her. It was like someone kept sticking something sharp into her heart to remind her that this happy state was all temporary.

Charlie didn't seem to have noticed. 'He's fine. My dad's a talker. Whether you want to know about his golf match or not, he's going to tell you.'

'I think over-chatty is better than under.' As a chatty person herself, she was always going to think that.

They went quiet for a bit while they both concentrated.

'Hey!' said Regan, when Charlie sprinkled her with a light dusting of brilliant white from his roller.

'Whoops, sorry.'

'I look like I've got rampant dandruff,' she said, inspecting her shoulders. At least she was wearing an old T-shirt.

'Sorry. What I was coming over to say was, you can tick "Helping out your dad" off your lottery list when we've finished.'

'Yeah. I will.' She didn't like to say that she'd already ticked off 'Get new hot boyfriend who doesn't nag or wear button-up pyjamas'. It was a little premature because she had yet to have confirmation of the last two points, but it had made her feel happy to put a great big tick next to it. She wasn't sure how many others she'd be able to tick off, but it was fun and it was definitely motivating her to get her life back on track – and out of the Nissan Micra lane for good.

They laughed a lot while they decorated. The conversation was easy and everything felt right. She was happy doing something mundane because she was doing it with Charlie.

'How's the business plan coming on?' He paused to wait for her response, his bicep taut as he held the roller. Regan remembered the cheesy firemen calendar she'd once received as a secret Santa gift and thought how she'd very much like a calendar where every month was a picture of Charlie, preferably with decreasing amounts of clothing as the year went on, finishing with December and a strategically placed Santa hat.

'Regan?' he prompted.

'Sorry. Miles away.' She gave herself a physical and mental shake. 'The market information you gave me was brilliant. They want stalls selling stuff that's quirky, shiny and vegan.'

'Apart from the vegan that could be your dad then.'

'Very droll.' She waved his comment away. 'I've had this idea about using the leftover fruit and veg that they're chucking away but I—'

'For like jams and chutneys?' He said it so effortlessly, like it was completely obvious, and yet she'd been mulling it over for a couple of days and only come up with cauliflower cheese and rhubarb crumble – both with questionable sell-by dates and neither of which she knew how to bake.

'Yes! That is exactly what I'm, um . . . thinking. Well,

I was thinking chutney but jam is a great idea too.' She broke eye contact. She at least wanted to claim a bit of it as her idea.

Charlie was looking pleased. 'I love it. It'll be low cost and once the fruit is in a jam it'll last for ages because the sugar preserves it. There's nothing like that locally. And people love home-made produce. I really think you're on to something here.' He waved the roller and another splodge landed on her shoulder, making it look like she'd taken a direct hit from a seagull. 'Whoops, sorry. Again.'

Regan didn't care about the paint splat. She was grinning; this really was a terrific idea. 'And chutney and jam are vegan . . . right?'

'Of course.'

'That's one box ticked. Now I need to work on the shiny and quirky.'

Charlie got back to work. 'I guess the quirky will be determined by whatever is being chucked out that day.'

This guy was a genius. 'Yes, because the other day it would have been cauliflower and rhubarb!'

Charlie gave her a look that said Brighton wasn't quite ready for that level of quirky.

After their decorating marathon, where they got one coat finished on everything, including Regan's T-shirt and the toaster – well they *were* only enthusiastic amateurs – they headed back to Charlie's with an Indian takeaway partly paid for by the ten pounds her dad had given her whilst peering suspiciously at his new-look kitchen.

Regan was keen to check out Charlie's place and also hopeful for a bit of bedroom action, given that their initial attempt had been thwarted by Cleo's chair and there hadn't been any other opportunities since. When a male voice shouted hello the moment the key was in the lock, she feared her plans may be derailed. She'd incorrectly assumed Charlie lived on his own.

'It's only Beanstalk,' said Charlie, leading her through to a small kitchen. It was a nice little house. Classic two up, two down, but modernised and stylish. 'Hi, Beanstalk,' she called.

'Evening, Reg,' came back the reply.

'Beanstalk moved in a couple of weeks back. My parents didn't like me being here alone what with . . .' he tapped the back of his head. 'They were threatening to force me to move back home, which would most likely have ended with me battering them both with Dad's golf clubs, so having Beanstalk move in here was a happy compromise for all of us.'

They decanted the food onto plates and sat in the kitchen at possibly the smallest table she'd ever seen. 'It's a garden bistro set,' he explained.

'I like it.'

They ate in silence, which gave her a chance to take in the surroundings. The units were modern in a gloss white, set against the dark granite of the surfaces, and everything looked spotless. Not quite what she'd expected from guys living alone. She hoped he wasn't a closet Jarvis. She couldn't cope with another neat freak.

Charlie caught her looking. 'My mum comes round to clean.' He looked a bit sheepish. 'Since . . . you know. She fusses a bit.'

They split the last onion bhaji and Regan licked her fingers flirtatiously when she'd finished.

Charlie didn't react. She did a very fake yawn and checked her watch, which made Charlie check his.

'Ah,' said Charlie. 'Sorry, I'd better clear up here and

get to bed. I'm on day shift again tomorrow and I want to go for a run before work.' He ferried the plates to the sink and she followed.

'Oh. Um. Right,' said Regan, failing to hide her disappointment.

'Sorry. It's just . . .'

She let the silence hang there until she could bear it no longer. 'Shame, because I wanted to check you weren't hiding any button-up pyjamas anywhere.' She ran a finger seductively along his shoulder.

'You're going to have to trust me on that one. Shall we catch up in a few days when I'm off?'

'Or maybe one evening, if you're on days?' He seemed to be going cold on her; or was she imagining it?

'It's two days, two nights and four off,' he explained.

She'd never get the hang of his shifts. 'Right.'

'I'll message you.'

She pulled a face. 'I've still not got a phone. But I'll be at the coffee shop in the day and the studio in the evening.'

'Sure thing.' He busied himself with filling up the sink. They washed up together, the silence only broken by Beanstalk shouting at the TV in the other room. She folded up the tea towel and waited for Charlie to put the last of the things away.

'I'd best be off then,' she said, sensing he was waiting for her to leave. He followed her to the door and gave her a brief kiss before letting her out. Nope, she wasn't imagining it – something had definitely changed.

Chapter Fifteen

By Friday, Regan found she was in a steady routine: early morning shower at the gym followed by a brisk walk to work. It was a bright blue-sky day and a shadow of the moon was still clinging on, making Brighton even more fairy-tale beautiful than usual. Her mind was mulling over great sets of quirky jam combinations; kumquat was leading the way, although this was mainly because the word made her giggle. Unfortunately Jag, who ran the fruit and veg stall, wasn't big on kumquats; he often had a glut of normal things, like tomatoes and melons, which didn't hit the mark for 'quirky' on their own.

She was wondering if rhubarb went with tomatoes when raised voices and frantic barking drew her attention. Up ahead, two youths were huddled over something on the ground, jeering. When one of them started kicking whatever it was, Regan automatically broke into a run. Nearing the scene, she could see it was a person on the ground. It was Kevin.

'Hey! I've called the police!' she shouted, and the hooded heads turned in her direction. Unfortunately they didn't flee as she'd been hoping. They stared her down. She hadn't thought this through. She looked frantically around. Elvis was tied to a cycle stand and was straining hard to pile in and help Kevin. When the shouting turned in her direction Elvis felt like her best option. She ran to him, but the rope was pulled tight and her fingers struggled to untie it.

She looked about for someone to help. On the other side of the street she spotted someone. It was Alex. In any other situation he would be the last person she'd want to see, but right now anyone who could lend a hand would be better than nothing.

'Oi, Alex!' He looked up and she waved whilst tugging at the rope pinning Elvis to the bike stand. Alex held up a hand but carried on walking. 'Alex?' This time he didn't look up at all.

The youths were shouting abuse at her and getting closer, although Elvis's strangled barks were keeping them at bay. *Shit*, she thought, struggling to free the knot. At last it came undone. Elvis bounded towards the youths, barking ferociously. They scattered.

'Elvis!' she shouted. The last thing she wanted was for them to hurt him; Kevin would be heartbroken. Elvis put the brakes on, halted in the road and continued to bark.

'That thing should be muzzled,' shouted one of the youths.

'Yeah, and so should I, so watch out!' yelled back Regan, her system swamped with adrenaline. She was ready to take on anyone.

Regan ran towards the crumpled figure on the ground. 'Kevin?' she said, crouching down. The smell of urine hit her. He was soaked in it. 'Kevin. Can you speak?' Kevin coughed and winced at the same time, but his eyes were open. 'You okay?' It was a stupid question. Why did she feel compelled to ask that when she could see quite plainly that he wasn't?

'Just kids,' he said, but his voice was weak.

'Can you sit up?' she asked. He looked pale.

A shadow loomed over them. Regan's head jerked up. She was ready to fight. But there was no need; it was Alex. 'Are you all right?' he asked, his eyes darting about sheepishly.

'Nice of you to wait until they'd cleared off,' she said. What a bloody hero he was.

'Don't get involved,' said Alex, turning his nose up at Kevin. She had to admit, he did reek, but that was no excuse.

'They attacked my friend – that makes me involved,' said Regan. 'Call an ambulance, will you?' She hated not having a mobile phone. The rice trick hadn't seemed to work so she was still without one.

'Your friend?' asked Alex, distaste written all over his face. 'Come away, Regan. You can't do any more. Look, I'll get you a coffee. I was heading that way – I have to buy my own since you left.' He gave her a cheery grin.

She shook her head and stood up. 'You're unbelievable.' This was a side of him she'd not seen in the office. It made her wonder how well she'd actually known him.

Kevin shuffled himself upright whilst clutching his side. 'I don't think I need an ambulance,' he said, but his contorted face said otherwise.

'Maybe not, but *he* will in a minute,' said Regan, stabbing a finger in Alex's chest. Alex stepped back in alarm. Regan was quite proud of the impact she had on him.

Regan could see Elvis approaching Alex from behind and she waited. 'Argh!' he squealed as Elvis took him by surprise, inspecting his nether regions. Alex stumbled out of the way.

'Bye, Alex! Thanks for your help,' called Regan.

Kevin started to laugh. 'Ow, that hurts.'

'And that's why we're getting you checked out. Come on, I think there's a first aider on the market.' She knew there was, because it was in all the blurb she'd read about the stalls. Regan put an arm around his waist and helped him to stand.

Nearing the market place a trader saw them coming and came over to help. 'You need a hand?' he asked.

'Please.' She was grateful when he took Kevin's weight and steered him to the back of his bread van.

'Here, sit on the edge there.'

'Some kids attacked him. I was after the first aider,' said Regan.

'You've found him. I'm Malcolm,' he said. 'Let's take a look at you, buddy.' He helped lift up Kevin's top and she saw him baulk at the taut red scars of long healed wounds on Kevin's torso. They matched his hands. 'Where's it hurt?' he asked. He ran his hands over Kevin's ribs, making him flinch.

'Right there,' replied Kevin.

'Sorry, mate. I'm going to call an ambulance to be on the safe side.'

'Thanks,' said Regan. She wasn't just thanking him for making the call, but for the kindness and respect he'd shown Kevin. Thankfully not everyone was like Alex.

Regan had to get to work and was grateful to Malcolm for offering to stay with Kevin until the ambulance arrived. She took Elvis with her, although she had no idea what she was going to do with him once she got there.

Penny was putting the sign out. 'I thought you'd quit

already,' she said, with a light smile. She spotted Elvis. 'What's up?'

'Kevin's been hurt. Some kids roughed him up.'

'Little sods.'

'They pissed on him too.' Somehow it seemed almost worse than the kicking: that they thought it was acceptable, that Kevin was so far down the food chain that he didn't matter.

'Bastards,' said Penny. 'Sorry, the werewolf can't come inside.'

'I know,' said Regan, ruffling Elvis's head. She felt sorry for him having to witness his owner getting attacked.

'There's a bike stand out the back by the bins. You could tie him up there?'

Regan nodded. With their heads low, she and Elvis plodded round to the back of the café.

It was a quiet morning, so Penny let Regan take a break. She took Elvis with her to see if there was any sign of the ambulance. Malcolm greeted her warmly. 'Hello again,' he said. 'He's going to be okay. Paramedics checked him out. Suspected broken rib.'

'Did they take him to hospital?'

Malcolm was shaking his head. 'Said it would heal naturally.'

Regan was taken aback. This was all wrong. 'I guess it would heal on its own, but that's if you've got a nice sofa to lie on and someone to look after you. Not if you're living on the streets like Kevin is.' The injustice of it made her cross.

'I know,' said Malcolm, who actually did look like he cared. 'One of the other traders gave him a lift to a local centre where they'll be able to get him some paracetamol, a hot shower and some clean clothes.'

'Thank you, Malcolm. I didn't know what to do.'

'Hey, any time. I'm always happy to help,' he said, stroking Elvis.

Regan bit her lip. 'Actually, there is something else. I was thinking of applying for a market stall. Any tips?' It was cheeky, but you didn't get anywhere if you didn't ask.

'Sure,' said Malcolm, looking chuffed to have been asked. 'Pull up a chair.' He passed her a plastic garden chair and she sat down behind his bread stall.

Ten minutes later, her brain was overflowing and a ripple of excitement was swirling in her stomach. She had never been surer of anything in her life: she was going to apply to be a market stallholder.

'I need to go. But thank you so much, Malcolm. I'm definitely going to apply.'

'Good on you,' he said, getting to his feet. 'And get your business registered with the council.' His head snapped in the direction of someone approaching. 'Stand by your beds,' said Malcolm, half to Regan and half to the traders chatting nearby. The others looked up and scurried back to their stalls.

Regan followed Malcolm's gaze. A rotund woman with masses of dark grey hair bouncing about her shoulders was bearing down on them.

Regan noted Malcolm's shoulders tense as he straightened the granary loaves in front of him. She could sense the tension growing until the woman marched past.

'Morning,' said Malcolm.

'Malcolm,' said the woman, her voice formal as she continued on her way. Malcolm let out a long breath and his shoulders relaxed.

'Who's she?' asked Regan, watching the woman gesticulate wildly at another stallholder.

'Boadicea,' he said, absentmindedly, whilst he too watched the drama unfold.

'Isn't it pronounced Boudicca these days?' asked Regan.

'What?' he turned to Regan. 'Not when I was at school.'

Regan opened her mouth but decided against labouring the point. 'But who is she?'

'The market manager. Someone you don't ever want to get on the wrong side of.'

Regan was grateful to have the café to keep her busy and take her mind off poor Kevin. Penny told her that, whilst she'd been on her break, Charlie had called in to say he was cooking dinner and she was welcome to go round. She'd been disappointed that he'd not waited to see her, but she guessed he was busy. The invite also sounded more casual than she would have liked, but maybe that had got lost in translation. Perhaps she was looking for problems? She had a distinct feeling that Charlie was cooling off, and with everything else, she didn't want to contemplate that. She'd grown very attached to him very quickly.

Regan tracked down Kevin after work, returning Elvis, who greeted him like he'd been at war, not in a shelter for the day. Kevin had had a hot meal but he still took the pepper and hummus wrap she'd brought him. He had a hooded look about him and he appeared distant, which wasn't surprising given what had happened to him. She didn't like leaving him, but he insisted he was all right although his flinching when he took a deep breath told her different.

Her biggest worry was that the youths would come back, but Kevin assured her he'd be sleeping in a different place tonight and that was one of the reasons he took care to move about. It upset her that people found entertainment in harming another human being and it made her feel helpless. He'd been pleased to be reunited with Elvis, who himself was over the moon, having been tied up most of the day with only the occasional visitor when Regan or Penny went to the bins.

She was all the more glad of Charlie's invite because she didn't want to be on her own. What she really wanted was to have a good rant over a nice bottle of wine. And a snog, obviously – and possibly some bedroom action.

Regan knocked on Charlie's door and held back her desire to launch herself at him the minute he opened it.

'Hey,' he said. She went in for a full-on snog but he managed to keep her at arm's length, kiss her lightly and turn away. 'Come on through.' She faltered for a second at his coolness.

The small table in the kitchen was in darkness and set for dinner. A candle was burning, making the room smell faintly of oranges and look almost bistro-like in its flickering glow. 'Wow, this is lovely,' she said, impressed he'd gone to this much effort. 'It looks very romantic.' She sidled over to him.

'I'm going to put the light on because I can't see to do anything otherwise.' He flicked the switch and the magical bistro atmosphere evaporated.

'Er, okay. Good, because I was hoping to go over my business plan and my market stall application with you too. I registered my business with the council today.' She rocked on her heels.

'Great,' he said. He ran his fingers through his hair. She could tell he was nervous.

'What's wrong?' She'd been worrying about the uncomfortable vibe she'd felt that evening after they'd decorated her dad's kitchen. It was still there.

He took a deep breath and looked her in the eye. 'The thing is, I thought I could do this . . . but I can't.'

'Is it a complicated recipe?' She peered in the cooker at a casserole dish.

'Not the meal. Us.' To his credit he appeared excruciatingly awkward.

Regan blinked. 'How do you mean?'

'It's hard to explain.'

'Try,' said Regan. She got the distinct feeling she was about to get dumped.

'Come and sit down,' he said, leading her through to the living room.

She sat on the sofa and waited. She had the same sinking sensation she got when Nigel did her performance review.

Charlie clasped his hands together in front of him. 'Regan, you're brilliant and I thought we could have some fun for as long as I'm here.' She didn't like to hear him talk like this, but she wanted an explanation. 'But the closer we get, and the more time we spend together, the tougher it's going to be for both of us. I don't want to make this any harder than it's going to be, so—'

'Hold on a minute,' said Regan. She knew he was speaking from the heart, which made his words hurt all the more. She needed to halt his speech. 'We can keep it on a superficial level. Fun only. I promise.' She crossed her chest and a glimmer of a smile crossed his lips. She was desperate to cling on to whatever amount of contact she could. They had a connection. She wasn't about to walk away from the best thing that was ever likely to happen to her.

'I don't know that we can.' The look he gave her made her insides puddle and a crazy paving of cracks shatter across her heart. 'I've been seeing my therapist again. I had been coping up until . . .'

'Meeting me?' she asked. He nodded.

'It's not your fault, Regan, but the thought of leaving you behind breaks my heart.' He puffed out a breath. 'And worse than that, I can't bear the thought of messing you up.'

She lifted her chin. 'I barely know you. Won't shed a tear,' she said, but the crack in her voice let her down.

Charlie raised one eyebrow. 'See? I can't be responsible for that. And I know it's selfish, but I want my last few months to be fun, not sad and guilt ridden. It hurts enough to think about how my passing will affect my parents, and that's more than enough for me to handle. I can't have you on my conscience too. Do you understand?'

'I think so. You're not a fan of the "better to have loved and lost" ethos then.'

'No, I want to leave as much happiness behind as I can. Not sad, screwed-up people.'

She let out a deep sigh. 'What do we do now?' She sent up a silent prayer that he wasn't going to ban her from seeing him. Her heart ached at the very thought. She reached for his hand and he gently pulled it away.

'I think we need to keep things formal.'

'I look great in a suit,' quipped Regan. She wasn't good at serious discussions.

'I meant treat each other more like colleagues. No physical contact.' She could see he was uncomfortable suggesting this and she could practically feel her uterus cop a strop.

'What . . . none at all?' It came out squeakier than she'd expected.

'I think it's best. I did look into moving away, getting a transfer to a different county,' she jolted her head back – moving to get away from her was a bit extreme, 'but it would upset my parents and be harder for them to sort things out . . . at the end.'

'I see.'

She realised she'd been too hasty ticking the boyfriend item off her lottery list, but at least he wasn't moving away; she was thankful for that. She was upset that he'd even considered it.

'Do you agree?'

She didn't have much of a choice. 'Okay. If that's really what you want. Let's keep it formal. I'm sure I can manage to keep my hands off you. You're not that irresistible, Charlie McGee.'

But he very obviously was.

Chapter Sixteen

The days that followed were only sunny on the outside. Regan saw Charlie a couple of times, but with the new regime things were stilted. She didn't want to complain though – she'd still rather see him like this than not at all. She put a brave face on and tried to appear nonchalant about the whole thing, but her disguise was paper thin. She was missing Cleo more than ever and had come close to calling her from the café when Penny popped out, but the calls would have cost a fortune and she didn't want to get Penny into trouble when she'd been so kind.

The routine of the café and evenings spent mapping out her new business venture gave Regan's messy life some much-needed focus and structure. Charlie had helped Regan revise her business plan, complete her application and fill in a number of other forms that the council needed. All she had to do now was get through her meeting with the market manager and she was almost home and dry.

She seized any overtime Penny had to offer and squirrelled away every penny by living on almost-out-of-date food from the café and drinking free coffee and tap water. She was low on essentials and had resorted to using the face cream samples she had accumulated but never got around to using. But none of it mattered, because she was following her dream. Even if it was a dream she hadn't even known she'd been harbouring until she'd made her lottery list. Plus, it was a good distraction to stop her mind dwelling on Charlie and what might have been.

The day of her meeting with the market manager dawned. Regan had done her usual trip to the gym and spent extra time styling her hair so she looked more business-y. Penny had brought her iron in, so Regan's clothes looked smart and not like Elvis had been playing tug-of-war with them. She had sent her off with a hug and a breath mint.

Regan waited patiently by the tiny office in the corner of the market building. It wasn't like her to be early and it was a little discombobulating. *Don't call her Boadicea*, she repeated in her head. She checked her watch again. The market manager was now fifteen minutes late. This wasn't a good start. Regan shuffled her papers, which included her hastily produced projected accounts. They were complete fantasy but better than a blank piece of paper. She was having a quick peek at the list of things she wanted to ask when a booming voice startled her.

'Mind your backs!' bellowed a man who would make Beanstalk look undernourished.

Regan jumped, bumped into the corner of the office wall and promptly chucked her neat pile of papers into the air. She watched some get trampled underfoot while the others landed on top of the booming man's trolley full of fresh fish. He halted abruptly and they both watched the ink bleed on her business plan as the wet fish seeped through.

He shook his head. 'Hope that's not important,' he said, snatching it up and handing it back, in a wet, and now, crumpled state.

Regan gagged at the fishy smell and made a mental note to ask that her stall wasn't near his. 'Thanks,' she said, holding the business plan at arm's length by the very tips of her fingers.

'Oh my,' said the market manager, arriving as Regan hurriedly gathered up the other sheets.

Don't call her Boadicea, thought Regan. 'Hello . . . Bernice,' said Regan, pronouncing her name slowly from her crouched position. 'I'm here about a stall.'

Bernice checked her watch. 'Then you're late.'

Regan stood up, hugging the papers to her chest, remembering too late that the business plan was liberally soaked in eau de fish. *Doh!* She followed Bernice inside and took a seat.

After initial introductions and the customary interest in her unusual name, they got down to business. Bernice read through Regan's application in silence whilst Regan listened to the thrum of her heartbeat in her ears. She'd never been so nervous. Usually she didn't get worried at things like interviews, but that was because she'd never cared about something as much as she cared about getting the market stall. All the other jobs she'd gone for were because she'd needed a job, any job. This time it was all very different.

Bernice eventually looked up. 'Your trading name is Sticky Situations?' There was the faintest hint of a smile on the edge of her lips.

'It's not firmed up yet. I liked Jam Packed but there's a company in Surrey called that already.'

'I see. And do you have any samples with you?'

'Ahh, no. Sorry, do you need samples?' Regan had read and reread the forms – there had been no mention of samples.

'It's not essential, but we like to see what is being sold so that we can check product quality, presentation and value for money.' *Then maybe put that on the sodding form*, thought Regan.

'Right. When do you need a sample by?' It sounded like a conversation with her doctor and it was putting her off her thread.

'Next couple of days?'

Regan tried not to appear as startled as she felt. She'd not actually got to the bit where she made anything yet. There hadn't seemed to be much point if she couldn't get a stall.

'If that's okay?' asked Bernice, with a hint of suspicion about her.

Regan tried to look nonchalant. 'Sure. Of course. Why not? Not a problem at all.' *Shiiiit – I've got to make jam samples in the next couple of days.* 'Here's a picture of the labels I'll be using.' She handed over the printout she'd spent a couple of hours designing at the library. Bernice barely glanced at it. She tried to look at the second page of the application, but it stuck to the first.

'Ah. Sorry,' said Regan. 'Marmalade.' She pointed at a splodge on the top edge. 'It was research.' Bernice pulled the pages apart with a harsh rip and carried on reading.

'There's a question mark in the box for organic. Do you not know if your jams and chutneys are from organic produce?' Regan could tell Bernice's suspicions were deepening.

Regan launched in to her rehearsed sales pitch. 'My

main USP – that's unique selling point – is that I am recycling fruit and vegetables that would otherwise have been thrown away.'

'Recycling fruit?'

'Yes. I am working with the other stallholders to reduce waste, keep the market tidy and provide a quality product for consumers.' Regan took a breath.

'How exactly?'

'By taking the other stalls' unwanted fruit and vegetables and turning them into jams and chutneys. So if they're organic then I am too.'

'I see.' Bernice consulted the form again. 'And what are your "quirky, original and tantalising flavours"?' she read from the form.

Regan had hoped Bernice wasn't going to ask that, because it all depended on what the grocery stall was chucking away. As Charlie had pooh-poohed her cauliflower and rhubarb suggestion, she had to think quick. Her mind whizzed to what she'd seen by the bins this week. 'Pineapple and . . .' *Don't say parsnip*, '. . . coconut.'

'Like a pina colada jam?' Bernice looked impressed.

'Yes!' Regan almost shouted it at her. 'Yes, exactly. Pina colada jam.' She grinned at Bernice, who appeared mildly terrified. Regan had no idea if there was such a thing, but if it got her a market stall then she'd damn well invent one.

Bernice stood up and shook hands with Regan. 'Thank you. I look forward to receiving your sample and after that I'll be in touch.' Bernice's nose twitched. 'Can you smell fish?'

'The business plan is a bit fishy, I'm afraid,' said Regan.

* * *

Regan was as hyper as a gerbil on Red Bull when she got back to the Hug In A Mug. 'Did it go well?' asked Penny, in between serving a customer and frothing milk.

'I think so, but there's one minor flaw in the plan,' said Regan, taking over the frothing. 'I need to make jam samples in the next couple of days.'

Penny gave the customer her change and joined Regan at the coffee machine. 'Why's that a problem? You're all set, aren't you?' Penny had managed to get Regan jam jars a few days ago from a wholesaler and had been keeping track of her progress.

'I haven't asked the person whose kitchen I want to use if I can use it yet.'

'You need to sort that. There's no cooker here, before you ask.'

'I know. And I need to speak to the grocery stallholder on the market about using his throwaway stuff. And . . . I've never made jam before.' She said the last bit really fast and scrunched her face up as if waiting for impact.

'Regan!' Penny's eyes pinged cartoon wide. 'You've based a whole business proposition on something you've no idea about?'

'I got a bit carried away with the other stuff. But it can't be that hard,' said Regan, ferrying the drink to the waiting customer and returning to Penny.

Penny was shaking her head. 'Don't you need a special pan and a thermometer thingy?'

'Do you?'

Penny nodded. 'Look, it's quiet. Why don't you go to the library and do some proper research? I'll hold the fort here.'

'I can't really afford the time—'

'I'll put it through as a full shift.'

'You're the best,' said Regan, whipping off her apron.

'Yeah, but don't go telling everyone or you'll ruin my reputation,' Penny quipped, with a smile.

Regan hurried outside and just stopped herself from stepping into the road as a small silver car careered past at an outrageous speed. The hoody-wearing passenger gave her the bird and tore past. She only caught a glimpse, but she was pretty sure it was one of the youths who had attacked Kevin. By the time she'd ordered her thoughts the car was gone, along with the chance to clock the number plate.

She looked about for Kevin, but she'd not seen him about much since the incident. There were quite a few pigeons around The Level today, so they were likely the reason he was keeping away from this part of town. She crossed the road, seeing the grocery stallholder heading for the bins already, and spied her chance.

'Hiya,' she called, and he turned and gave her a friendly smile. Good start.

After formal introductions, Regan was thrilled to hear that whilst Jag was trying hard to cut down on his waste, he was finding predicting buyer habits quite tricky at the moment and was blaming Brexit. They had a lengthy discussion, which ended with Jag agreeing to offer her all his 'going over' produce first in exchange for a regular supply of jam and chutney. She had expected to have to pay something for it, but Jag insisted that he wanted to 'pay it forward' and help someone else starting out in the market trade. She had thanked him profusely and merrily taken two trays of plums and onions. Jag had also thrown in a couple of pineapples and coconuts after she'd done a big sell on the pina colada jam idea. This was going to be a breeze.

She'd asked Jag if he'd seen Kevin or Elvis but he hadn't. Regan decided to keep an eye out for them on the way to the library. She walked via Pelham Square, which was one of Kevin's other regular haunts – a tranquil garden square away from the hustle and bustle with a few nice flower borders, some benches and some very impressive trees. She passed a group of students taking photos in and out of the traditional red phone boxes just outside the neat black railings. She balanced her trays on the postbox and scanned the square. No sign of Kevin or Elvis.

Regan read the sign at the entrance and realised that dogs were not allowed in Pelham Square, so it was no longer likely Kevin would be here now that he and Elvis were inseparable. She was running out of places he might be, and it was starting to worry her. She realised she had no idea how to track him down. Worse still: if anything had happened to him, how would she ever find out?

Chapter Seventeen

Regan spent a couple of hours in the library worrying about jam making, trawling the internet, scribbling down equipment and facilities she needed, things she'd over-looked and random questions that were bothering her. She sat back in the chair and stared at the very long list. This was more than a minor flaw in her plans. It was a great, gaping, cavernous disaster.

She checked her emails while she tried to stay calm. There were a few from Cleo, upset at not being able to speak to her. Regan fired one back explaining that her mobile had been unsalvageable and she was saving for a new one. Helpfully Cleo replied instantly, saying she had an old mobile phone in a drawer at the studio and as Regan had the keys she should pop round and get it. This was an excellent development. At least she'd be able to communicate with people again.

A friendly library assistant checked she was okay and she took the opportunity to ask about Kevin. But they hadn't seen him in the library since he'd got Elvis, because dogs weren't allowed inside. At least it was another place she could tick off her list. Regan gathered up her scribbled notes, stuffed them in her bag and left.

Outside she spotted Hillary, an older lady who had lived on the streets of Brighton for many years. 'Hillary!' called out Regan, to stop her crossing the street.

'Hello, my darling, how are you?' Hillary greeted everyone like a long lost relative.

'I'm good, thanks. Have you seen Kevin recently?' The homeless community was good at looking out for each other, so it was worth asking.

Hillary pouted hard and adjusted her crocheted hat, which sat on top of a mass of bouncy grey hair. 'Now you're asking.' Her mouth moved while she silently counted on her fingers. 'Yes!' she barked, startling Regan. 'I saw him and Elvis get turned away from the night shelter a couple of days ago. They don't take dogs, you see. And he's a bit of a brute is Elvis. Lovely, mind. I won't have a word said against him. Not. A. Word.' She shook a finger at Regan as she spoke.

'Me neither. He's a cracking dog.'

'What did you want with him?' Hillary narrowed her sharp eyes.

'I'm worried about him. I've not seen him for a few days and that's not like him. He usually calls by for a coffee.'

'Elvis drinks coffee?' Hillary's forehead was a mass of furrowed lines.

'No. Kevin drinks coffee,' said Regan, a little concerned that Hillary may not have been the best choice to track Kevin down.

'Coffee. Eurgh. I can't stand the stuff. A good old-fashioned cup of tea, on the other hand . . . now you're talking.' Hillary gave Regan a hearty slap on the shoulder. 'And a biscuit. I love a rich tea biscuit, me. Not those Bourbons. Not those things; they look like chocolate but they're just brown. Don't get me started on those.' Hillary laughed long and hard.

Regan waited for the laughter to subside. 'If you could ask around, that'd be great. And if you see him—'

'See who?' asked Hillary.

'Kevin,' said Regan, a little shocked at Hillary's question. 'Can you tell him to come to the café?'

'I will, my darling. Don't you worry.' Hillary waved her off like she was emigrating and Regan left feeling she was no closer to tracking Kevin down.

Back at the studio, Regan soon uncovered Cleo's old phone. It was literally stuck at the back of a drawer and covered in brown and cream paint, making it look like a melted choc-ice. She chipped enough paint off to make the screen visible, swapped over her SIM card and hoped for the best. It worked.

She leaned against the sink, checked there was nothing of hers in sight and FaceTimed Cleo. A sleepy looking Cleo answered the call.

'Oh, what time is it?' asked Regan, realising her error.

'Don't worry. It's lovely to hear from you,' said Cleo, with a giant yawn as she shuffled herself upright. 'How are things?' She was looking sympathetic.

'Brilliant. Have you ever made jam?'

Cleo did a slow blink. 'No. Why?'

'No reason.' Maybe now wasn't the time to explain. 'How are things with you?'

'Horrendous. As predicted, Oscar has flown home and left me to finish the tour alone.'

'What a bastard. Can he do that?'

'Apparently so. Thankfully so far the events have been small scale and I've got the gallery owners to say a few words while I've hovered around for a few photos and then slunk off.'

'You should try and make the most of it.' *Especially if it's all about to end*, thought Regan, but she didn't voice that to Cleo.

'It's really not my thing. But I have found something that is – or some*one*, anyway.' She sounded excited.

'Ooh. What do they look like? Anyone famous?'

Cleo gave a good-natured shake of her head. 'He's in his fifties and looks a bit like Yoda.'

'Bloody hell, Cleo. You need to aim higher.'

Cleo laughed. 'He's the university lecturer I mentioned. I've been coaching a couple of his star art students and I'm loving it.' She really did look different when she talked about it.

'That's great.'

'Is everything all right at the studio then?' asked Cleo, trying to peer behind Regan.

'Yes, it's all tickety boo.' *When had she ever used that phrase before?*

Cleo laughed. 'Only four weeks and I'll be heading home.' The words hit Regan like a medicine ball to the chest. She had been counting down to when she could take up the market stall; the fact she would have to move out of the studio in four weeks had almost passed her by. 'You all right?' Cleo was giving her an odd look.

'Yes. Fine. I'm fine. I should probably lock up here and go,' she said, making her way to the door, keeping the camera angled upwards so as not to reveal her stuff, which was mainly on the floor. Old habits died hard.

'Are you dashing off to this new bloke? Has he got you peeling grapes for him yet?'

Sadness instantly swamped Regan at the thought of Charlie. 'We're not . . . He doesn't want a relationship.'

'Why ever not? You're amazing. But I can't help thinking you've had a lucky escape. It didn't add up to me.'

'You were wrong. He really is dying, Cleo, and he can't handle the guilt of messing with my head when he goes . . . you see, I was kinda falling for him.'

Cleo looked shocked and a little teary. 'I'm so sorry. I should come home.'

'No.' Regan shook her head. 'This tour is important and I'm fine. Really. There's nothing you or anyone can do.'

A knock on the door made Regan jump. Cleo frowned hard. 'Who's that?'

'Good question. Let me see.' Regan held the phone tight to her chest while she opened the door a fraction.

'Oh, hello. I thought Cleo was back.' A grey-haired man in dark blue overalls was scanning Regan. 'Is everything all right?'

'Perfect,' said Regan. This neighbour's timing couldn't be better. 'I'm a friend of Cleo's and here is Cleo herself to tell you that I am allowed to be here.' Regan showed the phone screen to the man.

'Hello, Brian,' said Cleo, with a wave. 'Regan is getting something from the studio. I hope it didn't alarm you.'

'Well, the other night—' began Brian.

'Anyway,' cut in Regan, 'I expect you're busy, Cleo. We won't keep you any longer. I'll have a chat to Brian here and sort everything. You get off to your party.'

'It's one o'clock in the—'

'Byeeeee,' said Regan and she ended the call with relief. She turned to Brian, who was frowning a little. 'Brian, you are an excellent neighbour for checking on Cleo's property like this. She is very lucky to have you.' Brian looked chuffed about the comment. 'But you don't need to worry, because I will be coming and going quite a bit over the next few weeks. Important stuff going down in Japan for Cleo, so I'm managing things at the Brighton end.' Brian was looking frowny again. 'She's big in Japan . . .' said Regan, losing where she was going with this and trying hard not to repeat the ancient 80s song lyrics that were now whizzing around her head.

'Us small-business people stick together,' said Brian. Far be it from Regan to point out that Cleo really wasn't operating a small business from her studio, but there was something that might get him on side.

'I agree. I'm a market stallholder myself.'

'Are you?'

'Yes. Just starting out.' It wasn't a complete lie. 'Lovely Cleo has said I can store a few things here whilst she's away, so you may well see more of me and spot a few lights on. Is that okay?'

'Oh, that's fine,' said Brian, seeming far happier. 'Open Market, is it?'

'Yes. Sorry, Brian. Time is money, as you well know. I need to lock up properly and get on.'

'Of course. Nice to meet you,' he said, and he walked off to a unit a couple of doors down. Regan heaved a giant sigh of relief. Four weeks and counting. The clock was ticking and everything hinged on the market stall. Now was the time to get her arse into gear and make some jam.

Regan pulled a large saucepan out from the back of her dad's kitchen cupboard and wiped it down. She paused. Her father was in the doorway watching her. 'Shouldn't you be getting off?' she asked.

'When you said you wanted to do something in the kitchen I thought you meant more decorating.' Graham was putting on his coat, but he appeared troubled. She may have been a little misleading when she'd spoken to him earlier, but needs must. She was sure even Marks and Spencer had had to bend the truth a little to get to where they were.

'Ah, no, but you'll never know I was here,' she said, getting out yet another saucepan. 'What time will you be back?'

'What time are you leaving?' Her father looked quite alarmed.

She paused. *How long did jam take to make?* She wondered. 'I'll be gone by bedtime.'

Graham seemed to relax a little. He zipped up his anorak. 'Bye then.' His voice hesitant, he picked up a large holdall and a suit carrier and left.

Regan clapped her hands together. 'Right. This is where the magic begins!'

Her initial enthusiasm was short-lived. She read and reread the instructions for pineapple jam and realised there were a few things that didn't make a lot of sense. 'Add pectin.' What the hell was that? She'd seen it mentioned when she'd been scrolling through jam-making websites, but she thought it was something that was already in fruit. A quick Google check told her she was right, so she ignored the recipe's request for pectin and continued. She had purchased a lime and lots of sugar from the local shop, so she felt reassured that this would all be fine.

An hour later, she was ready to quit.

The pineapple was ludicrously difficult to prepare. By

the time she'd cut out the core and sliced off the bobbly surface and the sharp stalky bit that had nearly taken her eye out, there was hardly anything left. The recipe had told her to pulp it, but that was impossible without some sort of kitchen equipment, so she'd chopped it into oblivion.

If she'd thought the pineapple was a challenge, it was nothing compared to the coconut. Firstly, none of the recipes she'd printed had any mention of fresh coconut, only tinned coconut milk, which she didn't have; and she'd nearly lost a finger when the knife had slipped when she was trying to get into the sodding coconut in the first place.

She had managed to save a tiny amount of the liquid inside the coconut, which she'd chucked into the saucepan with her massacred pineapple. After that, it had taken a good hour to obliterate the coconut flesh into tiny flakes, but she'd done it. She added an unhealthy amount of sugar and the juice of the lime, and with an exuberant flourish she lit the gas under the pan. All it had to do now was boil. Job done.

She hoped the onion marmalade would be a lot easier. She'd bought some vinegar for this recipe and was planning on raiding her dad's cupboard for the few spices some of the websites had suggested. She was keen to invent her own flavour rather than steal someone else's, so she didn't want it to be too planned.

A lot of tears and swear words later, she had a pile of chopped onions and she hated every one. Her eyes were stinging and the finger she'd cut when attacking the coconut was smarting like hell. She tipped all the ingredients into the next two saucepans, added some chilli flakes she'd found, and went to wash her hands.

Returning to the pineapple and coconut mixture, she inspected it carefully. It was bubbling happily in the smallest saucepan, which seemed like a good sign. But it was looking very runny and didn't look to be thickening at all. She left it to bubble while she tackled the plums. All the recipes she'd found had been for plain old plum jam, but Regan knew that wasn't going to be good enough to impress Bernice. She needed a quirky edge. Something that made it different. Regan pulled out all of her dad's spices and gave each one a sniff. With the exception of the cardamom they all smelt like sawdust and were years out of date. 'Okay, cardamom and plum jam it is then,' she said, and she got on with the next batch.

Regan shut the door on everything gurgling merrily in the kitchen and took her shiny new jam jars to the bathroom to wash them properly before sterilising. She'd have more space to lay them out in the bathroom, and she'd already used every surface in the small kitchen. After washing them carefully and placing them on a brand-new baking tray exactly how she'd seen it in a YouTube video, she proudly carried them back through.

When she opened the door, it was like discovering a chemical weapons factory. The strength of the boiling vinegar in the onion marmalade took her breath away and most likely took a layer off her lungs. The pineapple jam looked like a mini volcano as it spewed merrily over the sides of the tiny saucepan, and the plum jam appeared to be trying to launch itself into space; splats were erupting out of the saucepan and all over the newly painted kitchen.

'Shittity shittington!' Regan wasn't sure where to start but, ever the optimist, she popped her clean jars in the oven in case there was anything she could salvage.

‘Hello,’ called her father in an uncharacteristically jolly voice.

‘Hel-lo,’ came Regan’s shaky reply.

‘What the blue blazes?’ Graham surveyed his once-pristine kitchen, which now looked like a mad professor’s laboratory.

‘You’re early,’ said Regan, switching off the gas and marvelling at the amount of jet-black jam that was now welded to the cooker top.

‘It’s . . .’ Graham pointed at the kitchen clock, ‘. . . tomorrow.’ It was ten past midnight.

‘Really?’ She stared at the clock, then checked her watch. Where had the evening gone? She’d spent most of it wrestling with pineapples and swearing at onions. ‘Sorry. I thought I’d be done.’

‘What have you done, exactly?’ asked Graham, holding his nose.

‘I’m making jam.’ They both looked at the mixtures in the various saucepans. None of them looked like jam, or certainly not any from planet earth.

The timer pinged to tell her the jars could come out of the oven now. Perhaps there was something she could salvage. She lined up the jars and hopefully tipped up the pineapple saucepan, but nothing happened. What was left inside was clinging desperately to the inside of the pan. The onion mixture was a little more mobile, but it needed help. She stopped scooping when she reached the black layer on the bottom. She’d work out how to clean the saucepan later – hopefully there was a YouTube video for that too. The plum mixture looked a little more hopeful, but what any of it tasted like, she really was past caring.

‘Please tell me this isn’t the business venture you were telling me about,’ said her father, unzipping his anorak.

'It's called Sticky Situations.' The irony wasn't lost on her.

'Well, that's appropriate.'

'If the jam stall fails at least I know I can make reasonable weapons of mass destruction,' she said, with a smile. Her father shook his head and went to hang up his anorak.

Chapter Eighteen

Regan let out a giant yawn as Penny unlocked the café and let her in. 'Out partying, were you?'

Regan pouted. 'I wish. I was making jam until silly o'clock this morning.'

'I'm proud of you. That's the sort of work ethic that will . . .' Regan was shaking her head. Penny took the hint and stopped talking.

'Only part of that time was making jam – the rest I spent chipping it off the kitchen surfaces.' Regan pulled two partly filled jam jars from her bag and placed them on the counter. Penny narrowed her eyes at them. 'Is that it?'

'Yep. Jam making is like some form of mystical alchemy. I did everything – well pretty much everything – the recipes said, and it was a total disaster. Dad's kitchen stinks – we'll probably have to redecorate *again*. And his cooker top is about an inch higher than it once was, thanks to a coating of hardened molten lava. Or my jam, which equates to the same thing. The only possible use for this stuff is to sell it to the council for road resurfacing.' Penny was looking doubtful. 'There was no way I could chip it off the cooker, so it's hardwearing stuff.'

Regan let out an *oomph* sound as she flopped onto a chair. 'Coffee?' asked Penny, starting to make the drinks. 'It'll all look better after a coffee.'

'That won't,' said Regan, pointing at the brown lumps in the two jars on the counter.

'At least you have some samples for Bernice. That's an achievement,' said Penny encouragingly. 'And you made it yourself.'

'Worryingly, that does look like a sample I made myself and should be handing in at the doctor's surgery.' Regan put her tired head on her hands. 'I give up.'

Penny plonked a large cappuccino down in front of Regan so hard the cup jumped in the saucer, making Regan jolt upright. 'Oh no you don't.'

'What is this – panto time?' said Regan. 'Oh yes I do.'

Penny sat down opposite. 'I didn't have you down as a quitter.'

Regan was too tired to fight. 'Sometimes you need to know when to quit.' She stared at the foam on the coffee. She didn't want to give up, but there wasn't even a glimmer of hope from last night's jam making that made her think it was worth trying again. This wasn't something she was going to learn overnight, let alone become an immediate expert in.

'What's it taste like?' asked Penny, tipping her head at the jam jars.

Regan shrugged. 'Dunno.'

'You don't know?' Penny was already up on her feet and heading for the kitchen. She soon returned with a plate, two knives and some crackers.

'I don't want to end up having my stomach pumped, thanks very much,' said Regan, clutching her cup for comfort. The coffee was slowly reviving her.

‘Drama queen,’ said Penny, opening a jar and sniffing it. Regan recoiled as if she’d opened a joke tin with a springy snake in it. Penny closed her eyes.

‘If you’re overcome with fumes you only have yourself to blame.’

‘Stop it.’ Penny scooped some out, spread a little on two crackers and handed one to Regan.

‘What’s this, a suicide pact?’

‘Eat it!’ Penny looked like she’d reached the end of her tether.

Regan took the cracker from her and sniffed it. ‘Onion and chilli,’ she confirmed, in a small voice. At least she could identify it. She looked at Penny, her cracker held in front of her. ‘On three?’

Penny shook her head and took a bite of the cracker. *Great, now I’ve definitely got to eat it*, thought Regan. She took a bite and chewed quickly. The sooner she got to the swallowing stage, the sooner it would be over and she could wash it down with coffee. This was not a moment for mindfulness. But as she chewed, the flavour that sprang across her tongue was a huge surprise. Regan slowed her chewing and watched Penny – she was grinning.

‘That’s bloody lovely. You really had me going there,’ said Penny, giving Regan a playful slap on the arm. ‘The sweetness of the caramelised onions works really well with the bite of the chilli.’ Regan was speechless. ‘And what’s this one?’ said Penny, opening the other jar and putting a big dollop onto a fresh cracker.

‘Plum and cardamom,’ whispered Regan. One was a fluke. This was bound to be vile.

‘It’s set well,’ said Penny, before taking a bite. Regan stared and waited. ‘Mmm, that’s really good too.’

Regan snatched up a cracker and spread some on to try for herself. Penny was right. It tasted good. The cardamom gave it a savoury flavour. 'I could eat that with a curry,' said Regan, sounding as stunned as she felt.

'Well done, Regan. I think you're in business.'

Regan was taking a break when her phone rang. 'Cleo. Hello, are you still in Japan?'

'Yes,' whispered Cleo. 'I've got a problem.' Regan was relieved and worried in the same moment.

'Why are you whispering?'

'Because I'm in Mr and Mrs Yomoda's toilet.'

That just gave Regan more questions. 'Again, why?'

'Because,' continued Cleo in hushed tones, 'they invited me to their house for dinner. I was going to watch an anime film in my room but I'm a bit sick of hotel food, so thought why not?'

'That sounds lovely,' said Regan, thinking that she could do with a nice home-cooked meal herself. 'What's the house like?'

'Er,' Cleo sounded momentarily thrown by the question. 'Simple. Boxlike. All painted white.'

'That's disappointing. I thought it would be all bright Japanese colours, silky kimonos and lanterns.'

'Me too, but it's less geisha and more IKEA.'

'So what's your problem?' asked Regan, checking her watch. She'd never been one for keeping to time, but working for Penny was different and Regan didn't want to take advantage.

'They gave me some sort of soup, but it had something large and black lurking in its depths like a bowl-sized kraken. And chopsticks to eat it with!' said Cleo, her voice rising for the first time. 'At least at the hotel I could use

Google Translate and get a rough idea of what I'm eating. Here it would be rude to ask.'

'Just copy what they do,' suggested Regan. 'Or ask for a spoon or a straw.'

'Right,' said Cleo, not sounding like her problem had been solved. 'I'd better go. Are you okay?'

'Yeah. I'm okay. Good luck with the kraken.'

'Thanks.'

The call ended and Regan smiled to herself. Even if Cleo didn't know it, she was making real strides. The Cleo of old would never have considered leaving the hotel alone – this was definitely progress. Regan was proud of her friend.

That feeling changed a little when just over half an hour later her phone rang again. Regan put her on speakerphone. 'I'm working . . . in the office,' she added. She wasn't ready to tell Cleo that she'd lost her job yet, or about the lottery debacle, because she couldn't see a way of telling her without revealing that she was living in the studio or making up more lies.

'Okay, I'll be quick,' said Cleo, still whispering but sounding brighter. 'I copied them like you suggested and hauled the black stuff up from its lair with the chopsticks. There was lots of the stringy substance so it took a couple of goes. And . . . it was okay. It was noodles.'

Penny glanced over at Regan and she gave her her best apologetic smile. 'Well done. That's great, Cleo. Anything else?'

'Yes, I'm looking up the next course. I asked what it was and they said *takoyaki* . . . which is . . . oh my goodness.' Cleo went quiet and Regan imagined her going pale at the other end.

'What is it?' called Penny over Regan's shoulder. 'Sorry, I couldn't bear the suspense.'

'Octopus balls,' replied Cleo in a watery voice.

Regan chortled and then stopped herself. 'Maybe now would be a good time to tell them you're a vegetarian.'

Penny gave a belated laugh.

'Who's that?' asked Cleo.

'Sorry, gotta go,' said Regan. 'Good luck!' She felt a bit guilty as she hastily ended the call.

Regan was apprehensive sitting in the market manager's office opposite Bernice, who was glaring at the two jam jars. They looked a little prettier since Regan had spent her break tying raffia round them and sticking on labels. Regan wasn't entirely sure what the end product would look like, but at least she'd made an effort. She'd not realised there was so much involved in producing something as workaday as jam.

Bernice prodded the top of each jar with her finger and the metal emitted a popping sound. 'They're not sealed properly.'

'I already opened them to check they were okay. I mean good. You know, first class.' Regan decided to shut up.

Bernice took a teaspoon from her drawer and tried the tiniest speck from each jar, wiping the teaspoon on a piece of kitchen roll in between dips. Regan held her breath.

Bernice studied the pots carefully. The anticipation was excruciating. 'I was hoping to try the pina colada,' she said at last.

Regan thought on her feet. 'I did make a batch, but I didn't feel it was up to the high standards I've set for myself.' Bernice's eyebrow gave a twitch of approval at this. Phew.

Bernice put down the teaspoon and locked eyes with Regan. 'All regulations adhered to?'

'Definitely,' said Regan, making a mental note to investigate what those regulations might be.

Bernice held out her hand in a Paul Hollywood-style handshake. 'Welcome to Brighton Open Market,' she said.

Regan grinned inanely as she strolled back to the café. Her phone rang and she answered it with a song in her voice. The song soon died in her throat. It was the council wanting to arrange an inspection of her food preparation area. *Shiiiit!*

A few seconds later she was on the phone to Charlie.

'Why did you give them my address?' asked Charlie, sounding perplexed and possibly a little cross.

'Because I panicked. Just like I'm doing now.' Regan spun around on the spot. There was no way she could have given her dad's address – there was still lava on the walls.

'And why today?'

'Because they had a cancellation and the sooner they do the check, the sooner I can sell stuff.'

There was a sigh from the other end. 'Beanstalk is home but he'll be asleep. He's covering for someone at the moment so he's on extra nights.'

'How do I get in without waking him?' asked Regan.

'Come to the station and I'll give you my key.'

'You're a superstar!'

'Hmm,' came the reply. Charlie didn't sound like he agreed.

'Thank you,' said Regan, doing another spin, but this time it was a happy one – and something caught her eye. 'Gotta go.'

Heading down a side street was Elvis's tail. Regan jogged across the road and caught up with him. 'Kevin!' she called. Kevin whipped round and scowled at her. His body was hunched and he looked terrified. Elvis stuck his nose in her groin, dropped his bottom to the floor and stared at her expectantly.

'What's wrong, Kevin?' She side-stepped Elvis and inched closer.

He covered his shaking head with his hands. 'Hit. Hit. Hit.'

Anger shot through her at what those kids had done to him. 'Nobody's going to hit you, Kevin.' Regan looked around for some help, but there was no-one nearby. 'Come to the café and I'll get you a coffee. Okay?' She reached out a hand to him and he retreated. Elvis manoeuvred himself under her hand in the hope of a cheeky petting session. 'Is Elvis taking care of you, Kevin?'

Kevin dropped his worried gaze to the dog and his features softened. 'Good dog.'

'Yeah, he is a good dog.' Regan crouched next to Elvis and gave him some fuss. He was feeling thin along his flanks. 'Shall we get Elvis some milk?'

'Thank you,' said Kevin, and as if it were an afterthought he added, '*carpe diem*.' This was a very different Kevin to the one she had shared a beer with under the pier. It was like he had retreated into a shell.

'Come on, then.' She held out her hand again and this time he took it. She felt the smoothness of his scars as she closed her fingers around them and gently led him out of the alleyway.

She settled Kevin and Elvis by the bins at the back of the café. She felt bad, but the tables at the front were all full and she wasn't sure that he would be allowed inside anyway. It was awful that people like Kevin were treated like a subspecies, but that was a battle for another day. If she could bring them some drinks and maybe get Kevin talking, she could get him some proper help. 'I'll be two minutes.' She held up two fingers for emphasis and Elvis tried to lick them. She dashed in the back of the café.

'Well, hello. Now didn't you used to work here?' asked Penny, pushing her fringe out of her eyes.

'I am *so* sorry,' said Regan, realising how long she'd been gone.

'How'd it go with Boadicea?'

'Bernice.' Regan said her name reverently. She was keen not to make the mistake of calling her Boadicea to her face, and now she liked her jam, Regan was warming to her. 'Bernice loved the jam.'

'Excellent.' Penny looked genuinely thrilled, like a proud mum.

'But I've found Kevin and he's in a bad way and the man from the council called and I need to meet him later so he can inspect my kitchen. And I'm sorry you've been on your own, but I'm going to need to leave early.' Regan scrunched up her shoulders; she knew she was taking the mick.

Penny's lips made a thin line and Regan felt instantly guilty. 'It's fine,' said Penny. Her tense expression said it wasn't really, but she'd tolerate it. 'I got you a present.' She handed Regan a paper bag and she peeked inside.

'A thermometer. Thanks.'

'It's a proper jam one. So you'll know when you've burned stuff.'

'Thanks, Penny. You're brilliant.' Regan popped the thermometer in her bag, put the bag in the back room and pulled on her apron.

'Before you get stuck in,' said Penny, 'There's a hot chocolate with cream on the side – customer error. Made in the last five minutes, so give that to Kevin. And then I could do with a hand with this queue.' She nodded at the line of people snaking to the door.

'You're the best,' said Regan, grabbing the hot chocolate and dashing back outside. But when she got there both Kevin and Elvis had gone.

Chapter Nineteen

Regan worked hard for the rest of the day. Both because she owed Penny, and to take her mind off Kevin. There was something wrong and she wanted to help him, but now he'd gone off again she was back to square one. She had also been trying not to think about her imminent kitchen inspection, which could pull the rug out from under all her plans. Mainly because she didn't actually have a kitchen, and she didn't really know her way around the one she was going to present to the council.

Regan finished early, rushed to the fire station and raced inside. She was slightly stunned for a moment at how big the station was; its huge doors were gaping open displaying three shiny fire engines. 'Can I help?' asked a stern-looking chap in uniform striding towards her.

'Hi, I'm looking for Charlie.' The stern man furrowed his brow at her. '*Debbie* McGee? I'm a friend. We go to mindfulness together.' Why she'd volunteered that information, she had no idea; it wasn't helping to unfurrow the stern man's brow.

'It's okay, Eric,' said Charlie, bounding into view. Eric grumbled something and disappeared.

'Eric?' she said with a smile. That must be another amusing nickname, she thought. 'Let me guess. His surname is Morecambe? Or Clapton?' Charlie was wearing the same furrowed brow Eric had had on a minute ago. 'Ooh,' she said as inspiration struck, 'he's a football fan. Ooh ah Cantona! Am I right?'

Charlie shook his head. 'No. He's just Eric Smith.'

'Oh. Right.' She couldn't hide her disappointment.

'Keys,' said Charlie, handing them over. 'Mum will have been in to clean this morning so your timing is pretty good.'

'Thank you so much for this.' She went up on her toes to kiss him and then, remembering their pact, stopped and hovered there like a trainee meerkat, unsure what to do next.

'It's fine. Although I'm not sure how much trouble you'll be in when they realise you're not actually cooking the stuff in my kitchen.' Charlie smiled. Regan pressed her lips together and lowered herself back to flat feet. She'd kind of assumed that he'd be okay about her using his kitchen for the jam making. She'd not revealed the true horror of what she'd done to her father's kitchen – although she had mentioned to Charlie that they needed more paint, so that might explain his now very troubled expression. 'You're not cooking in there, are you?'

'Not today. I'd better dash. Thanks for these,' she said, waving the keys.

'Regan?'

'Bye.' She scurried off without a backward glance.

Regan's phone rang whilst she was dashing towards Charlie's house. 'Cleo, I've got like two minutes before I have to go to a very important meeting.' At least this was true. So much was hanging on the council inspection.

'I'll be quick, I promise,' said Cleo. 'I've had a lovely evening.' She sounded bright, which was a relief. Regan had felt bad about cutting her off earlier.

'How did you get out of the octopus balls?'

'I looked up "vegetarian" and "sorry" in Japanese and then used them a lot. They were lovely about it and Mrs Yomoda whipped up some rice and vegetables for me which was delicious. I got to have proper Japanese tea in tiny handleless cups whilst sitting on mats on the floor . . .'

'Uh-huh,' said Regan, thinking this wasn't quite the kind of quick she'd been hoping for as she turned into Charlie's road.

'It wasn't tea like ours – it had a light flavour with a natural hint of sweetness. Sort of both cleansing and calming.'

'I could do with some of that right now,' said Regan, seeing Charlie's house up ahead.

'But the best bit was when Mr Yomoda produced a large folio case and showed me some paintings featuring Japanese cherry blossom. Each picture was unique, and yet they were all linked by the pop of colour of the cherry blossom. They were so beautiful – like happiness on paper—'

'That's lovely, Cleo, but I'm going to have to go.' Regan's agitation was rising.

'Oh, okay,' Cleo sounded crestfallen.

'Look, I'll call you soon for a proper chat, I promise. But for the record I'm glad you took the plunge and were brave enough to accept the Yomodas' offer. That took a lot of guts.'

'Thanks,' said Cleo. 'I'm pleased too, because I've had a really nice evening. The first since I left home.'

Regan ended her phone call and let herself into Charlie's house as quietly as she could. She wasn't entirely sure how she would keep from waking up Beanstalk, especially when the man from the council arrived, but she'd cross that particular rickety bridge when she reached it. For now she needed to check the kitchen was clean and tidy, and familiarise herself with it in case she was asked any tricky questions.

She shut the door carefully behind her and turned around. She came face to face with a woman wearing bright pink marigolds. 'Argh!' yelped Regan, trying to stifle the sound when she remembered a sleeping Beanstalk.

'Who are you?' quizzed the woman, giving her a once-over.

'Regan. I'm a friend of Charlie's.' She assumed this was Charlie's mum, so she stood up straight and tried to look like girlfriend material.

The woman pulled off the gloves with a snap. 'If you were a friend of his you'd know he was at work.'

Regan was slightly put out that he'd clearly not even mentioned her to his mother, but she tried to bury that feeling and deal with the issue at hand. She held up the keys. 'I went to the fire station and he gave me his key.'

The woman looked confused. 'Then why are you creeping about?'

'Same as you; because Beanstalk is on nights.'

The woman narrowed her eyes. 'Are you Beanstalk's girlfriend?'

'Beanstalk has a girlfriend?'

'I don't know; I thought you might be.'

'No. I'm a friend of Charlie's. He introduced me to

Mantra.' She was so close to wanting to ask: *has he really not mentioned me at all?*

'Oh . . .' She seemed to be considering this new information. 'I'm Joanna.' She held out a damp hand for Regan to shake. At least this was progress.

'Hi, Joanna. I'm Regan.'

'Oh, is it a nickname? Are you a firefighter too? You girls you can do anything these days.'

'No. It's . . .' Regan caught sight of the clock. The man from the council was due any moment. 'Anyway, you've made a fabulous job of the kitchen,' she said, popping her head round the door. 'Are you all done?' It was peculiar to have a whole conversation in whispers. Regan tried to steer Joanna towards the door but she wasn't budging.

'No. I was about to thoroughly clean the oven.'

'I'm sure it doesn't need it. Could you do it another day? It's just that I really need the kitchen.'

'What for?' The puzzled expression had returned to Joanna's face. This wasn't a good sign.

Regan decided to go for the honest approach. 'I'm starting my new business and Charlie said I could use his kitchen to make jam.' Well, it was honest-ish.

'You're making jam?'

'Not today. The man from the council food hygiene needs to check the kitchen first.'

'But it's spotless,' said Joanna, her voice rising slightly.

'I know,' agreed Regan, hoping to make an ally. A rap on the door drew their attention. 'That'll be him.'

'Right,' said Joanna, marching to the door.

The slightly built man on the other side was momentarily startled. 'Oh, um, hello. I'm Neil Peadon.' Regan stifled a laugh at his inappropriate surname. 'It's about your Food Hygiene inspection—'

'Shhh,' Joanna cut him off. 'There's a night-shift fire-fighter asleep upstairs.'

'Oh,' said Neil Peadon, and he scribbled something on his pad. Joanna craned her neck to try to see; he pulled his clipboard close to his chest.

'Here's the kitchen,' said Joanna. With a sweep of her marigold gloves she led him through. *She's staying, then,* thought Regan. *Just what I need.*

'Righty-o,' said Neil. Joanna followed him into the kitchen closer than his shadow. 'Let's start with your food hygiene certificate and product.'

Regan rummaged in her bag, passed him the two jars and pulled out a crumpled sheet of paper, which she tried to flatten out a bit on the worktop before she handed to him. He studied them all closely, before ticking something on his clipboard.

With every surface he checked, Joanna's eyebrows got a fraction higher. He studied the sink, checked the taps and jotted more things down. 'Waste disposal?' he asked.

Joanna pointed at the bin. Neil pursed his lips and Regan stepped forward. 'I take everything away with me and dispose of it properly. I'm recycling the fruit and vegetable peelings for compost.' Neil gave a brief smile and wrote this down.

'Refrigeration facilities?'

Joanna opened what looked like a cupboard and revealed the fridge. Regan scooted over to it and she and Neil looked inside – it was virtually empty. 'Most of my produce will be used same day so won't need to be refrigerated, but if it does I will use these trays.' Regan pulled out two spotless salad trays at the bottom of the fridge. Joanna nodded her approval and the small gesture buoyed Regan's confidence.

'Fire prevention?' asked Neil.

Regan faltered. 'Um . . .'

'Fire blanket,' said Joanna, pointing to a small packet on the wall. 'And extinguisher,' she added, opening the cupboard under the sink. 'My son's a firefighter,' she added, proudly.

'Excellent,' said Neil. 'Thermometer?'

Joanna looked at Regan. She scrabbled in her bag and produced the gift Penny had given her earlier. 'Thermometer,' she said, holding it aloft triumphantly.

'Righty-o. That all seems in order. We'll confirm in writing, but all that remains is to wish you the very best with your venture,' said Neil Peadon.

'Thank you,' said Regan and Joanna together.

'I'll see myself out.'

As the door clicked shut, Regan gave a fist pump. 'Get in!'

'Shhh,' said Joanna, putting a finger to her smiling lips.

'Thank you. You were brilliant,' said Regan, lowering her voice.

'I'm rather pleased the kitchen passed the council's food hygiene examination.' Joanna preened herself in a self-congratulatory fashion. 'Is this what you're making?' She picked up one of the jars. 'Plum and Cardamom?'

'Unusual flavours is my USP.'

'My grandmother used to make pear and lavender jam.'

'Blimey,' said a sleepy Beanstalk, appearing in the doorway. 'That sounds more like air freshener.' Joanna whacked him with her marigolds.

It all started to feel very real when Regan found herself with a choice of stall locations. Bernice was tapping a clipboard impatiently, but Regan felt this needed careful consideration. The first pitch was by the Ditchling Road entrance, which she really liked because it was nearer to the green area called The Level and the coffee shop, although Bernice had already pointed out that she might want to consider buying her coffee from the market café from now on. The other stall would be at the far end nearer to London Road, but also nearer to the grocery stall and handy for the loos, which would be useful.

'It's clearly a far bigger decision than I envisaged,' said Bernice, with a huff.

'Sorry,' said Regan, feeling pressured.

'Hiya,' said Malcolm from the bread stall as he strolled past.

'Malcolm – which do you think?' asked Regan. 'I've got to choose a stall location.'

'It doesn't have to be permanent,' said Bernice, sounding like she was losing patience.

'There's space down by me,' said Malcolm, nodding towards Ditchling Road.

Something caught Bernice's eye. 'Hey!' she broke into a run. 'Stop him!'

Regan turned to watch Bernice chase after someone in a hoodie. She grabbed hold of his hood, bringing him to an abrupt, if somewhat sweary, halt. A lot of shouting ensued and a passing police officer ran over and took charge of the situation. As the youth straightened his clothing whilst shouting about being assaulted by Bernice, Regan recognised him.

'You!' she shouted as she hurtled towards him. 'You attacked Kevin!'

The teenager used the police officer as a shield. 'I don't know no Kevin, you mentalist.'

'Hey. Calm down,' said the police officer, as Regan made

a grab for the youth. 'One thing at a time.' He guided Regan to stand a safe distance away.

'He took a speaker from that stall there,' said Bernice.

'She assaulted me!' shouted the youth, pointing at Bernice.

Yeah, and I want to do the same, thought Regan. 'And he attacked a homeless man a few weeks ago,' she said, anger rippling through her.

'Oh, him,' said the youth, with a sneer.

It was all she could do not to slap his smug face. 'See, he's admitted it.'

'No, I ain't. You can't prove nothing.'

Regan lurched forward. 'Regan,' came Malcolm's soft voice.

She took a step back and tried to remember her mindfulness techniques. She focused on her breathing and soon felt calmer despite the sneering looks the youth was giving her.

'Maybe leave them to it.' Malcolm tapped her arm and beckoned her away.

Bernice was studying Regan closely. She probably hadn't responded in the best way, but she hated the injustice. Kevin was missing again, and all because of the likes of this scumbag. Regan looked at Malcolm and nodded. She knew he was right. Reluctantly, she followed him.

'I don't suppose you want a coffee?' he said.

'Actually, I could do with one.'

'Come on then.'

Malcolm bought the coffees from the café in the Open Market and they went back to his stall where he thanked the person who'd been covering for him.

They sipped their drinks in silence for a bit. 'Bernice is pretty feisty,' said Regan, impressed with how she'd gone after the youth, and even more so when she'd hung on to him despite his colourful language.

'Good old Boadicea. She's a bit fierce but the market is her number one priority, and she's all right, when you get to know her.'

Regan figured that might take a while. 'How long have you been here?'

Malcolm sucked air in through his teeth. 'Seven . . . no . . . eight years in August. There's not a lot I don't know. So just ask. Okay?'

'Thanks, that's kind.'

'Which stall are you going for?' asked Malcolm. 'Up here or down on the dark side?' His voice had a touch of Darth Vader about it.

She felt like she'd found a friend in Malcolm, and as she didn't know the first thing about running a market stall he seemed like the sort of person she needed to stay close to.

'I think the pitch here will suit me just fine.' They pretended to clink their coffees in celebration.

Regan was disappointed that Charlie wasn't at Mantra on Saturday morning. She watched the door like a puppy at a rescue shelter and, when he didn't appear, she fired off another text to him before putting her phone away and joining the group. She got out a mat for Charlie, just in case, and Cressy started the session. But despite her best efforts, she couldn't relax. Her mind was all over the place. She fancied Charlie, that was a given, but he was also such a good sounding board. He listened to her, helped her order her thoughts – he showed an interest in her. She felt she could tell him anything, even without censoring it first. She wanted to talk to him about Kevin and the youth because it was rattling around her head most evenings – she blamed the lack of a TV.

She'd never clicked with someone the way she had with Charlie. She realised now how much she'd been looking forward to seeing him. And despite the fact they would have only been lying in silence next to each other on yoga mats, she missed him. She let out a sigh. Wendy let out a trump and someone started a coughing fit. Cressy rang her tinkly bell. Regan sat up and gave the door a hard stare.

'Any observations this week that anyone would like to share?' asked Cressy, her gaze falling on Regan.

'I almost lost my temper this week. I very nearly took a swipe at someone in front of a police officer.' She chewed the inside of her mouth. 'But I tried to remember what you'd taught me and it was enough to keep things off the boil.'

'Well done,' said Cressy, leaning forward. A muttered chorus of well dones echoed around the circle and Regan felt pleased with herself. At the same time, she wished Charlie had been there to witness it. She'd come a long way since he'd pulled her off Alex in the revolving door. She had picked herself up and started to sort her life out, and a lot of that progress was down to him.

She got chatting to Wendy in the break, although she was mainly watching the door in case Charlie made a late entrance. Wendy stopped talking about the benefits of alpaca wool and followed her gaze. 'Oh, Charlie won't be coming this week. Didn't Cressy say?'

Regan tried to appear nonchalant but it was a waste of time. 'Er, no. Why's he not coming?' She suspected he was probably off on a mission to save whales, or orphans, or both.

'Hot date apparently.' Wendy was trying to wink and failing badly. Regan was momentarily worried she was having another stroke and was relieved when she stopped.

'A hot date,' repeated Regan. 'Lucky him.' Her heart cracked a little bit more and she folded her arms across her chest as if to protect it from further damage.

Chapter Twenty

Regan caught up with Bernice as the market was closing down for the night. It had a different atmosphere with most of the people gone – sort of eerie. Regan followed behind Bernice whilst she strode about.

'I wanted to let you know I'd like to take the stall up by Malcolm, and I also wanted to speak to you about that kid who nicked the speaker yesterday,' said Regan.

'Don't let that put you off,' said Bernice. 'Thieving is rare. I've got a zero-tolerance policy for the vagrants, which keeps it under control.'

Regan bristled. She didn't like Bernice's assumption that the homeless were all thieves. 'That kid wasn't homeless. He's a thieving little sod.'

Bernice stopped to check a lock on a shutter. 'He's just out of control. Hopefully he can be helped.'

Regan struggled to keep calm. 'He doesn't need help. He needs locking up. I saw him kicking the cr . . . hell out of someone.'

'Well, that's a bit different.'

Regan feared that if Bernice knew the person was homeless she might change her view. 'I was after the kid's name so I could report the assault properly.'

'I don't have his name, but I do have a crime number, which should help the police to link it up. This way.' Regan dutifully followed Bernice back to her office.

Bernice rifled through the paperwork in a tray on her desk, pulled a sheet out and then paused. 'Have you considered the impact your accusation will have on the young man?'

Regan knew her eyes had popped wide. Was Bernice for real? 'I'm afraid I'm more concerned about justice for the victim he assaulted.'

'Yes, of course. Do you have any siblings?' asked Bernice.

'Nope. There's just me.'

Bernice openly sighed and her eyes wandered off. 'I've got a brother. Dale.' She glanced back at Regan. 'He's older than me, so I really looked up to him as a kid, but when he hit his teens, he went completely off the rails. Drove my parents round the bend. He got into all sorts of trouble. He even stole a moped once.' Regan raised her eyebrows. 'I know. But he changed. He straightened himself out and he joined the Royal Navy. My parents were so proud.'

Regan could see where this was going. 'I guess some people can change . . .' Regan wasn't convinced about the youth who attacked Kevin – that was malicious. 'But that's assuming there's some good inside them in the first place. This may be the wake-up call he needs to turn his life around.'

'Or it might seal his fate as a criminal,' said Bernice.

'Look,' said Regan. 'I'm glad your brother turned out well and you're a big happy family but . . .'

Bernice was shaking her head. 'We lost touch. I haven't seen him for years.'

'Right, well.' Regan was feeling awkward. 'I'm sorry, but even if you won't help I'm still going to report the assault.'

Bernice handed her the police reference number on a scrap of paper. 'Here you go.'

'Thanks, Bernice. I'll let you know how I get on with the police about the assault on Kevin.'

'Kevin?'

'He's the homeless guy that was attacked.'

Bernice's cheek twitched. 'Oh, there's really no need.'

Penny was grinning broadly as she flicked the bolt on the coffee shop door on Wednesday morning. 'Someone looks far too happy,' chided Regan, slipping inside.

'Mum's gone away.'

'You get on well, do you?' Regan asked, with a chuckle.

'Bit rocky. Anyway, it's my birthday tomorrow and I thought maybe we could go out for a few drinks and you can crash at mine . . . well, my mum's. You know what I mean.'

'Sounds good to me. Alcohol and a mattress – I'm a cheap date.'

Penny looked momentarily startled. 'You know it's not a date, right?'

Regan laughed. 'Of course I do. I'm not into women, Penny,' she said, taking her coat off.

'But you know I am?'

'Ah,' said Regan, a few things slotting into place. 'Makes zero difference to me. You're the best boss I ever had. And a top mate too.'

Penny looked relieved. 'I wish everyone took it like that.'

Regan shrugged. 'You're you. Who you fancy doesn't change who you are.' She pulled her apron off the peg.

'I wish my mother saw it like that.'

'I guess it's tricky if you live at home. Whoever you're dating, your parents rarely approve. That's not an exclusively gay thing. Trust me.' Her dad had never liked anyone she'd ever brought home and had always made that blindingly obvious.

Penny busied herself with wiping down the already clean worktops. 'I did have my own place . . .' Regan was nodding whilst tying her apron, '. . . and a husband.' Regan paused, and Penny glanced her way. 'I was a bit confused by convention for a while. I met a nice guy, thought getting married might sort me out. It didn't. I left him for a woman.'

'Ouch,' said Regan. 'That's gotta hurt.'

Penny agreed. 'I thought she was the one. I walked away from my family for her and then she upped and left me with so much debt I had nothing and nowhere to go.'

'Except your mum's,' said Regan, anticipating the story.

'It was the hardest thing I've ever had to do. Mum and I had said so many hurtful things to each other. It was painful for both of us, but we're ticking over okay now. She still doesn't understand it all but we'll get there. I've got some savings now so hopefully I'll be able to move out in the next year or so.'

Regan gave Penny a hug. Here was another person who had been just a couple of bad decisions away from living on the streets.

Regan opened the doors and the first customer was a familiar face. 'Hey, Beanstalk. What are you doing out in daylight? Don't you turn to dust or something?' said Regan.

'Don't. The night shifts are killing me.' He turned to Penny. 'Large mocha with an extra shot, please.'

Regan grabbed a large takeaway cup. 'So where are you having your birthday party, Penny?'

'Party? I'll come,' said Beanstalk, with a large yawn.

'Not my party,' said Regan, with an apologetic shrug.

'It's more of a pub crawl, and you are very welcome to join us,' said Penny. She gave a brief glance in Regan's direction. 'You and Charlie, obviously.'

'Charlie?' Regan tried to appear casual. 'I heard he had a hot date which was why he couldn't make Mantra on Saturday.' *And probably why he's not returned any of my texts*, she thought.

Beanstalk was scowling. 'Saturday he was at the launderette.' Regan gave him her best eye roll. Did he think she was an idiot? 'Seriously. The washing machine broke. He was probably joking about it being a hot date. And—'

'Well whatever the reason, he's obviously trying to avoid me.' Regan plonked the coffee on the counter and a spray of foam squirted through the hole in the top, making Beanstalk recoil.

'He's not seeing anyone else,' said Beanstalk. 'Look,' he added with a sigh. 'I probably shouldn't tell you this, but he went through a bit of a shagathon stage . . . but since he met you he's really changed. He's moping about, same as you are.'

'I'm not moping. I'm fine. I am very happy with how things are.' Regan was aware she was protesting too much.

Beanstalk's shoulders slumped. 'I feel like I'm caught in the middle. I can see it from both your side and his. Most of all, I see two unhappy people who could be much happier,' he held her gaze and then his eyebrows puckered, 'together.'

Penny leaned over the counter. 'If all else fails, we can bang their heads together tomorrow night. Eight o'clock at The Admiral.'

'Cheers to that,' said Beanstalk, and he bounded off with his coffee.

When there was a brief pause in customers, Regan quickly made a latte with some cooling milk she couldn't reheat and went in search of Kevin. She'd been doing this most days, in the vain hope that she'd catch sight of him. She walked a long way down Ditchling Road and circled back around The Level, but there was no sign of Kevin or Elvis.

In an odd way, she missed them. They had been part of her daily routine for a long time, and since the whole lottery prank debacle she'd got to know Kevin a little better. She wanted to find him so she could tell him that she'd given a statement to the police about him being attacked. She hoped it might make him feel a bit better to know that it had been officially recorded, although from the state she'd found him in last time this was probably wishful thinking.

The assault had clearly triggered something in Kevin, and she was worried for his mental health. She was certain the thief from the market was the same person who had assaulted Kevin, but the police officer hadn't sugar-coated the fact that it was unlikely to come to court because this particular youth was well known to them and always had a family member who was on hand to provide an alibi. But still, even if there was only a slim chance of justice being done, she was still glad she'd made the statement, because it was a step in the right direction.

She stood by the skate park and scanned The Level. A few people had picnic rugs out and were enjoying the glorious May sunshine. A toddler was running around the fountains while his mother fussed nearby. Cyclists whizzed around the outer edge of the park. A dog walker with a small pack of shared leads trotted by, scaring some pigeons into flight. All manner of life was here, but there was no sign of Kevin or Elvis.

Regan was thrilled to see Charlie enter the pub on Friday night with Beanstalk, but she tried to hide it. They spent most of the evening with a group of Penny's friends, and in the crowded bars talk was restricted. Regan barely had a chance to speak to Charlie, and when she did she wasn't sure what to say, so instead she focused on downing a few shots. That way she could forget about the gorgeous man she was hopelessly in love with, who wanted to keep his distance so as not to damage her already shattered heart.

They left the last bar, and after hugs and another impromptu verse of 'Happy Birthday' the group dispersed. Regan pulled Penny to one side. 'I'm not going to come back to yours if that's okay,' she whispered to Penny. 'I've not had much of a chance to talk to Charlie.'

'Good luck,' said Penny, with a wink.

'Oh,' said Beanstalk, catching on to the plan, 'I'll walk you home, Penny.' They hugged their goodbyes, leaving Charlie and Regan together.

'You missed Mantra. How was your hot date?' asked Regan, buoyed by a few vodka shots.

Charlie gave her a puzzled look. 'Oh that. I was down the launderette.'

'Really?'

'Honest,' he said. 'Washing machine died. Why? Were you jealous?'

'Nope. No. Nah-uh. No way.' She shoved her hands in her pockets.

'Did you have a good night?' asked Charlie.

'Yeah. I did. You know what could make it better?' She swung around to stand in front of him, making him bump into her. The alcohol had made her brave. She looked at him hopefully. Was one snog too much to ask? She could see the turmoil in his dark eyes. She reached up her hands to cup his face.

Charlie sighed deeply. 'Don't do this. Please.' His plea was pitiful.

She took her hands away from his face, because it was starting to feel weird now it was clear he wasn't going to kiss her. She switched to her Plan B. 'Charlie, I've thought about this and I think if we treat it like a holiday romance I'll be fine.' A smile flickered across his features. This was a good start, so she kept going. 'We can have a brief but amazing affair and then when . . . it ends,' she swallowed hard; she needed to show him she could cope even if she didn't believe it herself, 'I can look back on it as a fun time with happy memories, like a holiday romance.'

Charlie rubbed his chin, his expression more than doubtful. 'Have you had many holiday romances?'

'Yeah. Loads.' He raised an eyebrow. 'Okay, no, not loads. But a few. Brighton is where people come on holiday. I've got involved with tourists before, of course I have, and I've known it's only for a week and it's been fun and . . . why are you looking at me like that?'

'I guess I'm a little surprised.'

Regan was affronted. 'I'm not a tart.'

'I didn't say you were.'

'Your eyes did. Bloody hell, Charlie. You're no virgin. Beanstalk has filled me in on your recent escapades.' She liked the smug feeling she got from the change in his expression.

'That's different.'

Her hackles were not only up, but they were so far up they were picking up radio signals. 'What?' Her voice was rising to a shouty level. 'Because I'm a woman? Is that it?'

'Woah! No. That's not it. Bloody hell, Reg. I'm not a sexist. I freaked out a bit when I was diagnosed. Figured I had nothing to lose.'

'Okay. That is a bit different,' she conceded. She could feel the fight go out of her. 'So what do you say?' She playfully tapped her outstretched foot against his leg.

'It's just . . .' his gaze dropped to his shoes. She noticed it had started to rain.

'Just what?'

'I don't think I can do it. Not with you.'

'There's little blue tablets for that,' she said, with what she hoped was a cheeky yet seductive grin.

'It's not a joke.'

The look he shot her was almost a glare. She'd massively misjudged that one. 'I know. I'm sorry. But . . .'

Charlie turned up his jacket collar and shoved his hands in his pockets as the rain started a steady rhythm. 'Come on, or we'll get soaked.'

Reluctantly, she walked on, but this discussion wasn't over. Maybe she was going about it the wrong way. Perhaps her direct approach wasn't what was needed here. A touch of romance might be a better tactic. She didn't have the cash for wining and dining, but she could try subtlety. It wasn't a strength of hers, but for Charlie she could learn. They walked on in silence.

Through the rain, Regan spotted the familiar shape of

a large hound lolloping around the far end of The Level. She broke into a run. 'Elvis!' She shot across the road without thinking.

'Regan!' shouted Charlie, as she narrowly missed being hit by a car. It skidded to a halt. Charlie waved an apology to the driver and jogged after Regan.

The rain lashed at Regan's face, but the joy of spotting Elvis and the alcohol sloshing inside her was keeping her warm. She came to a halt near a bench covered in plastic and was immediately assaulted by the over-excited dog, who jumped about before abruptly sitting in front of her with a hopeful look in his eye, despite the rain trickling off his bushy eyebrows. She gave him a brief fuss and sadly noted how thin he was getting. Regan crouched down to the sleeping bag under the bench.

'Kevin?'

The sleeping bag moved and a face appeared. He looked haggard around his sunken eyes – it was as if the light behind them had gone out. His eyes crinkled at the sight of her but he didn't speak. 'Are you okay?' she asked. He nodded slowly. He didn't look okay. But his sleeping bag appeared to be on top of more plastic and a lot of newspaper to save him from the worst of the rain. Kevin's eyes darted above Regan's head when Charlie joined them.

'Hiya, mate. You all right?' asked Charlie. Kevin repeated his slow nod.

'Regan, you're getting soaked. We should be getting off.' Charlie was right, the rain was running off her hair and down the back of her neck and her showerproof jacket wasn't going to hold out much longer.

'Will I find you around here tomorrow?' she asked. Kevin looked blank and it pulled at her heartstrings. 'I'll bring your coffee here tomorrow. Okay?'

Kevin gave her the briefest of smiles. She was fighting back the tears. Kevin had been doing so well, and now he was a crumpled shadow of his former self.

Charlie put his hand on her shoulder. 'There's nothing you can do tonight,' he said. 'Time to go.'

She gave Elvis a fuss before standing up. 'I'll see you here, tomorrow morning. Okay?' She pointed forcefully at the bench, but Kevin pulled the sleeping bag over his head. For the first time, he didn't say *carpe diem*. As Regan walked away, Elvis tried to follow.

'No, Elvis. Stay,' instructed Regan. Elvis walked a few more paces and started to bark.

Charlie took Regan's hand and she looked up into his eyes. 'You're a good person, Regan. What the hell am I going to do with you?'

'Whatever you want,' said Regan. The rain went into monsoon mode and they hurried out of the park. She clutched his hand, welcome of the contact. He'd been so distant tonight. Charlie hit the pedestrian crossing button, but they didn't wait for the lights to change. The rain pelted down relentlessly and they broke into a jog as they crossed.

Regan heard the barking getting closer and a muffled shout behind her, but Charlie was propelling her along Oxford street. 'Hang on,' she said, coming to a halt. Charlie squeezed her hand gently. He was right, there was nothing she could do tonight. He tugged at her hand and she started to jog again.

The skidding came first. The sound of tyres on wet road. Of brakes not doing their job. Then the simultaneous yelp and dull thud. Regan spun around and wrenched her hand free from Charlie's so that she could run, but she needn't have done, because Charlie was already sprinting with her at full pelt back towards The Level. She heard the crunching of gears. Spinning tyres. She looked, but all she saw was a tail spray of water as the car careered away at speed, leaving two lifeless figures on the pedestrian crossing.

Chapter Twenty-One

The sight of Kevin and Elvis lying so still in the road punched the air from Regan's lungs. Her legs were leaden with shock. This couldn't be happening. Charlie reached them a moment before Regan and fell to his knees at Kevin's side. He quickly checked Kevin for vital signs whilst the rain continued its onslaught.

'I'll call an ambulance,' she said, and with fumbling wet fingers Regan dialled 999.

'Is he alive?' she asked, crouching next to Kevin, the whole time watching Charlie's face for a hint of hope. Her call was picked up and Regan asked for an ambulance, giving details of where they were. The rain was now bouncing back up off the road, having upped its ferocity. Charlie undid Kevin's coat and harshly pulled it open.

'He'll catch his death,' said Regan, alarmed to see Kevin's T-shirt darken from the rain. Charlie's expression was grim as he laced his fingers, locked his arms and commenced chest compressions with a force that frightened her. Charlie was using his whole body in an attempt to pump life back into Kevin. She looked about. She felt utterly useless. There was nothing she could do.

The 999 operator reassured her that the ambulance was

on its way. A few people sauntered out of the pub, but on seeing the rain most soon disappeared inside again. A barman came over with a golf umbrella and held it over Charlie and Kevin as best he could. He gave Regan a wan smile but after that he stared resolutely at the ground. Seconds ticked by, each one making the situation more hopeless. She couldn't bring herself to look at Elvis. He was a large grey motionless mass on the periphery of her vision.

A police car appeared first, its siren screaming to them long before the vehicle itself. The blue lights threw an unnatural glow on the scene. Two officers got out and one immediately started to speak into his radio. The other officer strode over and began asking questions, but Regan couldn't pull her eyes away from Kevin. She shook her head. 'I'm on the phone to the ambulance.' She knew it sounded lame but the 999-operator was still intermittently speaking to her, and right now it was too much to ask her brain to focus on what the officer was saying. She watched the police officer share a quick word with Charlie, who didn't lose his rhythm for a second – he was relentless.

At last the ambulance swung into view, pulling up at speed right next to them, and two paramedics jumped out. The female paramedic was quick to take over the chest compressions from an exhausted-looking Charlie. He sat back on his haunches with rain trickling off his hair and down his face. He looked at Regan but she didn't want to see the sadness in his eyes. Charlie got to his feet and left the paramedics to do their job. Without a word, he lifted Regan to her feet and ended the call on her phone. The police officer guided Regan and Charlie out of the road and onto the pavement and reminded them that they weren't to go anywhere without giving a statement.

'They'll save him, won't they?' Regan's eyes were fixed on Kevin's lifeless body. She needed to hear something positive; some hope that she could cling to; but, in her heart, she already knew the answer she wasn't ready to accept.

Charlie cleared his throat. 'It's been twenty minutes now.'

One of the paramedics shouted 'Stand clear' and they shocked Kevin. His whole body lurched, and for a second Regan was filled with hope. The other paramedic resumed the chest compressions. Minutes passed, until eventually the male paramedic shook his head and the woman checked her watch.

'Nooo!' yelled Regan, throwing herself forward. Charlie threw an arm out to intercept her. He held her tight, stopping her from running into the road. *How could the paramedics stop? They couldn't give up on Kevin.* She fought Charlie until he pulled her back into his arms. He held her firmly while she sobbed, letting out great heavy blubs. An ocean of sorrow engulfed her and she clung to him.

More police arrived and the area was quickly cordoned off. The first officer on the scene ushered them into the back of his police car, took their details and asked a few questions. He jotted down brief statements from them both and requested that they come down to the police station the next day to fill out proper ones.

By the time they got out of the car, great stretches of the road were cordoned off with police tape. A small white tent was covering where Kevin had been lying. It didn't go far enough to cover Elvis.

Charlie put a comforting arm around Regan's shoulder. 'Come on,' he said. 'There's no more we can do.'

'But I think Elvis was following me . . . and if Kevin ran after him, then—'

'Stop,' said Charlie, firmly. 'Don't even go there.'

Regan's whole body had started to shake and she couldn't control it. She wasn't sure if it was shock or because she was wet through to the skin. 'I can't leave Elvis like that,' she said, watching another police officer step over him. 'They'll dump him somewhere.' She choked back more tears. 'Kevin wouldn't have wanted that.'

Charlie squeezed her arm. 'Okay. Let's see if they'll let us take him back to mine. We could bury him in the garden.' Charlie went and spoke to the police officer who had taken their details and he waved Charlie under the tape. Regan watched Charlie crouch down and reverently lift the dead weight of Elvis into his arms. The sight was almost too much for Regan. Charlie put his cheek to Elvis's face and the gesture nearly made Regan's legs crumple.

Charlie's head jerked up. 'Reg!' he shouted, his face spreading into a grin. 'He's alive!'

Regan found herself on a plastic chair in the dimly lit waiting area of a charity-funded veterinary hospital. Charlie was asleep next to her. The kind barman who'd held the brolly had driven them there after calling his sister who was a veterinary nurse, and the on-call vet had been waiting for them when they pulled up. That had been three hours ago and she'd heard nothing since. She figured the longer they worked on Elvis, the better. It almost felt like they were making more of an effort with the dog than they had with Kevin – although she knew this wasn't the case. She couldn't comprehend why they had stopped trying to resuscitate Kevin, although Charlie told her he was pretty sure Kevin had died instantly and there would have been nothing anyone could have done. Elvis, it seemed, had come off slightly better.

Her mind had had time to mull over the evening's events – there wasn't much else to do in a closed vet's surgery in the early hours of the morning. She remembered the sickening sounds of the car, the sensation of the pavement jarring her limbs as she ran flat out, and the sight of Kevin and Elvis lying on the crossing – an image that was now etched behind her eyes. In the edge of her vision she'd seen the car driving off at speed, but in truth what she'd really seen was the flurry of spray it had left in its wake. She'd been too focused on Kevin to look at the vehicle that had killed him. She closed her eyes and tried to picture it. If she could recall a part of the number plate, or the car's make or model, or even its paint colour, it would be something to help the police, but it was a blur of teeming rain and rear lights. Nothing helpful at all.

She must have drifted off to sleep because a tap on her shoulder made her jolt to consciousness. Charlie did the same. They both sat up like expectant parents. The vet's expression was stern.

'We've done all we can . . .'

'Oh no,' said Regan, swallowing down tears. 'You can't let him die. You can't—'

The vet held up his hand and his expression softened. 'For tonight. We've done all we can for tonight. He's not out of the woods yet, but he is out of surgery, and he's sleeping. You can come and see him if you'd like to?'

Regan rubbed away a rogue tear as she got to her feet. They followed the vet out through the other side of a consulting room, down a corridor and into a very brightly lit room filled with built-in animal pens of varying sizes. Elvis filled the floor space of one of the larger pens. He had a drip up and was lying on a comfy-looking bed. Regan knelt down at the grille. 'Look at you, buddy. I bet you've never known such luxury.' Elvis didn't move.

'The bed is heated,' said the vet. 'The drip is to keep his fluids up; he lost some blood during surgery.'

'How much will all this cost?' asked Charlie. 'I think I explained that he's not actually our dog.'

'I know,' said the vet. 'We're a charity, so as the owner was homeless it'll be taken care of – but we're always grateful for any contributions you feel able to make. For now let's concentrate on getting him fit.'

'That's great, thank you,' said Charlie. He turned to Regan. 'He needs rest, and so do we. He's in the best place.'

Regan nodded and a giant yawn escaped. He was right. She wasn't sure she would be able to sleep but she felt she should at least try. She got to her feet. 'Thank you,' she said to the vet. 'When can we come back?'

'Call me in the morning, after surgery.'

'More surgery?' Regan looked pleadingly at Charlie, although she wasn't sure what she was expecting him to do. He reached out and gripped her hand.

The vet shook his head. 'Sorry, I mean morning surgery, not operating surgery.' He handed her a card. 'After twelve I'll be able to give you an update.'

A small thread of relief ran through her until she remembered that this didn't change anything for poor Kevin. But it was still a tiny dot of hope on an otherwise bleak canvas.

* * *

Charlie had set Regan up with a sleeping bag on his sofa, but she hadn't been able to sleep. At five she scribbled a note, folded up the sleeping bag and slipped out of the house. It was a crisp but bright May morning outside, and it somehow shocked Regan. She wasn't entirely sure what she'd been expecting – dark, sombre clouds? Crows on every lamp post, perhaps? She wandered down to King's Parade where a few cars were already zooming up and down. No, they weren't zooming; it just felt like they were. She found herself scanning each one for any sign that they might have been the driver who committed the hit and run, but she had no idea what she was looking for.

By the time she'd walked to the marina and back, things were starting to open up. The odd café here and there. Deliveries piling in to the seafront hotels. More cars, and now more people striding purposefully along. 'Oi!' shouted a cyclist as she veered into the pavement's cycle lane.

'Sorry,' she called, but he rode on, shaking his head. She hoped that was the worst thing that happened to him today. A few seagulls were on the railings hollering their morning demands, and the tide was on the turn. It was all a stark reminder that life really did carry on, and it highlighted to her how insignificant everything – and everyone – truly was.

She wasn't sure how far she walked, but a few hours later she found herself sitting under the pier. If she closed her eyes she could imagine the night she'd sat there with Charlie, Kevin and Elvis. The sounds today came from the pier's funfair – some distant music interspersed with squeals of delight from children. It should have been a joyful sound but it wasn't. She wanted to go up there and tell them what had happened last night. How one person's careless actions had changed lives forever. But they wouldn't care. And that was what hurt the most. There was nobody to care about Kevin. No-one would be grieving for him, except her and Elvis. The world didn't care about people like Kevin.

She realised now that Charlie was right. She couldn't enter into a relationship with him only to have him snatched from her. She knew, like he did, that any relationship they embarked on was going to be something special, and that would make parting all the more painful. She had to let him go, and the sooner she did that the easier it would be. She got up and walked some more. Hours passed, but her thoughts remained the same. Swirling over and over.

Regan was feeling a little chilly as she stared out towards the horizon. The sun was sinking into the sea, streaking colour across a sky as grey as the pebbles. The vibrant colours reflected in the darkening water, its surface pockmarked by the rain. The skeleton of the West Pier drew her attention away from the damp stones beneath her. The blackened metal frame was all that remained of the once-famous landmark. There was something about it that had always drawn Regan to it – perhaps its defiance at never completely giving in to the weather, the fires or the sea. After everything that had been thrown at it, it was still there. Not exactly as it had once been, but still there all the same.

'There she is!' She vaguely recognised the voice that travelled from far up the beach. 'Regan!' She heard the distant shout but didn't turn. She wasn't sure she could turn – every sinew was stiff. Her clothes were stuck to her. She hadn't moved for a while. The grinding sound of someone running across the stones grew louder until it was almost on top of her, jolting her back to reality.

'Reg?' Charlie dropped to his knees next to her making her turn to look at him. He looked so afraid. He reached forward and touched her cheek, wiping away the rain, and tears she wasn't aware were there. 'Are you okay?'

Regan swallowed. Nothing was ever going to be okay again. Seeing him this close, she wanted to settle in his arms and never move. 'Why do you think they didn't stop?' she asked. 'The driver. Why didn't they stop?'

Charlie blinked as if this was the last thing he'd been expecting her to say. 'Fear of prosecution, maybe. Drink driver. Who knows? We need to get you dried and in the warm.'

'I'm fine.' She turned back to look at the seagulls wheeling over the West Pier. Having him this close wasn't helping. She loved him, and it was the most painful thing in the world.

'I don't think you are,' he said, kindly. 'We've been looking for you all day. It's gone nine o'clock.'

'Where the bloody hell have you been?' said an out-of-breath Penny as she crunched alongside them. 'I've been worried stupid.'

Regan looked up and the sight of Penny's red face made her want to smile, although she couldn't. 'I'm fine.'

'No, you're not,' said Penny. 'You're soaked and I bet you've not eaten anything. Come on. You're coming back to mine.' Regan was about to protest. 'I don't want to hear any excuses. You've had a nasty shock and I'm taking care of you whether you like it or not. Sue me.'

Charlie reached out a hand to help Regan up and she pushed it away. The hurt in his eyes pained her, but she knew they were both vulnerable right now. He stood up and pushed his hands deep into his pockets. 'I rang the vet,' he said.

Regan hauled her stiff limbs upright. 'How's Elvis?' She felt awful that she'd forgotten to call. She'd been so caught up in everything else it had slipped her mind completely.

'He's off the drip and demanding food. The vet says the early signs are good.'

Regan choked back a sob. What a daft thing to cry about after all that had happened – but it was such a relief. She wasn't sure she could cope with losing anyone else. Regan moved to walk on the other side of Penny and distance herself from Charlie. And that was what she was going to have to keep doing.

Chapter Twenty-Two

Penny lived in a small, modern estate house, but Regan hadn't noticed much in the way of detail. After forcing her to have a warm brandy, Penny had tucked her up in a cosy bed and threatened her with all sorts of torture if she was to sneak out.

What with the trauma of the previous night, and a day spent wandering the seafront, she had at last been ready for sleep.

When she drifted back to consciousness, she could hear mumbled voices outside the room. She stretched her stiff body and strained her ears to try to hear what was being said. She recognised the timbre of Charlie's voice and her initial excitement was dampened by a dose of reality. She waited and, when it went quiet, she pulled on her clothes and slunk out of the bedroom.

'Morning. How did you sleep?' Penny must have been hovering outside. 'Coffee?' She held a large mug under Regan's nose.

'Good, thanks,' said Regan, taking the proffered mug and glancing surreptitiously around the landing.

Penny followed her gaze. 'Oh. He's downstairs.' Her expression changed. 'He's really worried about you.' She lowered her voice. 'I think he's a keeper.' Penny beamed a smile at her and she so wished she could mirror it.

'If only,' said Regan, the fear of losing him already a constant presence. She wandered downstairs. For a brief moment, she considered asking Penny to send him away – but what good would that do? They were in a rubbish situation, but at least they were now both on the same page.

'Hi,' she said, entering the living room.

'Hey,' he replied, twisting in her direction. 'You look rough.'

'Cheers.' She gave his head a nudge with her elbow as she walked past and immediately froze. 'I'm so sorry.' Could she do him damage doing that? She didn't know.

'It's all right. You don't have to wrap me in cotton wool . . . although I do have a bit of a thing about bubble wrap.' His eyebrows danced cheekily.

'Are you stalking me?' she asked, curling herself into the chair opposite.

'Oh yeah. One hundred per cent. Penny spotted me lurking outside, felt sorry for me and gave me coffee.'

'Okay. As long as you two aren't fussing.'

'Noooo,' said Penny, overacting as she joined them.

'I thought maybe we could check in on Elvis.' Charlie seemed cautious.

'I'd like that,' said Regan, taking a sip of the coffee.

'Once you've had a shower and done something with your hair.' Charlie peered forward for a better look. 'Do you backcomb it in your sleep?'

'It's the work of evil pixies,' said Regan.

'That explains it.' He smiled a warm *what might have been* smile at her and her insides melted. This was going to be so hard. He was like a giant magnet drawing her close, and she a tiny iron filing.

'How come you're not working?' asked Regan. Her mind was ticking; she knew he'd been off work since Wednesday – he'd told her that in the pub when he'd once again tried to explain his shift pattern. He'd spent all yesterday searching for her, and now he was off again.

'I was owed a few days' leave.' He gave a dismissive shrug. Regan felt something didn't add up, but she decided to leave it for now.

The vet's reception walls were covered in bright, jolly posters about fleas, ticks and overweight rabbits. A faint scent of disinfectant filled the air. An excited puppy – like something straight out of a toilet roll commercial – bounced towards them and seemed surprised when its harness bungeed it off its feet, making an almost-bald parrot with a Mohican squawk in protest. An elderly dog was sitting with its nose in the corner and its back to the room – clearly this wasn't his first visit.

'We've come to see Elvis,' said Regan to the receptionist, and she ignored the tittering that followed. Any other day she would have found it funny, but today was never going to be one of those days.

'I think you'd need a séance at Graceland for that,' she said, beaming bright white teeth through a fuchsia smirk.

'Hilarious.' Regan's face was stern and the receptionist's smirk slid from her over-made-up face. 'He's a dog.'

'Your dog?' asked the receptionist.

'No. He's . . . he's . . .' Why was this so hard? The very thought of Kevin conjured up a picture of his body on the crossing. No matter what she did it wouldn't go away.

Charlie stepped forward. 'He was the emergency on Friday night. We brought him in.'

'It's against our policy. Only the owner can have access, I'm afraid.' She jutted out her jaw.

Charlie beamed a smile at her. 'I'm afraid the owner—'

Regan cut in and locked the receptionist in a stare. 'His owner was the victim of a hit and run and is now lying dead in a morgue. If you want it to be front-page news of *The Argus* that you won't let us see his dog then you feel free to go ahead and enforce your policy.' Regan was now leaning over the counter. Charlie placed a hand on her arm to stop her getting any closer.

The receptionist swallowed. 'Ah. I see. I'll need to check with someone.'

'Yeah. You do that,' said Regan, feeling ready for a fight.

They took a seat and waited. Regan looked around at the other patients and their owners. She hadn't really noticed the woman with a fancy cat carrier until the cat inside let out an ear-piercing wail. *Poor thing*, thought Regan, eyeing the pretty tabby cat who was peering out at her. Maybe it was in a lot of pain.

'Fifi,' called the vet, and the woman with the cat stood up. 'Just a checkup today then?' he asked, as the cat continued to yowl its protest.

Blimey, thought Regan. *I wonder what noise she makes when she is in pain.*

Minutes later, the receptionist reluctantly escorted them through to a consulting room and handed them over to a veterinary nurse. She was far more pleasant and already seemed to have the measure of Elvis. 'Boy, is he a character,' she said. 'He chews everything.'

'Yep. That's Elvis,' said Regan proudly.

'He's quite thin, but that's easily fixed. We've treated him for fleas, ticks and ear mites so he should be a bit more comfortable now, too.'

Poor Elvis, thought Regan. She'd not thought about the sort of life he'd had living on the streets with Kevin. 'And after the surgery – is he all okay?' Regan held her breath.

'He's amazing. He's a bit sore and he's very unhappy about having to wear a collar, but the operation was a success. He just needs to heal.'

Regan's shoulders slumped in relief. 'Can we see him?'

'Sure. Come through. You can pet him but don't touch his stitches, all right?' They both nodded their understanding.

Elvis was lying in the same pen he'd been in after his operation. He wagged his tail excitedly at the sight of Regan and tried to stand up when the nurse opened the cage.

'Easy, boy. You need to take care,' said Regan. He looked a million times better than he had the other night, but she couldn't ignore his shaved fur and the long set of Frankenstein stitches on his abdomen.

'It's really okay,' said the nurse, seeing Regan's expression. 'They had to get in quick. He had internal bleeding and a ruptured bowel.'

'You poor thing,' said Charlie, joining Regan in giving Elvis some fuss.

Regan looked at the dogs in the pens around Elvis. Each one had a label explaining who they were. A beautiful black dog with more than a hint of Labrador in his genes pawed at the grille for attention. Regan checked his label. Barney. *I bet Barney has a home to go to and people who love him*, she thought.

'Thanks for everything you've done,' said Regan.

'You're welcome,' said the nurse. 'I've a huge soft spot for him – he's like the dog I had as a child. Next time you want to see Elvis, ask for me. My name's Deborah.'

Charlie and Regan exchanged looks.

'Thanks,' said Regan. 'I've got a good friend called Debbie.'

'You'll remember it then,' said Deborah. 'Try not to worry about Elvis. He'll soon be back to himself,' she added, shutting the cage again.

Elvis's big sad eyes stared out at Regan. 'You can't come out until you're better,' she said, pushing her fingers through the wire. *But what happens then?* she wondered.

She had no idea.

Chapter Twenty-Three

After giving the receptionist a surly look on their departure, they were back in Regan's little car. 'Right,' said Regan, noticing how close Charlie was to her when he leaned over to search for his seatbelt. A waft of aftershave caught her unawares, making her insides tingle mutinously. 'Home?'

'Actually . . . I was wondering, if I put some petrol in, would you mind taking me somewhere? It's a pain not being able to drive any more.'

How could she say no? 'Sure. Of course. To the garage!' She had no idea why she said it like cartoon Batman. She shook her head and focused on driving.

Charlie paid for a full tank of fuel, which she was very grateful for – but it did leave her thinking that maybe he was after a lift to Scotland. After filling up, they headed off in the direction of Hove in virtual silence with the exception of the odd direction from Charlie. It was a companionable silence – something she wasn't really used to. She had no idea where they were going, but it was good simply to be in his company.

When Charlie asked her to pull over, she was surprised to see they were outside an ordinary-looking bungalow. She was intrigued to know what he wanted here. An elderly relative perhaps? She switched off the engine and sat back in her seat. Charlie undid his seatbelt and then turned to look at her, a twitch of a smile at the corner of his lips.

'Don't get comfy, you're coming too,' he said.

Regan leaned forward to check the building. There was a nice tree in the garden and a door sign in the shape of a hedgehog. She wasn't really in the mood for making small talk with anyone, and the less she knew about Charlie and his family the easier it would be to keep her distance. 'You're okay, I'll wait here.'

'No, you won't. I've brought you here to tick another thing off your list. Come on.' He got out of the car before she had a chance to object, so with a slight huff, she followed him. She'd almost forgotten about her lottery list – but then a dumper truck of shit had landed on her life since then. And she'd thought Alex's prank was going to be her life's low point. How wrong could she have been?

They were greeted at the door by a rotund lady. 'Hello, I'm Mrs Tiggy-Winkle,' she said, her face deadpan. Regan snorted a laugh and resisted the urge to introduce herself as Jemima Puddle-Duck.

The woman noted Regan's snort. 'Of course I'm Philistia really, but it's what everyone around here likes to call me. And the local press love it, so why not, eh?'

'Why not?' agreed Regan, warming to the woman, who was either eccentric or a bit loopy. Either way, she liked her.

Charlie was grinning from ear to ear as they followed Mrs Tiggy-Winkle through the bungalow. Inside, it was like any 1950's bungalow: boxy, functional, with too much brown décor and not enough light. However, the building she took them to in the neatly ordered garden was a completely different affair. It was, without doubt, the biggest shed Regan had ever seen, and it covered a fair chunk of the garden. Calling it a shed didn't do it justice; it was more like a rustic log cabin. Regan still wasn't sure why she was here, or how this was ticking anything off her lottery wish list. Her list was now merely a vague memory – so much had happened since she'd jotted those things down – but she guessed this had nothing to do with cocktails and bare-chested waiters.

Philistia led them inside the log cabin, began rummaging in a cage and produced a small spiky ball, which was either a tightly curled-up hedgehog or a deadly scotch egg. She placed it carefully on a rainbow-striped towel and pointed at it. 'Watch,' she instructed.

Regan did as she was told, but it wasn't moving. Perhaps it was dead. She lost interest quickly but caught a glimpse of Charlie, who was watching intently. He had a few more days' stubble than usual and it suited him. He looked tired around the eyes and she felt a pang of guilt for having caused that, before realising she probably looked exactly the same but without the chiselled, stubbly chin. He seemed to sense her looking at him and turned, making her swiftly focus her attention back on the hedgehog.

At last the tiny creature began to move. The ball of spikes parted to reveal a smooth tummy, four of the cutest paws she'd ever seen and a twitching nose. Its dark eyes blinked as it lay on its back, taking everything in.

'This is Mr Pickle,' said Philistia. 'He was brought in last week. He'd been shut in a shed so he was undernourished and dehydrated.'

'Oh, the poor thing,' said Regan, feeling the urge to stroke it, then realising it would be exactly like stroking a toilet brush – only possibly less hygienic – so she returned her hand to her pocket.

'It's okay, love, you can pick him up.'

'You're all right. I don't want to get a prickle stuck in me, thanks.'

Philistia guffawed. 'Their spines rarely come out. He's not a porcupine. Go on,' she said, giving Regan a nudge. Charlie was watching her expectantly. She inched a finger closer. Didn't they have teeth and fleas?

Regan put her finger in front of the hedgehog. It sniffed it and recoiled sharply. *The feeling's mutual*, thought Regan. Mr Pickle slowly uncurled himself and she gently stroked his tummy. He seemed to like it so much that he weed. Regan pulled her finger out of the way just in time.

Philistia cackled with laughter. 'That's what his mother would have done. Licked his tummy to make him wee.' Philistia cleaned him up and passed him towards Regan.

'Ah, not if he's going to wee on me again.' She wasn't falling for that a second time.

'Don't be daft. He's all finished now. Here.' Philistia thrust a pair of gloves into Regan's hands, closely followed by the hedgehog, and she took him reluctantly. He was incredibly light and, thanks to the gloves, his prickles didn't scratch her skin.

'He weighs nothing,' she said, marvelling at the tiny creature.

'He needs feeding up. Once he's up to six hundred and fifty grams we'll release him back into the wild.' It made Regan smile to think of Brighton and Hove as 'the wild'. 'In a badger-free area, obviously.'

'Obviously,' chimed in Charlie.

'Don't they like badgers?' asked Regan.

'Would you like someone that saw you as convenience food?' Philistia narrowed her eyes.

'Er, no.'

Philistia busied herself with the other hedgehog cages while Charlie and Regan cooed over Mr Pickle. The shed seemed even bigger inside. It had rows and rows of shelves with small cages, and some bigger hutch-like structures at the other end. It was altogether a jolly nice hedgehog hotel.

'How amazing is this place?' said Charlie. 'I saw a clip on the news about the rescued hedgehogs, and I knew we had to come.'

'But why?' asked Regan, still puzzled.

'Because British hedgehog numbers are falling all the time. Loads get killed on the roads and their habitat is disappearing.' Regan was still wearing her blank expression – nothing he'd said explained why she was here holding a hedgehog who would likely wee on her without any warning. Charlie tilted his head forward. 'They're an iconic animal and they need saving,' he added.

'The British hedgehog is declining at the same rate as the tiger,' chipped in Philistia with gusto. 'They're being driven to the brink of extinction.'

'Really? I had no idea.' Regan stroked the inquisitive chap snuffling around her hands. 'Poor things.'

'This is where you come in,' said Charlie, widening his eyes like she should know what he was talking about. She gave a tiny shake of her head. 'You wanted to save an important animal from extinction. Remember?'

Regan let out an involuntary laugh when the penny finally dropped. 'I meant if I won millions I could set up an organisation to save the polar bear or something.' It wasn't like she'd actually thought it through – it was something she'd plucked from thin air that seemed like a good idea at the time. 'What can *I* do about saving hedgehogs?' She knew she was pulling what her dad called her 'duh face'.

'We're always after volunteers,' shot in Philistia, seizing her opportunity. She gave Regan a sandwich box filled with newspaper in exchange for Mr Pickle.

'Oh, I don't know.' Regan shot Charlie a glare for putting her on the spot like this, but he was busy cooing over the sandwich box. Regan peered inside. Four truffle-sized hedgehogs were snuggled together. Their wrinkly faces reminded her of walnuts. 'Awww.' The noise was involuntary.

'Hoglets. About five days old,' said Philistia, appearing unnervingly close to Regan's shoulder. 'Their mother was most likely killed. They need feeding every two hours. Here you go . . .' She handed Regan a syringe with a rubber bit on the end. Regan looked at it questioningly. 'Miracle Nipple,' explained Philistia.

'Aren't they all,' said Regan, under her breath.

By the time they left she was hooked, and she had signed up to be a hedgehog helper. Philistia had tried desperately hard to sign Charlie up, too, but as it was for a minimum of six months, he'd declined, saying very diplomatically that he didn't know where he'd be after the summer. Regan had concentrated on filling in her form and filling her head with images of suckling hoglets rather than thinking about Charlie not being there.

Charlie was looking particularly pleased with himself when they got back in the car.

'What?' said Regan, giving him a brief glance.

'You with the hoglets. It makes me smile, that's all. It's an image I'll treasure.'

'I have to admit it . . . they were the cutest things ever.'

'And now you can tick off another thing on your lottery list,' he said, looking mightily pleased with himself.

'I'm not sure being a hedgehog helper means I've saved the British hedgehog from rapid decline and extinction.'

'No, but it's a start.'

He'd done a lovely thing by getting her to go to the hedgehog rescue. She felt so much better. It was a precious thing to hold the baby hedgehogs and watch them guzzle from the tiny feeding syringe. Sometimes you just needed a hefty dose of nature to make you realise that simple acts could make a difference. It had given her quite a buzz. There was more chatter on the way home; the easy exchange she'd come to appreciate with Charlie was back, and she savoured it because she knew all too well it could be short-lived. Without thinking, she drove back past The Level. As she neared the crossing, the sight of a single bunch of flowers taped to the traffic lights brought a lump to her throat.

Regan needed some fresh air so after dropping Charlie home, promising that she'd stay with Penny for another night and doing a very awkward, hesitant air kiss, she walked to the library. It was quiet, so she got on a computer straight away. Two emails from Cleo were a welcome sight in her quest to get her mind to focus on something other than the accident.

Hey You!

Hope you're all right.

I'm still in Japan. I nearly cracked and came home (I know that makes me sound pathetic!) but lovely Mr Yomoda and his wife invited me to stay with them and I feel so much more positive now I'm not in a lonely hotel room. Mrs Yomoda doesn't speak any English but she keeps tempting me to eat with interesting morsels of food.

I told them I couldn't do the rest of the tour alone so Mr Yomoda volunteered to come along with some of his students so they can understand that being a successful artist isn't just about painting. For a very small man he's a huge tour de force – he's arranged it all! His efficiency at rearranging hotel bookings and contacting venues has been top notch. I've heard nothing from Oscar since he abandoned me and returned to the UK but I suspect his formal resignation as my agent will be waiting on my return.

How are things with you? It dawned on me that either you're still living with Jarvis – awkward! Or you've moved out?! I need to know details. Call me!

Love

Cleo

x

P.S. Miss you loads

Hi Regan,

Why don't you answer your phone? Hope you're okay.

I had a proper wobble about going to a gallery event and was stressing out, which was worse than normal because I was trying not to stress out in front of Mr Yomoda in case he thought I was nuts.

And when the student arrived I was getting chest pains it was that bad – and I was meant to be the one showing her the ropes. I thought all I was going to show her was how to have a public meltdown. But the student was more terrified than me! She was a tiny little thing called Hinata. It was her that painted the incredible cherry blossom picture – she's so talented, but cripplingly shy. We talked a bit about art which calmed us both down and I gave her one of my hair bobbles to fiddle with which hopefully helped.

Did you know 'anxious' in Japanese is 'shinpai shite'? I googled it! Turns out it's not pronounced how it's spelled, which is a shame because anxiety is shite.

Anyway the evening with Hinata was a success. Hinata was glued to my side the whole evening but I think that helped both of us.

Turns out Mr Yomoda knows about anxiety and has been actually quite helpful. He taught me an ancient Japanese relaxation technique where each finger represents a different emotion or feeling: anxiety, fear, anger, sadness and self-esteem. There's the strong possibility that it was ancient Japanese hokum but so far I've started each day calmer, so maybe it does work – who knows?

Hope to speak to you very soon. Call me!

Love

C

x

Chapter Twenty-Four

'I don't need babysitting,' said Regan, opening Penny's front door to Charlie on Saturday morning. She was feeling sorry for herself and didn't want someone with far worse problems trying to jolly her out of it. Kevin was dead and she was grieving.

He held up his hands in surrender. 'I wouldn't dare. I was after cadging a lift to Mantra.'

She huffed out a breath. 'I don't think I'll bother.'

'Oh, come on. For me?' he said brightly, coming inside and closing the door.

'You've walked almost as far to get here as it is from yours to the centre,' Regan pointed out.

'Oh, yeah. So I have. Silly me.'

She rolled her eyes at him. 'Do you fancy a coffee? Penny's at work.' Regan had worked the last four days but Saturday was her day off.

'Sure.' He followed her to the kitchen.

'Have you heard anything from the police?' They had been in to provide detailed statements but Regan had got the distinct impression that finding out who had killed Kevin was not their top priority. It had only warranted a tiny article in the local paper, too, whereas

Regan had been expecting a full-page request for information.

'No. They've not been in touch. But I guess it's early days,' he said.

'Do you think they're treating it as less important because he was homeless?' Regan held his gaze.

'No, they're not allowed to do that. But without a family banging on their door demanding answers . . .'

'Mmm, I think you're right.' She offered him a choice of mug. 'Hufflepuff or Slytherin?'

'Hufflepuff,' he said, looking affronted.

'I was just checking.' They could not be more compatible if they tried.

'So how have you been doing. You okay?' he asked, his eyes searching her face for clues.

'I'm okay. Just sad.' She was sad about losing Kevin and she was sad at the prospect of going through it all again when she lost Charlie. She tried to shrug it off.

'Cuddle?' he asked, with outstretched arms. She nodded. 'No funny business,' he added with a cheeky smile, and pulled her into a hug. She was happy and sad at the same time. The warmth of his body against hers and the light scent of him was enticing – she could have stayed there all day. It was safe; like coming home. She reluctantly pulled herself away. They exchanged knowing looks before she turned away and concentrated on making the drinks. They leaned against the cupboards, unconsciously mirroring each other, desperately trying not to make eye contact, while the kettle made a noise like a steam train coming through the tiny kitchen. The electricity between them was palpable. It was a relief to be able to finish making the coffees.

She handed him a mug. 'Thanks. And don't worry. I'm sure the police will do their best,' said Charlie.

'I think only having Kevin's first name is causing problems in identifying him. It's not a lot to go on.'

'Yeah. I got that feeling too. It sounded like there wouldn't be a funeral until they'd tried to trace his family. If he has any.'

'He did once mention something about his folks,' said Regan, leading Charlie through to the living room, 'but who knows if they're still alive. I'm guessing Kevin was in his fifties or sixties.'

They sat and sipped their drinks in silence for a bit. 'I'm glad you're staying with Penny now,' said Charlie, leaning back into the sofa.

Regan shook her head. 'I'm going back to the studio this afternoon. Penny has been great, but I don't want to overstay my welcome.'

'Why leave? Penny has space.'

'No, she doesn't.' Regan leaned forward. 'This is her mum's place. She's only gone to see her sister for a while. She'll be back in a few days.'

'Still, I'm sure her mum won't mind, and this sofa's comfy. It would be better than the studio. Just until things steady themselves.'

The last thing Penny's mother wants to see is another woman living off Penny's kindness, thought Regan, but it was difficult to explain to Charlie without outing Penny. 'I'm no charity case – I still have a little pride left. I don't want people to think I'm a freeloader.'

'You're using my kitchen for free.' He gave a cheeky pout.

'No, I'm not. I'm paying you in jam.'

He hid a smirk. 'Excellent. I hear diabetes is a lot of fun.'

She threw a cushion at him.

* * *

Mantra class seemed to take on a whole new meaning. Everything Cressy said, Regan was able in some way to relate it back to Kevin. All her thoughts seemed instantly to find a way to be about death and dying; although some mindful eating and a square of dark chocolate did help a little. They also learned a walking meditation, which Regan found difficult. She was usually quite competent at walking in a straight line, even after a few beers, but when she had to do it at a snail's pace and focus on the soles of her feet, she wobbled all over the place.

'Sorry. *Again*,' she said, grabbing hold of Wendy, who was wearing yet another gloriously colourful kaftan.

'Don't worry. I do it all the time. Bloody stroke. It's like my limbs aren't connected to me any more. You'll get the hang of it eventually,' said Wendy, with a kind smile.

'I'm not so sure,' whispered Regan, with another wobble. She caught Charlie trying to hide a grin and he immediately changed his expression to super serious. She gave him a hard stare and his grin returned. Despite her best efforts at trying to keep her distance, she still desperately wanted to snog that grin off his face. But it wasn't just physical with Charlie – he was the whole package; and that was precisely why she couldn't get involved. Regan closed her eyes, trying to concentrate on the walking meditation, and promptly toppled over, landing with a thud.

Coffee and custard cream time arrived, and Regan found herself chatting to Mandeep. Regan tried to remember what he'd said when they'd done introductions a few weeks before. 'So you said you come here because it helps you sleep?' She wanted to connect with someone that wasn't there because they were recovering from some awful, life-threatening illness. She needed a break from the Grim Reaper's shadow.

'Yeah. I do the body scan every night and it works a treat.'

'I think I need more practice,' said Regan, knowing that she definitely did. 'What made you give it a try?' She bit into her custard cream. Timing was important; you couldn't stuff in a biscuit if someone was about to ask you a question.

'My consultant referred me after I had a brain tumour removed.'

Regan spluttered and apologised profusely for spraying custard cream crumbs all over his Rolling Stones T-shirt.

'It's okay. I like that it surprises you. Wearing a turban hides a lot.'

'I'm so sorry. I had no idea.' He looked so healthy, but then so did Charlie.

'Really, it's fine. I get it a lot. But I'd rather that than people staring or muttering. This way I get treated normally.'

'I'm so pleased it worked out for you. You were very brave to have the operation,' said Regan.

'Didn't have a choice really. Literally do or die.' He laughed a hearty chuckle, one that made her feel she should join in, but she couldn't.

'You look so well.' It was hard not to stare.

'Because I am, now. I still need regular checkups and scans, but other than that I'm all fixed.'

Her eyes drifted to Charlie and Mandeep's followed her. 'It's a brave man that faces death the way he faces life,' he said.

'Wise words.' Sorrow washed over her. 'I don't know how he does it.'

Mandeep patted her gently on the shoulder. 'Because

he has no choice. To give up now is to let death win an early victory.' Regan was glad of Cressy's bell bringing them all back to the present.

The last activity was a full body scan, which Regan was now an old hand at – or so she thought, until she fell asleep. It turned out the power nap was exactly what she needed. Mantra class always helped her get some perspective on things; not just because of the meditation, but because of the people. They were still here after all that had happened to them, and they were carrying on and making the best of every second. She felt bad for having wallowed in the aftermath of Kevin's accident. The homework was to apply mindful techniques to focus on small things, and she pledged to give it a go. Maybe it would take her mind off the big things?

After work, Regan headed to Charlie's to make jam while Charlie was at the station. She was trying her best not to get in his way, although it wasn't entirely working out. She was standing on a chair trying to remove the batteries from the screeching smoke alarm when Charlie came home. He almost tripped over the two crates of strawberries she'd left by the door.

'Mind the fruit. Bumper day!' she hollered over the noise whilst she continued to wrench out the battery.

'Hey, don't do that!' he said, carefully lifting her down. For a moment she felt like a child as his strong arms effortlessly moved her to the floor – it was both comforting and frustrating.

'But it won't shut up.'

Charlie snorted a laugh. 'Because something's burning.' He poked his head around the kitchen door. 'What's burning?'

'Well, jam. Obviously.' She resisted the urge to roll her eyes. If she was in the kitchen then there was always jam burning. She had spent the last few evenings getting her market stall back on track. After the accident she'd drifted for a while, but she had no time for drifting if she wanted to have something to sell. Charlie hadn't had the heart to say no to her using his food-hygiene-approved kitchen, so she'd been making the most of the facilities.

Charlie was quick to take the giant pan off the heat. 'Don't do that,' she said, her voice laden with frustration. 'Now it'll never set. It's strawberry.' She had quickly learned this was a tricky jam to make.

He wafted a tea towel under the smoke alarm and it finally stopped. Charlie joined Regan in the kitchen and they both stared into the pan. 'Is it meant to be black?'

'No.' She was tired and beginning to feel a bit grumpy. 'I think I need to face the fact that I'm utter shite at jam making.'

'I think that's a little harsh . . .' She gave him a challenging look. 'Maybe you just need more practice?' *Why was he always so bloody positive?*

'I've been practising for days and I actually think I'm getting worse.'

'Now you're being defeatist. Think how much you've learned,' he said.

'I've learned that I'm utter shite at making jam.' Regan pulled off her apron and threw it on the worktop in defeat.

'Let me have a shower and I'll see if I can give you a hand.'

'You? Making jam?' At least it made her smile.

'Why not?' asked Charlie, straightening his back as if in challenge.

She gave a shrug. 'Don't rush the shower – this'll take some chipping off,' she said, pointing at the jam pan.

An evening making jam with Charlie was both brilliant and annoying. He followed the instructions to the letter, and already his batch of strawberry and black pepper jam was looking a whole lot more edible than hers.

'This is really fun,' he said, stirring the jam.

'Yeah. Wait till it gets to the volcanic spitting stage – it gets a whole lot less fun really quickly.'

Regan hovered over the pan with the thermometer and when it started to bubble she held it in the lava-like substance. Her fingers quickly heated up, which they always did, and she gritted her teeth in anticipation of the splatter of jam that would inevitably target her.

'Er, shouldn't you have gloves on?'

'Can't hold it – the oven gloves are too thick.' She was slightly insulted that he thought she hadn't considered this. She wasn't completely stupid.

'I was thinking the rubber gloves. They'll protect you, and they have grippy finger tips.'

Okay, that was a good idea. Grippy finger tips . . . who was he? Mary Berry in disguise?

Regan donned the rubber gloves and resumed holding the thermometer. It did make a difference. At least she wasn't wincing every time the jam spluttered – which was a lot.

Their heads were close together as they watched the temperature rise. When it hit the required number, Charlie began timing it on his watch. She noticed the flex in his muscled forearm. He wasn't a very muscly person, but he was clearly strong. She wasn't a fan of chiselled abs, but there was something reassuring about a man with understated strength.

'Regan?' said Charlie, as if this was about the third time he'd said it, which it probably was, because she'd been miles away contemplating the merits of a strong man.

'Yes.' She almost stood to attention.

'This is a mindful opportunity. Close your eyes for a second and breathe in the smell.'

Charlie leaned his head a little closer to hers and she closed her eyes. *A kiss right now would be quite nice*, she mused. The kiss didn't materialise, so she did as he suggested. Focusing all her attention on the smell, she got a whiff of freshly washed man mixed with strawberries, which was both delicious and slightly arousing – she'd never look at strawberry jam in quite the same way again.

'Why don't you get the plate out of the fridge so we can test it and see if it's set? Then you can line the jam jars up on the worktop.' And the moment was gone.

'Yes, boss.' She gave him a questioning look.

'Sorry, am I being bossy?'

'A bit.' She didn't mind him taking charge – in fact, she quite liked it, but she wasn't going to let him know that.

Charlie spread a little jam on the cold plate. They waited and then the two of them squidged it with their fingers, pushing the jam together in the middle. They both pulled their fingers out at the same time and licked them. There was something oddly erotic about it.

'Perfectly set,' said Charlie. Regan had almost forgotten what they were doing; she wanted to do the erotic jam tasting thing again.

Regan whipped the sterilised jars out of the hot oven and moved them carefully to the granite worktop. She turned her back for a second and 'BANG.' One of the jam jars had exploded. Charlie immediately stepped between her and the row of jam jars as a series of bangs signalled that they'd all done the same thing.

'What the actual hell?' Regan stared at the shattered glass scattered across the worktop and floor. She'd have to sterilise another batch. 'They didn't do that at Dad's.'

'Cold surface,' said Charlie, pointing at the granite worktop. 'The glass has contracted too quickly.'

'Ahhh,' said Regan feeling like a prize idiot. *Why was jam making so hard?* Her shoulders sagged.

'You know my mum would love to give you a hand with this. She's an expert jam maker.'

'Then why the heck didn't you say that before?' She clearly needed all the help she could get.

Chapter Twenty-Five

The next evening, Joanna came well prepared with three specialist jam recipe books, including a special edition Women's Institute book on preserves, and Charlie and Beanstalk made themselves scarce. Joanna handed Regan a pinny with seahorses on it; Regan tried not to show how she felt about that and was glad that Charlie wasn't there to see her wearing it.

'What fruit have we got?' asked Joanna, her eyes full of glee.

'I got cauliflowers for free but I bought some pineapples and some coconut milk because I really want to learn how to make pina colada jam.'

Joanna laughed, but fell quiet when Regan didn't join in. 'You're serious?'

'Yep. It was the clincher that got me the stall, but I kind of made it up under pressure so we need to make it an actual thing.'

Joanna's shock faded. 'I love a challenge. Hang on.' She disappeared and Regan could hear her rummaging in the hall cupboard. 'Here we are.' She proudly held aloft a very foreign-looking bottle of clear liquid.

'And that is?'

'White rum.'

Perhaps Joanna felt she needed to be steaming to make jam with her. Regan couldn't blame her – she'd come close to turning to alcohol after her previous disasters. 'Is it for us or for the jam?' asked Regan.

'The jam. It's what's in a pina colada.'

'Won't that make it alcoholic? I'd have to make sure people don't feed it to kids.'

'No, it'll be fine because the alcohol will evaporate when it cooks and just leave the flavour. You'll see.'

They set to work and Regan was impressed with Joanna's knowledge and her willingness to teach rather than tell. Joanna had also brought something called jam sugar, which held the answer to why some of her jams, especially the pineapple ones, hadn't been setting. 'Additional pectin,' said Joanna, tapping the packet.

'To make it set,' said Regan.

'Exactly.'

They worked surprisingly well together. The hours flew by, until eventually they sat to have a cup of tea and marvel at the rows of pina colada jam and bowls of cauliflower, which was soaking in salted water ready for them to make it into their own version of a fine piccalilli with a curry twist.

'Thanks, Joanna. This has been brilliant.'

'My pleasure,' said Joanna, raising her mug of tea. They clinked mugs. 'It's nice to be able to help you seeing as you've helped my Charlie.'

'I don't know about that.' Regan wasn't sure what Charlie had shared and it felt decidedly uncomfortable to talk about him with his mum.

'Well, he's definitely been happier these last few weeks. So it's either you or the fact the Grand Prix season has started again.'

'It's probably the Grand Prix.' Something unspoken passed between them. Two women who loved one man completely, but from two very different perspectives.

The front door opened and Beanstalk and Charlie appeared in the doorway. 'Hello, Mrs M,' said Beanstalk. 'Anything to eat? Ooh, jam.' He picked up a jar whilst inspecting the cauliflower bobbing in the bowl. 'Ew, that looks like brains.'

'It is,' said Regan, snatching the jam off him. 'From the last person who tried to steal my jam.'

Over the next few evenings, Regan ensconced herself in Charlie's kitchen, and with Joanna's help she made a mountain of jam. Not all of it perfect, but it tasted good, and she was growing in confidence with every batch. Joanna's help had been invaluable, but she was popping in less and less now as Regan improved. Joanna had been a superb taste tester too. Regan already had some favourite flavours and she was pleased with the quirky combinations she was conjuring up. Or, more accurately, what Jag's leftovers were dictating. Thanks to Joanna, she had a process now that worked; so she could set everything out, prepare the ingredients, make jam and deposit it into sterilised jars, all within a two-hour window. She almost felt like she knew what she was doing.

Despite Penny's protestations, she had moved back to the studio. She'd found that she'd grown quite fond of the little place – with the obvious exception of Cleo's torture chair – and with Penny's mum due home she was keen not to cause any issues for Penny.

Regan had been in touch with her dad and he'd invited her round for dinner. This was a very rare thing and showed Regan that he totally got how upset she was about

Kevin's death. Her dad had cooked for her throughout most of her childhood, but a weekly rota of fish fingers, beans on toast and pizza, with fish and chips on a Friday, was the full extent of his culinary talents – assuming you didn't count Marmite sandwiches and the ability to make a teddy-shaped jelly once a year for her birthday.

Regan leaned against the doorframe after ringing the doorbell. She could hear scurrying about inside and the faint shadow of someone dashing back and forth from the bedroom. Her stomach sank at the thought of sharing a meal with Tarty Tara. Then her stomach contracted at the thought she may have interrupted something. She tried to erase the image that had invaded her mind.

The door opened abruptly and her father appeared to be trying to smile, but he had the appearance of a startled chimpanzee. He rubbed his neck. Regan peered past him. 'Everything . . . um . . . all right?'

'Yes. Yes. Come in.' He held the chimpanzee grin for a moment more until it was too hard to maintain and he slipped back into his usual sombre but permanently puzzled face.

Regan had a good gander as she went in. Nothing seemed untoward. The bedroom door was closed. She wondered how much more stuff Tarty Tara had moved in since the last time she'd been there.

'You on your own?' She needed to be a hundred per cent certain; she didn't want Tarty Tara appearing, magician's-assistant style, during the arctic roll.

'Oh, yes. Just me.' He seemed more awkward than usual, which was quite a feat.

'You all right?'

'Yes, of course. Have a seat and I'll put the pizza in.' He

shot to the kitchen faster than she'd seen him move before. Something was definitely up. She sat at the table, but leaned to her left so she could watch him in the kitchen. He darted about and then slumped back against the cupboard, tilted his head to the ceiling and sighed deeply. He appeared to be trying to compose himself. Something was very wrong.

They ate their pizza in silence until Regan could take no more. 'So the night of the accident. I keep going over and over it.'

Graham nodded. 'That's understandable. But you need to try to forget about it now.' Regan frowned at him. 'Not Kevin. Don't forget about Kevin – but you do need to forget about the accident. It's not healthy to dwell on things.' He was nodding as though he was trying to convince himself.

'But if I could only remember more details about the car.' It was so frustrating. She knew she'd seen it, because she remembered seeing the spray of water as it careered away.

Graham shook his head and winced. 'No. You need to stop trying to remember. It won't do any good.'

She pondered this. 'Do you mean if I stop trying it might come back to me?'

'Um, no. Not exactly. Look, Regan, it's a terrible thing that's happened, but obsessing over who killed Kevin won't bring him back.'

Blunt as ever. 'No, but if I can get justice for Kevin then—'

'You'd feel better? Are you really doing this for you?'

How had he made it sound like she was being selfish? 'No, I want justice for Kevin. Nobody should be able to get away with what that driver's done.' Familiar bubbles of anger rose inside her. 'And if they're not locked up they could do it again.'

'Statistically that's not likely,' said Graham, cutting off a perfect inch-squared piece of pizza and putting it in his mouth.

She gave up.

'So no actual witnesses to the accident then?' he asked.

'No.'

'You didn't actually see it happen?' He paused with his knife and fork held above his plate.

'Nobody did.'

He shrugged a cardigan-clad shoulder and put his cutlery back to work. 'Then there's nothing you can do.'

Regan decided to change the subject. She should have known better than to try to discuss such an emotional subject with her father. 'I'm getting better at the jam making.' She knew she sounded a bit too pleased with herself, but it did feel like a real achievement.

'There was really only one direction for that to go,' said Graham, giving a hard stare at his kitchen.

She felt instantly deflated by his words. 'I'll see if we can get some more paint and redo that wall.'

'And the ceiling.'

'Okay.' Regan's shoulders slouched ever downward. He didn't mean to make her feel bad about things; he just had an uncanny knack for it. She took a breath and straightened up. No, she was proud of what she was doing, and she wasn't going to be pulled down by her father's unemotional approach. 'I'm really excited about starting on the market. I've made loads of different flavours of jam, so I've got a good amount of stock and I'm going to make two batches a week to start with, unless Jag is chucking away something I can't resist.' It was more like talking to herself when she got going, because her dad just nodded occasionally.

A thought seemed to strike Graham and his face brightened. 'Did I tell you I got marmalade from Lidl for fifty-nine pence? You can't beat that, now can you?'

He had a point.

Penny appeared uncomfortable when she opened the coffee shop doors to let Regan in on Wednesday morning. 'You all right?' asked Regan, already sensing that she wasn't.

'I spoke to Kasia last night.'

'How's the leg mending?' asked Regan, going through her usual morning routine. Penny didn't answer for a moment, making Regan pause to look at her.

Penny scratched her head. 'Her tendon has pretty much healed. The doctor says she can come back to work next week.'

'That's great news,' said Regan, and then the penny dropped. 'Oh . . . I'm out of a job.'

'I'm so sorry, Regan. I've loved working with you. But—'

'Hey.' Regan slapped a smile on her face and held up her palms. 'Penny, it's fine. I knew this was temporary. I'm mega grateful to you for giving me the job at all. Anyway, I need to focus on making serious amounts of jam so it's all good.'

'Really?' Penny was hesitant.

'Yes. Come here.' Regan spread her arms for a hug and Penny stepped in to it.

Regan had always known this was coming, but it didn't make the blow any softer when it landed.

* * *

Back in the studio after a busy last day at the café, Regan was sitting in the chair of doom surveying her growing jam stocks. She felt a little like Scrooge in his counting house. Pride was rippling inside her at what she'd achieved. None of it had been plain sailing, but then nothing worth having ever was. A reticent tap on the door had her jolt to attention. She threw a blanket over the jars and, in case it was the landlord, picked up the keys so it would look like she was leaving.

She opened the door to see Charlie and her heart soared higher than it should. 'Oh, hi,' she said, tucking her hair behind her ear and trying too hard to be nonchalant.

'I got you this,' said Charlie, stepping out of view and returning to thrust a very large white mass at Regan.

'Wow. A mattress!'

'It's an old one off the bunks we have at the station. They're not that great but it was being chucked out and I thought of you. Not the chucked out part . . . You know what I mean.' He coloured up a bit.

Regan hugged the mattress like an old friend. 'It's bloody brilliant.' She could feel her neck relaxing just at the thought of being able to sleep horizontal. 'Thank you.'

She went to kiss him and he stepped back, the movement tearing at her heart just a fraction.

'I also wanted to check you were okay.' He lowered his gaze.

She'd only seen him a few days ago, but it was lovely to think he'd felt the need to check on her, even if he couldn't bear to kiss her. At least he cared, and that meant a lot.

'I'm good. I finished at the café today. First day on the market tomorrow. Do you want to celebrate with me? Maybe get a bottle of wine?' But Charlie was already shaking his head. 'That's okay.' She waved it away with what she hoped was a casual air.

'As long as you're all right,' he said, turning to leave.

He was like an addiction she couldn't kick, and every tiny drop of time with him made her want more. She racked her brains for a reason to stop him leaving. 'I keep going over and over the night of the accident. I wish I could recall more about the car. Maybe if we talked about what we both remember it might trigger something.'

He paused and turned back. 'Maybe.'

'Well . . .' started Regan, 'we could go to the pub and discuss it there?' She bit her lip in anticipation.

'Hmm.' His furrowed brow told her he was considering it.

'I would invite you in, but I can't trust myself now I've got a mattress,' said Regan, trying her hardest to make light of the situation.

'Okay, it had best be the pub then,' he said, but he sounded reluctant.

She didn't give him a chance to change his mind, quickly flicking off the lights and pulling the door shut. 'Come on. The first glass of water's on me.'

They spent the first round of drinks going over exactly how each of them remembered the events of the accident, using beer mats for props. They had similar memories. The rain, the screech of tyres and brakes, the bodies on the crossing and the spray of water as the car left the scene.

'I think the car must have been an ordinary colour,' said Charlie. 'Because if it had been red or purple or something bright I reckon we would have noticed it more.'

'Good point. The rain made visibility really hard. Maybe it was rain coloured.' Charlie laughed. 'What colour is rain?'

Charlie took a swig of his pint. 'Oh, you're serious?'

'Completely.' Regan did her best serious face.

'Well, then . . . I'd say grey.'

'Brilliant. So the car was likely either grey like the rain or maybe black like the sky, which would explain why we didn't notice it.'

Charlie didn't look convinced. 'Or it was bright green with giant yellow spots and we just didn't look at it.'

Regan growled her frustration and whizzed the beer mats across the small table. She felt totally useless.

'Hey, I'm kidding. Even you would have spotted giant yellow spots,' he said. She gave him a thump and he feigned pain. 'Ouch. That'll be a bruise tomorrow,' he said, giving it a rub.

He made her smile, made her forget her frustrations with the world. She felt he had let her into his bubble where, for now, it was safe. She wanted to stay in it for as long as possible. She'd deal with the pain of the fallout later.

'How's Elvis?' he asked.

'Doing really well and starting to cause havoc.'

'That's good. And how are your plans for world domination of the jam industry?' he asked playfully, but at the same time engaging her with interested eyes.

'Stocks are good. I need to start making a profit by week two because Cleo will be back and I need to afford to rent a room.' She sipped her beer.

Charlie wasn't blinking. 'Isn't that a bit optimistic?'

'I have to be optimistic, because this has to be a success.' She had no space for contemplating the alternative. An image of her on her mattress in an alleyway loomed into her mind and she dismissed it.

The pub door opened and two blokes walked in laughing. 'I thought I was shit at barbecues!' said one. A waft of acrid smoke wafted in with them, and Charlie was off his seat and out the door in a heartbeat.

Regan downed her beer and followed him. She caught sight of him sprinting down Ditchling Road and she gave chase. And her father had always said to never run after a man.

He turned left into Hollingbury Road and disappeared. Regan had a stitch, but she kept going until she reached the source of the smoke, where it seemed a family barbecue had turned into a bonfire. There was no sign of Charlie. A group of people were gathered on the street.

'Is everyone okay?' shouted Regan, over the hubbub.

'Yeah. Knobhead tried to get the barbie going with petrol,' said a woman in heels, and the crowd laughed.

'Has anyone called 999?' The smoke was billowing now as the breeze coaxed the flames higher.

As if on cue, she heard the siren not too far away. She opened the back gate to see that half the shed was well lit and flames were lapping over the roof. Charlie was using a plant pot to scoop water from a small pond and chuck it at the shed in a rhythmic motion. 'Fire engine's on its way,' she called.

He looked alarmed. 'Get everyone the hell away! Send them down Hollingbury Crescent.' She didn't like the tone of his voice. Something was wrong. The shed was on fire, but it wasn't near the house and everyone was out of the garden. It didn't feel like they needed to get further away. She was considering challenging him when his expression hardened and he shouted at her. 'Now, Regan. Go!'

She didn't ask again. She was afraid and pissed off in equal measure, but if a firefighter was telling her to get further away then she wasn't going to argue. Well, not right now anyway.

She herded the revellers across the road and out of the way as the fire engine pulled up and lots of large, yellow-helmeted men, like giant Lego clones, all poured out.

She waved at the clone firefighters. 'Charlie is in there!' she shouted, and pointed towards the flames dancing over the roof of the garden shed.

Suddenly the atmosphere changed. A white-helmeted firefighter was shouting instructions and she and the others were ordered even further back. Police cars screamed into the area and Regan's pulse did the tango. *What the hell was going on?*

Chapter Twenty-Six

Eventually the flames disappeared, but now pyjama-clad families were being evacuated from nearby homes and they were all being pushed back down Hollingbury Crescent by the police officers. It made no sense. Surely the danger had passed? Regan felt like a spare part, but she couldn't leave without Charlie. Most of the barbecue party had gone home, the people who appeared to live at the house were talking to the police, and the few bystanders who had joined them had lost interest now the flames – and any Instagram-worthy footage – were no longer available.

A few firefighters returned to the engine and when the biggest of them took off his helmet she recognised him; it was Beanstalk. Police were still patrolling and stopping people crossing the street so she couldn't just walk over to him.

'Beanstalk!' she hollered. He spun in her direction and crossed the road. His face was grubby from the fire and his eyebrows knitted into a frown. 'Reg, what are you doing here?'

'I was having a drink with Charlie. Where is he?'

Beanstalk shook his head. 'He's getting a lecture from our watch commander.'

'Why?' Regan felt defensive. How many people would run to help on their day off? He'd probably saved that family's fences.

'Because the shed was next to the neighbour's full tank of heating oil. It could have exploded at any moment.' His expression was grave, and it chilled Regan's very soul.

'He could have got himself killed,' she said, in a small voice.

'You know what?' Beanstalk rubbed his forearm across his troubled face. 'Subconsciously, I think that's exactly what he's hoping. I think he'd rather go out like that than just slip away.'

A garden gate banged shut and they both turned to look across the street. An extremely cross-looking Charlie strode down the side of the house and back towards the pub.

'Charlie!' called Regan, but he didn't turn around.

'Maybe give him a bit of space?' said Beanstalk, gently. 'I know he acts like everything's fine, but deep down he's fighting demons all the time.' He always appeared so happy, but the turmoil he must deal with every day was immense – not knowing if this one would be his last. She wished she'd spent more time thinking about how Charlie really felt, rather than accepting the happy exterior he'd presented. They both watched Charlie stride out of sight.

'Beanstalk!' someone shouted from the engine.

'I gotta go. Will you be okay, Reg?' He gave her a worried look.

'Of course. I'm fine. I start on the market tomorrow.' She tried to find a smile from somewhere.

'That's grand. Good luck,' he called, and he strode back to the engine.

* * *

The next morning was bright and clear, just like a new chapter should be. Regan parked her car on double yellow lines, jumped out and began unloading the heavy boxes of jars from the boot onto the pavement. She paused as she had a thought. She couldn't carry the boxes all at once, and daren't leave them on the pavement because someone might steal them. She heaved two back in, shut the boot and picked up the last box. She lugged it inside and headed for her stall. A large woman with dreadlocks was unpacking ornate dragons from a wooden box.

'Erm, hi,' said Regan, shifting the weight of the jam box to her hip.

The woman looked her up and down. 'Hi,' she replied before immediately returning her attention to her dragons.

'I think this is my stall.' Regan nodded at the table, awash with dragons in various poses.

'I think you can see that it's not.' Dragon Woman shook her head dismissively.

'But when I spoke to Bernice she said I could choose and I chose this one.'

'You need to speak to Bernice, because I've been here for a couple of days so this is my stall and I'm not moving.'

The box was making Regan's arms ache. She didn't want to get off on the wrong foot. She made an attempt at a pleasant expression. 'Look, could you watch my box while I find Bernice and sort this out . . . please?'

'No.' The woman carefully unwrapped another dragon ornament. This dragon was about to land on a terrified-looking goat. Regan would have very much liked to be the dragon; but only if this woman was the goat.

'Right. Thanks.' Regan stomped out of the market and back to her car to see a parking attendant getting out his notebook. 'No, no, no!' called Regan, trying to run and realising it was impossible with a box full of jam.

The parking attendant spun in her direction and pointed at the car. 'This yours?'

'Yes. Please don't give me a ticket.'

'I should,' said the bearded attendant. 'You working the market?'

'Yes. First day and there's been some sort of mess-up with my stall.'

'Well you can't park here.'

'Where can I park?' Regan scanned the road, knowing it was hopeless.

'Plenty of car parks.'

'But they're miles away,' she said with a deep sigh.

'Your choice. Park here again and I'll ticket you.'

'Okay.' Regan reluctantly returned the jam to the boot and drove off in search of a parking space. Finding one that was both close enough to ferry the jam to the market and that she could afford for the day wasn't going to be easy.

After driving around for twenty minutes and inching up her annoyance level to one barely below 'spontaneously combust', Regan swung the car onto the wide pavement in front of the café. She marched inside with her frustration levels high and one of the boxes gripped tightly to her chest.

'I didn't expect to see . . . oh, is there a problem?' asked Penny.

Regan left the jam with Penny and charged off to abandon the car somewhere. A ten-minute walk later, she was red faced and at the point of muttering obscenities when she returned to collect the boxes. By the time Regan marched back into the market, she was ready to send a dragon where no dragon had ever gone before.

Bernice was in a serious-looking discussion with another stallholder. Regan made a beeline for her. 'Bernice, there's someone on my stall.'

Bernice glared. 'Then use another one.' She turned away.

Regan opened and closed her mouth like a confused goldfish. 'But, she . . . but . . .'

'Oh, really. You're not children. Surely you can sort this out yourselves.'

Regan huffed and shot a grade-A glare at Dragon Woman, who was looking smugger than Simon Cowell in a Who-Has-The-Whitest-Teeth competition. Regan lifted her chin and strode off to find an available table.

After a hurried setup, she almost felt like singing 'ta dah!' when everything was arranged how she wanted it. She looked up to see people milling about, so she fixed on a grin and waited for someone to show some interest.

An hour later, she had serious jaw ache and was still waiting for someone to give her stall the tiniest speck of attention. A few people had glanced in her direction, but her pleading puppy look hadn't enticed them over. At last, someone with a determined gait approached.

'How can I help you?' she asked. Was that the right thing to say? She hadn't thought this bit through. Perhaps she needed a jam patter that she could reel off.

'Yes. What's the code for the toilet?' the man asked.

'Oh, um, sorry, I don't know.' He quickly moved on. *Great start*, thought Regan.

The morning dragged on like a teenager doing chores. Her back started to ache, which made her feel old, and also realise that she needed to invest in a chair. All the stallholders had chairs, although they weren't using them much because they were busier than her. She leaned against the nearby wall, puffed out a sigh, slapped on a smile and called Cleo.

'Hey you,' said Cleo, looking thrilled. 'I was just thinking about you.'

'You were?'

'I saw a tiny dog dressed like a nurse.'

'Er, I have no idea what to say to that.'

'Well you work in pharmaceuticals and . . . well, anyway, the dog was really cute.' Cleo was bobbing her head about and it was making Regan dizzy.

'Thank you . . . I think.'

'Aren't you at work?' asked Cleo.

'Yeah. But it's slow . . . I mean boring.' It was difficult having a conversation when she felt she couldn't burden Cleo with all her problems. Cleo would worry.

'You should look for something else.'

'Yeah. I should. I thought about a market stall,' said Regan, with a tip of her head.

'Hard work. And it'd be cold in winter, being outside. But I could see you with a money belt doing "roll up, roll up, get your coconuts here!"' said Cleo with a giggle.

'I said market stall, not big top.' But Regan was laughing too. She needed to get herself a money belt, then maybe she'd feel more like she knew what she was doing. 'How are you?' she asked.

'I'm actually okay.' There was surprise in Cleo's words. 'I've done a couple of exhibitions with nervous students, but it's great to see the joy in them when they study the paintings. I think helping them has helped me, if that makes sense. And of course, they're wowed by the celebrities that show up and all the posh food they lay on.'

'But all that luxury and being treated like a princess

must be tough.' Regan studied her broken nails, damaged from moving around boxes of jam.

'It's not as glamorous as you think. I was—'

'Sorry, gotta go, there's a customer. I mean colleague. Anyway. Bye.' Regan hastily ended the call, scurried back to her stall and stood to attention.

An elderly woman with a stick had moved slowly through the stalls and was passing hers. Regan spied a chance. 'Good morning,' she said, trying to muster her inner professional (she hoped there was one in there somewhere, but they were exceptionally well hidden). The woman paused, possibly more to catch her breath than because of Regan. She seemed to be judging whether it was worth the effort of veering off course.

'Home-made jam. Lots of different flavours,' said Regan, hearing how dull it sounded. 'Melon and ginger?' she offered.

The lady wrinkled her nose, but was still squinting from her position a few feet away. Regan momentarily considered dragging her stall over in her desperation to make her first sale. 'Any damson?' asked the old lady.

Damson? What was that? Someone from a fairytale? Oh, no – that was damsel. 'No. Sorry.'

'Shame. You don't get damson jam these days.' It seemed to take an effort to get the lady going again. She meandered her way out of the market. Regan watched her only potential customer disappear, and with her, a little bit of hope.

Malcolm appeared about an hour later with a much-needed coffee. He handed it over.

'Thanks, I need this.'

'I did wonder if you'd changed your mind when you weren't on the stall near me.'

'I got ousted by a dragon.'

He smiled and eagerly scanned her stall. 'How many jars have you sold then?'

'None. Zilch. Nada. Bugger all.'

'Ah. First day is always tough. It'll get better. I promise,' he said, with an encouraging smile.

Regan cupped her mug with both hands, more for comfort than for warmth. 'I'm not so sure. There's not been a whiff of interest.'

'If it makes you feel any better, the Dragon has only sold one ornament.'

'Yeah, it does a little. Thanks.' Regan sipped her coffee.

There were a few more visits from other stallholders during the day; they wished her luck, but she got the distinct impression they were checking her out, which was understandable. A gruff bloke who insisted on telling her about every plant he stocked on his gardening stall seemed very surprised she'd been allowed to set up at all.

'Ken won't like it,' he said. Her blank expression did its job of conveying her lack of understanding. 'The honey man.' He pointed in the general direction of one of the permanent units that sat around the outside edge of the market. 'Been here years, he has. You'll be killing his business.'

'Not on what I've sold today, I won't. I've not made a single sale.'

'Oh, that's good then,' he said, with a jolly nod and returned to his stall. Regan felt another trickle of optimism evaporate. When the first people began packing up she decided to do the same. Her back ached, her feet were throbbing and she was thoroughly fed up.

She lugged a box down to Malcolm, and as she plodded

back to get the next one she was just in time to see someone grab a jar and run off. 'Hey!' she shouted, and everyone except the thief turned around. He sprinted out of the market, hurdling a pile of cushions as he made his escape. Regan couldn't be bothered to give chase. Today had been a total disaster, from start to thieving finish.

Malcolm helped her lug her heavy boxes to the café, where she slumped in the corner like a weary traveller.

Penny hurried over with a large coffee and flipped the sign to closed. 'How was your first day in charge of your own business empire?' She slid into the seat opposite and waited expectantly.

'Total and utter shit,' said Regan, and she relayed the catalogue of issues that had thwarted her day. Penny listened attentively, making sympathetic noises in the right places and shocked faces when she got to the bit about the thief.

'Look on the positive side,' said Penny, when she'd finished.

Regan scrunched up her features. 'There is no positive side. If there is, it's bloody well camouflaged, because I can't see it.' Regan was thoroughly glum.

'Well,' said Penny, 'at least someone wanted a jar of your jam, even if they weren't prepared to pay for it.'

Regan paused with her coffee at her lips. If that was the most positive thing Penny could find to say, it confirmed everything she was feeling. 'I've made a huge mistake.'

'You're not giving up after one day, are you?' Penny's tone was stern.

'No. I knew I wouldn't be putting Marks and Spencer out of business overnight, but I did expect to get rid of more jars.' Penny opened her mouth, but Regan continued.

'*Sell* more jars. Sell *something*. Maybe there is no market at all for unusual flavours of jam.'

'I blame the British,' said Penny.

'We're both British.'

'I know, and we're all stuck in our ways. We don't like change. We don't like things that are a bit different. We like things we can rely on, like . . .'

'Late trains and rain?' suggested Regan.

'Like pyjamas and toast and marmalade.' Penny froze.

Regan stared at her. 'Bloody marmalade. You're right. People like sodding boring marmalade. I'm doomed.' And she slumped back into the seat with dismay.

Chapter Twenty-Seven

Regan needed cheering up, and she knew precisely who could do it. She rang the vet's to check it was okay to visit, and half an hour later she skidded into the recently mopped waiting area and almost collided with a very large Saint Bernard. 'Out of the way, Holly!' said her owner. Regan righted herself, apologised to the dog and made her way to the desk. She was pleased to see the usual receptionist was having a day off. A kindly looking woman greeted her and, after checking the record, she showed Regan through to the back room where the animal pens were and told her the veterinary nurse would be through in a few minutes.

Elvis was lying in his cage all hunched up at the back, but the steady rise and fall of his side told her he was alive. 'Hiya mate,' said Regan, crouching down at the wire mesh. He opened his eyes but didn't move.

Instead of his usual overexuberant greeting, Elvis barely raised a bushy eyebrow. Regan flopped onto her knees. 'Elvis, what's wrong?'

Elvis's dark eyes studied her intently. He looked burdened with sorrow. It was like he knew what had happened to Kevin.

She felt for Elvis. It must be so confusing for him to have spent so long with the total freedom to roam, and then to find himself imprisoned twenty-four hours a day without his best friend. He'd gone from having constant company to being alone, with the obvious exception of the transient dogs that briefly occupied the other pens.

'Come on, Elvis. You need to get better,' said Regan, pushing her fingers through the cage. At last his tail thumped in acknowledgment. He looked desperately sorry for himself.

Deborah the veterinary nurse came in and joined Regan on the floor. 'How is he?' asked Regan.

'He's healing nicely, so we can start talking to the local rescue centres.' The nurse opened the pen, but Elvis didn't seem to want to come out. Regan reached in and stroked his head.

'Already?' Regan wasn't ready to let Elvis move on just yet, and he certainly didn't look well enough. She was worried by his lethargy. 'He doesn't seem his usual self,' she said.

'To be honest with you he's been like this for a couple of days. I think he's a bit down,' said the nurse.

'He's depressed?'

'Yeah, if you like. Some animals struggle in these sorts of situations.' She gave a sympathetic smile, but Regan was already worrying. She felt a strong sense of responsibility towards Elvis.

'That's not going to improve at the rescue centre if he's stuck there for ages.'

'Let's hope he gets chosen quickly.' The nurse patted Elvis and he twitched an ear.

He needed to cheer up a whole lot if someone was going to fall for the positive personality hidden inside.

But then, if he recovered fully, was his boisterous self too much for most homes? Regan surmised that somewhere in between was the sweet spot.

'You will let me know when he's moving to the rescue centre, won't you?' she asked, trying not to sound too pathetic. She knew it was what was best for Elvis, but she'd need to say a proper goodbye.

'Er, hopefully it'll be in the next day or so.' The nurse gave a wan smile. 'I'll give you a few minutes.'

Tears pricked at Regan's eyes. *Don't be daft*, she told herself. *This is the best thing for him*. She was in no position to offer him a permanent home – she didn't even have one for herself, let alone for a giant dog. This was his chance for a happy life in a nice home with a family who would love him. She looked into his big, sad eyes. She wanted to tell him everything was going to work out fine, but if she spoke she feared it would release the tears which were threatening to overflow. Elvis briefly stood up and flopped down again with an audible huff, this time with his head on Regan's knees. It was as if he knew this was goodbye, and it chipped away another piece from her shattered heart.

The next day was tough. No matter how hard Regan tried to focus on the stall, the lack of customers made her mind drift back to Elvis and how his big, sorrowful eyes had bored into her when she'd left him. She needed to focus on the now, but it was hard.

She had a tiny stool with her today; one from the studio, covered in paint splashes. Cleo was so neat in everything else, and yet she seemed to manage to get paint everywhere.

Regan stood and began trying to do the walking mindfully exercise. She managed to walk the length of her stall without thinking about Elvis, and only wobbled once. This was an improvement. In her periphery, someone meandered towards her stall. She prepared herself for them to ask where the loo was and rearranged her jars for the umpteenth time. She was fed up of thinking she had a potential customer approaching, only to be asked for the code for the toilets.

'Hiya,' said a familiar voice.

Just when she thought she'd reached rock bottom, some bastard introduced lower ground. Alex was standing a few safe feet away.

'Alex.' She kept it formal. It wasn't likely he was after jam.

'Is this what you're doing now?' He managed to make it sound like she was cleaning toilets. It irked her beyond reason.

'Yes. I am running my own business. Being my own boss. Calling all the shots . . .' She ran out of suitable clichéd phrases. 'How about you? Still kissing butts at BHB Healthcare?'

He looked amused. 'Yeah. I meant to tell you that you got me with the candied onion. Good one.'

That seemed such a long time ago, but she couldn't help her sense of pride at getting one over on him. 'Good of you to let me know.'

He stepped closer, but still looked afraid – she liked that. 'I feel so bad about everything, Regan. Can I buy you a drink sometime?'

'No, thanks. I'm fine.' She broke eye contact and straightened her sign. She looked past him as if she had a queue of customers but there was no one there.

'Right. I'd better go,' he said. He had the good grace to look embarrassed. 'Nice to see you.' She couldn't say the same, so she said nothing. He turned to look over his shoulder. 'What's with all the flowers on the crossing?' He pointed vaguely towards the Ditchling Road entrance.

'My friend Kevin was killed there.'

His expression changed. 'Oh. I'm so sorry.'

'You met him. You remember the lads beating up the homeless guy and you wouldn't help?'

'Er . . .'

'Remember?' She gave him her most challenging look. It made him whip his head back and walk straight into the fish trolley. He toppled slightly and saved himself by plunging a hand into the fish.

'Hey!' said the fish man. 'Get your hands off.' Alex scurried away shaking his wet cuff. That would stink for hours.

Regan glanced about. There were worse places to be. She tried a little mindful thought – she had plenty of time. What was good about the market? It was dry, and she had her own designated space – even if it wasn't the one she'd agreed. She shot a glare at Dragon Woman as she walked past, shaking her head as she went. It was sunny outside, and most importantly she didn't have to answer to anyone else. She let out a slow breath – things were okay. She was okay.

Glancing at the market entrance, Regan saw the old lady. Obviously Regan still didn't have damson jam, but with the speed this woman walked, she had ample opportunity to try to sell her something else. She picked up a jar of her most conservative offering and darted out from behind the stall.

Regan realised she'd made her move way too soon, and she was now stuck in no man's land holding a jar of jam. Poor woman, arthritic sloths could overtake her. She waited awkwardly for what seemed like an age.

'Is that damson jam?' asked the old lady, a hopeful look in her bespectacled eye.

'Er, no, it's rhubarb and ginger,' she ignored the old lady's disappointed twist of her lips, 'which is a very traditional flavour combination. All home-made.' She held the jar with a hand on the top and the bottom and smiled.

'Hmm.' The woman shuffled closer and read the label. 'It's not damson though, is it?'

'No, it's not,' she had to concede.

'Oh, well. Bye now.' It took her another three minutes to move past the stall.

Her day didn't get any better. Regan was stacking the last jars into a box and wondering how the hell she was going to get them back to the car when another stallholder appeared and introduced himself as Ken.

'Oh, you're the honey man,' she said. His face brightened. 'If you're worried about me killing your business then I wouldn't. I've had another crap day and I probably won't be back.' It was petulant, but it was how she felt – and if he was going to moan at her it would be the thing that would tip her over the edge.

Ken laughed like he had a front-row seat for comedy night. 'You'll hear "killing my business!" a lot. Along with "guess what management have done" and "watch out Romans, Boadicea's on the rampage again".' His good humour made her smile. 'It's a hard life on the market. One day up, another down. If you are serious about making it successful, you' – he pointed at her – 'have to be resilient.' He leaned a little closer. 'Are you serious?'

'Yes, I am. I've put hours into this already.' If she was honest she'd thought the hard bit was doing all the setup and learning how to make jam, but she was fast realising that wasn't the case.

'Good. Want some advice?' She nodded eagerly. 'Get to know the other stallholders. Lots of people come and go, so make it known you plan to stick around. Improve your signage.' They both stared at her A4 page bull-dog-clipped to the table – he had a point. '"Sticky Situations" is funny and it will intrigue people, but only if they can see the sign from a distance, so it needs to be much bigger. Do you have any jam samples?'

'I can't afford to give any away.'

'Come here a sec,' he said, and she followed him back to his stall.

A large rustic table had three tiers of neat jars of honey – probably about fifty jars in all, each one clearly labelled. Ken picked up a pot of what looked like wooden coffee stirrers. 'Here. Try some.'

She took a stick and perused the many jars. So many different flavours of honey; she had no idea. She'd thought honey was honey. A jar labelled *wildflower meadow* caught her eye. She dipped her stick in, picked up a tiny dribble of honey and popped it in her mouth. It tasted divine. Ken took the used stick off her. 'It's good, isn't it?' he asked, and she nodded eagerly. 'That one is a more delicate flavour. Would you like a small jar of that, or do you want to try something more intense? Or perhaps something a bit more exotic, like honey with cardamom, or chocolate and vanilla?'

She blinked a couple of times. 'Umm, well . . . ah . . .' Bloody hell, she'd lost money today – she couldn't go buying anything.

Ken dissolved into hysterics. 'I'm kidding with you. But that's how you get people to buy your stuff. I'm trying to show you the difference.' He pointed at his stall and then back at the sad sight of hers. The contrast was huge.

'That was really clever.' If she'd had the cash she would have bought a jar. The layout of his stall was enticing, and the big labels helped you find what you wanted. But tasting it was the clincher.

He nodded proudly. 'Years of practice.' He dropped the used stick in a bin. 'And one more thing. Listen to your customers: they might just give you an idea.'

Regan went back to her stall feeling like the day had no longer been a total waste of time. Mostly, but not totally. Maybe today wasn't the day she'd give up.

'Here you go,' said Jag, plonking down a large crate of red peppers. 'All yours if you want them.'

'I don't suppose you've got any damsons, have you?' she asked, the tiniest ray of optimism permeating the gloom.

As Regan was leaving the market she was pulled up short as, for the most fleeting of moments, she thought she saw Kevin. Malcolm came to join her where she was standing fixed to the pavement.

'Bernice will be on the warpath if she spots those shelters,' said Malcolm, pointing to where a couple of homeless people had set up tents on The Level. 'When they put them up near the market last year she rang the council every hour until someone came and took them away.'

'That's awful,' said Regan, unable to drag her gaze away from the person she could now clearly see didn't look much like Kevin at all. 'People need shelter. They need proper housing, but at least a tent keeps the worst of the weather off.'

'I agree, but Bernice worries it gives the wrong impression to people visiting Brighton.'

'Some people don't get that being homeless isn't a lifestyle choice,' replied Regan, at last pulling her eyes away.

'No car?' asked Malcolm.

'Yes, but it's parked a marathon away.'

'I can run you over,' he suggested.

'What?' asked Regan, her head snapping round at his turn of phrase.

He looked horrified at his own words. 'I'm so sorry. No. I didn't mean run you over. I meant drive you to wherever you left your car.' He looked mortified.

'It's okay. And thanks, that'd be great.'

Malcolm was kind enough to give her a lift in his battered little van back to her car. His had so many bumps and scrapes it almost made hers look smart. Despite being there six days a week, she figured he wasn't making a fortune. 'Malcolm, I've got an idea.'

'Oh dear. Does it involve me buying jam?'

'No . . . not exactly.' He shot a brief but worry-filled look across at his passenger.

'What do people put jam on?'

'Erm, toast?'

'Exactly. So if people came to my stall . . .'

'Which they don't,' he joked with a smile, which faded. 'Sorry.'

'That's okay. But when they *do* buy jam from me, I could point them at your stall and recommend which bread would make the perfect toast to go with the flavour they've picked.' Malcolm was looking sceptical but she continued undeterred. 'Like . . . "Ooh, pumpkin and vanilla jam goes really well with a seeded loaf. You should pop along to Malcolm's stall and if you show him that jar, he'll give you ten pence off.'" She said the last bit very fast.

Malcolm sucked in a breath so hard, she thought the steering wheel might go with it. 'Ten pence discount! Do you know what my profit margin is?'

'It was just a thought. We could do it in reverse. They buy a crusty white bloomer and you say "Balsamic strawberry jam goes lovely on that. If you take that loaf over to Sticky Situations she'll give you ten pence off a jar." *That* direction costs you nothing.'

'Hmm.' He stared straight ahead. 'How about I send them to you for a discount and, *if* the ones you send to me become regulars, I'll think about a discount. Deal?'

'Sure thing. Thanks, Malcolm – you're a star.' She was delighted with the thought that tomorrow he might send some people in her direction, even if it did mean a little loss of profit. Right now she had zero profit anyway.

He pulled over next to her car and put on his hazard lights. 'It's a good idea. You're thinking like a business owner. We'll start it tomorrow and see if we can't strong-arm a few folk in your direction.'

She didn't care how they got there, as long as they bought jam.

Chapter Twenty-Eight

Regan let herself in to Charlie's house and almost collided with him and a full mug of coffee. 'I've had a brilliant idea!'

'Hello, Reg. Hello, Charlie. How are you?' he said, shielding his mug.

She waved his pretend conversation away. 'No time for that. We need to save Elvis, and here's how we're going to do it. You are going to adopt him and—'

Charlie was shaking his head. 'I can't do that, Reg.'

Regan was affronted. 'Why not? You like him, don't you?'

'Yes. Of course I like him, but . . . I can't even commit to a magazine subscription right now, let alone the long-term care of an animal.'

Something squeezed her gut. 'Okay. I get that, but—'

'How about Penny?'

'Her mum's allergic.'

'I'm sure he'll find a good home.'

It was her turn to shake her head. 'I can't let him go. I'd keep him if I had my own place. How about you say you're the owner but really it would be me? He'd just be living temporarily with you.' She beamed a grin at him. Surely that was a clincher?

He dragged his bottom lip through his teeth. 'He's not house-trained.' They both glanced at Charlie's neat living room.

'Nor's Beanstalk, and you let him stay.' *Humour is always worth a go*, thought Regan. 'And he's hairier than Elvis too.'

'Beanstalk doesn't chew the furniture or pee on the carpet . . . apart from that one time. And he paid for it to be cleaned.'

'I'll train him.' Regan wasn't easily deterred. 'Elvis. Not Beanstalk.'

'You'll be working on the market. I'll be at the station. You can't leave him shut in here all day; he'd trash the place.'

There was a pause while they both thought. Inspiration struck, and Regan raised her hands. 'In the day I'll take him to the market.' She was bobbing up and down on her heels.

'What, and leave him here at night? Sorry, Reg, I know you're trying to help, but taking on a large dog right now isn't a good idea for you, me or Elvis.'

She stared at him trying hard not to pout. 'I disagree. Who else is going to take on a giant, untrained, hair-shedding mutt like him?'

'You're not really selling him.' He smiled, but she didn't.

'He has no-one else now that Kevin's gone.' She pulled back her shoulders. 'I won't let him down.' Charlie kept quiet and sipped his coffee. 'Right. Thanks for nothing.'

'Come on, Reg. I'm—'

She didn't hear anything else, because she marched out of the house and slammed the door. She hoped he'd be out later when she came back to make jam, or it might be slightly awkward.

* * *

Regan was thrilled to find that Elvis had not yet been collected by the rescue centre because they had just taken in a load of dogs from a recently discovered puppy farm. After a heartfelt plea from Regan, Deborah conceded that she clearly cared a lot about the dog, so she exercised her discretion and agreed Regan could take him. She felt she could argue that if Regan had said he was hers at the start there'd be no question about her taking him now. Regan made a donation to the veterinary hospital for as much as she could spare. Deborah gave her a run-through of his wound care and medication and handed over his vaccination and microchip records, and before she knew it, Elvis was officially hers.

Regan gave the records a brief scan. *Breed: Irish wolfhound*? Not a giant mongrel werewolf after all. She thanked everyone at the vet's and left with the dog plodding behind her on a second-hand lead that Deborah had conjured up from somewhere. Regan wasn't sure taking on Elvis was the smartest decision she'd ever made, but she was certain it was the right one. Although seeing him wearing his medical collar, looking like he'd speared a lampshade, did give her some doubts.

Elvis had his tail between his legs and his head down. 'Come on, Elvis. It'll be fun, you and me against the world,' she said, negotiating herself, the lead and him out of the vet's through the double-door affair. Elvis kept his head low – it wasn't a good sign. They stepped outside, and a fragrant breeze ruffled his fur. The change in Elvis was instant. Once his nose caught a whiff of fresh air, it was as if it breathed life into him. His head shot up, his ears pricked and his tail gave a cursory flick. The prisoner was now a free man.

'Elvis has left the building.' She gave a light tug on the

lead and he trotted after her; then he tried to gallop past, magnificently pulling her over and dragging her along the gravel. 'ELVIS!' she shouted, and he halted, turned and looked at her with a tilt of his head, which seemed to say, 'Why are you lying down?'

Regan dusted herself off and opened the passenger door of her car. Elvis sniffed inside, groaned and lay down on the gravel. She took off his medical recovery collar so negotiating getting inside would be easier for him, but he still refused to get in.

A woman with a French bulldog on a pink harness strolled over to the large, sleek Audi next to Regan's little Fiesta. The woman opened the Audi's back door. The dog hopped in and sat down without a word of command.

'That'll be us next week,' said Regan, with a confident nod. Elvis put his head between his paws – he didn't seem to agree.

Forty minutes later, Deborah was leaving for the day. She looked surprised to see Regan trying to drag Elvis into the back of the car.

'Having problems?'

Why did people ask bloody obvious questions? 'Just a bit,' said Regan, through a mouthful of fur. She spat it out.

Deborah came over, walked to the other side of the car, opened the other back door and held out a dog treat. Elvis trampled Regan in his attempt to get to the small morsel.

'Ow!' she rubbed at her chest. Right boob, direct hit – ouch. But the key thing was – Elvis was in the car. They shut the doors in unison. 'That was smart.'

'I always carry treats. Take care, now,' said Deborah, with a jolly wave.

Regan slumped against the car door, exhausted. A

sudden bang on the glass made her take off. Elvis barked his protest from the driver's seat and then leaned his paw on the horn. The elongated honk made the nurse look as she drove away, and Regan waved serenely like everything was completely normal.

It took a while to convince Elvis that he wasn't driving and eventually settle him in the back of the car. Well, part of him was in the back; his front half was wedged between the front seats, where he kept trying to chew the gear knob, despite Regan telling him repeatedly that it wasn't a ball on a stick. Twice she tried to change gear with his nose.

Getting him out of the car was far easier; he was keen to investigate new smells. Steering him in the right direction was somewhat trickier – Regan imagined it to be a lot like water-skiing on the pavement. She didn't want to let him off the lead in case he wandered off, but it would have been a whole lot easier than hanging on to it. She opened the door to the studio, and while she keyed in the alarm code Elvis trotted in to investigate.

Within seconds there was a crash, which was followed by what sounded like a helicopter in a box. She shut the door quickly. Elvis was humping her mattress with his head completely through a painted canvas. His face was now precisely where a nipple had once been. He was an actual right tit. Cleo was going to kill her and then feed her remains to the seagulls – and who could blame her?

Elvis tried to have a scratch and managed to make the canvas spin around his neck, hit an easel, which toppled and knocked over another canvas, which, in turn, clattered onto her stacked jam jars and knocked them to the floor. 'No, no, no!' Regan watched the domino effect in horror.

How could he do so much damage in under thirty seconds?

A text message popped up from Cleo. **Oscar rang me. Can you believe his cheek? Said he thought he'd had some sort of breakdown but was now fully recovered! He was surprised I was still in Japan. He must have been desperate to get hold of me because he said he'd been to the studio. He was so full of b*llshit.**

It made Regan smile that Cleo didn't even swear in text messages.

What did he want? Regan texted back.

He wants to focus on my future lol. He offered to meet me in Taiwan. He's seen some press articles about me attending events with Mr Yomoda's students and thought it was a PR stunt. I see now what an *rse he is. I told him I didn't need him and that my lawyer would be in touch about him being in breach of contract for abandoning me. The line went dead.

Regan texted back: **Well done you! You don't need him. You can do this on your own.**

Not sure about on my own but I can do it without Oscar.

It made Regan feel good to see the change in Cleo.

Go you! she texted.

I am looking forward to coming home and catching up with you and all your news. Regan stared at the text and the messy studio; she couldn't really say the same.

Regan woke the next morning to the sensation she'd often heard heart attack victims describe, like having an elephant sitting on their chest. In her case, it was a snoring Irish wolfhound whose doggy breath could wilt a stone rose.

'Eurch, Elvis! Gerroff.' She wriggled from underneath him. Elvis sat up and began merrily licking his doggy nether region. She popped his medical collar back on and he shook his head about in protest.

Dilemma number one – she usually went to the gym first thing for a mini workout and shower. There was only one thing for it. She lured Elvis into the car with a beef and onion crisp, after her first attempt using a banana failed. She popped round to her dad's, and as she was going up the steps she remembered that she'd not called ahead. She knocked on the door anyway and busied herself trying somehow to get Elvis to sit so he didn't look quite so imposing. With his medical cone, he looked like a furry standard lamp sitting next to her.

A shadow appeared at the door moments before her father opened it.

Graham was wearing his usual cardigan and dark trousers, but today he had the addition of a surgical collar. Regan looked from her father to the dog and back again. The resemblance was uncanny. 'I don't have a lot of time, but this is Elvis. He's your grand-dog.' She gave her best goofy, but hopefully loveable, smile. 'And I need to use your shower because there's a problem with Cleo's. Please.'

Graham blinked several times in quick succession. 'Does it have fleas?'

'No, *he* doesn't. He's Kevin's dog . . . well, mine now.'

'Oh. I see. All right. Come in.' Graham stood well back as they passed.

'What happened to your neck?' asked Regan, a little concerned.

Graham seemed to jolt at the question. 'Nothing.'

'You're wearing a surgical collar. It can't be nothing.' She looked around for where to put Elvis. There was nowhere ideal. He was already using up a large amount of the space.

'Minor . . . um . . . accident. Took a tumble. Grazed my elbow and did something to my neck.' Graham rubbed his elbow.

'Be careful. You're not as young as you once were.' She'd bet anything Tarty Tara had something to do with his injuries; she shuddered and tried to block the X-rated image that popped unwelcomingly into her mind. 'Stay,' she told Elvis, showing him the palm of her hand, more in an attempt to show her dad she was in control. Elvis licked it.

She only had time for a super-quick shower and hair wash, but it was better than not having one at all, especially as she'd been used as a dog bed for most of the night. She dried herself off and checked her wet hair in the mirror. She noted the make-up smeared on the hand towel by the basin. Evidence that Tarty Tara had been here recently; though, thankfully, she didn't seem to be about this morning.

When she heard growling, she threw on her clothes and hurried out of the bathroom to find Elvis hanging on to her father's much prized 1994 Manchester United scarf. It was Graham who was doing the growling. Elvis was very happy playing tug of war.

'It's eating my scarf!'

'*He's* . . . oh, never mind. Elvis, drop it.' She didn't know why she was bothering; there was no way he was letting go without a much better incentive. She went to the fridge and returned with a sausage roll. Elvis let go in a heartbeat, and Graham tumbled backwards, the victor.

'You all right?' she asked.

'I think so.' He sat up and checked his scarf. 'Yes. It's

okay. I've recently taken it out of the back of the car because the sun was fading it, but—'

'Not the scarf. Your neck.'

'Oh, yes. Hey, that sausage roll was for my lunch!'

Regan knew it was time to leave. This was far too much to handle before breakfast.

Chapter Twenty-Nine

Regan felt like she was trying to solve a puzzle – how was she meant to deposit a box of jam *and* Elvis at the market? She pulled up at the coffee shop and shut the door quickly so Elvis was trapped in the car. Regan ferried the first box of jam inside, but by the time she got back, the car was rocking like a troop of demon monkeys had invaded it. There was so much fur flying around the inside of the car it looked like a giant snow globe. Elvis didn't like being left; but then he had spent all his time outside with Kevin, so it was understandable.

Regan ferried in the rest of the jam and moved the car, then she and Elvis walked back to collect the jam from the café. Elvis switched between walking calmly at her side and trying to yank her arm out of its socket when he spotted anything he had to investigate. It was Saturday and it felt odd not going to Mantra, but the stall now had to come first. Her mind drifted off to Charlie. He was becoming less of a presence in her life and she didn't like it. They'd not spoken since the argument over Elvis.

'The Dragon isn't here today,' called Malcolm, pointing to the nearby stall when they entered the market. Elvis's nose went into overdrive, and Regan tried to tug him in Malcolm's direction. Apparently there were far too many interesting smells, so he had to stop every other centimetre to check them out. She left Elvis with Malcolm trying to teach him to give his paw on command and went to retrieve her jam from the café.

She eventually got the stall set up and Elvis settled down underneath it. She popped the loop of his lead under the leg of the stall so he didn't wander off, because he was still meant to be resting after his operation – although everything was going very well in that regard. Regan had no stool today, because she couldn't manage it with everything else. She had planned to do new signs for her stall at the library, but she'd not got around to it what with everything else, and she started to make a few notes of what she needed to do. Somehow the market stall had slipped down the list, and she needed to put it firmly back at the top. A few people glanced over as they walked through the market – it was a popular cut-through first thing in the morning – but, unfortunately, nobody stopped.

A few hours in, she left Malcolm minding the stall and Elvis while she went to get drinks from Penny. Along with two coffees, and milk for Elvis, she'd also grabbed a spare paper cup and a handful of coffee stirrers because she was going to offer people a taste of the jam like Ken had suggested. She was on her way back when she saw a hooded youth take a jar of jam from the edge of her stall and slip it in his pocket. With his head down he walked towards her. Regan stopped in front of him and blocked his path.

'You've got something of mine.' She sounded a lot calmer than she felt.

His head snapped up and his eyes pinged wide when

he realised who she was. He shoved her hard in the chest, sending the hot coffee all over both of them.

'Shit!' shouted Regan, making a grab for his hoodie and holding on. On her shout, Elvis started barking and tried to run to her aid, but unfortunately he had the minor encumbrance of a market stall attached to his lead. Despite this he kept going anyway.

'No!' yelled Regan, letting go of the youth and running back towards Elvis, who looked like a budget version of Santa's sleigh dragging the red-and-white cloth-clad stall behind him. Jars of jam toppled off the stall in all directions and shattered around him. 'Sit!' she yelled, but he was intent on getting to her. She raced up to him and he greeted her happily. His tail was wagging at high speed. He sniffed at her coffee- and milk-soaked jumper; his bum hit the ground and he stared up at her hopefully. Regan surveyed the devastation, with her obedient-looking dog, who was totally oblivious, sitting in the middle of it. When she thought it couldn't get any worse, Bernice came thundering towards them.

'What on earth is going on?' boomed Bernice.

Regan steeled herself. 'There was a thief, and—'

'Did he try to make off with your stall?' She was staring wide-eyed at the skewed stall and shattered jars. Elvis wagged his tail in welcome.

'No, just one jar, but—'

'I take it this thing isn't the thief?' she pointed at Elvis.

Regan unhooked his lead. 'No, this is my dog, Elvis, and the thief was the same little scrote as before. All this mess is *his* fault. We need to call the police so they can add it to the list of charges against him.'

Bernice shook her head. 'We've dropped the previous charges.'

'You've done what?' The level of challenge in Regan's voice even surprised her. She noted Malcolm pull back his head in shock.

Bernice's eyes bore an icy glint. 'He agreed to attend a diploma course in plumbing and straighten himself out, and—'

'Well, that's not exactly going to plan now, is it? He's just stolen something else!' Regan tried hard not to yell.

'People don't change overnight—'

'Or at all,' snapped Regan. She was furious. Bernice and her softly, softly approach meant the youth would never face any charges for anything – including what he'd done to Kevin. 'You can't just—'

'I think this discussion is over. And you have some clearing up to do,' said Bernice, infuriating Regan further. 'Oh, and how much longer are those dead flowers going to litter the pedestrian crossing?' Bernice called as she walked away.

'Why, you—'

Malcolm grabbed Regan and restrained her long enough for Bernice to get a safe distance away. 'You okay?' he asked, letting Regan go. She clamped her jaw together to stop the emotion overpowering her and gave him a brief nod of reply. 'Don't let her wind you up.' She knew he was right. Malcolm silently picked up a broom and started to sweep up the glass.

With Malcolm's help, things were back to some form of normality quite quickly. She'd checked Elvis's paws multiple times for any signs of broken glass but he seemed to have avoided it all. She stood behind her pitiful-looking stall, which now only had the six remaining jars that had survived being towed across the market by Elvis. She should probably have packed up and gone home, but her stubborn streak wouldn't let her.

The little old lady made her way slowly through the stalls. 'Ooh, you've sold a lot today,' she said, with a cheery wave. Regan didn't have the heart to tell her.

After she'd packed up her stall, which took a lot less time than usual, Regan really needed to replenish her jam stocks – she had gone from overrun with the stuff to not much at all, thanks to Elvis inventing the first mobile market stall – but she had a shift booked with the hedgehogs, so jam would have to wait. She'd made a commitment to Mrs Tiggy-Winkle; and it may have been the name, but she couldn't bring herself to be the person who stood Mrs Tiggy-Winkle up.

She was fast discovering that being a dog owner was a full-time job. She literally couldn't leave Elvis for a minute. She drove over to Hove and decided that someone like Mrs Tiggy-Winkle must be an animal lover and would surely understand her dilemma with Elvis. She daren't leave him in the car because he'd taken to chewing the headrests – chewing stuff appeared to be his favourite pastime.

Mrs Tiggy-Winkle – or Philistia, as she reminded Regan – was very understanding, and even had some top tips for her on how to train Elvis. Because he was so food orientated – Regan took this to mean he ate anything that wasn't nailed down – she suggested that Regan could use his dry food as a reward mechanism, rather than giving it to him all at once in a bowl for no other reason than it was dinner time. This made perfect sense, and Regan vowed to give it a go from tomorrow. While they were chatting, Elvis was quiet, which always meant trouble: on this occasion it transpired he had been chomping his way through a large bag of hedgehog food. Regan apologised, but Philistia didn't seem too worried, blaming herself for leaving the bag open. Philistia shooed Elvis outside and let him have the run of the garden, where he trotted around cocking his leg on every plant. It kept him occupied and thoroughly happy.

Regan set to work on cleaning out the hedgehog cages as instructed. It wasn't taxing, but it was helping, and that mattered to her. Philistia disappeared to answer her front door, and Regan watched as Charlie came into the garden and did a double take when Elvis barrelled up to him.

What was Charlie doing here?

They both looked at each other through the warped glass of the hedgehog cabin. He still looked handsome, even when the glass made his face all wobbly. Charlie's troubled expression changed when Philistia appeared and ushered him inside the shed.

'Hiya,' said Regan, giving him an odd wave – it was like someone had dialled up her awkwardness setting and now she wasn't sure what to do with her hands.

'You got the dog then.'

'Good spot.' She couldn't help it.

'I'm sorry I couldn't take him, but I'm glad you've worked something out.'

Regan pulled a face; she couldn't let him think that everything was rosy. 'We're both living at the studio and Cleo is back in five days. So you were right, it wasn't a good decision; but I really had no choice.' Charlie opened his mouth, but then seemed to change his mind. 'Anyway,' she continued. 'Something will come up. It always does.' She tried to sound hopeful, although voicing the situation did send a mild panic through her now. She wasn't making any money on the market and she was about to be made homeless again, and this time she had a giant dog in tow – she was going to end up living on the streets like Kevin. In fact, exactly like Kevin; because now she had Elvis too.

'Are we okay?' he asked. He was studying her closely.

'Yeah. You're forgiven.' How could she not forgive Charlie? Those eyes, that face – he was all very forgivable. 'I didn't expect to see you here, but it's a nice surprise . . . for the hedgehogs.' She didn't want to get too mushy.

'I figured if you're volunteering here, they'd need all the help they could get,' said Charlie, lifting down a cage.

She stuck her tongue out at him and tried to ignore the sight outside of Elvis attempting to hump a garden gnome.

That evening, she had her head down and so did Elvis as they walked along the seafront. It had been good to see Charlie; it always was. It was always bittersweet: the more she saw him, the more she wanted to see him . . . and snog his face off . . . and drag him to bed. She realised she wasn't a lot different to Elvis, with his 'taste it, hump it' approach to the world.

Up ahead she heard the unique laugh of Tarty Tara – a sound like someone strangling a hysterical hyena. There was nowhere to escape to, but thankfully the light was fading. Regan cast a quick glance at the shadowy figures approaching. Tara was walking arm in arm with another woman. Regan kept her head down. Elvis pulled at the lead as the women approached, and she did her best to yank him back. The older woman lurched away looking startled – or was that just her over-the-top make-up? 'Sorry,' said Regan, hoping Tara didn't recognise her, because she wanted to avoid any awkward conversations.

They carried on in their separate directions and Regan heaved a sigh of relief.

Her phone lit up and she answered the FaceTime from Cleo. 'Hi, how's things?' asked Regan, safe in the knowledge that a background of Brighton seafront gave no hint of her deceptions.

'Where are you?' asked Cleo, who seemed to be in a car.

'I am walking my dog,' said Regan, proudly. She angled the phone for Cleo to see Elvis, who was still straining to get a look at Tarty Tara and her friend.

'Oh, wow. What a cutie.' Cleo seemed genuinely pleased, which was good. 'You must have zoomed in because he looks ridiculously huge.'

'Well . . . he's definitely not handbag sized.'

'Anyway. I've got a surprise . . .' Cleo left an ominous pause. 'I've decided not to go to Taiwan so I'm home!'

Regan almost dropped the phone. 'Home! Where? What? How? Home?'

Cleo laughed. 'I knew you'd be pleased.' How the hell did she interpret this level of stunned panic as pleased?

'When you say *home . . .*' *Please don't go to the studio*, she thought.

'My flat is still occupied so I'm checking in to the Grand Hotel.' Regan breathed a tiny sigh of relief. 'I'm popping to the studio first, and then—'

'Oh, no, no, no . . .' Regan was panicking. Cleo was looking alarmed.

Regan started to speedwalk and an excited Elvis lolloped alongside her. She needed a reason to stop Cleo going to the studio. 'I'm not far from the Grand. Meet me there,' said Regan, trying to cross her fingers and nearly dropping the phone.

'I thought I'd best check the studio because—'

'The studio is fine,' cut in Regan. 'Better than fine. No need to check. I've been . . . um . . . keeping a regular eye on it for you.'

'Okay. Great. Thank you. I'll see you at the Grand in about twenty minutes then?'

'Perfect,' said Regan, slowing to a walk and ending the call. At least that bought her some much-needed thinking time. Although all she was thinking right now was *Shiiiiiiit!*

She had twenty minutes to come up with something resembling an explanation as to why Cleo's studio was a temporary squat and dog rescue.

Chapter Thirty

Elvis stopped to water the railings, so Regan paused and looked out to sea. There was something soothing about the ocean, but it wasn't having its usual magical calming effect, which she needed right now.

She wandered along to the Grand Hotel and her stomach growled, reminding her that she hadn't eaten. Elvis was probably okay, having munched a year's supply of hedgehog food.

Regan stood outside the hotel and watched the taxis and posh cars pull into the semicircular drop-off zone. The doorman watched her and Elvis closely. At last a large black car glided in, and Cleo waved from the back seat. Regan still didn't have a coherent explanation for her. She'd considered elaborate stories about burglars, travellers and a swarm of cockroaches, but they were all too far-fetched. And in her heart of hearts, she knew her friend deserved the truth, however embarrassing that may be.

Cleo flung herself out of the car and into Regan's arms, making Elvis bark excitedly. It was so good to see her again. Unexpected emotion made Regan give herself a mental shake. She'd been through a lot over the last few weeks, and doing it without her best friend by her side had made it doubly difficult. Above all else, it was wonderful to have Cleo home.

'Look at you,' said Cleo, holding Regan at arm's length like a proud auntie. 'I'd almost forgotten what you look like.'

'No, you hadn't. And look at *you*. Still pale and interesting.'

Elvis pawed at Cleo's expensive-looking dress, which wasn't great, but at least he wasn't chewing, peeing on or humping it, so it was a massive result in Regan's book.

'And who is this?' said Cleo, making a fuss of him.

'This is Elvis.'

'Great name. Irish wolfhound?'

'Yes. Yes, he is.' Regan was relieved that Cleo had taken to him – maybe it would soften the blow about the trashed canvas.

'Good luck, Elvis,' said Cleo, addressing the dog directly. 'She's never managed to keep a pot plant alive until now, so you're a real test.'

Regan frowned at the implication. 'Hey . . . some cacti are sensitive.'

The chauffeur appeared at Cleo's side. 'I've left your bags at reception, Miss Marchant. And the doorman says the dog is welcome inside.'

They all looked up to see the doorman tip his head at them. *Today is full of surprises*, thought Regan.

Inside, Regan found that the Grand truly was dog friendly. Elvis was welcomed by staff like a movie star, which he of course lapped up. They settled in the lounge, and Cleo passed Regan a menu. 'On me,' she said.

Regan scanned the food choices greedily. She hadn't eaten out for so long. Elvis crashed out under the table, allowing the women to catch up over dinner. Cleo filled

Regan in on the dramas of Japan and Oscar and her decision not to do the Taiwan leg of her tour. Regan nodded and oohed in the right places. Even Cleo's tales of disaster were glamorous.

'Now, tell me what you've been up to.' Cleo leaned forward expectantly. 'Oh, and him.' She nodded towards Elvis, who was twitching in his sleep. 'He's adorable.'

'Well, basically, if he can't eat it or shag it, he pees on it.'

'I've known men like that,' said Cleo.

'Me too.'

'And what about the whole Jarvis, job, fireman thing?' Cleo's eyes were bright.

Regan thought the world of Cleo, and seeing the hopeful innocence in her eyes, she knew once and for all that she couldn't lie to her. 'Right, well get comfy because I've a shitload of crap to update you on.' Cleo's eyes widened but she remained intrigued. 'And there's bits of this that you're really not going to like.' This time it was Cleo's turn to make noises in the right places – although hers were mainly *ouch* sounds and wincing. She hugged her and they both shed a tear when Regan retold the night of the hit and run.

'So to conclude,' said Regan, 'I am homeless, Elvis is orphaned *and* homeless, and we're squatting in the studio. For which I am genuinely sorry.' Regan felt wretched. She knew she'd let herself down and that she'd deceived Cleo, which was the worst thing.

Cleo pursed her lips, and Regan waited for the bollocking she knew would come – it would be a civilised bollocking, but it would be a bollocking all the same.

'It's fine,' said Cleo, at last.

'Fine?'

Cleo nodded. 'I can't say I'm thrilled, but if I'd been here I could have helped you, and I wasn't, so . . .'

Regan didn't let her have any time to reconsider. 'You're the best,' she said, flinging her arms around her friend.

'And so are you,' said Cleo, hugging her back tightly.

Cleo insisted that Regan stayed at the Grand for the night, because she was a little concerned about breaking the terms of the studio's tenancy agreement. She still wanted to keep it on so she had somewhere to paint when the mood took her. They had connecting rooms, and after the initial excitement of having a toilet to drink out of, Elvis had settled down on the end of Regan's bed and he and Regan had both had a blissful night's sleep.

As Elvis wasn't allowed in the main restaurant, they did a relay with him at breakfast. Regan took him for a walk while Cleo had her granola, and then Cleo sat with him in the lounge while Regan ate hers, although she spent considerably longer at the buffet than Cleo had. Afterwards, Regan joined them, flopped into a nearby chair and rubbed her full stomach. 'Everyone should start the day with a five-course breakfast,' she said, checking her watch. Cleo didn't comment. 'I need to get going and set up the stall.'

'Great. I'll come,' said Cleo, getting to her feet.

Regan chuckled. 'Nah, you don't want to do that.'

'I do. I'm interested . . . and I've missed you.'

'I've missed you too, but I don't want to come to work with you.' Regan thought the world of Cleo, but she simply couldn't imagine her behind a market stall. It would be like the Queen working in McDonald's.

'But I can help . . . work the stall? Is that what you say? It's been a while since I've watched *EastEnders*.'

'And that's your only experience of markets?'

'Pretty much.' Cleo shrugged, looking apologetic.

'I don't have any customers, so there is literally nothing to do there. But I am working on that.'

Cleo put on her best hurt face. 'Then I'll mope around the studio all day. Alone. Being lonely.'

'Look. The studio is . . . let's just say it's not quite how you left it. After work I'll go round and tidy it up and move out.'

Cleo looked concerned. 'Move where?'

Regan pointed a finger emphatically. 'That is a bloody good question. I have no idea. But I'm still moving out.'

'Move in here.' Cleo splayed out her arms in a sweeping gesture. 'It would be almost like a holiday.'

Regan laughed, and then seeing that Cleo was serious, she stopped and leaned forward. 'Cleo, you are the sweetest person, but I can't afford to stay—'

'But I can.'

'And that's kind of you, but I need to do this on my own.' Regan wobbled her head. 'Well, as much as I can. Okay?'

Cleo pouted. 'Okay. But I still want to see the stall, and I would really like to help. Please let me?' Her voice was pleading, but that frequently worked on Regan's stubborn streak.

'I think you'll be bored, but if you really want to . . .'

'I do. And if I get in the way, you can tell me to butt out. Deal?'

Regan smiled. 'Yeah. Deal.' And Elvis barked his approval.

It was lovely to have Cleo back for many reasons, but especially because she was majorly enthusiastic about the market stall. Cleo was like a mother hen and waxed lyrical about virtually every stall in the market; it buoyed Regan a little, which she very much needed. With the lack of sales and the numerous disasters, her excitement had waned considerably.

She did have one reason to feel more positive. Malcolm had fully embraced the discount scheme she'd dreamed up and was highlighting it to his customers. Whilst she hadn't been swamped by people, there had been a few who had come over to try some jams. She'd even sold two jars, which felt like a huge achievement.

Regan and Malcolm covered each other's stalls for breaks, so she was able to sneak away with Cleo to the café for a quick sandwich, as long as they sat outside with Elvis and he didn't wee on anything.

Penny brought their lunch out on a tray so she could join them, and Regan did the introductions. She was still quite full from her mammoth breakfast, but that didn't stop her having lunch.

'Are you vegetarian?' asked Penny, passing Cleo the Mexican bean wrap.

'Yeah, I'd like to be vegan but I can't seem to give up cheese.'

'Nor me,' said Penny, sliding into the seat next to Cleo.

There followed a lot of veggie chatter while Regan tucked in to her sausage and bacon baguette. Penny and Cleo nattered like old friends, and it was nice to see – but Regan was keen to tap into Cleo's talents now she was home.

'Cleo . . .' She began, and Cleo twisted to look at her as if she'd completely forgotten she was there. 'Are you still up for helping me with the business?'

'Of course. Anything.'

'Signage. My signs are rubbish. Could you do something more professional?'

'I'd love to,' she said to Regan before turning back to Penny. 'I'm a bit arty,' she explained.

'Understatement,' said Regan, through a pretend cough. 'She's the famous artist whose studio I've been living in.'

Penny looked suitably impressed. The conversation veered off into the world of art, which Penny seemed to be quite knowledgeable about. After another five minutes of feeling like she was invisible, Regan arranged to meet Cleo at the studio when she finished at the market and then headed back to the stall with Elvis. She glanced back as she crossed the road to see Penny and Cleo were still deep in conversation.

The afternoon was erratic, but thanks to more referrals from Malcolm she sold another two jars of jam and her first jar of chutney. She was busy jotting down options for where to stay for the night when she became aware of someone approaching. It was like a cloud passing in front of the sun when Beanstalk loomed over the stall, but his beaming grin made up for the lack of light. 'Hiya, Reg. How's it going?'

'Good, thanks.' And today it actually was. Today she felt like she was starting to get a feel for what being a stallholder meant. Taking cash and handing over her own product had filled her with pride and, along with Cleo's positivity, it had renewed her enthusiasm.

'We need a favour . . .' She looked at him standing there apparently alone. He stepped to the side to reveal a sheepish Charlie, lurking behind him.

'Oh. Hi.' It was like being a teenager again. She turned

her attention back to Beanstalk – it was far easier to concentrate on him. 'Sure. What's the favour?'

'The fire station is getting an aerial appliance. I've been put forward to fly to the factory in Germany and learn how to use it and how to train the others,' said Beanstalk.

'Congratulations,' said Regan. She figured the puffed-out chest meant Beanstalk was quite pleased.

'Thanks.' He grinned. 'Anyway, I'll be away for three weeks and my flight's on Monday.' He was looking at her hopefully. Charlie was studying the ground. 'And you see, Charlie would be on his own . . .'

'This is not necessary,' said Charlie, his expression a mixture of embarrassment and irritation. 'Beanstalk has been on lots of night shifts recently and look, I'm still here.'

Beanstalk turned to Charlie. 'Do you think I like leaving you?'

Charlie shrugged. 'I'm only saying that you're out a lot.'

Beanstalk looked affronted. 'I work. What am I supposed to do?'

'I don't know. I'm just saying we could go out together more.'

'I'm tired after night shift,' said Beanstalk, rubbing his face. They reminded Regan of a married couple.

'You're always tired.'

'How many times do I have to apologise for that?' Beanstalk threw up his hands.

'We used to do more stuff together before you moved in.' Charlie studied his feet.

'After Germany, I'll make more time. And when I'm back on the standard shift pattern I won't be as tired. Okay?' said Beanstalk.

'I guess.' Charlie shrugged.

Regan cleared her throat to remind them she was still there, and they both virtually stood to attention. 'What's the favour, exactly?' she asked.

'Sorry,' said Beanstalk. 'Would you be able to move in to Charlie's for three weeks just to . . . you know . . . keep an eye on him.'

'In case I die,' said Charlie, bluntly.

'I'd love to,' said Regan almost at the same time, making her sound rather callous. 'I mean . . . You've helped me out. So it's only putting us square.'

'You're a star.' Beanstalk leaned over the stall to hug her, and she feared the whole thing would collapse like matchsticks. She looked at Charlie. That was not the face of a man happy about his new lodger. 'You can move in when you like,' added Beanstalk.

'Great! I'll be round later,' said Regan.

Charlie leaned forward. 'You sure you're okay with this?'

'Yeah. It's perfect.' She was going to be homeless in a few hours, so things couldn't have worked out better from her perspective.

'Is it? Three weeks in a house . . . together. When we're not . . . together.' Charlie was frowning hard.

'Ah, right. I see what you mean.'

Maybe this was something else she should have thought through.

A little while later, Regan was rearranging her jars when she saw two police officers walk into the market. She made eye contact and they headed towards her. 'Can you tell us where we'll find Bernice Keegan?'

'Better than that; I'll take you.' Regan shot from behind her stall, giving Malcolm the nod to watch her stuff, and led the way to the office. If they had news about the youth, she wanted to be first to know. She marched them through the market, aware that others were watching.

Regan knocked on the glass office door. Bernice looked up and beckoned them in.

'Er, thanks,' said the policewoman, trying to keep Regan on the other side as she tried to shut the door.

'If it's about the thefts, I was one of the stallholders who lost stuff,' said Regan, wedged in the doorway.

'It's not,' said the male officer, putting a little pressure on the door; but Regan stayed put.

'Well, if it's about Kevin being beaten up by those kids, I should definitely be here, because I was his friend – and that is his dog.' She pointed back to where Elvis was doing an impression of a hairy rug. 'And I have a few theories about who might have killed him.'

Something passed between the police officers, and Regan's interest was piqued. 'It's a private matter,' said the male officer, giving Regan's foot a nudge and successfully shutting the door with her firmly on the other side.

She wondered what the private matter was that they needed to see Bernice about. Bernice wasn't the sharing kind, so unless they carted her off in handcuffs she'd probably never know. She wandered back to her stall.

Regan was packing up when the male police officer appeared. 'Miss Corsetti, would you mind joining us in the office?' he asked.

She looked at Malcolm, who with a tip of his head said he would watch the stall again. This was weird. Why would they want her if it wasn't to do with the thief or Kevin? *Ooh, maybe they are arresting Bernice and I need to lock up the market*, she thought, and she quickened her stride behind the policeman. When they reached the office, the blinds were down and an uneasy feeling settled over

Regan. She was waved inside where Bernice was dabbing her eyes with a tissue, clearly very upset.

'What's wrong?' asked Regan, not feeling that she knew Bernice well enough to give her a hug.

'Shall I explain?' asked the female officer, and Bernice nodded.

'Sadly, we've just delivered the very sad news that Miss Keegan's brother has died.'

'Oh, I'm so sorry,' said Regan, moving round to try to comfort Bernice – although it felt mightily uncomfortable, since neither woman had been in any way close before. Regan gingerly patted Bernice's arm.

Bernice looked up at the policewoman. 'You need to explain who my brother was,' she said, blowing her nose. Bernice gave Regan a meaningful look, but Regan had no idea what she was trying to convey.

The male officer cleared his throat. 'The gentleman who died was Dale Keegan.' He was looking at Regan like this should mean something to her. She gave a tiny shake of her head to indicate she had no idea what he was trying to tell her. 'He was known in the Navy and locally by his nickname, Kevin.'

Chapter Thirty-One

Regan couldn't imagine how Bernice was feeling. To find out your brother was dead was one shock, but to find out he had been living rough just a few metres away was something else. Regan was wrung out – she thought she'd cried all her tears for Kevin, but apparently she hadn't. In the last hour, she and Bernice had set each other off a few times. After the police had taken some details and left, Malcolm had got them some drinks and Bernice had called her uncle, who was coming to pick her up so she had some company for the weekend. The women sat silently drinking their coffees whilst they waited for him to arrive.

Elvis was keeping them company and had fallen asleep stretched out across Bernice's feet – something Regan was sure she would have fiercely objected to an hour ago, but everything had changed, and Bernice was now viewing the hairy creature in a very different light.

'I thought my brother was living a happy life in New Zealand,' said Bernice. 'That's what my parents had told me. Always trying to protect me. When I found no details after they died I tried to track him down but drew a blank. I figured we'd just lost touch.'

'Did the police say how they traced who Kevin really was?' asked Regan. The last time she'd spoken to the police they hadn't been hopeful of tracking down Kevin's family, so something must have changed.

'He had a tattoo on his calf. Something else I didn't know about. Apparently it was of his Royal Navy trade badge and it had his service number on it.' Bernice looked up from her coffee. 'He was a weapons engineer. They said he was scarred. Burns, apparently. Did you ever notice anything?'

Regan nodded; she wasn't sure what else to do. 'His hands and his torso.' She could picture the red, twisted skin. She had wondered how Kevin had been hurt.

'He was in the Falklands conflict. I knew that, but what my parents hadn't told me was that he was on HMS *Sheffield* when it was hit by a missile. Dale was lucky to get off alive.'

'How awful.' Regan didn't know much about the Falklands war. She wasn't born when it happened, but she vaguely remembered something about it at school when it had been the anniversary of the conflict.

'The Navy are sending me a letter to explain everything, but it seems he was badly burned and after treatment it was clear he was suffering from post-traumatic stress disorder.'

'That explains a lot. Sometimes he was fine, but after those kids attacked him . . .' Bernice looked alarmed. 'They just roughed him up a bit, nothing serious,' – telling her the details now wasn't going to help her – 'it kind of sent him off somewhere. He wasn't the same afterwards. I guess it was the PTSD.'

'It's like we've known two different people.' Bernice wiped away silent tears. 'I remember my big brother so vividly. Strong and funny. He was twelve years older than me and he was my hero. But I've not seen him since I was eight, and I'm forty-five now.'

'That's a very long time.' Regan hoped that didn't sound like she was implying Bernice was old.

'What was he like? The Dale . . . Kevin . . . you knew?' Bernice asked.

Regan smiled. 'He was a truly lovely person. He used to cheer me up. There he was, a guy living on the streets, and yet he looked out for me more than once. Every morning he used to tell me *carpe diem* – seize the day. I used to buy him a coffee and . . .'

Bernice sobbed openly. 'Thank you.'

'It was nothing really.' She pulled up the blind and looked out of the office window to give Bernice a moment to compose herself. Regan could see Malcolm directing an older gentleman towards them. 'I think your uncle's here.'

'Regan, I'd like to talk some more about my brother. Another time maybe?'

'Sure, I'd like that too. Whenever you're ready.'

'And I'm sorry if we didn't see eye to eye over . . . things.' She gave Elvis a pat. He stretched and let out a fart.

Regan waved both the comment and hopefully the smell away and stood up. 'Forget it. We're on the same page now.' She hoped that with a family member to give them a poke, the police might actually make some progress on finding Kevin's killer.

She'd never get used to him being called Dale. He'd always be Kevin to her. Regan's dad was such a big football fan she'd grown up hearing all the old players' names. Kevin was such an obvious nickname with a surname like Keegan. She almost chuckled. If only they'd known his surname, he and his sister might have been reunited; but then it struck Regan that perhaps he knew who Bernice was all along and that was why he was there. Maybe it was why he stayed by the market, and somehow he couldn't bring himself to explain who he was. Sadly, they would never know.

It brought a lump to her throat, and she was grateful for Bernice's uncle coming in and taking over. Poor Bernice – she broke down again, and Regan left her crying in her uncle's arms. Strolling back to her stall, Regan thought of the times Bernice had complained about the homeless people hanging around the market and her comments about the floral tributes on the crossing where he'd been killed – they must have been haunting her now.

Despite the delay, Regan managed to get to the studio before Cleo and have a bit of a tidy-up. She found her lottery list and checked it over. She'd been able to tick off a surprising amount, including pedigree puppy now that she had Elvis – he appeared to be a pureblood wolfhound and, whilst he technically wasn't a puppy, he still thought he was, so that counted. The market stall was doing okay, so she ticked off 'Run my own successful company' too.

She looked at the tick next to the last item. She tore off the corner to remove the tick next to the hot boyfriend line. She'd ticked it off prematurely, but hopefully there might be another one sometime in the future. Regan folded up the list and stored it carefully in a box. That list had got her back on her feet – she owed it a lot.

She was wondering if there was anything she could do about the canvas Elvis had trashed when Cleo arrived.

'Sorry,' said Regan. 'Look, I'm making a tit of myself,'

she said, holding it up and poking her head through the hole for comic effect.

Cleo chuckled. 'Nutter. It may even be worth more now. That's what happened when they shredded the Banksy painting.'

Regan removed her head and had a look at the gaping hole. 'I doubt it.'

There was a knock on the door making them both pull puzzled faces. Regan hoped it wasn't the landlord. That would be just her luck; to be moving out, yet still get into trouble. Cleo went to answer it.

'Hello, Brian,' she said, warmly. 'Is everything all right?'

Regan recognised the grey-haired man in dark blue overalls as the man who had spoken to her when Cleo was away. 'Hello, Brian,' she called with a wave, and he waved back.

'Ah. You are back then,' he said, to Cleo.

'Last night. What can I do for you?'

'It's nothing really.' He scratched his head. 'There was a bloke here a couple of Fridays ago. I thought he was going to kick the door in.' Cleo twisted to look at Regan and she shrugged in response. She couldn't have been there when it had happened. Brian continued. 'I told him I'd call the police if he didn't sod off.'

'Did he say who he was looking for?' asked Regan, joining Cleo at the door.

'He was after Cleo. I think he was drunk. He was ranting a lot, so it didn't make a lot of sense. He had shiny shoes and a highfalutin voice.'

'Oscar,' said Cleo and Regan together.

'Sorry you had to witness that, Brian. Oscar is . . . *was* . . . my agent. We've parted company.'

'As long as you're okay. He seemed like a nasty bastard.

Drove out of here at high speed and bounced off the pavement.' Brian was shaking his head.

'I'm fine. He shouldn't be bothering me again.'

Brian gave her a thumbs-up and went back to his own unit.

'I'm glad I missed Oscar's visit,' said Regan, stacking up some jam jars.

Cleo shut the door. 'Oscar's all mouth and designer trousers. But I'm glad you weren't here. You know you don't have to move out. If you've been here nearly seven weeks without anyone raising the alarm, I don't see why you can't stay on a bit longer.'

'Thanks, but I don't need to. Something has turned up. Like I said it would.' Cleo looked surprised. 'Charlie needs a babysitter for three weeks so I'm moving in with him.'

'You're moving in together? Isn't that a bit quick? You've just met him.'

Regan shook her head. 'It's so very not like that at all. It's actually the opposite of that. He can't cope with a relationship that already has an end date stamped on it.' Regan wasn't sure how else to explain it. 'I'm there in case he's taken ill. I *would* be flattered that he's asked me, but it was me or his mum, so . . .'

'I see. I guess spending some time together will give you some nice memories to look back on.' Cleo gave a little wince. 'Sorry, was that the wrong thing to say when he's still here?'

Regan smiled – it wasn't just her that felt like she was constantly putting her foot in things. 'You're right. I'll make sure we do that. I'll take some photos.'

The sound of someone pawing at the toilet seat drew her attention. 'Elvis!' He seemed to think it was a drinks dispenser. 'We'd better make a move.'

'Okay. Before you go . . .' Cleo flicked the hairband on her wrist. 'Penny . . . I'm guessing you know her quite well from working with her?'

'Penny's lovely. She's loyal, hardworking and caring, but it's all underneath a bit of a crust. Don't let her fool you into thinking she's tough, though, because she's really a pussycat underneath.' Elvis barked and scanned the room diligently.

Cleo gave the hairband another twang. 'Does she have a boyfriend at all?' She seemed tentative.

'Ah. No, there was a husband once but . . . not any more.' She pondered whether to say anything else, but decided against it. She grabbed hold of Elvis before he destroyed anything else and steered him out of the studio and towards the car.

'Hi, honey, I'm home!' called Regan through Charlie's letterbox. The door soon opened and he looked a bit grumpy when Regan merrily thrust two boxes of cherries into his arms. 'There's more stuff and the dog in the car.'

'I want to talk about house rules,' Charlie called after her whilst she ferried stuff back and forth.

'Sure thing. Whatever you say,' she said, following him inside with Elvis at her heels. Elvis started snuffling around like a highly trained sniffer dog. She wasn't sure about his ability to detect drugs, but he could track down a sausage roll from a mile away.

'No getting on the furniture,' he said. 'No sleeping on beds—'

'Hey, I am housetrained, you know,' she said, with a grin.

'I mean Elvis, as you well know. He's not allowed in the kitchen at all and if you can stop him shedding hair everywhere that'd be great.'

Regan gave him an amused look. 'Other than making him wear a onesie, which would be highly entertaining, I can't think how you might achieve the last one.'

'I'm not trying to be awkward, I just don't want the place covered in dog hair because then it will smell of, well, dog,' said Charlie.

'I understand. He's pretty good. Aren't you, boy?' Elvis trotted over to stand in front of Charlie. He gave himself a good scratch with his back leg and a flurry of fur puffed into the air. And with a dramatic full-body shake, he distributed another pile onto the living room carpet.

'Okay, maybe we'll have to live with the fur thing,' said Charlie good-naturedly, opening a cupboard and pulling out a vacuum cleaner.

'Sorry.'

Elvis eyed the vacuum suspiciously until Charlie turned it on; then he went bonkers, barking at full volume and trying to bite it every time Charlie pushed it forwards. Once the pile of hair was sucked up, Charlie switched it off, but there was a delay where Elvis continued to bark at it. Charlie went to put the vacuum away, which was handy – because that was the moment Elvis chose to lift his back legs up in the air in front of him and drag his bum along the carpet. Thankfully Regan was able to grab his collar and usher him into the hallway, but she couldn't hide her giggles – it was without doubt one of the funniest things she'd ever seen.

'What's so funny?' asked Charlie, shutting the cupboard door, still oblivious to Elvis's bum wiping antics.

'Nothing.' Regan tried to look innocent.

'And I wanted to check you were still okay with our agreement.' He broke eye contact.

Regan waved her hands at him. 'Look, I think I've

shown I can keep my hands off you. Your virtue is safe with me, Charlie McGee.'

'Sorry. I just thought it was better to be clear than to have any . . .'

'Awkward advances? No, you're safe. I've decided I'm into hairy males now.' She tipped her head at Elvis. 'So unless you're planning on turning into Hagrid, you'll be fine.'

'I'll make sure I shave every day.'

'No need to go that far.' She liked his stubbly look.

He pushed his hands into his pockets and hunched up his shoulders. 'Do you want to see your room?'

Elvis was still meticulously inspecting the hallway so she figured he'd be occupied for a few minutes at least. 'I'd love to.'

Upstairs was compact and matched downstairs with its white walls and grey carpets. 'Here you go,' said Charlie, opening a door to reveal a nice-sized bedroom with a double bed, wardrobe and tub chair. 'Beanstalk has cleared a shelf in the wardrobe and asked that you don't wear his underwear.'

'Great.' She flopped onto the bed and lay down. 'Ahhhh.' The involuntary sound came out with more of a sexual tinge than she'd intended; but it was so comfy.

'Right. Well . . . my room is next door. And there's a lock—'

'Bloody hell, Charlie. You make me sound like some sort of sexual predator. I promise I won't jump you.' She snuggled into the thick duvet; it was bliss. 'Anyway, you'll never entice me off this bed.'

'I was going to say there's a lock been put on the bathroom door, and I've even scraped the mould off the tiles especially for you.'

She opened one eye. 'Bloody hell, I am honoured. Now who's sounding seductive?'

He fixed her with a long-suffering look. 'Any questions?'

'Yes.' She propped herself up on her elbows and she could have sworn he inched behind the door for safety. 'What's for tea?'

'Me and Beanstalk usually have a takeaway on a Sunday night.'

'Brilliant.'

As it turned out it wasn't entirely brilliant, because they left the pizza on the side while they fought over who was paying and then over who was tipping, which gave Elvis enough time to figure out there was food in the odd, flat-shaped box. He hadn't worked out how to open it, so he had simply eaten half the pizza box as well.

'Elvis!' shouted Regan, dragging him out to the small back garden and giving Charlie her best apologetic face on the way.

Charlie was laughing. 'He's a four-legged dustbin. I'll order another pizza. Same again?' he asked.

'Please.' Elvis was busy smacking his lips whilst trying to seize the other half of the pizza box. 'Apparently it was delicious.'

Chapter Thirty-Two

Their first evening living together had been very civilised: pizza, a couple of beers and the Grand Prix on the telly. Elvis had eventually stopped rolling around the carpet and spent the evening asleep by the door like a giant furry draught excluder.

'Right. I'm going to walk Elvis round the block for last wees, and then I'm off to bed,' said Regan. 'An actual bed.' She was excited at the thought of it.

'I can take him out, if you like?'

'Are you sure?' She didn't want to turn out again if she didn't have to.

'Sure,' said Charlie, getting to his feet. 'I'll shut him in the hallway.'

Regan realised Elvis didn't have a dog bed, but it was too late to do anything about it now. He was used to sleeping in worse places than Charlie's hallway. 'Okay. Night then.' She wasn't sure what to do. If she was leaving the house, she would have kissed his cheek, but she was only going upstairs. She jigged on the spot awkwardly for a moment.

'You okay?' Charlie tilted his head questioningly.

'Yes, I'm fine. I'm going to bed.' She pointed at the door. Charlie raised an eyebrow as if she were suggesting something. 'On my own. Alone. Just me in the bed. Which is fine. It wasn't an offer. I should go now,' she gabbled, whilst her cheeks heated up. She turned to leave, but Elvis was against the door and blocking her exit. After a great deal of effort and an agonising delay, she managed to push the dog over enough that she could open the door a few inches to squeeze out. How embarrassing.

She was in bed when she heard Charlie and Elvis come back. She waited to see if she'd need to go down and settle Elvis.

'Now, listen, Elvis,' said Charlie, his voice low and gentle. 'This is your space. Sleep wherever you like. Doormat might be good. Regan has gone to bed and I'm going up too. Night, night, mate.'

'Night, Reg,' he called from the landing.

'Night, Debbie,' she called back, and she heard him chortle.

She closed her eyes and tried to stop grinning. This wasn't perfect, but she was somewhere very comfortable with Charlie in the next bedroom. She closed her eyes. Within moments they pinged open again, because something was scratching at her bedroom door. If it was Charlie then her day was made. She hopped out of bed and opened it a fraction but the large hairy face that poked through dismissed her little fantasy.

'No, Elvis,' she whispered. 'Downstairs.' She held her palm in front of his eyes so he'd know she meant it. He licked it. 'No.' She tried to make him reverse onto the landing. There was a small scuffle when Elvis pushed back. A door clicked open.

'Are you sneaking him in?' asked Charlie, his voice reproachful.

'No. I'm trying to sneak him back downstairs without the landlord seeing him.'

Charlie smiled. 'I'll take him down. Come on, Elvis. No creeping into girls' bedrooms uninvited.' He strode onto the landing wearing a Superman T-shirt and black boxer briefs, making it almost impossible for Regan not to stare. Her teenage self was about to spontaneously combust into a giggling mess.

She muttered a 'Thanks' and hurried back to bed, stifling her nervous laughter with her pillow.

She was beginning to fall asleep when the scratching at the door was repeated, this time accompanied by a whimper. She and Charlie opened their doors at the same time. She concentrated hard to maintain eye contact. 'What do we do?' she asked.

Charlie ruffled his hair, which lifted his T-shirt enough for her to get a glimpse of his slim midriff. 'When I took him downstairs before, he just sat there looking at me. I don't think he knows where to sleep,' said Charlie, lowering his arm.

'He's not got a bed.'

'Hang on. We can make him one.' Charlie turned and gave Regan a nice view of his bum in the tight black briefs, and she sighed involuntarily. He looked over his shoulder. 'Don't, you'll set me off.' He yawned, and she faked one of her own. It was far better he thought she was yawning than sighing at the glorious sight of his tight little bum in stretchy underwear.

Charlie reappeared with a body warmer, complete with fur-trimmed hood. 'He can try sleeping on this.'

Regan was grinning. 'Is that yours?'

'I've been meaning to give it to charity.'

'What was it – your East 17 phase?' she asked, with a splutter.

He headed downstairs and Regan and Elvis followed. 'No. My mum brought it back from Canada.'

Regan took the furry body warmer off him, her face beaming with glee, and she laid it out on the doormat. 'Elvis,' she patted the body warmer, 'bedtime.' Elvis came and gave it a sniff, pawed it a bit and then curled up on it to repeated *good boy*s from both Regan and Charlie. Once he seemed settled, they padded back upstairs and into their respective bedrooms.

When Elvis woke them up again shortly afterwards, Regan opened the door to him to see that this time he had brought the body warmer with him. Charlie peered around his door. 'I think he'd like to return the body warmer. He says he looks ridiculous in it,' said Regan, with a grin.

'I give in,' said Charlie, throwing up his hands. 'He can sleep with you.'

'Thank you,' said Regan, but Charlie had already disappeared.

Regan had a spring in her step when she left for work the next morning. She had slept incredibly well despite having to share the bed with Elvis, who liked to stretch out but at the same time be right up against you. She guessed this was what he'd been used to – he and Kevin sleeping close to keep each other warm. She stopped at the café to unload her boxes and Penny popped out to take them from her.

'Good morning,' said Penny, taking the first box. 'You look cheerful.'

'I am,' said Regan, following her in with another one.

'I slept well, had a hot shower and a chat over breakfast with my favourite fireman.'

Penny spun around so fast she nearly fell over. 'A hot shower with a fireman?'

'No. Hot shower on my own, worse luck. Then breakfast with the fireman.'

Penny pulled a commiserative face. 'Have you got time for coffee when you've parked the car?'

'Er, yeah, go on. Quick one,' said Regan. They weren't expecting Bernice back for a few days, but she didn't want to take the mick.

When she returned from the car with Elvis, Penny was bringing the drinks to a table outside. The June day was starting to warm up around them and Elvis looked expectantly at Penny. She pointed to a water bowl. 'It's new and just for dogs,' said Penny. Elvis huffed his disapproval and slunk under the table.

'Thanks. How are you?' asked Regan, taking the coffee.

'Good.' She had her shoulders hunched. 'I met Cleo for a drink last night. Sort of a last-minute thing.'

'Oh, good. Did you have a nice time?'

Penny's shoulders relaxed. 'Yeah, I had a great time. She's lovely . . . I'm really sorry we didn't invite you.'

Regan shrugged. 'It's fine. It's kind of nice that you both get on.' Often good friends fitted in to separate groups and didn't mix, so it was lovely that they all got along.

'We thought the three of us could have a girls' night in at Cleo's once she's got her flat back,' said Penny. 'You know . . . takeaway, wine and film.'

Regan scanned Penny's face; she seemed different somehow. She was certainly very excited about the prospect of a night in. 'Sure.' Regan gave a shrug.

'Cleo's incredibly glamorous, isn't she?'

'I guess,' said Regan, knowing that she was; but she'd known Cleo long enough to know that wasn't the real her. Underneath she would always be the anxious nail-biter who preferred woolly jumpers to party dresses.

'It must be amazing to think of your works of art hanging on the walls of the rich and famous. It's just paint and canvas, but because it's been made by Cleo Marchant people pay thousands to have one of their own. Kids are going to be queuing up to join her mentoring programme,' said Penny, checking her watch.

Regan was nodding without really listening, but now she tuned in fully. 'What mentoring programme is this, then?' She dismissed a brief prickle of hurt at not being the first person Cleo had discussed it with.

'Oh, it's just an idea she has.' Penny seemed to realise her mistake. 'She said she was going to talk to you about it once it's finalised. She knows you've been dealing with a lot recently.'

It was true, but it hadn't stopped Cleo sharing her ideas in the past. Perhaps them all being friends wasn't going to work out quite as well as she'd thought. *Three's a crowd*, thought Regan.

On the morning of Kevin's funeral, Regan was woken by a tap on the bedroom door. Elvis sat up and almost fell off the bed. Charlie stuck his head around the door. 'I'm off to work and I wanted to say I hope it all goes okay.' He carried in a mug of coffee. 'Are you sure you don't want me to come with you?'

'Thanks.' She took the coffee. 'And no, I don't want you playing hooky from work for me.'

'And you're sure about taking Elvis?' His tone of voice said he had reservations. Elvis was lying on his back waiting for someone to scratch his tummy, and Charlie obliged.

'Yes, I am. I know you all think it's crazy, but Bernice has spoken to the vicar and they've all said he can come. And I know it's a bit mad . . .'

'Barking,' said Charlie, with a grin, and she ignored him.

'But to Kevin, Elvis was family, so I think he should be there.'

'And if he cocks his leg on anything?'

'Then he will be removed by a verger and be condemned to the fiery pits of hell.'

'Okay then. I'll be thinking about you,' he said, and he reversed out of the door. She knew what he meant, but she wanted to say "I'll be thinking about you too. Because that's what I do most of the time. And it's really bloody annoying when you pop up in my head like whack-a-mole."'

'Regan?' Charlie was waving at her. 'Are you sure you're okay?'

She pulled herself back to the moment. 'Sorry, I zoned out there. Go on – you need to leave and I need to make copious amounts of jam.'

Charlie faltered. 'Right. Well, don't burn the place down.'

'I'll try not to . . . but if I do, it's okay because I know a fireman.' She fluttered her eyelashes in a very non-Regan way, making Charlie shake his head and leave.

Regan wasn't working today. The market was still running, but the funeral was in the middle of the day and it hadn't seemed worth it to set up just for a couple of hours. But she still needed to keep herself busy until it was time to leave.

Jag had handed over a large tray of strawberries before

she'd left the day before, but strawberries were the last thing she needed. She had a big stock of strawberry and black pepper jam and of balsamic strawberry jam, and she wasn't sure what else to put with them to make the jam unusual and 'Reganify' it. She'd done some googling but nothing had popped up that had seemed to tick the right boxes.

She sipped her coffee and considered her dilemma. She was still pondering when she entered the kitchen, Elvis at her heels.

'Nuh-uh. You know the score.' She shooed him out and he skulked away with his head held low, bestowing maximum guilt.

She got everything out ready to make jam, but still had no idea what to put with the strawberries. She decided to hunt through Charlie's cupboards in the hope of finding something to trigger some inspiration. Tinned tomatoes – yuck. Marmite – double yuck. Regan measured out the sugar and hulled the strawberries, and while they began heating up she had another hunt through the cupboards. There at the back was the answer to the question she had been trying to figure out.

With a twinkle in her heart, she set about creating another unique jam for Sticky Situations.

Chapter Thirty-Three

A few hours later, Regan had swapped an apron for her black interview suit and was waiting outside the crematorium for Elvis to have a final wee. Regan had brushed out so much hair from Elvis's coat she was surprised he wasn't bald. He'd fluffed up quite nicely. Elvis found a watering can and peed against that, the empty metal vessel making a spectacular noise and alerting gathering mourners to their presence. She gave the gawpers a curt smile and scuttled inside.

Regan slipped into a seat near the back in case she needed to make a quick exit. Elvis had a good sniff around and then flopped down at her feet. The crematorium was echoey and, despite the sunshine outside, there was a chill in the stale air. Regan wasn't very comfortable in churches and this seemed somehow worse. It was the first funeral she'd been to, having been too young to attend her gran's, and luckily all her other close relatives were still alive.

Bernice arrived and smiled at Regan on her way down the aisle. She paused. 'You should be at the front with me and the family.'

'It's okay. He might kick off,' said Regan, with a nod at Elvis.

'That's fine – he's family too.' Bernice ushered her out of the pew and down to the front, where they sat in silence. At last some music started. It was 'The Scientist' by Coldplay, one of the songs Regan had suggested. She didn't know if it was a favourite of Kevin's, but he'd whistled along to it the night they'd sat under the pier and it was a time he had been happy, so in Regan's books that meant it qualified. It was somehow appropriate too. She took a deep breath and Bernice gripped her hand.

Regan turned to see Kevin's coffin being carried in. She choked back the tears. Elvis jumped up onto his back legs and she feared she'd have to take him out, but he steadied himself against her like he was trying to get a better view or give her a cuddle – she wasn't sure which. She got the feeling he knew there was something wrong. When the coffin was set down, Elvis slumped back to the floor.

Regan looked around; there were only a handful of people there. Malcolm had come and he was sitting at the back. Hillary was also there, and another older man she recognised from the homeless community. Then there were a couple of smartly dressed men who she guessed might have been naval friends, and that was it. So many people would have seen him and walked past him every day, and yet when it came to it, so few people actually knew him.

The civil celebrant taking the service was excellent. Talking about Dale's time in the Navy and his time on the streets, he painted the picture of the kind and caring soul she had known. The service went by in a flash, and soon they were watching the coffin disappear behind a curtain to the *Titanic* theme tune – not one of Regan's suggestions. Elvis began whimpering and Regan bent down to comfort him, rubbing tears from her own eyes at the same time. Elvis pulled her forward as if he wanted to follow the coffin. 'No, mate. It's time to say goodbye,' she whispered in his ear, and with a deep groan he lay heavily on the floor. Perhaps animals understood more than humans gave them credit for.

They watched the curtains slowly close. There was something horribly final about the drawn curtains. She didn't know what she'd been expecting, but it didn't seem enough to end a life by closing a bit of material. Surely people deserved to go out with something more impressive, like fireworks, or one of those video montages they did when people left reality shows? *Let's have a look at your time here . . .*

'You okay?' asked Bernice, dabbing at her mascara with a tissue.

Regan blinked. She'd shed a few tears, but she was better than she'd expected – no full-on blubbering, which was a result. 'Yes. How about you?'

'I think Mum and Dad would have approved.'

Regan knew what was required here. 'I'm sure they would say that you'd done him proud.'

Bernice smiled. 'Pub?'

Regan liked this side of Bernice; it was a shame it had taken something so traumatic for it to be revealed. 'Definitely.'

The pub was dog friendly and Regan was well prepared, having brought along a large chew bone to keep Elvis occupied. A few people stayed for one drink before making their excuses and leaving. Bernice's aunt and uncle led the conversation, reminiscing about Dale as a child – they frowned every time Regan referred to him as Kevin, but she couldn't help it. When they left it was just Regan, Bernice and a snoozing Elvis.

'The other day you said you knew who had killed my brother.' Bernice fixed her with a stern eye.

Regan sipped her drink. 'I've got a theory.'

'Which is?'

'That thieving little sod in the hoodie.' Regan knew they had very differing feelings about the youth, but Bernice had asked.

Bernice pursed her lips. 'I take it you've told the police?'

'Not exactly. You see . . . I'm lacking evidence.'

'Lacking? What evidence do you actually have?'

Regan pouted. 'None. But I've got a hunch.'

'You can't accuse someone of something this serious because of a hunch.' The Bernice of old had returned in an instant.

'I can't believe you're still sticking up for him. He's not Kevin. He's nothing like him. Kevin was kind and gentle, and that kid is a thug who has no respect for anyone or anything.' Regan stood up to leave.

This time Bernice was calmer. 'Sit down. Please.' Regan paused, but Elvis hadn't moved and she still had some beer in her glass, so she did as Bernice asked. 'I hoped you had something more concrete to go on.' Bernice looked disappointed and suddenly tired, sinking back into her seat.

'Look,' said Regan, leaning forward, 'I can't be completely certain because of the rain that night, but I don't think the car that hit him was coloured.' Regan sat back.

Bernice looked puzzled. 'But all cars are a colour. It's a big selling point. That's how I pick mine.'

'What I mean is it wasn't red or yellow. It must have been something that blended in. Like grey.'

'Grey?' Bernice didn't sound convinced.

'Or possibly black . . . maybe silver.'

'That narrows it down then,' said Bernice sarcastically, taking a long swig of her wine.

'Don't dismiss it. I know it was a small car, so if we could get local businesses to have a look at their CCTV footage we might be able to spot something.'

'Aren't those cameras in black and white anyway? So wouldn't all cars look grey on CCTV?'

They both visibly slumped – perhaps this was an impossible quest after all. They finished their drinks in contemplative silence.

Another Monday came around and Regan's feet were throbbing. She'd never realised how hard it was standing up all day. The market stall was doing okay, but she needed to work the stall six days a week to stand any chance of making a living out of it. She stepped inside Charlie's front door and kicked off her shoes – bliss.

'Hey, you.' Charlie's smiling face peeped from round the kitchen door and Elvis trotted over to greet him. 'Good day?'

'Yes. The little Indian restaurant want me to make them some exclusive mango chutneys in special combinations. I just need to work out an interesting twist and the pricing.'

'That's brilliant. Well done you!' He seemed thrilled. 'You want a coffee or a glass of wine?'

'Wine. I need wine,' said Regan. 'Or beer. I'm not fussy.'

'Okay. Well, you sit down because dinner is under control.'

'Ooh, what are you making?'

'Don't get your hopes up because I've not done it before, but I'm making scallops wrapped in bacon to start, followed by mushroom risotto.'

'You'd make someone a lovely wife,' said Regan and

Charlie stuck his tongue out. 'What's the special occasion?' she asked, slumping onto the sofa with a groan that made her sound like a pensioner.

'None really. I guess having you here makes me want to try a few new things out.' He handed her a chilled glass of rosé.

She took the glass, but her eyes were fixed on his. The number of new things she'd like to try out with Charlie was endless, but she couldn't say that. It would make him feel awkward. She blinked and sipped the wine. 'I am happy to be your guinea pig.' She gave a little squeak and Elvis dashed over, sniffing the air wildly.

Charlie shoved his hands in his pockets. 'There's a new film on Netflix that the guys at work are raving about. Action thriller with that guy you like.'

Regan gave him a look. She knew him pretty well by now. 'Or we could binge-watch *Gavin and Stacey*.'

Charlie's face lit up. 'Yeah, that'd be perfect.' He cleared his throat. 'You know. If that's what *you* want to watch, then sure . . . I don't mind.' He gave a cheeky smile and her heart smiled along too.

Regan felt smug and virtuous as she waltzed out of the gym, having handed in her membership card and asked them to change Jarvis's membership to a single. Yes, she had taken a while to do it, but the important thing was that she had got there in the end. Jarvis had clearly forgotten to change it too, so she didn't feel too bad about it – she'd just maximised his monthly membership by showering there most days.

The gym had been a little bubble she could escape to – with its nice-smelling body wash, clean towels and hair-dryers, it had helped to keep her going over the last few weeks. She had two weeks left at Charlie's, but ultimately Cleo's return had signalled the end of Regan's austerity period. She was still determined to get herself back on her feet, but knowing you had a backstop made a huge difference. Especially when that backstop had a beautiful flat and loads of money.

She walked to the barrier, and instead of the bar turning when she pushed it, it jammed, and she almost dived over the top. She gave it a jiggle but it didn't move. Typical. They always hated you cancelling your gym membership – she was probably trapped there for all eternity. She reversed out and was about to go through the next turnstile when she saw Jarvis leaving the gym with his sports bag slung over his shoulder. Regan did a little jolt but quickly composed herself. She'd managed to avoid him since the split, but here he was. He was checking his phone and she put her head down, hoping he'd not notice her. She gave the next turnstile a nudge and thankfully it let her through. She was free.

'Regan.' Jarvis touched her arm. *Oh, so close to escaping.*

'Jarvis. Hello,' she said, spinning around. 'Fancy seeing you here.' Why did she suddenly sound like her grandmother?

'I've been a member here for six years. I come at the same time most days. So it was fairly likely.' He was giving her the look that always made her feel stupid. Not any more.

'I thought you would have cancelled the joint membership, but you hadn't, so I've done it for you.' She held her head high – she could do this. She could be polite and aloof.

He was scanning her up and down. 'Right.'

He could have at least thanked her for saving him a

few quid. 'Anyway, I'm very busy running my own business, so I must dash.' Now she sounded all showy and a bit posh.

He seemed to be considering her statement. 'I heard you were working on the market.'

'Yes. That is my business. You arse.' And no-nonsense Regan was back.

'There's no need to be abusive.'

'Excuse me.' A lycra-clad woman skulked past them, and Regan realised they were causing an obstruction. She pointed outside and Jarvis followed her into the car park.

'I have been to hell and back these last couple of months. You have no idea what I've been through, so don't you dare belittle my business.'

Jarvis looked bored. 'You are the architect of your own misfortune, Regan.'

What did that mean? 'Are you saying it's all my fault?'

'I'm saying you don't consider the consequences of your actions.'

Regan's blood was beginning to heat up. 'Consequences! I lost my job and nearly ended up on the streets because of Alex's pranks.'

'You see. You're still not taking any responsibility.' He checked his watch. 'Whilst this has been interesting, I need to get going.'

She wasn't done putting over her argument, so she followed him across the car park. 'I do take responsibility. It was not my fault—'

'You entered into these silly games of one-upmanship with Alex. It was bound to end badly.'

He was so infuriating. 'Well, not any more. I'm my own boss.'

'Market stall. You said.' He stopped at a red Audi and opened the door.

'New car?' Jarvis hadn't had the silver one very long. She clocked the registration. It was the same age as his last one, so not a huge upgrade.

'Yes. It was time for a change. It's the sports model.' He really did look bored. 'I really do need to go. Good luck with the market stall,' he said dismissively, and he got in the car.

'In case you didn't know, Marks and Spencer started on a market stall,' she said, as he shut the door. It was one of those moments she really wished she could conjure up the perfect insult, but it had escaped her – and she'd spend the rest of the day reliving the conversation until she found the perfect parting shot.

Chapter Thirty-Four

Thankfully the rest of Regan's day went slightly better. She had a good day on the stall, not only selling a few jars but also getting her first returning customer, who brought back empty jars for a discount. After she'd packed up for the day, she met Cleo at the library so she could go through the designs Cleo had sketched for her logo.

'I *love* them,' said Regan, marvelling at the professional job Cleo had done.

'It was fun to do something different. I've been stuck in a rut since the first collection started selling. And Japan has given me so many new ideas. None of them Oscar would be interested in, because in his view I was just there to churn out big-ticket pieces.'

'You sure you're okay about walking away from all that?' Regan struggled to see how Cleo was so calm about it. Partly because she was voluntarily walking away from a large income, and also because Cleo usually worried about things like this – but this time she seemed quite chilled.

Cleo paused and looked off into the distance as if really considering the question. 'Yes, I'm really okay with walking away.' She looked back at Regan with a smile. 'Now let's get these images loaded.'

With Cleo's help, Regan managed to set up a free website for Sticky Situations – something she had been meaning to do for ages – and they scanned in the new logo and some photos Regan had taken of her jams. By the time Cleo had finished tweaking things, it looked like a very professional job.

Whilst Cleo tinkered with the pictures, Regan jotted down some online tips for marketing her website. 'Has your tenant moved out?' she asked.

'Yes. He managed to drop a bottle of aftershave through my sink, but otherwise the place is fine. Once the sink is fixed and it's been thoroughly cleaned I'll be moving back in.'

'Great.'

'How are things at Charlie's?'

Regan paused and chewed the end of her pen. It was one she'd taken from BHB Healthcare. 'You know that feeling you have at Christmas, that even when there's shit going down, it doesn't matter because it's Christmas? It's like that. It's blissful.'

'Oh, Regan. You're falling for him, aren't you?'

'I think that happened long before I moved in. But living together has cemented my feelings.' She blew out a heavy sigh.

'But you're only there for a couple more weeks.'

'I know. How many before I qualify for squatter's rights?' She tried to make a joke of it, but leaving Charlie was going to be incredibly hard. They had quickly slotted into a domestic routine. There had been no petty squabbles, and he'd even seemed to accept Elvis and his hair shedding – although now she brushed him every evening it was greatly reduced. Elvis was settling in too. He had found the introduction of carpet and a television all very confusing to start with, but now he took them, and even the vacuum, in his stride.

Regan was a far better housemate than she'd ever been before. When she was a student, she had done the bare minimum; and only after someone had complained or they had been on the verge of kicking her out. With Jarvis, she had been generally lazy although nothing she had attempted in the early days had been to his standards, so it had been easier to let him get on with it. With Charlie they were on an even keel and she wanted to pull her weight. She realised how much her outlook had changed since she'd met him.

Regan uploaded a photo and Cleo adjusted it until it looked perfect. 'What does that label say?' Cleo was squinting at the screen.

'Unicorn jam,' said Regan, proudly.

Cleo laughed and then studied her carefully. 'What on earth is in that then? Apart from boiled unicorns?'

'Ha, ha. It's strawberry jam with edible glitter. As it says on the label – it's what unicorns eat for breakfast so they're sparkly all day long.' She was very proud of her latest flavour, thanks to her root around Charlie's cupboard on the day of Kevin's funeral.

'And they do sparkly poos, no doubt.'

'Exactly. I should add that in,' said Regan, taking over the keyboard.

'Why unicorn jam?'

'Two reasons. One: I had too many strawberries and no idea what to put with them to make them unique until I found the edible glitter. And secondly, it had been bugging me since I filled the form in for the market that they asked for market stall produce to be lots of things, like vegan friendly and healthy, and one of the things was shiny. And I've been racking my brains for how to include shiny, and now I've found it. And thirdly . . .'

'You said two reasons,' pointed out Cleo.

'This is a bonus one: it sells really well. Kids love it. And there are worse things to have for breakfast, which means parents love it too.'

'I'm delighted this is working out for you,' said Cleo.

'Thanks,' said Regan, and she gave her friend a hug.

When they were happy they had everything on the website as perfect as they could get it, Regan pushed the button and put the website live. Now all she had to do was hope she got lots of online orders flooding in. The market stall alone wasn't going to be enough for a viable income and, although she'd been saving, she was still a long way off being able to afford to rent somewhere of her own.

'I'm meeting Charlie and Elvis on the beach. Do you want to come?' she asked, logging out of the computer.

'Um . . . Actually, I'm meeting Penny for a drink.'

'Oh, right. Okay.' Regan couldn't hide that she was slightly miffed not to have been included again. They'd only met each other thanks to her, and now she was being left out.

'You can join us if you like?' said Cleo, belatedly.

'I need to get Elvis. He's probably been driving Charlie round the bend. Another time?'

'Sure.' Everything felt a little uncomfortable. They said their goodbyes and went in different directions.

Regan spotted Charlie and Elvis on Black Rock Beach. She watched them unnoticed. Charlie was throwing stones and Elvis was chasing after them like a demented greyhound, going slightly potty every time one landed and seemingly disappeared into all the other stones on the beach. He was like a child watching a magician. As she drew closer, she could hear Charlie's laughter carrying on the breeze – it was a wonderful sound.

At last, as if Charlie sensed her watching, he turned to look straight at her and she waved. This was a big mistake. Elvis followed Charlie's gaze, clocked Regan and set off towards her at high speed, skidding slightly on the pebbles. On any other beach this wouldn't be a problem, and Black Rock was a designated dog-friendly beach, but it was also home to Brighton's naturists, which meant that Elvis was now careering through their small section of beach quite literally willy-nilly. Naked people were diving out of the way and body parts were swinging in all directions. Charlie didn't know where to look. Elvis leapt straight over a sunbather, spraying him with sand. 'Sorry!' shouted Regan, which only seemed to draw the attention – and full-frontal views – in her direction. Elvis slowed down when he neared Regan, but instead of barrelling into her, something caught his attention: an elderly, naked gentlemen was bent over, folding up his picnic rug. Momentarily distracted, Elvis gave the gent his usual greeting of a nose in the nether regions. Regan thought the poor man was going into space, he jumped so high. But then a cold, wet nose up your bottom was always going to be a shock. The man turned around quickly and Regan just managed to grab Elvis's collar and stop him from having another sniff. Goodness knows what the poor man was going to say; he must have been furious.

'I'm very, *very* sorry,' she said, shielding her eyes from the dangly bits and trying to drag Elvis away, which was virtually impossible one-handed.

'That's all right,' said the man, with a chuckle. 'You're

only saying hello, aren't you?' Regan peeped one eye out to see the elderly man was now making a fuss of Elvis. How awkward. She'd rather the old man were furious – that would have been far easier to deal with than his being friendly and chatty. 'What's his name?' He smiled at Regan.

'Elvis.'

'Well, he's got his sideburns all right.'

She stifled a nervous giggle and dragged the dog away. 'He's very sorry. Bye!'

Charlie was running towards them, holding his sides from laughing at the same time. 'That's the funniest thing I've ever seen.'

'You were no help,' she scolded, before bursting into hysterics. They held onto each other for support as the giggles gripped them. Elvis sensed the excitement and began barking and leaping around.

'Come on,' said Charlie, putting an arm around Regan. 'It's your turn to cook. What are we having?'

She started to laugh again. 'I was thinking of sausages but now I'm not so keen.'

The next morning Regan was dropping her jars off at the café and Penny was giving her a hand. 'Have you got CCTV here?' asked Regan.

Penny laughed. 'Come on, you know how tight Mr Hughes is.'

'What's that then?' She tipped her head at what looked like a bubble camera on the front of the coffee shop.

'It's a fake. Why do you ask?'

'Me and Bernice are doing a bit of sleuthing. The police don't seem that interested in tracking down Kevin's killer . . . actually, that's a bit unfair. They have done quite a bit, and they've checked the road cameras, but there's nothing that covers the crossing so we thought we'd do some investigations of our own.'

'Ooh, good idea. The nursery a few doors down has a camera. A real one. But you wouldn't want to see most of the footage they catch on it.' Penny gave a chuckle.

'It's a start though. We need to see if we can catch a glimpse of the car speeding off. I can pinpoint the time so we don't need to trawl through hours of tape like they do on the cop shows.'

'I can ask them to check,' said Penny. 'We all want to catch this bastard.'

Regan shut the boot and paused for a second. Penny was looking tired. 'Are you all right?'

Penny tilted her head to one side and pursed her lips. 'Not great.'

'What's up?

'Mr Hughes called me last night. He's selling up.'

'But you'll still have a job, won't you? This place is a gold mine.'

Penny was shaking her head. 'He's hoping to sell to a big chain.' She slapped a fake smile on her face. 'But at least he's given me lots of notice so I've got time to look for something else.'

'I'm sure something will turn up. Look at me – it could be the best thing that's ever happened to you.'

'I love your optimism, but I'm not so sure,' said Penny, with a deep sigh.

'Bloody hell,' said Charlie as he opened the front door that evening. 'Are you making chemical weapons?'

'Yes, it's a big order for the Ministry of Defence and it doubles as beetroot and orange chutney,' said Regan, opening the kitchen door. She scanned Charlie up and down. The sight of him in his uniform was always a thrill and something she would never tire of.

'Thank goodness it's not dinner.' He screwed up his nose and she threw a tea towel at him. Elvis expertly intercepted the throw and grabbed it. 'Hey,' said Charlie, and Elvis growled playfully in response. Elvis and Charlie had a tug of war until Charlie conceded and Elvis trotted off happily with his prize.

'Good day?' asked Regan, with only a short glance at Charlie because she was concentrating on decanting the last of the chutney into jars.

'Meh,' he said. She could tell even from a brief look that he'd had a bad shift. Sometimes he opened up and sometimes he didn't. It seemed to depend on what he'd had to face.

'You want to talk about it?' She put the large pan down.

'Maybe after I've had a shower. How was your day?'

'Pretty productive. I've made so much unicorn jam, I'm out of glitter. Actually, I've been meaning to ask you why you had edible glitter in your cupboard.'

Charlie grinned. 'It was for Beanstalk's birthday.'

'Aww, did you make him a cake?'

'No.' Charlie looked almost offended. 'I put it in his beer. You know, so it was birthday beer.'

'*Obviously*,' Regan quipped, trying hard not to roll her eyes. 'Here, try this?' She scooped the remains of the chutney out of the bottom of the pan with a teaspoon and fed it to him. She could tell from his expression he was sceptical, but he dutifully tasted it anyway. It was when his lips slowly closed around the end of the spoon that she realised what an intimate gesture it was to feed someone.

'Wow. That's tasty.'

'See? It's like I almost know what I'm doing.' She was in a steady routine with her jam and chutney making and now had a tried-and-tested list of flavours, which she was still adding to.

'You're awesome,' said Charlie, holding her gaze for a heartbeat too long. They both looked away.

'I had good news today,' said Regan, clapping her hands together for emphasis – and also to detract from the sexual tension fizzing between them.

'Go on,' said Charlie, taking the spoon from her and dragging it around the pan to find a bit more leftover chutney.

'Sticky Situations had its first online orders!'

'You star. That's brilliant news. Orders? Plural?'

'Yes. Two customers and a total of three jars. I'll not need a juggernaut for deliveries, but it's a start.'

Charlie picked her up and twirled her around – she thought she'd pop with excitement like a shaken champagne bottle. When he put her down, he didn't let go. They couldn't pull their eyes away. Was this it? The moment they gave in to the attraction that was consuming them both? Charlie's lips tweaked at the edges.

Elvis started barking and running up and down the hallway, followed moments later by a knock at the door. Charlie squeezed his eyes shut and let her go. 'I'd better get that.' They both knew they had come close to breaking their agreement.

Charlie opened the door to an apprehensive-looking Penny.

'Hi, Charlie. Is Regan in?' asked Penny, peering past him.

'Sure. Come in.'

'Blimey, that burns your eyeballs,' said Penny, doing elaborate blinks.

'Chutney. It tastes much better than it smells,' said Charlie. He was loyal to a fault.

Regan was standing in the kitchen doorway drying her hands. 'Everything all right?' Penny had never paid her a house call before.

'Sorry to drop round unannounced, but I thought you'd want to see this.' She held out a USB stick. 'It's the nursery's CCTV footage from the night Kevin died.'

Regan was awash with an odd sensation: a mixture of excitement at possibly having a lead, and horror at the thought that the person who mowed Kevin down was on the footage.

Charlie quickly got out his laptop and they all crowded round. The whole clip was only fifteen seconds long. The camera was angled so that it covered the front of the premises rather than the road – which was completely expected, because that was the whole purpose of having CCTV, but it wasn't entirely helpful to Regan. The entire pavement was visible, including some of the road, and all in slightly grainy black and white.

'Wouldn't the car be on the other side of the road?' asked Regan.

'Yeah, but there is a bit visible,' said Penny.

Charlie put a hand on Regan's arm. 'Let's watch it and see.'

The first twelve seconds of video showed a group of youths walking past, going towards town and away from the pedestrian crossing, all with their heads bent down against the rain.

'Watch on the top left corner of the screen,' said Penny, pointing unnecessarily.

There was a brief flicker of reflected light on the wet road and a small car weaved briefly across the topmost corner of the screen before it was gone. Regan stayed watching and the screen went black as the footage ended.

'Play it again,' said Regan, not taking her eyes off the screen. They watched it three more times and each time Regan tried not to blink – she didn't want to miss something vital. When it finished its fourth play, Regan slumped back on the sofa and Charlie and Penny looked at her.

'It's a small, light grey or possibly silver, two-door car . . .' She screwed up her face because she wasn't entirely sure.

'I think it might be the same car that nearly ran you over a few minutes before,' said Charlie, his voice steady but quiet.

Chapter Thirty-Five

Regan had had a busy day on the market. She wasn't complaining, but her feet were. She'd not sat down all day. She'd been covering for Jag on the fruit and veg stall, which was always busy, and Malcolm had nipped off a few times because he and his wife were trying to book a last-minute holiday. Plus, thanks to Cleo's new signs, Sticky Situations had also had a steady run of customers.

'Love the new design,' said Ken the honey man, pointing at the banner across Regan's stall. 'Much better.' He gave a thumbs-up.

'That's thanks to you,' she replied.

He waved her comment away. 'You're doing great. You're killing my business,' he said with a friendly wink.

The new signage was much larger and more eye-catching and had definitely increased interest. The new logos on the labels made everything look more professional, and people really liked to stop by and try the jam, especially if she had new flavours. The unicorn jam was still a winner, but the pina colada was a close second. Apparently the mango and aniseed chutney had become a firm favourite at the local Indian restaurant, and they had popped by to order a batch of twelve.

She'd gone straight from the market to the police station to hand over the CCTV evidence to the very bored desk sergeant, who took her details again and nodded in the right places but gave her zero hope that anything at all was going to come of it. She couldn't blame him; the footage wasn't exactly conclusive. A two-door car was all they were certain about. The make, model, age, colour and number plate were all still a mystery.

From the police station she had gone back to Charlie's, which was feeling increasingly like home; she had to keep reminding herself that she would be moving out in twelve days' time. She didn't want to think about that, and instead busied herself making a batch of melon, lime and ginger jam – which was a new recipe thanks to a glut of melons from Jag – and tidying up.

When she knocked on Cleo's front door, she was ready to drop into a heap and snooze. Elvis was having a good sniff around, but when Regan put a hand in her pocket he immediately sat to attention. The regime of feeding throughout the day for good behaviour was starting to pay dividends.

'Hello. Come in,' said Cleo.

'For you,' said Regan, handing Cleo some gerberas, their bright faces bobbing about as she handed them over.

'My favourites. Thank you. Coffee?'

'Yes, please. Where can Elvis sit?' asked Regan, realising the small but stylish apartment was not designed for large clumsy dogs who liked to chew stuff.

'He's fine anywhere. Actually, hang on.' Cleo disappeared and returned with a real sheepskin, which she put on the floor by the sofa. Elvis went straight to it.

'Are you sure? Because what he's going to do is . . .' Elvis demonstrated what he was going to do on cue by bunching up the sheepskin and starting to shag it.

'Ah . . . oh well, never mind. He can take it home with him.' Cleo turned away. 'Should we give him some privacy?' she whispered.

'No, he's not shy, and he usually falls asleep afterwards. He's like most men, just a little hairier – apart from one bloke I went out with at university. You could have plaited his chest hair.'

'Eurgh,' said Cleo.

'Yeah, it was gross. Anyway, have you settled back in?' She sat at the breakfast bar whilst Cleo set about making the coffees.

'Yes, I salvaged something of that picture.' She pointed to a small canvas on the wall. Regan tilted her head and she could see it was part of the canvas that Elvis had stuck his head through, but minus the torn section. It made for quite a tasteful picture.

'Nice job,' said Regan, giving a nod of approval.

'I've not done much else because I've been so busy sorting out the . . .' There was a dramatic pause and Regan smiled at the twinkle in Cleo's eyes, '. . . Cleo Marchant Art Scholarship and Mentoring Programme.' She followed it with a tiny squeal of delight.

'That's fantastic! Well done, you.' Regan gave her a tight hug. She was really proud of her, but also so pleased to see her looking bright and happy.

They chatted over coffees while Elvis snoozed next to his new love – the sheepskin. Cleo talked a lot about how Penny had inspired her to extend her original idea to underprivileged kids. In fact, Penny came up a lot in the conversation.

Cleo checked her watch and Regan took it as a cue to

leave. 'Right, I'd better get back. Charlie's making a curry tonight.'

'You two have got domestic bliss sussed, haven't you?'

'Oh, we're exactly like an old married couple, all right. Meals together, but we sleep apart.' She tried to make it sound like a joke, but it didn't quite hit the mark.

'I'm seeing someone . . .' Cleo was biting the inside of her mouth.

'Ooooh,' said Regan, with childish excitement. 'Out with all the details.' Cleo had been single for such a long time. It made Regan happy that she was dating again.

Cleo's cheeks flushed with colour and she suddenly looked very nervous.

'What would you say if I said I think I might be . . . gay?' Cleo slowly raised her head and made eye contact. She looked so afraid.

Regan smiled. 'I'd say: I've known for ages.'

Cleo's eyebrows danced something akin to the tango. 'How can you have known? I've only recently worked it out for myself.' She looked indignant.

'Painting giant tits was a bit of a giveaway.' Regan pointed at the painting on the wall and they both began to laugh.

Bernice returned to work the next day and intercepted Regan as soon as she started setting up. 'The police are investigating that CCTV footage you handed in,' she said, her voice chipper, although she herself looked drawn and weary.

'That's good,' said Regan, trying to sound upbeat but falling a little short.

'Could you see who it was?'

'I'm so sorry, Bernice. The footage wasn't great. It's a

small, two-door car in a light colour – possibly grey or silver – but that was all.'

Bernice's expectant expression expired. 'You sound like you're already resigned to not catching them. You're not giving up, are you?'

Regan straightened up. 'Goodness, no. Never. It's just really hard. But we'll keep going.'

Bernice bent down to give Elvis a fuss, but Regan had brought the sheepskin so he was otherwise engaged. 'The car was heading towards town, right?' asked Bernice.

'Yep.'

'Then it must come up on other shops' CCTV. There must be other cameras on whatever route the killer took.'

'But once it gets too far away from the scene it's less and less likely that it's the same car.' Regan didn't like the despondent air in her own voice.

Bernice stood up quickly like a jack-in-the-box. 'You *are* giving up.' Her voice was getting louder.

'No. I'm only repeating what the police said.'

Bernice mumbled something else and went to shout at Jag who had left a load of empty crates by his stall.

'You okay?' asked Malcolm, appearing from behind a pile of crusty bloomers. 'I see Boadicea's not got any mellower.'

'Ah, give her a break. She must be going through hell. And she's kind of right.' Regan didn't want to admit it, but she was moving on. She felt awful, but life did go on and with each day it seemed less and less likely they were going to find the hit and run driver. She felt guilty that it was no longer her number one priority, but it was the truth.

She had the business, she had Elvis and she had a multitude of other stuff going on which had all pushed poor Kevin down the list. She felt shitty about it. Kevin was her friend and maybe there was more she could do. She crouched down to stroke Elvis but he was busy rolling on the sheepskin so she left him to it. 'Can you hold the fort, Malcolm? I'm going to do some more door knocking.'

All the businesses she approached were really keen to catch the driver but unfortunately most of them had their CCTV trained on their property. She'd walked right down to Valley Gardens looking for stores with cameras on. Two shops and a pub did have working cameras that caught a glimpse of the road and they all pledged to check the films for the night of the accident and get back to her. It wasn't much but at least she could go back to Bernice with a clear conscience and show that she hadn't given up on Kevin – someone who was important to her too.

She walked back up London Road because, where she could, she avoided Ditchling Road. It was odd, but she could picture Kevin and Elvis lying there and it freaked her out, so it was best to avoid going that way. She racked her brains for what else she could do to help. Perhaps they could get a still image of the car from the nursery and put that on a poster. It may be enough to trigger someone's memory or better still flush out the driver if they had any shred of conscience at all.

Back at the stall the slow old lady was perusing the jars. 'Still no damson?'

'No, but you can try the others if you'd like?' said Regan, slipping back behind the stall.

'You get some toast and I will do, love,' said the old woman with a cackle.

* * *

It was Regan's turn to cook, and she was trying her best. She'd gone for bought pasta and sauce, but she had chopped her own basil to go on top and grated the cheese. Unfortunately, she had also managed to grate one of her knuckles, but she doubted any had actually gone in with the cheese.

'Emergency, emergency,' said Charlie as he came through the door, although his jovial voice didn't match his words.

'What's up?'

'Mrs Tiggy-Winkle called me. She's having a bit of a crisis and she needs our help.'

'But I made dinner.' Regan pouted. She gave her sore knuckle a suck.

'It's okay. I said we'd be over in about an hour. So I'll have a quick shower, we'll eat, and then we can go. If that's all right with you?'

She didn't catch what he said at the end because he'd pulled his shirt off whilst he was talking and she'd been transfixed. It wasn't the most ripped body she'd ever seen – he wasn't all carved abs and baby oil – but he was lightly toned, with nice muscle definition on his arms and a neat trail of hair running down his taut middle and disappearing into his trousers.

'Hellooo,' said Charlie, waving a hand in front of Regan's eyes. She blinked rapidly. 'You all right?'

'Yes, Mrs Tiggy-Winkle. I mean Charlie. Shower, food and hedgehogs. Got it.' She smiled, spun around and promptly walked into the doorframe.

Dinner had been a success and Charlie had ladled on oodles of praise, which Regan lapped up. They decided to risk leaving Elvis on his own for an hour. He'd managed to doze at Regan's feet for most of the day and he was in a good routine with his toileting, so it felt like it was time to give it a go. They chatted in the car, mainly about Elvis, like parents having their first taste of freedom after the birth of a new baby.

Mrs Tiggy-Winkle appeared at the door cradling what looked like a woolly hat. 'Thank you both so much for coming to my rescue. Now, I've got them all ready for you and I've got an instruction sheet I made a few years ago when we had a similar crisis.'

Regan was peering into the woolly hat. A tiny, pale hoglet was wriggling about in the middle. 'Oh, wow. He's so tiny.'

'He's a newborn. Yours are slightly bigger, but still need to be fed every two hours.'

Regan looked from Mrs Tiggy-Winkle to Charlie, and then at the hoglet. 'Our what?'

Mrs Tiggy-Winkle stepped aside. 'Sorry, didn't I explain?' Charlie and Regan shook their heads in perfect synchronised confusion. 'We've been overrun with orphaned hoglets.' Regan couldn't suppress the 'aww' sound that escaped. 'My daughter has some, my neighbour has two and volunteers have the rest, but I had more come in this afternoon and I knew I wouldn't be able to cope. You see, if they aren't kept warm and fed every two hours they'll die.' She stepped back to reveal a hessian bag and a wooden crate on the floor with a small fleece blanket inside. 'There's syringes and Esbilac formula in the bag, along with fresh bedding and a tepid hot water bottle. The instruction sheet I mentioned is in there too. Next feed will be nine o'clock.' She turned back to the bemused pair. 'Any questions?'

'Um, when do you want them back?' asked Charlie.

'I'd like you to keep them for as long as you can.'

They looked at each other. 'I'm busy the next couple of days but then I'm off for four,' said Charlie.

'Terrific,' said Mrs Tiggy-Winkle brightly. 'Call me if you have any problems. But I'm sure you'll be fine. Good luck!'

Chapter Thirty-Six

Charlie had fussed about making sure the hoglets were safe in the crate in the passenger footwell and Regan noted her own subdued, extra-careful driving on the way home. When they got back to Charlie's, Regan went in first to calm Elvis before they brought in the new arrivals. The house was surprisingly and thankfully all intact and he greeted her with much excitement, celebrating her arrival home with a quickie with his sheepskin. While he was occupied, Charlie brought in the hoglets and their paraphernalia.

He put them down on the table in the living room, and they both sat on the edge of the sofa and stared at the crate. A tiny nose was poking out. It twitched.

'What do we do now?' asked Regan.

Charlie checked his watch. 'Get ourselves prepared for the nine o'clock feed, I guess.' He pulled the instruction leaflet out and they both read it, whilst surreptitiously keeping an eye on the crate.

'So shall we take one each at nine o'clock?' suggested Regan.

'There's no point us both being up every two hours during the night.'

'You're not suggesting I do it all, are you?' Regan gave him a look she hoped he understood.

'No. We've both got work tomorrow, so I'm saying we could take it in turns. I'll take eleven o'clock, you take the next one and so on. Okay?'

Regan was working out her shifts in her head. 'Hang on. That means you're only up once in the night with the three o'clock feed, but I've got one o'clock and five.' She wasn't going to be hoodwinked.

'I really don't mind. I thought you'd prefer to get to bed earlier and get a few hours in but I'm happy to swap.'

Regan's brain was whizzing. Which was the best option? She wasn't sure. 'Okay. I'll stick with—' A tiny squeak from the crate drew their attention. They inched forward until they were both peering over the side of the crate.

Inside, two tiny brown blobs with pale spines were wriggling about. They were the oddest sight. They looked like someone had stolen some of their prickles, and they were blind as their eyes hadn't opened yet. They were the most helpless creatures Regan had ever seen. 'Oh, look at them. Aren't they the cutest?' She pulled the blanket back slightly for a better look.

'Mind they don't get cold,' said Charlie, poking the blanket back into place.

'I'll introduce Elvis to them so he doesn't feel left out,' said Regan, opening the living room door.

'No, don't let—' But Elvis trotted in and went straight to investigate the crate.

Charlie whipped it out of the way, making Elvis even keener to get his nose inside. 'Get him away, Reg. He'll eat them.'

'No, he won't.' She was defensive of Elvis but she grabbed him by the collar and pulled him away all the same. 'You're overreacting.'

'Am I? We all know Elvis's rule of three: eat it, shag it or pee on it. And I don't want any of those things happening to the twins.'

'The twins?' said Regan, with a splutter. She liked the way Charlie was protecting the hoglets, but he made them sound like actual human babies. 'Come on, Elvis.' And she encouraged him out with the lure of food. 'We'd better leave Charlie Poppins to it.'

Regan had heard new mums complain about night feeds and being tired, and now she had a tiny window into what they were on about. When her phone buzzed into life again at five o'clock she could have merrily thrown it out of the window or fed it to Elvis. Elvis buried his face in his paws and she wished she could do the same.

She padded downstairs and heard an awful noise coming from the living room. She rushed in and both babies were making a high-pitched whistling noise. They looked okay, so Regan figured it was them demanding their next feed. She got the formula ready in between giant yawns. She felt like a reheated zombie. Her brain wasn't functioning properly whilst she hunted for the syringes. Where had Charlie left them? They were in the sink but hadn't been washed. She grumbled and banged about whilst sterilising them.

Her frustrations vanished when she cradled the tiny hoglets and they stopped their baby shrieks and began guzzling. It was a slow process because they were so little; they only took a tiny amount of fluid with each suck. And the syringes had to be small so needed regular refilling. She watched them nodding off as their tummies filled up.

'Come on,' she whispered, 'just a bit more. Mrs Tiggy-Winkle's instructions say you have to drink it all.' But she could feel her own eyes growing heavy too. Having her sleep interrupted was a killer. She had slept between feeds, but it had felt like it had taken ages for her to drop off, only to be woken shortly afterwards by the next alarm. Thank goodness Charlie was taking his share of turns or she'd feel even worse than she did.

'Reg. Wakey wakey,' came a distant voice. Regan stretched.

'Whoa,' said Charlie, quickly taking the bundle of hoglets from her arms. 'You fell asleep.'

She opened a blurry eye. 'What time is it?'

'Seven. It's my turn.' He took the hedgehogs and empty syringes off to the kitchen while Regan tried to pull herself awake.

'You want a coffee?' he called cheerfully. He was so cheerful, she wanted to smother him with Elvis's sheepskin. How come he was so bright? She'd definitely picked the wrong shifts.

By quarter to five that evening Regan was dead on her feet. If she wasn't feeding the hoglets, she was cleaning them, checking they were safe and warm, or thinking about the next time she had to do all those things. Trying to run the stall at the same time was quite the challenge. Elvis was having a playful day and he wanted to greet anyone who came within six feet of them. Regan was convinced he was acting up because he was jealous of the new arrivals.

Despite her feet aching, she could have fallen asleep standing up. Sales-wise it had been an okay day, and the online business was steadily picking up now Cleo had got a friend to examine her SEO, which apparently stood for 'search engine optimisation'. Regan wasn't that clued up on how to manipulate the internet, so she was very grateful for any help she could get.

She had six orders that needed packing up and posting, and she needed to make more jam. She was now in the odd position where she was having to buy strawberries from Jag because her unicorn jam was a bestseller. This had made Jag very happy, and he was sharing with the other stallholders how he had 'paid it forward' to help her get started.

Regan started to pack her stall away but was interrupted by Bernice striding over. The sight of her looming into view didn't have its previous effect now the two women were getting to know each other better.

'Regan, take a look at this.' Bernice placed a sheet of A4 paper on the stall and Regan tried to focus on the picture. 'One of the shops got in touch and this is the shot we got from their film. I've given the film to the police, but I've printed off fifty posters of this image. It should be enough for someone to identify the car.' She tapped a finger on the blurry image. It was the back of a small, light-coloured car. The number plate was obscured, but part of a Manchester United scarf was clearly visible hanging in the back window. Regan recognised the scarf and a wave of nausea washed over her.

Regan had thought she was going to be sick but she'd held it together and packed up the stall in record time. Now she was on her way to the fire station. She swung into the small car park, carefully picked up the baby hedgehogs and beckoned Elvis out of the back seat. She nudged the car doors shut with her bum and rushed inside, where she found Charlie chatting to Eric. His face fell at the sight of Regan.

'What's happened? Are they okay?'

'They're fine. I have to go. I can't explain. But you need to take these.' She thrust the crate into his arms. 'And Elvis too, because I don't know when I'll be back.'

'Hang on. I'm still working.' He tipped his head at Eric. 'I'll be finished in thirty minutes.'

'Sorry. Can't wait.' She was already walking away. 'I'll explain later.' And she broke into a jog.

'Reg? Regan!' he called after her, but she kept going.

She was on the brink of tears when she reached her dad's place. She went to knock on the door. She needed to see him; to speak to him and try to understand what had happened. There must be some explanation, but try as she might she couldn't think what it could be – other than that her father had mown down her friend and driven off. There was no answer from his flat, so she knocked again. Inside she saw a shadow move. Either he was in there or he had burglars.

'Dad, it's me. It's important,' she called through the letterbox, hoping she didn't sound like she was about to burst into tears. A mix of anger and hurt coursed through her, but she needed to stay composed. Shouting and wailing wasn't going to make this any better, although it might have relieved the tension building up inside her.

A shadow appeared at the glass and the door opened, but only by a few inches because it was on the chain. Who ever used the chain on a door? The face on the other side wasn't her father's.

'Tar . . . Tara.' Regan couldn't hide her surprise or disappointment. 'Is my dad in?'

'Umm. No.'

Clearly a woman of few words. *No wonder she gets on with my dad*, she thought.

'I need to speak to him urgently. Please.' It pained her to have to be polite to the woman.

'He's out.'

'So I gathered. When will he be back?'

'Well, the thing is . . . he won't be back until later,' said the sliver of Tara's face that was visible. It didn't look like she was wearing any make-up, so perhaps that was the reason for the door chain.

'Okay.' Regan was losing patience. 'What time is he back?'

'About one . . . tomorrow morning.' Tara went to shut the door. Tara's behaviour was fishier than a mermaid's armpit.

'Hang on.' Regan was struggling to control her escalating temper. 'This is serious. I need to speak to him before then, so—'

'Sorry,' said Tara and she shut the door.

'Hey! You can't . . .' but Regan could see Tara had moved away from the door, so shouting on the doorstep was pointless.

Regan banged on the door, but when that elicited no response she went and sat in her car. Her father didn't have a mobile phone, so waiting it out seemed like the only option. She didn't know what to do. She picked up her phone and rang Cleo.

The phone was answered but all she could hear was laughing. 'Hello?'

'Shhh. Sorry. Regan. Hi,' said Cleo, with giggles in her voice.

'Is this a bad time?'

'No, it's an excellent time . . .' said Cleo, and more laughter and shushing followed.

'Oh, bloody hell. I've interrupted something. Sorry. Bye.' She ended the call.

What the hell was she meant to do now? While she was pondering her options, she had another look at the photo of the car on the poster. There was no doubt, with that scarf in the back window, that it was definitely her dad's car. Her heart sank.

If she approached him he was sure to deny it. But it had to be done. She took a deep breath and tried to order her muddled thoughts. The only shred of hope she had was that it wasn't him driving that night. Her brain sparked with possibilities. This made so much more sense. If Tara was driving, that would explain her cagey nature with the door chain. It was all starting to fit together.

It was likely her poor dad knew nothing about any of it. But if she waded in there now, Tara would be full of excuses and lies. She couldn't risk her getting away with this. Regan needed to be calm and act rationally. She needed to think this through. Perhaps she could present her dad with the evidence when he was alone. Or approach Tara on her own. Or go straight to the police. There were too many options.

She sat for a while mulling things over whilst keeping watch on her father's front door. Her phone rang, distracting her, and she scrabbled around to answer it. It was Charlie. 'What's wrong? You're scaring the life out of me.'

'I'm really sorry, but there's some stuff going on with my dad and Tara and I need to sort it out.' She rummaged around in the passenger footwell for the poster she'd grabbed off Bernice earlier.

'Is there anything I can do?' Charlie sounded sincere.

'Just look after the kids for me.'

'Okay. But you can't—'

'I need to go. Bye.' Her dad's car was taking off up the road. She went into autopilot and drove off after it.

Her heart was racing. It was like being in a slow-motion police chase – her dad didn't drive all that fast. She held back a bit so she wasn't right up behind him at the lights. They set off again and she tried to think where he was heading at this time of the evening. There was nobody in the passenger seat, so he was alone.

They meandered through Brighton until he pulled in quite quickly. Regan had no alternative but to drive past, hoping he didn't see that it was her. She found a parking space further down the same road and waited, watching as a figure got out of her dad's car and moved to the pavement. He was going to walk right past her car: this was her opportunity to catch him and show him the evidence that put his car and, most likely, Tara at the scene of Kevin's accident.

Regan's hands went all clammy. She watched through the mirror as the person came closer. There was something not quite adding up about the movement of the figure approaching. She opened her door a fraction, ready to hop out at the opportune moment. She could hear the sound of heels on the pavement. It must be Tarty Tara.

Regan had a wobble. If she confronted her, could she wreck any chance of a police conviction because she was tipped off? She pulled the car door shut just as the other person drew level. They stopped dead and turned to look at the car. Regan was rumbled, so decided to brazen it out.

She got out of the car and dashed around to the pavement. The person in front of her was wearing a long, pale mac with a sequinned dress just visible underneath. 'Oh hello, Tar . . . Dad?'

Regan thought she was gong to topple over with the shock. Her dad was standing there in a long, flowing wig and full women's make-up. Regan opened her mouth and did the best impression of a goldfish she'd ever done. She could not conjure up a single word, despite a million questions all invading her head.

Graham cleared his throat. 'We should probably talk.' He pointed at her car; silently, she walked round to the driver's side and got back in. Graham got in the passenger seat. At least in the car she didn't have to look at him. She didn't need to; the image was etched on her mind forever.

'I expect you're a little surprised,' he said.

That was the understatement of the century. 'Yeah. A bit.' She clearly didn't know him at all. 'Does Tara know?' She wasn't a fan of the woman, but this would be a shock for anyone.

'Yes. She's been very supportive,' he said. If she shut her eyes he sounded the same.

What were you meant to say to your cross-dressing father? Nice eyeliner? He had actually done a good job with it. She always found eyeliner quite tricky. 'How long have you . . .'

'A few months. When I invited you round for pizza I was going to tell you, but when it came to it I didn't know how. And then, when I fell off my stilettos and strained my neck, I thought I'd have to explain the neck brace, but I felt foolish so I skirted around it.' Regan was aware she was doing a lot of blinking. It was a lot to take in. 'I'm sorry if it upsets you, Regan.' He touched her arm and she jumped. 'It's still me. And I'm happy doing this. It makes me happy.'

She felt the tension in her shoulders slide away. What right did she have to judge? If Tarty Tara was supportive, she could be too. 'Then I'm happy too.' She made her best effort at a smile and turned to face him. He'd overdone the eyeshadow and blusher, and those eyelashes were extreme, but otherwise he actually made a quite striking older woman.

Graham looked down. 'What's that?' He took the scrunched-up poster from her hands. She'd almost forgotten about it.

She cleared her throat. 'Dad. Your car was caught on CCTV. Just after Kevin was killed.'

He peered at the picture and smiled in recognition, his magenta lips lifting at the edges. 'My Man United scarf.'

Why was he smiling? 'Dad, it's your car. Either you or Tara were driving it when it hit Kevin.' Her voice went all weird and shaky and the rest of her joined in.

'It's my car, yes. And I was driving, but I promise you I didn't hit Kevin.'

His well made-up eyes were sincere. 'I had just finished a gig and I was heading to Tara's, so I didn't go past The Level that night—'

Regan blinked a few times and held up a hand to stop him. 'A gig?'

He went all perky and his voice changed. 'I'm Virginia Flowers.' Regan's face must have registered her total lack of comprehension. 'I'm the drag queen on the pier.'

'A drag queen? You?'

'Yes. Why else did you think I was dressed like this?'

'Drag queen,' she muttered, feeling relief mixed with a new wave of embarrassment swamp her.

'Yes. Seems quite popular – they've signed me up as a regular.'

'That's, um . . . great news. Congratulations.' And she meant it.

‘Thank you.’

He looked so proud, and it made her smile – but this was only one question answered. ‘How come your car was on CCTV swerving down Ditchling Road after the accident? Just before it turned into Richmond Place and was captured on camera a second time?’

‘I wasn’t on Ditchling Road. I went up Gloucester Place and then into Richmond Place and up that way.’

‘Away from town?’

‘Obviously.’

She snatched up the poster and scanned the photograph. ‘So this is your car, but the one on Ditchling Road moments before can’t have been yours.’ Regan’s whole body slumped in the seat like a deflating airbed.

‘That’s right. But now I think about it, a car did come flying down Grand Parade.’

She sat up again. ‘And can you remember what that car looked like?’

He looked thoughtfully out of the windscreen before turning back to Regan and giving a slow blink with his heavy false eyelashes. ‘Yes. I can.’

Chapter Thirty-Seven

Regan hoped her offering of fish and chips would help smooth things over with Charlie. She wasn't proud of having dumped the animals on him earlier, but at the time she couldn't see another solution.

She came inside hugging the chippy bag. 'I am so sorry. But you see—'

'Shush,' said Charlie sharply, sticking his head out of the living room. 'They've just stopped squeaking.'

'I bought fish and chips,' she said, waving the paper bag like a lumpy white flag of surrender. Elvis was already circling her like a starved shark.

'You can't dump these guys on me when I'm at work, Regan.' His tone and his use of her full name weren't good signs.

'I'm really sorry but I honestly had no choice. Did you get into trouble?' She took the food through to the kitchen and decanted the fish and chips onto plates. If she'd been on her own she'd have eaten them out of the paper.

'Eric wasn't impressed. Especially when Elvis peed up the pole and got his head stuck in a bin.'

'Ah.' She bit her lip. 'I really am sorry, Charlie.' There was a pause where they both surveyed each other. Charlie broke eye contact first and ran his fingers through his hair. She could see the fight was going out of him and she was relieved. She didn't want to argue with Charlie. She grabbed knives and forks and he followed her to the table.

'What was so urgent?' he asked.

'Oh, where to begin?' she said, spearing a chip.

Five minutes later, Charlie had gasped and spluttered in all the right places and was now up to speed. 'Blimey. I have to say I've heard your dad sing and he – well, Virginia Flowers – can really belt out a tune.'

Regan felt an odd sense of pride. 'Yeah, he can sing. I guess I'll have to go along and watch him perform.'

'Have you told Bernice that she's got the wrong car?' he asked, changing the mood somewhat.

'Calling her is next on my to-do list.' Regan put down her fork. 'She's going to be gutted. Not least because she's had loads of those posters made.' Regan tapped the crumpled sheet. She wasn't looking forward to telling Bernice her only lead went nowhere.

A high-pitched squeal came from the living room. Elvis sat up in the hallway and whimpered. Charlie put his cutlery down. 'No, you finish your meal,' she said, getting to her feet. 'I'll get this one, and I'll cover the night shift to show how sorry I am for dumping the kids on you.'

'You don't have to.'

'No, I know I don't; but we're a team.' She patted Elvis and he flopped back down.

At two o'clock in the morning she was very much regretting her gallant gesture. The hoglets had had her up every hour. They seemed to have decided that they didn't like being fed together and they preferred their pipettes separately, which meant the whole process took longer. One of them wasn't taking all the milk so Regan had painted her toes with pink nail varnish so she could keep an eye on her. She'd decided it was a female because she was showing diva-ish tendencies and, inspired by the flamboyant nails, she'd called her Virginia. She hoped hedgehog Virginia was okay but she really wanted to get some sleep herself. It didn't matter how much she'd clanged about, Charlie hadn't stirred.

She'd moved the hoglets into her bedroom, but that had disturbed Elvis; so Regan was now curled up under a soft throw on the sofa while Elvis and Charlie slept soundly upstairs. She'd heard of sleeping like a baby, but she wanted to sleep like Charlie. She didn't begrudge him his sleep – he had another twelve-hour shift ahead of him and she had a day off with the spiky duo – but she could still do with a few hours' shut eye.

She thought back to her awkward telephone conversation with Bernice. She had struggled to accept Regan's information that the car in the picture was not the one that had killed her brother. She had gone on to insinuate that Regan was covering for her father, which had been the low point of the conversation. Although Regan didn't blame her for lashing out. She didn't like being the one to rub out the only lead they'd had, but she wasn't going to let an angry mob hunt down her dad when he was innocent.

It had made her see that they should have left the sleuthing to the police; and to an extent, that was what they were going to have to do. After some persuasion, due to the involvement of his alter ego Virginia, her dad had agreed to go to the police and make a statement. He only had a snippet of information about the car he'd seen that night, but Regan was very much in the every-little-helps camp.

Despite vowing that she was now leaving it all to the police, she still had one thing niggling away at her. She'd have to investigate it for herself or it would drive her potty. Something her dad had said about the speeding car was ringing bells in her own mind but she couldn't quite work out why.

Regan saw every hour of the night. She wasn't proud of how Charlie found her when he came down at seven o'clock. He was startled to see her sitting in the kitchen, huddled over a jar of jam, with her hair displaying crazy scientist qualities.

'You all right?' he asked, with a yawn.

'I'm eating unicorn jam with a soupspoon. What do you think?'

'Um, not great?' he ventured, automatically getting out two mugs for coffee.

'I've hardly slept. One of them's not feeding properly. And they're not sleeping like they were. I even put *Peppa Pig* on for them.'

Charlie furrowed his brow. 'Can they watch that?'

Regan almost lost it. 'Jeez. It's not *The Walking Dead*, Charlie. I don't think they'll have nightmares or turn out to be hoodlum hedgehogs.'

'I meant because their eyes aren't open, not because it's not suitable.' He was laughing at her. She wished she wasn't too tired to laugh at herself.

Regan refilled her spoon with sparkly jam. 'I think one of them is ill. Virginia.'

'Aww, you named one after your dad,' said Charlie with a chuckle, and he went to get them from the living room and put the crate carefully down on the table. He peered inside like a doting father. 'Is she the one who's had a manicure?'

'Yep.' Regan licked more jam off the spoon. The sugar hit was starting to kick in.

'She looks okay.' He was peering closer.

'She's not taking all the milk formula. I'll keep an eye on her.'

'What shall we call the other one?' There was a sparkle in his eye and it made her heart melt. 'Spike?' he suggested.

'Too corny. I like Trevor, Alan, Dave, or . . . this one is a bit controversial – Badger.' Not that she'd spent half the night mulling over her favourite baby names. She'd had to stop her mind wandering off into the dangerous territory of 'what-would-Charlie-and-I-call-our-baby'. 'Badger' hadn't appeared on that particular list.

'Which of those works best with McGee-Corsetti?' he asked, his face serious.

'I think you mean Corsetti-McGee. And it's definitely Trevor.'

'I agree.' He beamed a smile over the crate. 'Trevor and Virginia. I'm a little bit in love.' *Yeah, me too*, thought Regan.

Regan had taken the day off, but because Charlie was worried that chutney fumes might choke their babies she had decided to get out of the house.

She poked her head around the coffee shop door. 'Woman needing caffeine,' she called to Penny, who was wiping down tables.

'Come in,' said Penny.

'Can't, I've got the kids.' She pulled an apologetic face.

There was a massive thud on the glass as Elvis jumped up and began licking the window.

'It's just like old times,' said Penny, watching Elvis. 'I'll bring your drinks out.'

Regan managed to manhandle Elvis to a sitting position, but he refused to take his eyes off Penny making drinks inside. Regan took the table nearest to him and settled herself down with the crate.

'Hi,' said Cleo, sashaying into view and pulling out a chair. 'I thought you'd be working the stall today?'

'I took the day off to get jam orders up straight but I've been hijacked by this pair.' She pointed into the crate and pulled the blanket back slightly.

Cleo recoiled. 'What's wrong with them?'

'They're baby hedgehogs. There's nothing wrong with them,' she said, feeling defensive towards her charges.

'Oh. I thought it was a mouse with some awful disease with those spikes on its head.' She leaned over for a better look. 'Aww, they're sort of cute, in a weird way.'

A noise drew Regan's attention. 'Elvis.' Her voice was stern as Elvis pawed at the window. He stopped, blinked his hairy eyebrows at her and returned to licking his lips obsessively. 'This parenting lark is hard work,' said Regan, yawning and flopping back in the seat.

'Parenting?' Cleo was giving her a comical stare.

'It's like parenting, but because it's with animals it's probably harder.' Cleo's expression didn't change. 'Anyway, what are you doing here?'

'Ah. Well . . .' Cleo's cheeks coloured up.

Penny came out carrying drinks, neatly sidestepped Elvis, placed the drinks on the table and kissed Cleo firmly on the lips. Cleo froze and Penny sat down between them.

A smile spread across Regan's face. 'So *that's* what you're doing here.'

'Oh, sorry. Had you not told her?' said Penny. She was back to her usual effervescent self and it suited her.

Cleo shook her head. 'Not officially.' She reached for Penny's hand. 'We're dating,' she said proudly.

'Brilliant. I'm thrilled for both of you.' Regan gave them both a hug, being careful not to nudge the hedgehog crate.

Elvis flopped his head impatiently onto the table, making the drinks wobble precariously and jolting the hoglets awake. Immediately they began screeching. 'He's jealous,' said Regan, picking up his milk and dribbling it into his mouth. He soon gulped it down and settled under the table.

'While I feed these two, you can tell me what your plans are now Mr Hughes is selling up.' Regan was overheating so she unzipped her hoodie.

'Blimey, I thought you were going to breastfeed them for a moment,' said Penny. Regan glanced skywards and carried on. She got out a jar of formula she'd got ready earlier and a syringe and starting feeding the babies. She was pleased to see Virginia latching on quickly and guzzling away – she was obviously feeling better.

'Good morning,' said a smartly dressed man. Penny nearly toppled over backwards in her haste to stand up.

'Mr Hughes. I was just taking a quick break. I'll get back to work . . .'

He waved Penny's words away. 'It's fine. You can do whatever you like now it's yours,' he said. 'I called by to say I've—'

'Hang on,' said Penny, waving her hands in front of Mr Hughes. 'What did you say?'

Cleo cleared her throat. Regan whipped out another

syringe in an attempt to shut up Trevor, who was still squealing to be fed. She didn't want to miss the drama unfolding around her.

'I was going to say something tonight, over dinner . . .' said Cleo, her voice all wobbly. 'I bought the café . . . for you.' She looked glassy-eyed. Regan felt quite emotional witnessing it.

Penny was frowning hard. 'You bought the Hug In A Mug?'

'Yes, I did.' Cleo was grinning.

'So now I work for you?' Penny was shaking her head and her smile was long gone.

'No, it's yours. It'll all be in your name,' said Cleo.

'She drives a hard bargain,' chipped in Mr Hughes.

'I can't accept this. It's like you're trying to buy me.' Penny waved her arm perilously close to Trevor, making Regan inch her chair back.

Cleo was shaking her head and Mr Hughes joined in, most likely sensing his quick sale was about to crumble. 'It's just a gift,' said Cleo, still forcing a smile.

'You buy people flowers and chocolates, Cleo, not a sodding café.' Penny looked around as if she was assessing her best escape route. 'I need to get back to work. Is that okay?' She stared at Cleo.

Cleo dropped her gaze and fiddled with the hair band on her wrist. 'Of course.' Regan felt for Cleo – she had seemed so happy a few moments ago; they both had. She hoped they could sort this out.

Mr Hughes straightened his tie. 'Right. Well, I've signed the paperwork so I trust this doesn't alter things.'

'Don't worry, I'll still buy it,' said Cleo, her tone glum. Her phone rang and she excused herself to answer it.

'Great,' said Mr Hughes, perking up. 'How old's the

baby?' he asked, nodding at the blanket bundle Regan was cradling.

'We're not sure,' she said, and Mr Hughes's eyebrows did something akin to the worm. 'Probably a couple of weeks old.' Regan angled the bundle so he could see.

Mr Hughes was so startled by the sight of the wriggling hoglets that he almost sat on the table in his haste to retreat.

'Hoglets,' said Regan, trying not be offended by his dramatic reaction to her babies.

'Oh, I see. Lovely,' he said, with a twitch of his nose. 'I need to get going. Bye.' Regan watched him shake his head all the way to his car.

Cleo ended her phone call and returned to the table, her expression one of bewilderment. 'That was Oscar,' she said. 'He's been arrested.'

Chapter Thirty-Eight

'You're home early,' said Regan, when Charlie strolled in at five o'clock. 'You can feed the twins if you like.'

'Sure,' he said, and he followed her through to the living room.

'You won't believe what happened today . . .' started Regan, but then something in his eyes stopped her. 'What's wrong?'

'I'm fine.' She held him with her stare and he shrugged. 'Okay, I went for a scan today.'

Her guts plummeted to her feet as she felt the now familiar sensation of her world crumbling. 'Why? What happened? Do you feel all right?' Her voice constricted in her throat. The thought he might be getting worse scratched at her eyes.

'It's routine. Nothing to worry about.'

'Has the . . .' she pointed to his head.

'The tumour,' said Charlie. 'You can call it by name – it's not Voldemort.' He managed a smile.

'Has the tumour grown?'

'They don't tell you anything on scan day. I'll see my specialist in a week or so and he'll update me.'

She was struggling to see what had affected his mood

so greatly if there wasn't any news. 'Then what's wrong?'

Charlie lifted a hoglet from the crate. He cradled Trevor and his blanket in his arms. 'They show you a slide show whilst you're in the scanner. Just a bunch of pretty pictures.'

'To take your mind off what's happening?'

'Exactly. It's all landscapes and scenery. It's quite calming.'

'Like looking at someone's old holiday photos. Sounds like my granddad after he's been on a coach trip,' quipped Regan.

'Yeah. It is a bit. There was one of the Northern Lights. It was stunningly beautiful.' His eyes drifted off when he spoke, like he was seeing it again. 'It's something I've always wanted to see. And I guess I thought that one day I would. And then today, when it popped up, this wave of reality hit me . . .'

Regan gripped his hand and he returned the squeeze. 'I'm sorry, Charlie.'

'It's okay. It's the oddest things that bring it home.' He took a deep breath. 'I'm wondering if I should have done a bucket list after all.'

Regan pondered this. 'I think your live-each-day-the-best-you-can plan is better. I know someone who spent a fortune going to see the Northern Lights and when they got there they weren't on.'

Charlie was laughing. 'You know they don't get switched on by a celebrity like Brighton Christmas lights?'

'Ha, ha. You know what I mean. I think we could all learn from you.' She didn't like to admit it, but there were things she regretted. She'd only recently really taken control of her life – she'd wasted a lot of time coasting. 'There's a list of things I wish I'd done differently.'

'Hang on, I'll call the *Guinness Book of Records* because that's going to be a very long list.'

'Oh, you're funny,' she said, tickling him in the ribs.

'Hey, I'm holding the baby. You can't do that.' He wriggled away. 'Anyway, how was your day?'

'Sit down, because I need to update you on lesbian hook-ups and police arrests.'

'Blimey, you have been busy,' he said, with a chuckle.

The next day, Regan had already taken two calls from an anxious Cleo, who was struggling with the guilt she felt thanks to Oscar pleading with her to drop the charges after his arrest for stealing money from her. Cleo's accountant had done a sterling job of uncovering the deception and, now he'd been found out, Oscar was woefully apologetic and, as usual, was trying to manipulate Cleo. Thankfully she was standing up to him so far. Poor Cleo was also feeling guilty because Penny was still steaming like a volcano thanks to her generous but somewhat mistimed gift. Regan had juggled the calls in between customers, and now there was a lull she took a quick break from the stall.

She was on her way to do a coffee run when she spotted Alex looking in a shop window. She made a detour to join him; it was an ideal opportunity to put things straight between them. She was trying to take a leaf out of Charlie's book and be the best she could be every day. It wasn't going to be easy but she was willing to try.

'Hiya,' she said, coming up behind Alex.

He jumped. 'Oh. Um. Regan. You okay?' He was already backing away.

'Yeah, can I buy you a coffee?' He looked wrong-footed. 'Come on, I'm not going to attack you. I promise.'

He checked his watch. 'Okay,' he said, but he sounded unsure.

Regan didn't want to sit and reminisce with Alex. All she needed to do was assuage her conscience. They strolled towards the coffee shop. 'How's work?' she asked, bored by her own dullness – but she was trying to be polite.

'Yeah. It's good. Busy since you left. I've been covering.'

'Sorry.' She said it automatically rather than because she was.

'It's okay. I think it's impressed the bosses, so hopefully I'll get something out of it in the long run.'

They continued their bland conversation in the coffee queue. Regan paid and handed Alex his cup. They walked out in silence.

'Thanks for the coffee,' he said. 'I am really sorry about everything.'

'Yeah. Me too. The coffee is really to say sorry about losing it that day. And hopefully bring an end to it all.'

'You know you could come back to work,' he said, pausing by a silver car.

'No, you're all right. I'm doing okay, thanks.' She glanced at the car behind him. Something about it spiked her memory. 'Are they different hub caps?' she asked, distracted by the odd mismatch of the circles on the wheels.

'Different wheels. I bumped the alloy and twisted it about a year ago.'

'Right.' Her lips had gone suddenly dry. 'You could get that swapped to match the others for next to nothing,' she said, trying to think on her feet. She might have put two and two together and got fourteen, but she had to go with her hunch.

'Nah, I don't think you can. Alloys are quite expensive.'

She shook her head. 'I know this guy, Brian. He runs

a tyre place. I'll message you his number and he'll sort it for you. Probably won't even charge.' She was sailing close to the wind now.

'Really?' He was frowning hard.

'Yes. I'll text you his details.'

'Great.' Alex unlocked the car. 'Thanks for the coffee, Regan. It was good to see you.'

'You too.'

Alex paused and jiggled his car keys, pulling Regan's gaze away from the wheels. 'You're seeing someone, right?'

'No. What makes you say that?'

'Oh, my mistake. I saw you out with some guy and assumed. But if you're not, maybe we should go out for a drink sometime?'

'Yes. We should do that,' said Regan. Her brain was churning so fast it was going to turn to butter. She waved him off as he drove away and got straight on her mobile.

'Cleo, I need a huge favour. I've got a hunch I know who killed Kevin.'

Regan came flying into the house with Elvis at her heels and almost skidded to a halt in the hallway. Charlie was standing there cradling the crate, his face a picture of sadness.

'What's happened?' she asked, her heart doing a flutter.

Charlie looked up. 'Mrs Tiggy-Winkle called. There's room for them to go back to the rescue centre.'

Regan's bottom lip wobbled. How could you get so attached to two squealing little bundles so quickly? 'Is this goodbye?'

'Until we go over next week for volunteering. We'll see them then.'

They both stood and stared at the sleeping duo nestled

protectively in Charlie's bicep. Virginia stirred in her sleep and scratched her nose with her painted toes. It was like she was waving goodbye. Regan cleared her throat to hide the fact that she was choked with emotion.

'Do I need to drive them back tonight?' she asked.

'Yeah, but we don't have to go until after we've had dinner. I cooked meatballs so we just need to boil some pasta.'

'You're the best boyf . . .' Regan stopped herself and lifted her chin. 'You're the best.'

'Like you said. We make a great team.' His voice was wistful. He was right, they were brilliant together. It felt like they could do anything, achieve anything, as long as the other one was there. She'd waited her whole life for the right one, and now she'd found him, he had months left to live. There was so much Regan wanted to say, but she was struggling to keep a lid on her bubbling emotions. She blamed the hedgehogs for making her turn soppy and sentimental.

'Right. Pasta.' She needed to keep her mind busy.

Charlie returned the hoglets to the living room before joining her in the kitchen and laying the table. 'How was your day?'

'Interesting . . . I might have a lead on who killed Kevin, but it's wafer-thin and based mainly on my dad's memory.'

'Anything I can do?'

'Don't suppose you know any tame coppers who would check out a car on the sly, do you?'

'No, but I know one who owes me a favour. I could probably ask him to do a routine check or something like that.'

'You get better and better,' she said, unable to resist giving him a hug. She wrapped her arms around him and he didn't resist. He held her and she didn't want to pull away. It felt right when they were together. It felt right all the time. Unfortunately, Elvis agreed and tried to join the hug, effectively shoving them both into the table and sending the cutlery clattering to the floor. From the other room they heard the squealing begin; the clatter had woken the hoglets.

'You know, maybe I won't miss them quite as much as I thought I would,' said Regan. Charlie went to check on the hedgehogs for the last time.

A few days later Cleo was pacing around the studio when Regan arrived. 'This is a wild goose chase. What are the odds of it being the same car?'

'Minuscule, I know, but I have to check. Charlie's policeman mate is going to look the car over while I have a drink with Alex. We're not doing any harm.'

'And when it's not the car that killed Kevin, Alex is going to want to know why he's not got a new matching alloy.'

'I've thought of that. Brian's going to say the bolts are seized up.'

Cleo shook her head. 'It's bonkers.'

'But I have to know. Dad said the wheels on the speeding car were different. If we can match anything about Alex's car to the CCTV footage the police will pull him in for questioning. It's not much, but I owe it to Kevin.'

Cleo was still shaking her head when a text came through on Regan's phone from Brian to say the policeman had arrived.

'Where's Charlie?' asked Cleo.

'Hmm?' Regan was concentrating on replying to Brian. She was finding all the subterfuge quite exciting.

'I thought Charlie was going to be here?' said Cleo.

'He was, but he dashed off first thing . . . said something had come up.' Regan sent the text and tried to hide the smug smile that was threatening to slap itself across her face. 'I think things might be changing with Charlie. He gave me such a tight hug when he left this morning. And he paused – you know like when they're going to kiss you? And I swear my heart missed a beat. That or I've got arrhythmia.' She let out a sigh, but on noticing Cleo's expression she tried to be less gooey. 'Sorry. How's things with Penny?'

'She's not talking to me. Still refusing to run the place after the sale goes through.'

'That's awkward,' said Regan.

Cleo sighed. 'I don't know if we can recover from this. I've been such a fool.' Their conversation was interrupted by the sound of a car pulling up outside.

'Right. Showtime,' said Regan, straightening her shoulders and rubbing her hands together.

'Be normal,' said Cleo. 'Well, you know; as close to it as you can get.' Cleo gave her a brief hug and Regan steadied her breathing. This was it.

Chapter Thirty-Nine

Regan strode up to where Alex had parked outside Brian's garage.

'Hiya.' She felt a bit jittery meeting Alex. There was an awkward air kiss and she had to keep reminding herself that he didn't suspect anything, so all she had to do was not alert him to what they were up to.

'Thanks for setting this up,' said Alex.

'My pleasure,' said Regan, not sounding like herself at all. 'We need to forget what happened at work. Move on.' She was glad when Brian appeared and took over. Brian played his part beautifully – even mentioning that the bolts looked like they'd take some elbow grease to get them off. Alex handed over his keys and they got in Regan's car. With great relief, she drove away. Stage one: complete.

They went to the Caroline of Brunswick pub, because if he was guilty she felt returning to the scene of the crime might prick his conscience. She parked up nearby and was pleased that her pulse had settled to a steady rhythm. She glanced at Alex, but he was busy checking his phone and appeared perfectly normal. It was beginning to look like a wild goose chase.

They crossed the road and she saw him looking at the

flowers on the crossing. 'Horrible accident,' she said. 'It was a wet night. The driver probably didn't see him.' She had her eyebrows raised in hope.

'Yeah. Tragic. So this Brian bloke, he's legit, right?'

Regan sighed inwardly – it was never going to be that easy. 'Yeah. He's a friend of Cleo's.'

'Artist. Posh sort?'

'Yep, that's her.'

They crossed the road and went into the pub. Regan got the first round in and they found some seats and a table.

'Not drinking?' Alex nodded at her Diet Coke.

'I'm driving.'

'You can have one proper drink.' He clinked his pint with her glass.

'I'd rather not. Maybe that's what happened to the person who killed Kevin.' She leaned forward in anticipation.

'Look, Regan. I get that it must have upset you and everything, but do you think we could talk about something else?' He looked apologetic. He didn't look like someone racked with guilt who wanted to offload the burden of his crime. It didn't look like Alex was the killer.

'Of course. Sorry.' She threw her hands up in submission and she could see Alex relax. 'What's new in the world of pharmaceuticals?'

Alex jiggled in his seat. 'You know Jackie and the Milk Club Mafia?' These were a group of ladies who ran the tea and coffee fund with a rod of iron and Sharpie black marker so they could keep track of who was using the milk and be sure they were paying in to the fund. This was the sort of office shenanigans Regan was not missing. She nodded to Alex and feigned interest. 'The rumour is she's gone for a job at the council to work for Melanie's husband!' She took a chance to glance at her watch; it was going to be a very long hour.

Regan was sipping her second Diet Coke and trying to conjure up a variety of facial expressions other than the I'm-so-bored-I-think-I-might-just-give-up-living one that was currently in place. Alex had talked about all the things she didn't miss about working in an office: the gossip, the backbiting, the petty politics and the crap printers.

'Don't you miss it?' Alex was studying her.

'Nope. Not for a second.'

'But a market stall . . .' His tone was condescending. She had to remind herself she was here for a purpose. She only had another ten minutes and she could take him back to his car and forget she'd ever conjured up the stupid idea that he'd been involved. It was her dad's fault with all his daft 'the car had different wheels' malarkey – if it was going so fast, how could he be so sure? She tuned back into Alex. 'It must kill your feet standing up all day.'

'As much as sitting in an office kills your arse.' She gave a sarcastic smile and he laughed.

'But how much is the markup on jam? You must have to sell a shedload to make what you were making at our place? You'll never match the supermarkets for value.'

'I get most of my fruit for free. It's the ultimate in recycling. That appeals to my customers too, and they're happy to pay a fair price for a home-made product.'

'But still . . . must be tough.'

'I'll be honest, Alex. I've come close to giving up, but then I remember I have a load of arseholes to prove wrong and it spurs me on.' She gave him her sweetest smile and finished her Coke.

'You're funny, Regan. I've missed you.' He reached across

the table to take her hand, making her retract it sharply and knock over her glass.

'It's okay. It's empty,' she said, picking it up. 'Right. Time to go.' She stood up and a confused-looking Alex downed the rest of his pint and followed her.

She was keen to get back and forget the whole sorry episode. She stalked out of the pub and across the road. A screech of brakes and Alex's hand on her shoulder stopped her from being run over.

'Shitterama,' she said, her heart pumping at warp speed. She waved an apology at the bloke in the white van, who was shaking his head. It was exactly like the night of the accident when she'd stepped in front of a car – the car that most likely killed Kevin. 'History repeating itself,' she said, with a glance at Alex. 'Poor bloke looked terrified.'

'Yeah. I know how he feels.' Alex seemed to freeze.

All sorts of things ran through Regan's mind. The rain the night of the accident. Seeing Kevin in the park and running into the road. The car that almost ran her over. 'It was you.' Her voice was so much calmer than she thought it would be. 'The night of the accident. The car I stepped in front of. It was yours.'

Alex was biting his bottom lip. 'Don't go jumping to any conclusions.'

'I'm not, Alex. You're my friend.' It was maxing out her acting skills not to rip his head off and boot it into The Level. 'I stepped out. It was my fault.' She could see it now: a flash of silver. She'd been completely focused on getting across the road. 'But that was your car I stepped in front of, wasn't it?'

She held her breath. Alex rubbed his chin. 'Yeah. But it wasn't me that . . .'

She waved his words away. Her mind was racing.

Charlie was sure the car that had almost hit her had done a lap of The Level and had been the same car that killed Kevin. 'Like I said, it was an accident. It wasn't intentional. The dog runs out, the homeless guy chases him. You can't see properly. You try to brake, but . . .'

Alex scratched his eyebrow, glanced furtively around and let out a slow breath. 'I know this looks bad . . .'

Regan pushed her balled-up fist into her pocket. She needed to stay calm. She shrugged and tried hard to look like she didn't care, whilst she silently focused on her breathing. 'Hey. Accidents happen. You getting locked up won't bring him back.'

'Exactly,' said Alex, with gusto. Relief swamping his features. 'That's exactly it. It was just an accident. It all happened so fast.'

You bastard, thought Regan, clenching her teeth. Her breath was shaky, but Alex didn't seem to notice.

'It was awful.' Alex was shaking his head. 'I felt sick and I panicked. But then when I found out it was this homeless guy, I figured my luck was in and I might get away with it.'

Regan's body was fizzing from the inside out like a bottle of shaken Coke. 'Hmm.' She swallowed and nodded. She needed to get him back to his car before she was the one doing time. 'We should get back.'

The atmosphere in the car was tense. Regan kept her eyes fixed on the road and gripped the steering wheel until her knuckles were white. As they neared the studio Alex started speaking. 'Regan, you're very quiet. You do understand about the accident, don't you?'

'Sure,' she said, hardly able to speak for the tightness of her jaw.

'You won't say anything, will you?'

She glanced at him. His face was ashen. 'You could say something.' This was his opportunity to do the decent thing. She pulled the car into the kerb outside Brian's unit.

'Why? Why would I do that?'

'Because it's the right thing to do.'

'I can't. I'm scared, Regan.' He shook his head. 'Look at it this way. The bloke's dead. Nothing is going to change that. What would be the point of me getting nicked? I would lose my licence. Possibly even lose my job.'

'You might end up on the streets,' said Regan, her face deadpan.

'Exactly! And for what? The guy was probably a junkie anyway.'

Regan got out of the car because she feared if she didn't she'd hit him. She slammed the door shut and ran towards Brian's. Alex chased after her, catching her on the threshold. 'Regan. Think about it. Why should I lose everything because some homeless guy stumbles in front of my car?'

'He was on the crossing!' Her voice was spiralling out of control.

'I didn't see the red light until it was too late. I tried to brake but everything locked up. God knows what speed I was doing . . . I was looking for you, Regan. One minute you were there, the next you'd gone.'

'It's my fault. Is that it?'

'No. But it's not mine either. You said it earlier. It was just an accident.'

Regan was incredulous. 'You didn't stop!' She thumped his chest with her fists and he lurched back. Tears of anger streamed across her cheeks.

Someone behind the open door cleared their throat

and Regan and Alex spun around. A tall police officer pulled out his warrant card.

'Mr Alexander Lowe?'

'Yes,' said Alex, his voice barely a croak.

'I'm arresting you on suspicion of failing to stop at the scene of an accident. You have the right to remain—'

'Hang on! You can't take an overheard conversation as fact. I was joking anyway.' Alex spluttered a laugh. 'We do this all the time. Her and me, we wind each other up. It's what we do. Isn't that right, Regan? Regan? Tell him.'

The police officer lifted his jaw in a questioning manner. 'I've spent the last hour collecting samples from the front of your car, sir. The front of your *damaged* car.'

'There can't be anything on it,' said Alex, his voice adamant.

'Not on the new bumper, no, sir, but around the grille there's something that looks very much like dog fur. But we'll need the lab to confirm that.'

'That could have been from any animal.' Alex tried to snort a derisory laugh, but there was a sheen of sweat forming on his brow and he looked agitated.

'We'll be doing a thorough match to determine that, and to check any other microscopic traces that may remain. We've seized the vehicle for further tests.' Alex hung his head and the officer went through his rights. A police car appeared from around the corner and Alex's head snapped back up again, his mouth almost a smile.

'You set me up.' Alex was glaring at Regan, but his voice was even.

'No. If you had nothing to hide it would all have been a big waste of time.'

'Bloody hell, you got me this time, Regan. You win.' He shook his head as he was led away.

Tears were brimming in her eyes. 'No, Alex. This time nobody wins. Least of all Kevin.'

It took a while before Regan felt calm enough to drive home. Home. Charlie's place felt like home, but then she guessed wherever Charlie was would feel the same. She had a renewed sense of determination. Life could change on a coin toss – the Alex and Kevin situation had taught her that. Two lives had been changed in a few seconds.

The time had come to tell Charlie how she felt. She had nothing to lose. He could still stick to his guns and say they weren't to enter into a relationship, but perhaps if he knew how much she loved him . . . perhaps it would be enough to make him rethink. Because she didn't care about the pain that was coming. It was coming anyway – she may as well face it knowing they had enjoyed every moment to the maximum. She just hoped he felt the same.

The lights were on when she unlocked the door. This was good – he was home.

'Charlie!' she called, excitement bouncing around inside her like Elvis on a trampoline.

She saw the shadow fill the living room door and spun in that direction. This was it – this was the moment she wanted to remember. Her broad grin was almost making her face hurt.

She looked up and baulked. 'Oh, Beanstalk. Hi.' She self-consciously tucked her hair behind her ear. 'We weren't expecting you back until Friday.' She tried to look behind him, but he was a sweatpants-wearing barricade. 'Where's Charlie?'

Beanstalk's face twitched. 'You need to come and sit down.'

If Regan's stomach had been a gymnast, it would have just done an elaborate somersault and faceplanted the floor. Beanstalk stood back and she went and sat on the sofa. He joined her. There was an awkward moment where he sat down and his weight made her slide towards him and she had to shuffle away from the middle.

Beanstalk blew out his cheeks. 'Bloody hell, this is hard,' he said, and without warning, tears trickled down Regan's cheeks. 'Oh, no. No,' he said, shaking his head. 'Charlie's not dead. It's not that.'

She angrily brushed the tears away. 'Shitting hell, Beanstalk. Then what is it?'

'Charlie changed his mind a few days ago . . . about risking the operation. He went in this morning to have the tumour removed. They were operating at lunchtime.'

Questions flooded her head. What had changed his mind? Why had he suddenly decided to go ahead knowing the risk it entailed? And what were the odds of him surviving this intact?

'And . . . ?' She could barely breathe. 'How is he?'

'There's been no word yet.'

'Then let's go to the hospital. Which one is he in?' She was already on her feet, but she found she wasn't moving forwards because Beanstalk had hold of her arm.

'I'm sorry, Reg. He was quite explicit. He only wants his mum and dad there. Nobody else.'

'Why do you think he didn't tell me?' she asked.

Beanstalk did a slow blink. 'He didn't tell me either. His mum rang me this morning. She said he'd been considering it for a while, but once he'd made his mind up, he didn't want anyone trying to talk him out of it.'

'But what if we don't get to say goodbye?' Her voice caught in her throat.

'We can't think like that. We just have to stay positive and wait.'

They both twisted to look at the clock.

'It's been hours,' said Regan. 'When will we know?' She rubbed at a stray tear.

'His mum's gonna ring my mobile.'

'Right. Then we sit tight and wait.' She sat back down and patted the sofa for no apparent reason.

'Actually, I need to check in at the station.'

'What? Tonight?'

'Yeah. A few things got rushed because I had to come back early and I want to check everything's in place for the aerial appliance delivery. I'll be an hour, tops.'

She had things she should be doing too. 'Actually I need to collect Elvis. Penny's had him for a few hours and he'll need a walk.' Sitting in the house on her own was not going to make time go any quicker. 'Will you call me if you hear?'

Beanstalk rolled his lips together. 'How about we meet back here in an hour, okay?'

Regan nodded. She understood Beanstalk's pessimism; she knew he wouldn't want to tell her bad news over the phone. Charlie had been so adamant about not taking such a huge risk. What if he'd just hastened the end?

She reminded herself that she needed to stay positive. 'Agreed,' she said. 'And one of us should get some alcohol, because whatever happens tonight I'm going to need a stiff drink.'

'You and me both,' agreed Beanstalk.

There was a chill in the air as Regan walked along the beach. The sound of the pebbles crunching underfoot was somehow helping to calm her troubled mind. Elvis was oblivious, charging about like the wild animal he was. She called him when they neared the pier and he trotted over to her like the best-trained dog ever. Occasionally he surprised her.

'Sit,' she said, and he did. His tongue lolled out of his mouth as he panted after his exploits. She rewarded him with a morsel of food, put on his lead, and they continued along the promenade to the pier. She walked down the slope and stood to look at the spot under the pier where she, Elvis, Kevin and Charlie had spent an evening listening to music. She almost smiled. It was a happy memory, and she hoped so much it would be one she could recall with Charlie.

She closed her eyes and tried to use the mindfulness techniques to stop her mind spiralling into the gloom of her worst nightmares. She could hear the sea, its gentle lapping of the stones. She could hear music on the pier and she tried to concentrate on that. Someone was belting out 'I Will Survive' by Gloria Gaynor. There was something very familiar about the voice. 'Virginia Flowers, you old dog,' she muttered to herself, and Elvis whimpered a reply.

Her dad really could sing – she'd always known that from parties, because at the end of a good night someone would pull out a guitar and Graham would be in his element. She was pleased for him that he'd found something he enjoyed. It wasn't your usual run-of-the-mill, dad-type hobby, but then in Regan's life, she never expected run of the mill.

She turned away from the pier and they strolled past the beach cafés, now enjoying their evening trade, until they reached the i360 tower. Regan sat on the wall and Elvis settled at her feet whilst she looked out to sea. This was her favourite spot. There was something both comforting and haunting about the remains of the West Pier, its skeletal structure black against the vibrant colours of the sunset. She loved it just as much as she would if it looked like the Palace Pier. And she knew she'd feel the same about Charlie, whatever the outcome of his operation.

She watched the sun being slowly and deliberately devoured by the sea. A shiver ran through her. She needed to get back to Charlie's – she'd been gone more than an hour. It hadn't been intentional, but she knew deep down that she was putting off finding out. Although being in limbo while they waited was awful, there was an innocent sort of peace in not knowing.

It was almost dark and she quickened her pace as she passed the back of the big seafront hotels. She wouldn't have gone that way without Elvis, but she was pretty fearless with a large dog at her side. She heard shouting up ahead, but her mind was on other things. As she neared, the tone of the shouting changed and she tuned in. A yelp of a shout for help was shortened by a punch and someone fell to the floor. A group of youths were crowded around someone, and when the individual dropped to the floor, that was their cue to pile in. Regan saw red.

She hit the emergency button on her phone so it auto-dialled 999 and she broke into a run. She wasn't letting this happen again. The domino effect of Kevin being attacked would always haunt her.

'Hey! The police are on their way!' she hollered. Elvis was running at her side and barking. She let his lead slip from her fingers and he raced towards the group like a greyhound after a rabbit. 'Look out, rabid dog!' she shouted. The youths started running in all directions and quickly dispersed, leaving the victim crumpled on the ground. Elvis stood nearby and barked loudly while Regan crouched down next to the person on the ground.

'They've gone. Are you okay?' she asked. The person rolled over and, despite the crumpled face, she could see who it was. She sprang upright in surprise and the youth on the floor looked startled. It was the one who had attacked Kevin and stolen from the market stalls. 'You?'

'I'm fine.' He shuffled upright, wincing as he did so.

'Sure?' Her voice was clipped. He nodded. A noise from her mobile distracted her. She apologised to the emergency services operator and ended the call. 'Elvis!' She called him to her, but he was too busy barking into the street.

'I know what you're thinking,' said the youth, clutching his ribs. 'That I deserved it.'

'I do believe in karma,' said Regan, 'but, no, that wasn't what I was thinking.'

He looked surprised. 'What then?'

Elvis trotted over. He sniffed the youth's trousers, lifted his leg and peed on his trainers, oblivious to the youth's shouted expletives.

'That was what I was thinking,' said Regan. 'Exactly that.' She picked up Elvis's lead and they headed home, feeling that on at least some level, Kevin had been avenged.

She slowed down as she approached Charlie's front door. This was it. It was all about Charlie, and yet she knew her own life was going to change the moment she walked inside.

Elvis pulled on the lead. Regan took a deep, steadying breath, unlocked the door and went in. 'Hello?' she called. There was no answer. Beanstalk wasn't back. She sighed in frustration. How long was this torture going to last?

She flipped the switch on the kettle and turned around to see an envelope lying on the table. Beanstalk had scrawled on a sticky note 'Read this. Gone for alcohol.'

Regan snatched up the envelope. Her name was written on the front. With shaking hands, she pulled out a letter written in Charlie's handwriting. She read the first line and slumped into the chair.

My dear Reg,

I'm so truly sorry. If you're reading this then sadly I'm no longer here because my gamble didn't pay off.

Chapter Forty

Tears blurred her vision and she could read no more. Her heart was in pieces. Despair engulfed her, stealing her breath and stripping away her resolve. She slumped onto the table and sobbed. Great, heaving, blubbery sobs; but she didn't care – there wasn't much left to care about. Why had Charlie taken such a risk? She'd not even had a chance to say goodbye. Her tears overwhelmed her. Elvis whimpered and she briefly looked up to see his big sad eyes, level with hers. He pawed at her leg, and when she pushed the chair back he rested his head in her lap. He knew there was something wrong.

She clung to Elvis and cried. He was a comfort. Her world had imploded. She and Charlie had spent the best part of two months in each other's company and it had been the best time of her life. And now it was over.

She heard the front door open and Beanstalk came striding in. 'Oh, Reg.' His voice was soft and he wrapped his arms around her, almost squeezing the air out of her. 'It's okay,' he said.

'Nothing will ever be okay again,' she said, her face buried in his rock of a chest.

She felt him take the letter from her grasp. 'Oh, shit,' said Beanstalk. She pulled away to look up at him towering over her. She knew she must look a mess, but the way Beanstalk was scrunching his face up wasn't really warranted.

He pulled another envelope from his back pocket. 'Whoops. Really sorry. Wrong letter.' He gave an awkward grin and shoved the other envelope at Regan.

She sniffed back the tears. 'What?' Her voice was barely a croak. The front of the envelope just had her name on – it was exactly like the first one. She slowly opened the envelope and unfolded the letter inside. Once again, Charlie's words swam in front of her. She blinked hard to control the tears.

My dear Reg,

I'm sorry I didn't tell you before about having the tumour removed, but I needed to do this alone. And if you're reading this it means I've made it through the operation. It'll be a few days until we know if it's successful or if there's any damage, but this letter means I'm alive.

God only knows what my future holds but I know I want you to be a part of it . . .

She couldn't read any more. She dissolved into yet more tears, but this time they were happy ones.

'Shitting hell, Beanstalk!' she said, giving him a wallop as she laughed through the sobs. She took a deep breath to try to steady her shaking limbs. He handed her a length of kitchen roll and she could see he'd been crying too.

'I am so sorry. I'm such an idiot,' said Beanstalk. 'Charlie left the envelopes in my locker at work and his mum gave me instructions as to which one was which, but then I got a bit confused. When she rang with the news, I came straight here but you were still out, and I'd forgotten the alcohol so I left the envelope in a rush.' He paused, his eyebrows knitted together. 'I'm really sorry I upset you, but I got the best champagne the corner shop stocks.' He held up the bottle proudly.

'Get me a straw,' said Regan, her heart feeling lighter than it ever had before.

'I bought a few bottles.' He pointed to some bags in the hall. 'And now I've got some calls to make.'

Within half an hour the small house was full of friends and firefighters. Beanstalk had dragged out anyone from the fire station not on shift. They'd managed to get hold of a few people from Mantra too, and Penny and Cleo were both there, but studiously avoiding each other. There was music and chatting and lots of drinking. It was probably all a bit premature, with poor Charlie still in a hospital bed, but whatever happened next this was something to celebrate. The tumour was gone and Charlie was alive. He'd beaten the odds.

Cleo had arrived with a case of champagne and a case of beer, because she knew Regan's preference. It was one of the many things Regan loved about her.

'I'm so pleased for you,' said Cleo, giving the hair bobble around her wrist a ping.

Regan looked around the room. 'Too many people?'

'Yeah, but I'm okay. I wanted to check you were all right.' Regan had cried down the phone when she'd rung her, mainly out of relief.

'I'm fine. Well, I will be when I can see for myself that Charlie's okay.'

‘That’s so lovely.’ Cleo was a bit teary, but that was probably due to the champagne consumption and because she and Penny were still struggling to work things out over the coffee shop.

‘Cleo, can you give me a hand with something in the kitchen?’ said Regan. ‘People need more crisps.’ Cleo followed her into the kitchen and Regan handed her a large packet and a bowl. ‘Oh, hang on – I’ll be back in a minute.’

Regan returned with Penny. ‘What’s wrong with the kettle exactly?’ asked Penny, turning to see Cleo. ‘Oh, I see what’s wrong. Nice try, Regan, but—’

‘No, no, no,’ said Regan, blocking the doorway and Penny’s exit. ‘You guys need to sort this out. Look at the pair of you. You’re making yourselves miserable. I’m happy and I want you both to be too.’

‘I appreciate what you’re trying to do,’ said Cleo, starting towards the door. ‘But I should probably go.’

Regan held out a hand to stop her. Penny and Cleo were now side by side. ‘Running away is not the answer. Come on, look at Penny. You think the world of her, don’t you?’ asked Regan.

Cleo glanced at Penny, embarrassment colouring her pale cheeks, but she nodded anyway. ‘And Penny. Look at Cleo . . . She’s way out of your league,’ said Regan with a broad smile, and Penny laughed.

‘Cheeky cow. I mean, you are right, but you’re a cheeky cow.’ Penny twisted to look at Cleo. The way she looked at her was how Elvis looked at his cup of milk; though thankfully with less dribbling. It was love – pure and simple.

Penny and Cleo exchanged the tiniest of smiles and Regan saw her cue to leave. She slipped out and closed the kitchen door. She'd done what she could, and now it was up to them – they were adults and, like most people, were guilty of making bad decisions, but Regan was confident that being together was most definitely the right thing for both of them.

She found Beanstalk, who was quizzing Mandeep about his brain tumour operation, and in particular his recuperation. Mandeep was giving a few cautions around how tired Charlie would be and that it would likely be a long road to recovery. But this was fine; Regan was prepared for that. She knew that with an operation of this scale and invasiveness it was going to take time for his body to recover, and she wanted to be there by Charlie's side every step of the way. She would support him like he had supported her in getting her life back together.

'It's good to meet you,' said Beanstalk, giving Mandeep's hand a hearty shake. 'You're living proof he can get over this.'

Beanstalk's phone rang, and on seeing who was calling he shushed the room. 'It's Joanna, Charlie's mum.' Regan's breath caught in her throat. *Bad news? Good news?* Beanstalk answered the call. 'How goes it, Mrs M?'

The room fell silent and Regan held her breath. Beanstalk listened for what felt like forever, but could have only been a few seconds. Eventually he gave a thumbs-up to the room.

'He's awake!' yelled Beanstalk. The place erupted. Everyone cheered, and he shushed them again before sticking his finger in his ear to block them out while Joanna carried on talking.

Regan was hugged by virtually everyone in the room. She felt almost high from the adrenaline coursing through her. She went to get another beer and catch her breath. Penny and Cleo were coming out of the kitchen holding hands and Regan beamed to see it. 'All okay?' she asked.

'Penny is buying into the business,' said Cleo. She was glowing with happiness.

'Equal partners,' said Penny, looking as happy as Cleo.

'That's brilliant,' said Regan, hugging them both. 'Free coffee for me!'

'No,' said Penny; a little harshly, Regan thought. 'But we are going to run a scheme, so people can pay for coffees for the homeless, which we can give out when needed. So people like Kevin will always have a drink if they need it.' Regan felt the tears well up again and she threw herself into Penny's arms.

'You guys are the best.' It was such a lovely gesture and meant so much to Regan.

When Beanstalk came off the phone, he took Regan to one side. 'Charlie's in Critical Care, but that's what they expected. He's not speaking or anything, but it's a good sign that he's awake. He's over the worst.' Beanstalk wiped away a tear.

'Come here, you great softie,' said Regan, trying to pull him into a hug. Realising he was an immovable object, she went to him instead.

He cleared his throat and pulled away. 'Time for a toast.' He refilled glasses and everyone gathered round. 'I'm a man of few words, but what our friend has done today was the bravest thing I've ever known. And we've seen some stuff, right, boys?' He nodded at the firefighters and there was mumbled agreement. 'The thing is: he had this operation not to be a hero, but because he loved someone so much it was worth risking his life to stay with her. And because of her, my mate is going to be sticking around a whole lot longer. So I want to make a toast to two awesome people – to Debbie and Reg!'

'Debbie and Reg!' chorused the room, and Elvis joined in with a howl.

Epilogue

Six Weeks Later

Regan was more than confused as she turned down the dirt track. Her little car bumped along until she reached a large barn and a farmhouse. She checked Charlie's note. This was the right place. She got out of the car to be greeted by a bearded man in a body warmer and wellingtons.

'Regan?'

'Yes. I'm here to collect something for Charlie McGee.'

'So pleased to meet you,' he said, giving her a very physical handshake. 'Charlie's told me all about you. This way,' he said, striding off down the side of the barn. They walked quite a way until they reached a lake. A sign told her it was for registered fishermen only. Why had Charlie sent her here?

'I'm sorry, but do you know what I'm collecting?' she asked, taking in the picturesque location, the water gently rippling on the surface and the smell of jasmine in the air.

'Yep,' he said with a huge grin, and he tapped his nose. *Not helpful*, thought Regan. He walked onto a wooden fishing platform and pulled on a rope that was tied there until a rowing boat appeared. 'In you get,' he said.

'I think maybe I should call Charlie.' The farmer type man seemed nice, but this was turning really odd really quickly.

'No need. All will be revealed shortly,' he said with a wink, and he held the boat steady. 'Now, in you get.'

She'd probably regret it, but if the worst came to the worst she was a good swimmer. She got in and held on tight while the grinning chap joined her. He turned the small boat around and started rowing off across the lake. Behind him a small clump of trees in the middle of the lake was growing closer: she could see it was a small island . . . and there was a picnic rug laid out on a patch of grass . . . and there was Charlie. Her heart soared at the sight of him.

He was standing on the bank of the tiny island in smart black trousers and a crisp white shirt – he was a sight to behold. He'd left the house early with his dad saying he was off for a checkup. He had them regularly, so she hadn't queried it; nor had she questioned it when he'd said she needed to collect something important from the farm. She couldn't stop grinning. Just the sight of him up and about filled her with a happiness she'd never thought possible. The little boat pulled into another landing stage and Charlie helped Regan out.

'This is a strange place for a brain checkup.' She put her hands on her hips and gave him her best school ma'am look.

'I *might* have lied about that,' said Charlie, with a cheeky grin. His hair was still shorter than before, but it had grown back well and it was even starting to sprout a little around his scar. He looked so well. If it weren't for the eight-inch scar across the back of his head you'd never know he'd had major surgery. He was a marvel.

'Um . . . Where's he going?' asked Regan, when she noticed the farmer had rowed away.

'It's okay. He'll be back later.' Charlie opened his arms. She stepped into his embrace and felt the now-familiar senses of belonging and ecstasy. 'What is all this about, Charlie McGee?'

'Ah . . . patience, Reg.' He sat down on the picnic rug and beckoned her to join him. He opened the picnic basket next to him, took out two cocktail glasses and a cocktail shaker and proceeded to shake it with relish.

'Steady on. The doctor said no exertion.' She knew she was being overprotective. He had come so far in the last few weeks, but she still feared something could happen that would set him back. It had all gone so well since the operation. He'd had some headaches and some sickness afterwards, but otherwise he had improved day by day with no side effects. Despite all the risks, the operation had gone well. The surgeon said you never really knew exactly what you were dealing with until you operated, and thankfully Charlie's brain tumour had been easier to remove than expected.

'I'm fine,' said Charlie, giving her a long-suffering look. He gave a last flourish with the cocktail shaker before pouring the pinkish-red liquid into two conical glasses.

'What sort of cocktail is it?' she asked.

'It's a cosmopolitan.' Regan licked her lips and reached for a glass. 'Uh-uh. Not yet,' he said, getting to his feet.

She watched with interest while he slowly unbuttoned his white shirt. 'The doctor said—' she began.

'The doctor said I could resume sexual activity when I felt ready.'

'Resume?' Regan gave a chuckle. This was something they had not quite got around to, mainly because Regan was terrified of Charlie straining himself. It had taken all the will power she owned – and Elvis guarding the bed – to stop her from sleeping with Charlie, but it was somehow easier knowing that eventually the right time would come.

He pulled off his shirt and she whistled like she was watching a stripper. Oddly, he still had white cuffs in place. He reached into the picnic basket and pulled out a bow tie and a small silver tray. He put on the bow tie, checked it was right, placed the cocktails on the silver tray and stood up straight.

Regan was enjoying the show, but she still wasn't sure what was going on. 'What now?'

'Here.' He pulled a scrap of paper and a pen from his pocket and handed it to her. 'You've a couple of things to tick off your list.'

She unfolded the crumpled paper. It was the lottery wish list she'd drawn up all those months ago. She scanned down to where it said, 'Bask on a deserted island and drink cocktails served to me by bare-chested waiters'. She tapped the page. 'It says *waiters*, plural,' she said, chewing her lip. 'I mean *technically* . . .'

'Tick it off now, or else,' he said, threatening to pour her cocktail away.

'Okay, okay.' She marked the paper. 'There, it's ticked off.' He passed her a cocktail glass and she took a sip, licking her lips appreciatively. It was strong, zingy and very alcoholic. She went back to the list. Top of the list was: 'Awesome home'. They'd not wanted to waste a second – as soon as Beanstalk had moved out, she'd moved in with Charlie so she could definitely tick that one off now.

It wasn't a flash mansion, but living with Charlie was absolutely the kind of awesome she wanted. 'Now what about "Get new hot boyfriend who doesn't nag or wear button-up pyjamas". Where do we stand on that one?' she asked, tilting her head and surveying Charlie in his Chippendale-esque outfit.

He took his glass from the tray and knelt down next to her. 'I promise you, I do not own a pair of pyjamas. Button-up or otherwise.' He leaned forward and she spotted something behind him that distracted her. He followed her gaze.

'What sort of berries are those?' she said, pointing at the small, purple, grape-shaped berries on the bush behind him.

'They're damsons,' he said, turning back to her and getting even closer this time.

'Really? That's brilliant. I need some of those. You don't happen to have a Tupperware pot in that picnic basket, do you? Because I know exactly what I'm going to do with them.'

Charlie laughed. 'As a matter of fact, I do . . . but first, I know exactly what I'm going to do with you.'

He leaned in and kissed her, and all thoughts of damsons disappeared from her mind completely.

Acknowledgements

It takes so many people to get a book from a spark of an idea to the finished article and here are the wonderful folk who have made this book possible:

As ever my huge thanks to the fabulous team at Avon – Katie Loughnane, Molly Walker-Sharp, Sabah Khan, Ellie Pilcher and so many others. Thanks to my agent Kate Nash for her ongoing encouragement, support and tactical shoves in the right direction.

Thanks, too, to all the wonderful experts I have had the joy to spend time with whilst researching this book:

Heather Guppy for a fun morning making jam and lots of excellent jam disaster stories.

Leo Fielding for letting me peep into the world of the firefighter and answering my many questions.

My resident medical expert Dr David Boulton for detailed explanations of the brain and various medical scenarios.

Will Pointon, Market Manager at Brighton Open Market, for letting me use a snapshot from their website and introducing me to amazingly helpful stallholders.

Kris, the real honey man at Brighton Open Market, for bringing me up to speed on life as a market trader and for his wonderfully original honey flavours. Please check them out here: https://greenvalleys.uk

Mary Dunmore, Centre Manager at St Anne's Centre, Brighton, for answering my questions about the local homeless community and the support available.

Del Sharp, Environmental Health at Brighton & Hove City Council, for pointing me in the right direction regarding food regulations.

Faye Tapping RVN BSc for answering my many weird questions about animal ailments and veterinary procedures.

Kyra & Sophie from Hedgehog Friendly Town for helping with the hedgehog details and for doing such a brilliant job at raising awareness of the plight of the British hedgehog. Here's their website: http://www.hedgehog-friendlytown.co.uk

Also to hedgehog carer, Lynda Harris, for coming to my aid when we had a real-life hoglet emergency.

Any mistakes are entirely my own.

Special thanks to my Readers Group for being so dedicated and supporting me through the writing of this one.

Thanks to Tina Wilkinson for suggesting the name Mr Pickle for one of the hedgehogs, and Deborah Jennings for offering up her name to be used for the veterinary nurse in the story.

Congratulations to my lucky competition winners whose pets all get a cameo:

Marie Carter and Fifi

Kaisha Holloway and Barney

Lynne Beeston and Holly

A huge thank you to all of my readers. Whether you've found my book through the library, local bookshop or online, I appreciate every one of you and if you have a moment to leave a review that would mean the world.

Escape to the Cotswolds with Beth and Leo . . .

Available in all good bookshops now.

Tempted to read another heart-warming romance by Bella Osborne?

Available in all good bookshops now.

As the sun begins to set on Sunset Cottage, an unlikely friendship begins to blossom . . .

Available in all good bookshops now.